Death *at the* Point

ANDREW DUTFIELD

FriesenPress

One Printers Way
Altona, MB R0G 0B0
Canada

www.friesenpress.com

Copyright © 2023 by Andrew Dutfield
First Edition — 2023
Jacqueline Dutfield, photography

All rights reserved.

No part of this publication may be reproduced in any form, or by any means, electronic or mechanical, including photocopying, recording, or any information browsing, storage, or retrieval system, without permission in writing from FriesenPress.

ISBN
978-1-03-916700-1 (Hardcover)
978-1-03-916699-8 (Paperback)
978-1-03-916701-8 (eBook)

Fiction, Crime

Distributed to the trade by The Ingram Book Company

DISCLAIMER

Death at the Point is a work of fiction. All situations, incidents, events and dialogue, and all characters with the exception of one historical person are products of the author's imagination.

ACKNOWLEDGMENTS

I would like to give credit and thanks to my wife, Jackie for her steadfast support during the writing and editing process. It was an item on my bucket list and it was encouragement all along the way. This book is dedicated to you, the special lady in my life.

Thank you also for the front cover photgraph that so perfectly captured the isolation and the atmosphere of the point.

I would like to thank my Mother and Father, for encouraging me to be tenacious. Little did I know that writing a book and getting it published would require so much of this quality to get the job done. They also said it was my responsibility to make the best of my talents, so thank you Mum and Dad you were the best and I have done my best.

For our kids, Stewart, Katie and Laura and their significant others, Kathleen, Matt, and Phil, Many thanks for your support.

After a life time of working in the construction industry, I discovered a passion for writing, especially writing for and about things I care about.

I have always loved murder mysteries and history and the book contains a little of both. All the characters except for one are fictional.

I would like to specifically thank the following people who have supported this project in one way or another: Marilyn Slobogian, Matt Wilms, Armande Martine, Danie Botha, Xanthe Zarry, who all read my draft and gave helpful suggestions and advice.

To Jaime Cox, my first editor, who's efforts helped turn my rough manuscript into a book, many thanks for your fun approach to life and work and taking on the challenge of my manuscript.

Also thanks to Anne Claros-Ristau, my Friesen Press Publishing Specialist for keeping me on track and to Paul Schultz for the map illustrations.

I am grateful to my friends at the Manitoba Writers Guild, who have heard me read sections of the book in the making and gave me suggestions along the way.

Many thanks to the Manitoba Historical Society for an article number 35, published in spring/summer 1998, which formed the inspiration for the one real character in the book.

Finally I must thank you the reader, for buying the book. I hope you enjoy the read and get a feel for Manitoba, and Hecla Island in particular. Maybe take a visit out here and get a sense of the people and the place and what inspired the book.

"

If you don't leave your past in the past, it will destroy your future

Live for what today has to offer. Not for what yesterday has taken away

Anonymous

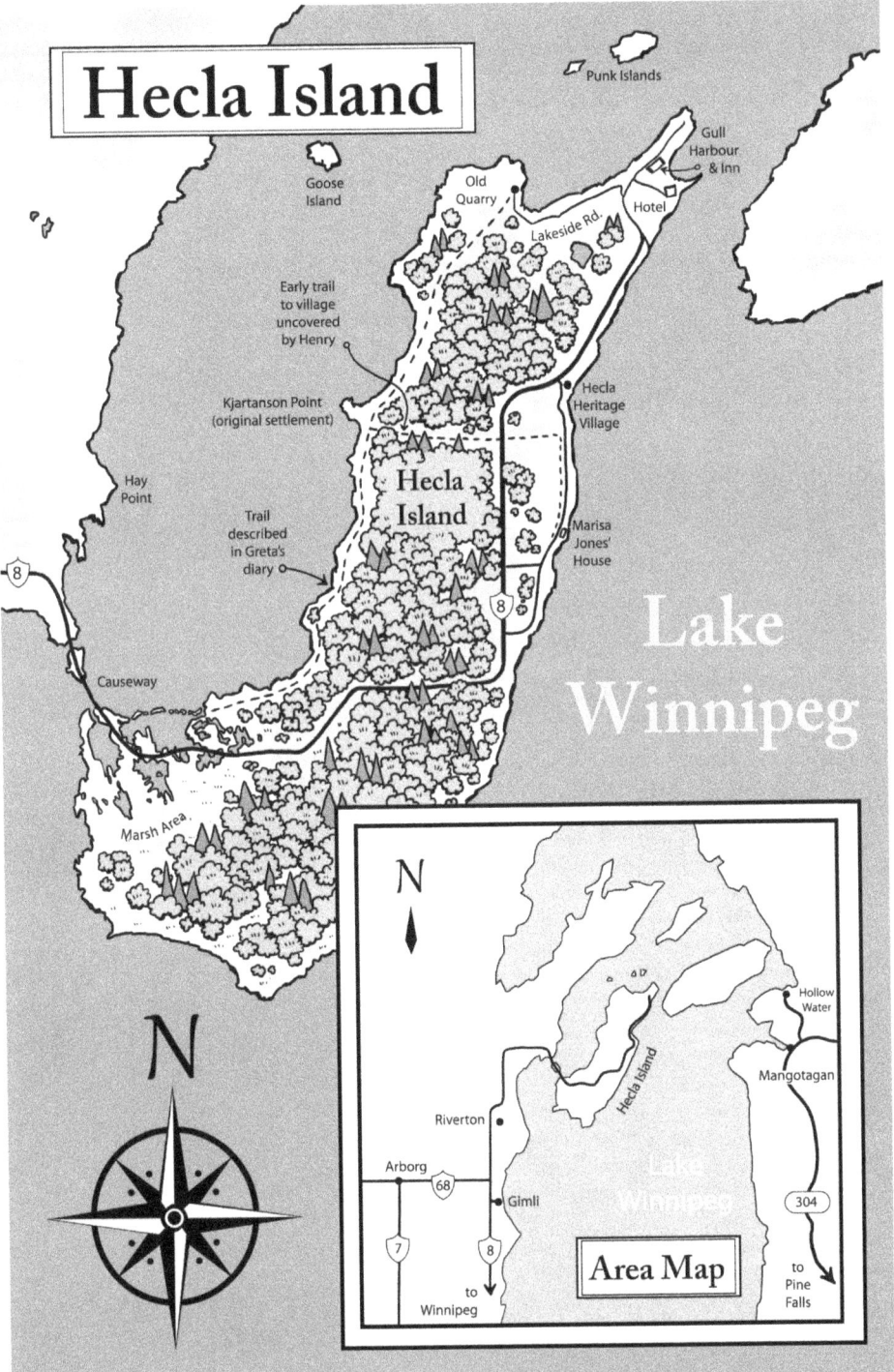

PROLOGUE

July 9, 1914

John finally woke from a restless night, shivering, the thin blanket inadequate for warmth or comfort. It was early morning, and pale light was slowly filling the high-walled room through the small, barred window close to the ceiling. It threw a dim shadow of itself on the west wall of the cell. He sat up, rubbing the sleep out of his eyes.

The peeling, white-walled room held nothing but the cot to lie on, along with a hole in the floor for calls of nature. The cell was musty, cool, and damp, even on July mornings, and the odour from the rudimentary toilet was nauseating—especially given his empty stomach. There was a piece of paper, a pencil, and an envelope on the floor next to the bed, which had been provided to him by a guard the previous day. John looked up at the heavy steel door.

It was deadly quiet. John knew what any sound would mean. His senses were heightened, almost tingling, like never before. He had butterflies in his stomach, but this time, not in a good way. This was not the first time he had been in a tight spot—he had always managed to stay calm—but this was different, completely different. His heart pounded in his chest. He took a couple of deep breaths in an effort to regain his composure.

They would be coming for him soon; he was *not* resigned to his fate. His failed escape attempt had not stripped him of the hope that he had always held onto when he found himself in a bind. Unfortunately, even he had to admit that he had run out of ideas and was really left now with only a bleak chance of a late clemency.

John reached for the paper and pencil, then paused. Writing this letter felt like acceptance of defeat and resignation to fate, so he hesitated for a couple of minutes, considering not writing anything at all.

His mind turned to earlier, happier times, when he was a young child living back in the old country. His memories were not clear, but they seemed to be there when his mind wandered: a simple world, with simple wants and needs, a time when he was just a cute kid, a time before his violent temper had developed into the rage it became after he came to Canada and got him into a short lifetime of trouble.

He thought of his twin cousins, close to his age, who had lived next door. He hadn't seen them since he left the old country with his parents, but imagined them as they were then, not as they probably were now. They would be twenty-eight years old. They had played together a lot and he had only sweet, innocent memories of them and that time in his life.

John had struggled to have strong positive feelings about *anybody* since he had moved to Canada. His parents were dead. Even his wife had deserted him and run away with someone else. His stepmother, who his father had married after the early death of his first wife, was the only person who had loved him in spite of who he was, and she had campaigned tirelessly the past months for the commuting of his sentence. She deserved all that he had secured away, but he knew she wouldn't take anything from him.

Reluctantly, John picked up the pencil and started to write in his childhood language. The letter, in its way, was his last will and testament. He greeted his two cousins and enquired about their health and happiness. He left specific instructions as to the whereabouts—at least, as far as he could recall them—of the metal box that he had carefully salted away. Giving no further details, he wished them well and signed his name. He decided to address the letter to the original home that they had lived in, hoping that one of them lived there still. His childhood village seemed almost idyllic now... his mind wandered again.

Snapping back to his grim reality, he picked up the pencil and finished writing the address. He took pride in his handwriting and took particular care writing it as he wanted to ensure that the letter made it to its destination.

DEATH AT THE POINT

The waiting was getting to John, and he felt the familiar rage building up. He started to pace the room like a caged beast. He contemplated making a blind rush for the door as soon as it opened. Not much of a strategy, but he had run out of other options.

He was fixated on this thought when he heard the distant sound of the clinking keys on the guard's belt echoing down the halls, then the distinct sound of a key turning in a lock—definitely he was thinking for the security gate of the cell block he was in. John did not hear the sound of that gate being relocked behind him, nor did he hear the sound of anybody else. That was strange, but good, as he knew he could overwhelm a single guard. There was still hope.

Eventually though, he heard muffled voices, saw movement through the small viewing screen in the door, and then heard his door being unlocked. It was now or never. The guard shouted to him to stand back and move to the rear of the cell. He refused, swearing aggressively. He was suddenly sweating profusely.

To his amazement, the cell door burst open, and the room was instantly full of guards. They had anticipated his belligerent behaviour and had decided that strength of numbers would be required for what they needed to do. Two burly guards threw him face down on the bed while two others handcuffed and shackled him. John struggled violently but was no match for them. The guards finally managed to place a hood over his head.

A priest arrived, attempting to offer John his last rites, but he was in the throes of rage, anger, and panic, and was shouting and swearing like his life depended on it. The priest nevertheless said the words, though he was drowned out by the commotion. It took all four guards to drag him to the small single gallows at the end of the cell block. The whole fiasco had taken no more than a couple of minutes. The cell was silent again. It would be silent until the next condemned man filled it.

Still in the cell, the priest looked relieved for the moment of silence. He saw the letter on the floor and kneeled to pick it up, then put it in his jacket pocket. Suddenly, he rushed out—the pandemonium had begun again—and raced down the hall to catch up with the guards and the condemned man.

When John's execution was announced, the citizens of Winnipeg and indeed those of Manitoba breathed a sigh of relief.

CHAPTER ONE

Henry and his family had survived his midlife health concerns and everybody in his family, at least in his opinion, had benefited.

A retired police officer, Henry was waiting impatiently for his wife, Julia, who had an irritating habit of putting work first on a Friday afternoon. He was parked near her building and was watching for her impatiently. *Surely whatever is holding her up could wait until Monday,* he thought.

After calling her number numerous times, he concluded she had at least left her office. The short walk to the building's entrance wasn't far, but Julia knew everybody, and everybody knew her. She was a popular member of staff at an advertising company and getting to the building's main doors without at least a couple of conversations was next to impossible.

Suddenly, there was an aggressive bang on the driver's-side window. Henry looked up, and immediately jumped aggressively out of the car as a man turned and walked away, shouting.

"Turn your car off!" he said. "Save the planet for the grandkids!" He glared at Henry as he pointed to the sign that said, "No idling" and walked away.

Henry was a little surprised by his own assertiveness and realized he was responding to being caught unaware, something police officers past or present are taught never to be. Reluctantly, he turned off the engine; he was as keen as anybody to save the planet, but as he opened the driver's window, hot and humid air quickly filled the vehicle. Skip, the family Labrador, immediately began panting in the back seat. Henry sat, frustrated, as perspiration beaded on his forehead. *Where can she be?* It was over a two-hour ride. *It's going to be way past 6:30 p.m. before I'll have the barbecue going,* he thought.

Finally, there she was, hurrying through the doors. "Sorry, Henry! Got caught up a bit," she said as she reached the car.

Henry rolled his eyes. Julia was such a likeable person and had such a kind soul and a smile that always melted his heart, which was one of the reasons he was originally attracted to her. And so, he couldn't really get angry. *At last,* he thought, *now we can hit the road.*

"You look a little flustered," Julia said concerned, as she put on her seat beat and turned to look at her husband. "Is your atrial fibrillation under control? You look a little red-faced.

"Sure, Henry replied. "Just had a guy bang on my window and caught me by surprise; I was a little over-assertive in my response. Just because I am retired doesn't mean some resentful criminal is not going to come after me or the family."

Julia didn't respond. She'd had a lifetime of this, and she had learned to put it to the back of her mind. Henry had always struggled with this risk and the responsibility it carried. Fortunately, there had never been a serious attempt to hurt anyone in his family.

The first section of the route heading north was to go around Winnipeg on the Perimeter Highway, forty-five minutes if one headed west, but the interchange had been completed on a northern section so, paradoxically, it was now quicker to go east. For Henry, the journey around the city was a grind.

The Perimeter was built at a time when Winnipeg was the largest urban centre in western Canada and looked as if it were to be the first city of a million people. Something had gone wrong with that plan, and it was only in recent years that sections of the city had grown out to the highway.

Julia, now in the car, was still very much in work mode, sending emails and texts to colleagues to finish her day to prepare for the week ahead. "Sorry; just replying to a few urgent things," she said. It was a small lie. Julia felt Henry drove too fast, so she preferred not to look out the windshield and instead mostly looked down to check social media.

Henry didn't mind as it was better than picking her up later. He understood from his own working years the difficulty of extracting yourself from a busy job at the end of the week.

By the time they had traversed the Perimeter, Julia was a little more relaxed. Turning onto Highway 8 had always felt to Henry like the point at which the weekend officially began.

Typically, they didn't talk a lot on the journey—Julia needed to unwind, and Henry had to concentrate on the busy single-lane highway. North of the city and past St. Andrews Airport, it immediately became rural: small crop farms and pastures for animals. The topography was very flat with large drains at regular intervals and deep ditches on either side of the road to drain the fields—essential in the spring or after downpours to keep flooding at bay. Treed sections of birch, poplar, and fir at the fields' edges and in between broke up the monotony.

After forty-five minutes or so, the first signs for Gimli appeared. They used to stop in Gimli to buy groceries and alcohol, but since Henry had retired, they purchased and stowed everything in the car in advance.

If leaving the Perimeter felt like the start of the weekend, then passing Gimli was like shedding the woes of city life for the quiet, peace, and tranquility of another world. The sun now was lower in the sky and made a brief appearance on their right as they approached Hecla Island, driving along the spit of road leading to the causeway that ran south. The water level in the marshlands on either side of the road was high, something that was not missed by Julia as she glanced up and looked through the passenger window.

"Great," she said, "the mosquitos will be eating me alive this weekend." For whatever reason, the island's mosquito population found Julia a tasty treat and she had correctly concluded that the first of the season would be out and about, given the wet spring and warming weather.

Why would anybody not born and raised in Canada suddenly want to take on the expense, hassle, and extra work of owning and maintaining two properties, when one was more than enough work? Henry's midlife crisis at fifty-five was definitely part of the answer. A lifetime of long-distance running and some heart enlargement probably led, ironically, to Henry's spell in resuscitation at the local hospital, where four unsuccessful chemical cardioversion procedures and, finally, the paddles were used to bring his heart rhythm back to close to normal. Henry, now resigned to not running anymore races, was grateful for the drugs he now took to manage his atrial flutter and fibrillation. This life crisis did cause Henry to take stock of his life.

At the time, he had been working as the head of the major crime unit with the Winnipeg Police Service, which amounted to "being on" seven days a week—a very stressful job, to say the least. He had needed to get away from the rat race and the criminal community of Winnipeg to clear his head. He wanted to "see nobody" and "hear nothing" except the wind in the trees, the waves crashing against the rocky shore, and the occasional sounds of the birds as they patrolled past the cottage along the water's edge.

He and Julia had looked for places a little closer to home, but they were just not quiet and out the way enough. He was so glad they had found their Garden of Eden on Hecla Island.

Even Julia had had to admit that although she didn't like the drive, it was a special spot. After all, she was still working. Henry had since retired, and she needed the rest and relaxation the cottage provided, as much as he did.

As they drove over the causeway, they could see the remains of the mooring spot for the old ferry sticking out of the water. In the wetlands on the south end of the island, there was water on both sides of the road, full of the geese that weren't waddling alongside the road. There was even the welcome sight of a pair of returning trumpeter swans.

They arrived at the park entrance just as a couple of young skunks scurried across the road, stopping at the kiosk, which was nicely decorated with hanging flower baskets. Henry lifted their park's pass from its spot against the windshield and presented it to the pretty young lady whose head was hanging out of the kiosk window.

"Good evening. How are you doing?" Henry asked in his happy, I'm-at-the-lake voice.

"Good, thanks, Sir," she said, smiling broadly at Henry. She glanced briefly at the park pass he held out of the window. "I like your accent," she said, smiling as they pulled away.

"What is it about your accent?" Julia laughed. "The number of women who have commented on your accent is amazing. Men have never commented on mine, and it's the same as yours… I don't get it," she said, shaking her head.

The twenty-mile island road cut its way north through the forested section, past the right turn to the original village, until it finally traversed the island to the northeast shoreline. It then ran alongside the lake through an avenue of trees that always looked the most beautiful after a snowstorm had dressed them in white. There were a number of white-tailed deer chewing away at the bushes on the side of the road. Henry pumped the brakes—deer could be skittish, and he didn't want to spook them and have them run into the path of their vehicle. Sadly, it was a common occurrence in this part of the world.

Once past the deer, he continued on the road. It was a clear evening. Judging by the whitecaps on the water, Henry could tell the wind was blowing strongly from the southeast. The sun was setting, and the water looked dark and cold; the ice from the frigid winter had only just melted.

Henry turned left onto the gravel of Lakeside Road and drove slowly to the bend, still keeping an eye out for deer. A short distance along, they hit the entrance to their lot.

Paradise found, yet again, for another blessed weekend.

Both Henry and Julia were born in the UK and had met in London where they had both lived and worked. After earning a degree in physics, Henry had joined the London Metropolitan Police and after his general training and some working experience, he had opted for officer's school rather than forensics, which was his first interest. When they first met, he was an up-and-coming officer in the Fraud Squad, later moving to the Major Crime Unit.

Julia was the second daughter of an Italian father and an English mum and was a budding actor in London's West End.

They became acquainted at the opening night event of a new play. Henry had been there with a young woman friend he had just met a couple of weeks before, who turned out to be a friend of Julia's.

Henry had felt the chemistry the moment they were introduced. Julia's beautiful Latin features, her captivating smile, and her bubbly personality swept him away. It took Julia awhile, but she grew to appreciate Henry's suave sense of dress, charm, intelligence, and his rather wacky sense of humour. It was not long before they were an item and it was clear to anybody who knew them that this relationship would end up at the altar, which it did, a couple of years later.

After marriage, their three kids, Harry, Christine, and Diane, came along fairly quickly. It was good to have the support of family so close by when their children were young. Life had been hectic, just as it was for all working parents.

Henry, by that point, had worked his way up in the Major Crime Unit despite the erratic hours. Julia had resigned herself to voiceover and other freelance work, which paid well, had flexible hours, and enabled her to be a devoted mum. As the kids grew, Julia and Henry spoke more and more about getting out of the rat race and moving to a small centre in the UK or even moving overseas.

A number of Henry's colleagues had moved to Canada, and he started to keep an eye out for opportunities. Eventually, he found a posting for a senior officer in the Major Crime Unit in Winnipeg. Winnipeg was having serious challenges due to the growth of drug crimes, and they were looking for big-city expertise and experience to head up the department.

That had been more than twenty years ago, and after the normal "immigrant challenges," Winnipeg felt like home. The kids adjusted quickly and had done well at school, then university, too. The eldest, Harry, had retained his English accent but the two girls, Christine and Diane, sounded as Canadian as anybody else. Henry still chuckled at the thought of his kids having their "Canadian accents."

After fifteen years or so, Henry and Julia decided to get their Canadian citizenships. They found the citizenship ceremony very moving, and it had a profound effect on them both as they took great pride in being Canadian.

Henry had been a little taken aback when he shared the good news with his parents a couple of days later. His father was very disappointed Henry and Julia had taken this step.

"So, being British isn't good enough for you anymore?" he had asked. Henry was upset initially, but this was a typical Dad comment and Henry had to admit to himself that he had expected nothing less.

Henry and Julia worked out regularly and appeared generally to be in good health. They had a small number of good friends and were grateful for where they were in life. So, the cottage was an unexpected blessing. Hecla Island ended up being its location least in part to Julia's hard negotiation stance with Henry when his relentless demanding they buy a cottage could no longer be resisted. The right property appeared during their search.

"I insist that it be lakefront, have three bedrooms, and I definitely need at least one bathroom with a real bath, not just a shower… Oh, and it needs to be a new build." Julia was in a good bargaining position.

Henry remembered the day they moved in. It was June and the heat of the summer had yet to make itself evident. Although the building had only been completed the previous year, no yard maintenance had been done, so the lot was overrun with weeds and wildflowers. It was wet and cutting the weeds down to a mowable height had been challenging.

With the yard now tamed, they could look out onto the lake from the deck, barbecue sizzling, white wine in hand, and watch as bald eagles and pelicans flew past the property's lakeside —often too quickly to photograph. This was truly God's country.

Not only was it an incredibly beautiful natural space, a sense of history pervaded the place and gave it an almost haunting dimension. As a bit of a history buff, Henry made it his business to learn the Island's backstory and found it fascinating. The Icelandic connection with the area was evident in the special sign boards with the country flag posted outside any homes that housed those with Icelandic backgrounds. The main churchyard also contained the graves of countless settlers to the area. The architecture of the buildings in the preserved heritage village captured the time when the Icelandic community had established itself and built the community infrastructure.

Henry and Julia realized what a privilege it was to be part of Hecla's community and never took the time spent there for granted. For Henry, in particular, Hecla had an almost spiritual dimension, which he shared with anybody that would listen. Julia noticed, when they arrived on the island, Henry was elated and when they drove off Hecla, a little sad.

Little did they know that the seeds of an old mystery were about to germinate, sprout, and disrupt the sense of peace and harmony, and challenge the emotional connection Henry had with Hecla Island.

CHAPTER TWO

A couple of weeks later, Henry and Julia were looking forward to a special weekend. Old friends from earlier days in London, Elliot and Sarah Sutcliffe, were popping into Hecla as part of their cross-Canada holiday.

They could hear the faint sound of their car coming down the gravel driveway from the other side of the house. It was turning out to be a lovely sunny day.

"Looks like they have arrived, Henry!" Julia called as Henry looked up, steel barbecue brush in hand.

"Be right there," he called back, putting down the brush and reaching for his other glasses. He made it to them just as they were getting out of the car and giving Julia enthusiastic hugs and kisses. Henry joined the throng of happy embracing people then walked to the back of the car to unload their suitcases.

"Nice vehicle," Henry said, looking enviously at the brand-new rental. "Still got that new-car smell," he said, laughing at his own observation as he lifted the hatch.

"Yes, we splashed out a bit," Elliot said. "We needed a larger comfortable car as we'll be putting on a good number of miles on this holiday."

"Good point," Henry replied. "You are finding out, no doubt, Canada is an enormous country."

"Come on, Sarah," Julia said. "Let me show you to your bedroom and then I can give you the tour." After a brief wander through the house, Julia offered Elliot and Sarah chairs on the deck overlooking the lake.

"Wow! It's beautiful, folks. I've never seen such a wonderful sight," Elliot said, genuinely blown away by the view.

"Yes, it is a special place. To be only two hours north of Winnipeg and be surrounded by such unspoiled beauty is amazing," Julia added.

"Yes, this used to be part of New Iceland, an area designated for Icelandic people who settled here from 1875 onwards," said Henry. "Apparently, Iceland was going through dire environmental and economic conditions at the time, caused by volcanic eruptions, the ashfall was heavy enough to poison the land and kill the livestock and a large proportion of the population emigrated over the next twenty years."

"Thanks, Henry, for the history lesson," Julia said with a smile. She sensed their friends were not as fascinated by Hecla's history as he was in telling it, which was probably true.

Henry refocused in a moment. "So, what would you like to drink?" he asked as Elliot and Sarah settled into their chairs.

"A white wine for me," Sarah said.

"A beer for me. Surprise me with something local," Elliot said before Henry had a chance to run through the list of beer options.

"I guessed you'd still love your beers," Henry laughed. "Some things don't change. Julia, what would you like?"

"A white wine is good for me, too, Henry. Can you get us some snacks while you're inside please?"

Henry nodded and slipped back inside, closing the screen door to prevent any mosquitoes from sneaking in.

Between the sound of glasses tinkering, the uncorking of a wine bottle, the pouring of the beers, and the filling of snack bowls, Julia regaled them with stories from their early experiences at the cottage. Elliot and Sarah leaned forward, intently listening as Julia had a well-deserved reputation for telling a good story.

"We purchased the place ten years or so ago. It of course took time to make it feel like home. It had to be furnished, blinds put up, bathroom vanities hung, and tons of other things, but it was fun."

"We moved the older furniture and appliances here from the house in Winnipeg and replaced with new ones. After Henry's push to buy the cottage, he was in no position to be restricting my wish list for purchases," Julia said, laughing.

"Good for you, Julia," Sarah replied, smiling. Elliot also smiled but decided no comment was necessary; he didn't want to be seen to be taking sides.

"In short order, we made the cottage nice and cozy in time for the coming winter. With the house made comfortable, it was time for the yard," Julia continued. "The cottage is situated, as you can see, on flat ground, but it is probably six metres at least above the lake. This presents a wonderful view of the lake and islands from all the lake-facing windows, but it was practically a vertical cliff down to the water. This end of the island is an outcrop of limestone, which grows in height the closer to the north end of the island that you go.

"The wind is often blowing and the water crashes into the rocks just like the sea. You can get wicked storms on this lake. Henry had decided he wanted to purchase a couple of kayaks so we could explore the islands and get some exercise. No motorized boat for him, at least for now—we really didn't have the spare money, anyway."

Henry, you should tell them about the 'project,'" Julia said.

"You've always had a project, even back when you lived around the corner from us in London," Elliot said, chuckling.

"As you know, I always liked a challenge." Henry liked to tell stories, too. "The cliff was certainly something that required a lot of thinking. It wasn't long before I was scribbling ideas for a deck, stairs, and access for storage and launching of the kayaks.

"I found out from the neighbours that the lake levels would vary a lot depending on the seasons, spring thaw, southern runoff, rainfall, and hydro dam demand upstream. During the course of that first summer, lake levels were low and the 'beach' in front of the property was exposed as loose, flat, shale-like rock that was very difficult to walk on and would often be covered with algae that made it very slippery.

"The deck and stairs ended up being more of a project than I expected—they were completed at the end of that first summer—but over a number of years received some necessary modifications. Originally, the steps went right down to the water. That turned out to be a mistake as I had totally underestimated the power of the lake in a storm. After coming up one early fall weekend, we discovered the lower steps had been ripped away and the remnants were nowhere in sight. I rebuilt the lower level with aluminum sections that could be lifted like a drawbridge every time the steps aren't in use." Henry continued talking as Sarah, Eliot, and Julia sipped their drinks, listening intently.

"We purchased the kayaks in Winnipeg. They're strong, robust crafts but are heavy and lifting them up and down the steps proved to be difficult, dangerous, and extremely hard work, particularly after a long kayak when your legs and arms felt like jelly. I eventually built a small deck to store the kayaks closer to the bottom of the steps to reduce the effort, which made a big difference."

"Sometimes it felt like one step forward and two steps back," Julia joked. "Henry is generally a reasonably cautious person by nature and considerate about taking risks. He does have his moments, however, on occasion, of being a little over-enthusiastic and may have been guilty of not assessing risk correctly from time to time. I know I can be more risk averse, particularly around my family, and often my concerns would be a frustration for Henry. An example is the time he decided to kayak, not along the edge of the lake, which was his normal practice, but to attempt to reach Little Punk Island, which is three kilometres offshore. I was not happy.

"He put his shortwave radio in a plastic bag in the pocket of his life vest and packed an energy bar and a bottle of water—nothing else to consider, really. It was a warm day, with only a slight breeze blowing towards Little Punk Island.

"I had carried a chair down from the cottage and was sitting on the deck as Henry started to paddle out. He was actually making good progress as the breeze was blowing offshore. After a while, the wind intensified, and the water became rougher. He had trouble keeping the kayak facing in the right direction as it did not have a rudder. Henry discovered that distances are farther than they look when you are on the water, and the island didn't seem to be getting any closer. I'll leave you to finish the story, Henry."

"Sure Julia, I was wondering when I would get my chance to speak," he said chuckling. "After much effort, I did eventually get to the island. I struggled a bit to get out of the kayak; it was slippery underfoot and my arms and legs were exhausted. I secured the kayak against the increasing wave action, ate my energy bar, and drank my water. Through the binoculars, I could just see Julia in the distance, still sitting high up on the deck. After a couple of seconds, I could hear Julia's voice coming from the radio, which I pulled out of my life vest.

"So, you feel proud of yourself Henry?" she said a little mockingly through the radio. "Planted a flag on the island?"

"No flag, but I did take a selfie with my cellphone," I said to her. She warned me the wind had picked up and I could see a lot of whitecaps on the water, and clouds approaching. It was definitely time to head back. The tree branches were soon bracing in the wind and the waves were breaking harder on the beach—no time to lose. I pushed off and took a little water into the kayak as I attempted to get the boat aligned to get into it. It was no mean feat with the waves breaking over the boat. The water was now a vastly different experience. The oncoming wind was creating large swells, which I had to go up and down and often a wave would be cresting and washing over the deck. I didn't have a spray-skirt on to keep the water out.

It was now double the effort, the wind was blowing in my face, and the spray was stinging my eyes, making it difficult to see. The only good news was that it was easier to keep the kayak straight as the cottage was directly into the wind; it was just damn hard work. Halfway across, the sky went dark, and it started to rain. The radio crackled. Julia was obviously concerned and attempting to know how I was doing. She meant well, but it was totally impossible for me to take my hands off the paddle; I was barely keeping it upright as it was. The boat was now more than half full of water and required even more effort to move it forward." Henry's voice lowered to dramatic effect.

"Just when I was starting to panic and was gravely concerned, the wind died down a little. The water closer to the shore was partially shielded by the land and paddling got a little easier. I was totally exhausted, and I could see Julia walking down the steps to meet me and help me out of the kayak.

"I was a totally spent. Julia kept me upright long enough for me to regain enough strength to clamber out of the kayak and drag it out of the water. I had heard how quickly the lake could whip up a storm and now I had witnessed it firsthand—pretty scary. Important where possible to stay close to the land."

"Well, it looks pretty calm out there now, Henry," Elliot said. "Maybe we can do a kayak tour a little later, along the shoreline of course." He grinned.

"Come on, tell us more," Sarah said, obviously intrigued by what was an alien environment to two born-and-bred Londoners.

"That summer, we also learned about bugs," Julia said. "That first year was quite hot and wet, and bugs of every variety had their season. No-see-ums, black flies, horse flies, fish flies, wasps, and of course our all-summer-long friend, the mosquito. Unfortunately for me, they all find me very attractive, and it was—and continues to be—an issue for me at the lake in the summer. Not my favourite season, for sure—a little sad if you consider how short the summers are in this part of the world!" Julia paused to take a sip of her wine.

"That first summer was over far too soon, but we discovered how beautiful the fall can be. The oppressive humid heat was gone, along with the mosquitoes, and the leaves on the trees turn a wonderful palette of colours. Truly a magnificent season on the island. The mornings are generally crisp and sunny, and the days warm up to a reasonable temperature where a light jacket suffices. We got into quite a routine. Henry would drive us up on the Friday night and we would arrive sometime after 6:00 p.m. We would cook dinner together and enjoy a bottle of red wine, watch a DVD, and then head for bed. There is something about country air that makes you sleepy, leaving the challenges of the week behind. The next morning, Henry would be up early, taking Skip our energetic labrador for his walk. After breakfast, he would mess around outside, cleaning up the yard, cutting down trees which were growing too close to the house or power lines, or preparing the property for the winter—something he was learning about by talking to the neighbours. For example, the last time of the season we cut the grass, we loaded the cuttings in bags and lay them around the holding tank; it's a neat little trick to reduce the possibility of the tank freezing! Also, emptying out the gutters of newly fallen leaves reduces the possibility of ice build-up under the eaves in the spring."

DEATH AT THE POINT

"Wow, a lot of things to learn," Elliot commented.

"Yes, to be frank, it was a bit of a new adventure," said Henry. "How much snow is too much when you arrive at the lake at 7:00 p.m. in the middle of the winter, with no snow shovel, and Julia says 'just gun it,' and you have the embarrassment the next morning of digging the snow out from under the car—all four wheels off the ground—while the neighbours snigger as they walk past. I am ashamed that this has occurred more than once. I should stop listening to Julia," he said, laughing.

"How full is 'too full' for the holding tank, especially when you have invited friends around to share your place for the weekend? What do you do when you turn up on a brutally cold night and the lock on the front door is frozen? Who do you call when the electric furnace goes on the blink, and it quickly gets below ten degrees in the cottage?"

Elliot and Sarah were in stitches as they listened to Henry and Julia's adventures.

"Thirsty work, listening to your stories," Elliot said, touching his empty glass.

"Oh, sorry folks. Anybody want another drink? I'm not a good host—too busy talking." After taking everybody's orders Henry had just disappeared into the kitchen when the doorbell rang. *Maybe it's a neighbour*, he thought. Skip, who had been lying in the lounge, rushed to the door, barking. Henry grabbed the dog by the collar as he opened the door.

A tall red-headed stranger clad in brown corduroy pants and a checked shirt was staring down at him. His face was tanned, and he had crow's feet around his eyes. In very broken English, he said that he was looking for donations to support a float at the village celebration of Icelandic Day coming up in August. Henry was a little curious. The man had what he guessed was a strong Eastern European accent. He didn't get the impression he was a local, but Henry reached into his pocket and found a twenty-dollar bill to give him. The man nodded his head in thanks and turned away very abruptly, retreating down the driveway. As he closed the door, Henry was unsure whether he'd just been scammed. He went back to the kitchen, poured the beer and wine, and headed back outside to the group on the deck.

"You were a while," Julia said.

"Yes, the doorbell rang, and I made the mistake of answering it," Henry said smiling. "A tall guy I didn't know was looking for a donation for one of the floats at the Icelandic Day festival in the village in August. He had Skip a little spooked, which is strange because Skip is a pretty friendly dog."

"Oh, OK," Julia replied. She didn't seem inclined to dwell on Henry's suspicions. "It's a pity you won't be here in a couple of weekends," Julia continued, "the Icelandic Festival is the highlight of the year and attracts a large crowd from all over. The parade of floats is a lot of fun."

"That is a shame," Elliot said smiling. We are always up for a good party.

"Excuse me for a moment." Henry stepped back indoors.

"So it was quite an adaption for two 'city folk,' but you two have seemed to have done OK. We could never dream of a second property like this," Sarah said, looking a little jealous.

"Property is relatively cheap in this part of the world," Julia said, "and the prices are not escalating like they are in the bigger cities. The downside is we could now never afford to move to a bigger city or back to the UK. But that's OK; we have our family here and we feel very much part of the community. This is now home for us."

"Henry has definitely grown. I never saw that adventurous side of him when we lived in London," Julia continued. "The last twenty years we have taken risks, but everything has worked out. The cottage, like other things, was a little unexpected—unusually impulsive of him, but in the end, I agreed to go with it. I have to say I like the new, slightly unpredictable man he has become."

"So Henry is now retired?" Sarah asked.

"Yes, not so long ago. The job took a lot out of him. Drugs fuel a lot of crime in this part of the world, the top dogs are very violent people, and staying on top of the situation is a challenge when you are always a little short of manpower. I think he misses the adrenaline rush a little more than he cares to say, but his health issues did change his perspective on life. The Winnipeg Police Service organized an elegant event to mark his retirement, and the family were invited. It was a lovely occasion and Henry gave a humorous and appreciative speech. He was proud to have his family there to share the special moment in his life—"

"What health issues?" Elliot interrupted.

"He has developed heart arrhythmia issues, Julia replied, "but it is controlled with drugs, and he can still do most things, but he misses his road running."

"Yes, I suppose he does," Elliot replied. "I remember the day after he finished the London marathon that first time; he was so pumped."

"Well he hasn't let the grass grow under his feet," Julia continued. As soon as the party was behind him, he seemed to be re-energized and wasted no time seeking out new opportunities to give his life purpose and have some fun. He continued to jog gently, joined a badminton club, then a writer's group, he decided to volunteer at a local shelter, and picked up his guitar after twenty years, and found a friend to practice with. These activities, as well as maintaining the running of the home and cooking dinner, has had Henry running around almost as much as he was when he was working. However, there were no more long erratic hours or the stress that goes with working in the police force. Life is good."

Henry reappeared with more drinks and the conversation continued. After so many years apart, there was much to catch up on.

The four packed a lot into the next three days they spent together. There was some uneventful kayaking, beach time, walks along the coastline, barbecues, and more than a couple of beers and glasses of wine. Henry and Elliot even managed a couple of beers at the local hotel by themselves, while the girls took a grocery trip to Arborg.

"Reminds me of our evenings out before we were married," Elliot said. He picked up his glass and toasted, "Two off-duty police officers out on the town," clinking glasses with Henry. "Great times."

"A lot of water has gone by since those days, Elliot," Henry said smiling, a little froth on his upper lip that he instinctively felt and licked off.

"Do you miss the cut and thrust of the Major Crime Unit?" Elliot asked.

"Not really, but I have to say I do like solving mysteries, whether it's a leaking pipe or something I have mislaid," Henry said, grinning.

"Not sure you would have people mysteries up here. The population of the island looks like it must be tiny, especially in the winter," Elliot said.

"Yep, it is so peaceful, and in the winter it feels like we have the island to ourselves, which I love. It's a real contrast to Winnipeg, which in some years has had the highest per-capita number of murders of any city in Canada. Many involve gangs and drugs. Having a murder up here would spoil the innocence of the place," Henry continued, thinking aloud. "Hecla has got in my blood, and I feel personally protective of it, strange I have never felt like this about a place before."

Both men were quiet for a second or two, reflecting on his words.

"Want another?" Henry asked breaking the odd silence.

"Yes, but it's my round," Elliot said as he waved to the waiter. "Same again?"

"Sure, thanks," Henry replied, feeling pretty mellow.

"So how are things at the Met these days, Elliot?" Henry asked.

"Very much the same: the occasional terrorist attack. Which you know are notoriously difficult to get ahead of when they are lone-wolf events. Of course, we still have the criminal gangs from the old Eastern bloc, particularly Russia. We have a number of good informants, but the Russians are particularly vicious when they catch a snitch, and we don't pay enough to really motivate anybody to turn on their own organization to get the really good information, which is frustrating."

Slightly worse for wear after a couple more beers, they stumbled the mile or so back to the cottage. Fortunately, Elliot and Sarah were not leaving for a couple of days—the boys were likely to feel a little delicate in the morning.

All good things must come to an end. It was a little bittersweet when it came time to wave Elliot and Sarah goodbye. They were such good friends that after many years, they could still instantly reconnect, like they had never been out of contact. They had so much common history. And yet another wonderful memory had been formed in connection with the island that had come to be a special place in Henry and Julia's lives.

As they walked back down the gravel driveway to the house after saying goodbye to their friends, Henry spoke up a little out of the blue.

"So Julia, do you know a tall red-bearded guy with a foreign accent who lives around here?" Henry always was curious about people.

"No, I can't say I do. We know people and we have been to quite a few events, and you know I am quite the social butterfly, but I cannot recall meeting him. Why did you bring it up?"

"I don't know. Something didn't feel right—I gave up twenty dollars too easily."

"We can afford it, Henry. Don't worry about it."

The next weekend was the annual Icelandic Festival. Henry and Julia had invited their elder daughter Christine and her husband Johnny, and their kids up for the weekend.

It was a blazing hot couple of days and the kids loved the parade. There were countless floats and lots of craziness and fun. Henry remained on the lookout for the tall red-headed guy, but he was a no-show on any of the floats. Everybody was wearing costumes and many of the participants wore masks. However, Henry was pretty sure he would have spotted him if he was around as he was exceptionally tall. Henry concluded he had been scammed, but he still felt something was not quite right.

CHAPTER THREE

Julia's Retirement

Henry and Julia spent every other weekend at the lake, enjoying their lives, sometimes with Johnny and Christine and their family. Christine was the only one of their children who had stayed in Winnipeg. It was great to share the place with them. As the years went by and grandchildren came along, Henry had built a fence on the edge of the cliff to ensure that they were safe, and they loved helping Granddad with the chores around the cottage and Grandma in the kitchen with the baking.

One day after they had returned home to Winnipeg, it occurred to Henry that Julia was not her regular self. She was normally the life and soul of the party but recently that was no not the case. Eventually, over dinner that night, Henry asked Julia what was preoccupying her.

"Sorry, love. I am not really down, just thoughtful. I have had such a great time at the cottage these past number of years and I realize how precious time is, as we have lost some good friends in recent years. The grandkids are growing up fast, and you are retired. I can go on an unreduced pension in three months when I turn sixty, and I am thinking of calling it a day at the advertising company."

"That's great news, Julia. You've always said you would retire when you're ready and it looks like now is the time. Good for you."

"Will we be OK financially, Henry?" she asked. "I had not planned to retire so soon."

"Don't worry," Henry replied. "We will be fine. These are our best years, and we cannot get them back."

The next day Julia woke up with a smile on her face—her old self was back. She didn't really know why it had been such a challenge, but like a lot of things in life, once you've agonized and made the decision, you often struggle to understand why it took so long. Retiring marks the end of one era and the start of another, *the final one*, and that can be a little scary to contemplate.

"First point of business: inform the boss of my decision, then make an appointment with HR to start the paperwork process," Julia said between spoonful of cereal.

Henry drove Julia to work, and she gave him the biggest smile and kiss as she exited the car. "Looks like I am joining the retirement club real soon." With that, she closed the car door and walked purposely to the entrance of her office.

As Henry drove away, he was still feeling a little stunned by Julia's decision. He knew something was up, but Julia had always been a working mum and it had never occurred to him that she would quit. She loved her job; it used the talents and passions she had, and she had built relationship with the people she worked with. She quite rightly knew she made a difference for the business and was well respected by everyone. She had worked her way up in the hierarchy and yet she still had time for everyone. Henry was confident that with her love of people she would re-invent herself once retired.

Still it is going to be an adjustment for Julia, Henry thought as he turned onto the back road leading to the house.

Julia was elated when Henry picked her up that evening,. She had managed to get an appointment with the HR people that very afternoon and the paperwork was already completed. The pension would be in place by her retirement date, her sixtieth birthday.

"Let's go out and celebrate! Dinner is on me," Julia said.

"That's no problem for me," Henry replied, "I haven't started preparing anything, and this is a big deal." Since retirement, Henry had taken over the role of cook in the house. Picolino's was Julia's favourite neighbourhood restaurant, and it was early enough that no reservation was required.

"Wow! You look happy, Julia—like you have won the lottery," Joe, the owner, said as he greeted them at the door.

"I have decided to retire," Julia replied.

"Well, congratulations, Julia! Well deserved. That advertising company is going to miss you," he said, scanning the room for an appropriate table. "Julia the wine is on me," Joe said. "This is a special occasion."

"Well thank you, Joe. It's appreciated," said Julia.

"Looking forward to seeing you here more often now you will have more time on your hands." Joe smiled as he pushed the chair under Julia as she seated herself at the table.

Henry knew Joe had a soft spot for Julia; it must be the shared Italian blood.

Joe returned with menus and a wine list. "By the way, if you are having a retirement party? We can put together a good spread for up to fifty people in our function room if you're interested. Special price for you of course, Julia. No pressure," he said, filling the water glasses.

"So what do you think, Henry?" Julia said excitedly. "I would like to celebrate. It will be a birthday–retirement party," she said chuckling at her own humour.

"Let me talk to Joe and see what we can do," Henry replied, happy that his old Julia was back. Julia picked a nice Super Tuscan wine and they each had a Caesar salad and a pasta dish. They spent the evening going over the potential guest list.

"I think I'll do something separate for all my work colleagues one afternoon, so we can focus our list on family and friends for this event," Julia said.

"OK," Henry said." You finalize the list and I'll coordinate the event."

Julia loved a good party and being the centre of attention was not a problem. She had stage presence from her years in theatre and an extroverted personality.

"You know we can spend more time at the lake now, Henry," she said with a smile. She knew how much Henry loved being up there.

"Good," Henry replied. "I can cut back on my volunteer work a little, and now we can go up in the week when it is a little quieter. Are you OK with that?"

"No problem, but I think we should invest in an air conditioner if we are going to spend more time up there," Julia suggested. "Also, I am planning to have activities of my own, but no rush for that. I aim to take it easy for a while and enjoy having time on my hands," she said smiling.

"You are probably right about the air conditioner. It can get a little sticky in July and August and if we're going to be up there more, I think we can justify the expense," Henry replied, smiling.

As Julia went to the washroom. Henry contemplated all the things they could be doing at the lake, un-encumbered by the commitments of work. No more rushing around. It seemed crazy to think that in the winter when the roads were bad and it was safer to travel in the daylight, they would often leave on the Saturday morning and come back Sunday afternoon. There would be more time to be spent in their tranquil, peaceful place, untainted by the world around it. It would also be good to get to know the community a little better. For most of the time they had been coming up here, they had been seeking peace and quiet and socializing had never been the priority.

Henry felt blessed but always in the back of his mind he was very aware that as much as he tried to shield Julia and the kids from the seriousness and violence of his previous job, it hadn't always been possible, and it had taken a toll on him and the family. It had always been a concern to him—both in the UK and Canada—that he, or more importantly, Julia and kids, may have been targeted by the people that he and his unit were trying to investigate and bring to justice. Murder, kidnapping, or blackmail of some type was always a possibility. He felt relieved and blessed that they had gotten to this stage of life and nothing serious had happened.

In the time they had been in the restaurant it had gotten dark, and a cold wind had blown up. They both instinctively pulled up their collars as they approached the door.

"Thanks, folks," Joe shouted as they left. Julia smiled and waved, and Henry said, "Will call you Joe. Sounds like the party is on."

As they closed the car doors and Henry leaned forward to start the ignition, Julia reached out to hug Henry.

"Looks like a start of a whole new chapter in my life has begun today. I am so excited. We are going to have some fun, Henry," she said, a broad grin on her face.

Julia completed the list in a couple of days—mainly of friends as Henry and Julia's Canadian family was limited to a few second cousins, who Henry had discovered in British Columbia and Saskatchewan, relatives of one his great uncles.

Johnny and Christine would be joined by Diane who would be coming from Montreal, and Harry and his wife Karen from Toronto.

It was decided it would be an early evening occasion. Julia wanted her grandkids to be there, and she also wanted it to be a little dressy: suits for the men and eveningwear for the women. Julia was going to start her new life in a memorable way, she would pick out a nice outfit for her special evening.

The snow came early that year—a little before Halloween. The snow that was falling by the middle of frigid November would be around until mid-April. It was a very white Christmas that year and Henry was definitely considering buying a snow blower for the lake and a better shovel for the house.

Winnipeggers love Christmas, but as soon as it's over, the lights are off the houses, which emphasizes the coldness of January. However, on January 31 that year, there was a big party to look forward to.

Henry had worked hard with his daughters to put everything together. They sent out invitations early to secure the day in everybody's calendars and there was positive RSVPs from everyone. Banners were made up to hang in the room, short speeches were written, and Henry had even crafted a special song, "It's Good to Be Sixty." Diane, their youngest, who was flying in from Montreal, who enjoyed photography and was quite talented, would be the "official" photographer for the event.

The afternoon came around all too soon. Everybody arrived in their finery, including the grandkids who were soon playing quite happily in the incredibly crowded room. The sound of happy voices and laughter rose in volume as more and more guests arrived.

It was a special time for Julia who looked the belle of the ball and was clearly enjoying being the centre of attention as always. She was dressed in a classic long blue dress, her dark hair, with just a hint of gray, hanging long down her back. Her beautiful face barely revealed her age. Henry looked across the room in admiration at his wonderful, attractive, and vivacious life partner, the most precious person in his life.

He played his song, proposed a toast for a happy birthday and a long, healthy and happy retirement, and gave Julia the biggest kiss, before she grabbed the microphone and proceeded to have everybody in stitches with funny anecdotes from past birthdays and humorous family moments. Diane quietly snapped away, ensuring the evening's festivities were captured for posterity. Henry noticed that Diane seemed extra vibrant and smiled a lot. He fleetingly wondering if she had finally met the right man.

Tables were laden with empty champagne flutes and porcelain cocktail plates, the crowd thinning to a handful of close friends and family as the evening wound down. The guests said their goodbyes and the family removed the decorations and helped load the generous pile of cards and presents into the back of Henry's car that was nice and warm from being started earlier. Eventually, Julia reluctantly left the restaurant and shivered across the parking lot to the car. Henry opened the car door and ensured her coat was not trailing outside before he shut it, then walked around to the driver's side and climbed in. When he turned to her, she had a big smile on her face and tears streaming down her cheeks.

"Thanks, Henry. This was the best party ever," she said between sobs. "I don't know why I am crying when I am so happy. I only used to cry when I was mad."

Henry laughed. "You are becoming more sentimental, like most people get in their old age," he replied, still grinning. "Let's get home."

Now we will be free to spend more time at Hecla... no more racing up and down, Henry thought, smiling to himself. *A little more peace and quiet in our life.*

CHAPTER FOUR

Early spring was not Henry Trevellyn's favourite season. In this part of the world, spring never seemed to make its mind up but always felt colder than it should be. Cold winds blew off the still mostly iced-up lake and the little melting and thawing that was occurring created slippery and icy conditions under foot and made for more unpleasant weather compared with Winnipeg farther away from the lake—no daffodils in sight until well into May. Spring was often overcast, and the lake seemed desolate again for a while. The ice fishers were now off the lake, their coloured tents and snow huts gone, as the once-thick surface was starting to melt, making it no longer safe.

As Henry pulled up the bedroom blinds and stared out the window in the early morning light, he could see the northwest wind blowing snow squalls towards the islands—the smaller islands offshore progressively disappeared behind the wall of snow. In about ten minutes the snow and ice pellets would reach the cottages on their side of the lake, so he decided to wait until the storm blew through. After twenty minutes or so, it was finally just gently snowing.

"This is a harsh but beautiful place. There is something magical about this island and its situation," Henry would often say to anybody who would listen. For most of the year, with the exception of summer, there were few people around. Some folks lived year-round on the island as they had for most of the past 150 years—mainly fishers, who were descendants of the original Icelandic settlers, The village general store closed around Thanksgiving. The harbour inn and store stayed open as did the main hotel. This attracted some cross-country skiers and people on Ski-Doos, more so on the weekends, and those who just wanted to get away from the city.

Although he had been retired awhile, Henry still kept active, spending time in the city, volunteering, working on the odd project, and then heading back to God's country to enjoy the peace and quiet and the sounds of the natural world—a constant wonder to him.

Julia had joined an amateur theatre company in Winnipeg, which she was really enjoying, but she was cautious about committing to anything else as she just loved the time to take it easy and be spontaneous.

At the lake, Henry's usual morning walk with Skip was along the gravel road and then off road between the trees and along the cross-country ski tracks down to the old, abandoned quarry and back. He would only occasionally see someone else—a fellow cottager or a guest walking out from the hotel that was a mile or so away. That was how Henry liked it; he needed his quiet time. He was a morning person and up at the same time, winter or summer, seven days a week. For him, life was just too precious and fleeting to spend too much time in bed.

At this particular time, he and Julia had been at the lake for a couple of weeks. Henry, a man of routine, headed to the kitchen where Skip was sleeping. The dog reluctantly opened an eye when the light flicked on, but when he saw Henry, he was up and pacing and scratching at the door as Henry put on his coat. Henry seldom put Skip on a leash. There was rarely anybody around and he was a disciplined dog with a good temperament.

As they walked along the road, they were sheltered a little from whatever wind was still blowing. By the lakeside band of trees, the snow was falling vertically, rather than blowing in his face.

Many cottages were closed up, so there was still deep snow in their driveways, with just the occasional set of tire tracks to indicate somebody had been out to their property recently to check that everything was OK. There were plenty of deer tracks. Other than the cawing of a couple of crows, there was only the sound of the wind and the trudging sound of Henry's boots as he walked through the falling snow.

As they entered the woods, the sound of the wind died off and a silence filled the frigid air. He stopped walking for a moment to take it in. Skip stopped, too, and looked up at Henry, awaiting the nod to continue

DEATH AT THE POINT

walking on the path. When he did so, the sound of his boots crunched on the icy snow and drowned out the quietness as he walked between the groomed ski trails. Every so often he would stop and listen to the wonderful sound of silence, that was almost impossible to find in the city.

The trail in the woods was no more than a couple of kilometres, generally flat, and followed the curve of the lake. Henry always carried his cellphone, but it was difficult to keep it charged in the extreme cold, and the signal at the lake was never the best. Henry was always careful to let Julia know which trail he had picked for that particular morning. He was aware that anything could happen: a fall, a heart issue, or potentially a bear attack, and that it was best to be prepared for the worst.

Halfway along the trail, Skip started to behave strangely, running up the pathway and back. After a couple of minutes, he began barking and growling.

"What's gotten into you, Skip?" Henry said, walking onward. When they reached the crook in the path, he saw what looked like an unusually large set of boot prints, which led up and away (to the left path) from the main route to the quarry. Whomever they belonged to had chosen to go deeper into the woods. A strong smell of a wood fire lingered in the air. Henry and Skip continued on the path to the quarry. Skip's anxiousness died away as they walked, and he quickly settled to his normal self.

The lakeside limestone quarry had been worked for a short while in the early 1900s but quickly closed. After a hundred years, the workings were now overgrown with trees. Henry and Skip walked down to the beach. What remained of the jetty, built so long ago to carry the limestone to Winnipeg, was now a number of black timbers protruding defiantly out of the ice. It was difficult to assess exactly where the water began because of the way the jumble of ice contorted in so many ways, littered the foreshore. He could see the warming hut a little farther down the beach and smiled: a place to warm up hands and paws.

Henry looked out across the water and could clearly see Punk and Little Punk islands as they were now bathed in sunshine—at least for a couple of minutes as there was a temporary break in the clouds. The cliffs and trees projected through the expanse of broken ice like an oasis in a desert. Henry exhaled deeply at the scene spread out before him, ice fleetingly sparkling in the sun. After a couple of minutes, the low clouds and snow squalls and cold wind started to build again.

With Skip on his heels, Henry approached the clearing just off the beach where the public warming hut sat, pushed the snow away from the door, and stepped inside the wooden building. It was spartan, with one small window and a bench on two sides of the room. There was a chill, but at least they were out of the wind. A metal fire box was against the opposite wall, with a crude metal flue that rose up through the roof. It had a faint wood fire smell, much like they had encountered on the trail a while ago. There was a pile of firewood, some matches, and newspaper to kindle the fire. The fire box was clean, ready for someone wanting to warm up in the cold. Henry was not staying long enough to start a fire. He shrugged off his rucksack, took out a mug and bowl and his thermos. Henry put the bowl on the floor and filled it with the hot light yellow liquid, following suit with the mug. Skip liked his herbal tea on their walks as much as Henry did on a cold morning. Skip lapped the rapidly cooling tea quickly and then looked up at Henry for a little more.

"Wait until I have finished my mug, Skip," Henry said, thinking that Skip's begging face was quite a picture.

Farther south along the north west side of the island was where the original Icelanders had settled, the area around Kjartanson's Point. The cold winds that blew from the north made it a less-than-ideal site for development and, apparently, according to what Henry had read, the east side of the island quickly became the more favoured place for settlement. Although he was a bit of a history buff, Henry had yet to explore the original settlement area. He'd been told that there was little to see of the original settlement; the houses and barns built of wood had long rotted back into the earth. Also, the area was now only accessible by water as the old rough-cut path from the main track across the middle of the island had become totally overgrown.

A local developer had been lobbying to put a proper road through and build some kind of development on this side of the island but there wasn't a lot of support from the cottagers in general and the Descendants of the Original Settlement Association in particular. This group was formed many years ago to celebrate and protect what was left of the legacy of the original settlement around Kjartanson's Point. They were specifically anti-any-disturbance of this area. The settlement had never been properly protected or excavated from an archeological point of view. Henry thought there was a fat chance of the developer being successful, which was fine with him; he didn't want to see any more development on the island.

It would be difficult to imagine how tough life had been back in the 1870s. The island was cut off from the mainland and was a long way from a town of any size. Also, the extreme cold and poor soil made for little more than subsistence farming. Fishing was the island's main industry, which had attracted the Icelanders to New Iceland, an area on the west side of lake Winnipeg. In the early days, long before overfishing destroyed their way of life, fish were abundant, and after a couple of tough establishment years the community started to prosper.

What remained of the village, the schoolhouse, community centre and church are located in the heritage area on the east side of the lake. By the late 1960s, many people were leaving the island, due to the decline of the fishery. Apparently, the community banded together and petitioned the Manitoba government to make the island a park, at least in part to provide some employment for those folks remaining. The park officially opened on July 26, 1975. From what Henry had read, there had been some bad blood caused by the value paid by the province in expropriating the land. In the 1990s, the government decided to sell the original homesteads back to the original families or their descendents.

Henry and Skip enjoyed a little more tea from his flask in the warming hut. Henry reflected on the incident on their walk. *Surely the person couldn't be sleeping rough.* Henry wondered. Eventually they headed back down the trail and home for breakfast.

Henry and Julia had a little morning ritual. Since Julia was not a morning person, Henry would put the coffee on after he and Skip got back from their daily walk. While the coffee brewed, he feed and watered Skip, then take two coffee mugs down to the bedroom where he'd sit on the bed, staring out across the lake while Julia slowly woke up. They would talk about the day ahead and send a quick text or two to the kids.

Henry mentioned the stranger on the trail, and Julia's first sentiments were of irritating disinterest. With his police background, Henry always saw the suspicious in every situation while Julia was more likely to see the good in everybody and everything. It was the strong smell of fire that suggested to him that this person could be camping or living outside—a very strange thing to be doing at this time of the year. He had seen many unfortunate folks living on the streets in the city, but at least they could find a warm spot and good meal from time to time at one of the shelters.

In spite of his curiosity, Henry didn't give it a lot more thought. He was looking forward to the warmer weather, spending some time on the water, and further developing the vegetable garden they had started working on last season.

He had also gotten into woodworking and had made a number of wine racks for the kids the past Christmas. Now, Henry was working on this year's project, benches to sit on while putting on your shoes by the front door.

Over the next couple of weekends, neighbours reappeared as the weather got warmer and the thaw really set in. The Briars, Jim and Ingrid, lived on one side and the Krugers on the other: both couples were good neighbours. The Briars were there year-round except for a couple of months they spent down south in Texas in the winter. They had spent many years coming up to the island before they built their cottage and retired, seemingly knowing everybody on the road. The Krugers were still working and came up less often.

Although sociable by nature, Julia and Henry didn't know all their neighbours, as they had come up to the lake mostly on weekends while they were working to ensure some alone time. Things were different now and Henry welcomed getting more involved in the lake community and getting to know more people. Julia's heart was really more in the city, being close to the grandkids, but she enjoyed the lake and enjoyed meeting the neighbours and sharing good times.

CHAPTER FIVE

Summer 2016

Spring turned into summer and Henry and Julia went up regularly to the cottage in the week to avoid all the visitors to the island. It gave them an opportunity to spend time at home in the city with the grandkids who were still small; their parents worked shifts and often had to stay in town on weekends. Neither Henry nor Julia appreciated how busy the island got in the summer and every year it seemed to get busier.

When their kids were not working they would all get together at the lake, have great times and create fun memories. The grandkids loved the water, and it was good for them to get away and really explore nature. All manner of wildlife populated the island, deer, fox, moose, bald eagles, pelicans, and black bears. Deer particularly, were regular visitors, which fascinated the grandchildren.

Henry spent quite a bit of time building up the vegetable patch, taking lots of tips from Jim Briar next door who had built quite a setup. Jim, a slender and fit guy, had a friendly, always-help-you-out demeanor, and a wicked sense of humour. Sometimes Henry didn't even know when he was being had. Jim had imported some topsoil, fenced off an area on his land to keep out the deer, and already he had a lot of green shoots coming up. Henry was working hard to emulate his neighbour.

One early morning, Henry was weeding while Jim was out doing the same thing. After an hour or so, Jim suggested a coffee break and the two friends headed down to the Harbour Inn. It was a beautiful morning, the sun was shining, a slight breeze blowing from the east. They decided to sit outside and watch the fishers coming in, dragging their catches up from their boats. Shouting rather than talking among themselves, it sounded to be light-hearted banter: the catch must have been good. A couple of small sailing boats were on the way out of the harbour, and there were young folks in kayaks, paddling back to the jetty.

The sun was still relatively low in the sky and was shining right in Henry's eyes, so he stood to change seats. As he moved, he suddenly smelled the same wood-fire aroma he had encountered in the woods a while ago. As he seated himself, he was vaguely aware that somebody had simultaneously disappeared through the screen door into the restaurant.

Henry was curious of who this stranger could be, but not curious enough to get out of his seat and follow the person into the restaurant.

"Henry? Are you still with us?" said Jim.

"Oh, sorry Jim, just daydreaming," said Henry, a little distracted.

Somehow the subject of murder mysteries came up. Henry and Julia were great lovers of this slightly macabre entertainment and they always had a new series on the go that they had purchased from PBS—no streaming at the lake, only DVDs.

Henry was yakking away when Jim muttered almost under his breath.

"What did you say?" Henry asked.

"I was wondering if there has ever been a murder on the island."

"Now that's an interesting thought," said Henry. "How would you even find out? Though who would care?"

"You would, Henry. You love the whodunnit stuff. I am sure you would have the curiosity to find out."

They finished their coffees, paid, and headed back to the truck.

"You know what, Jim? You've gotten me intrigued. A community of fishers and their families living in a remote place like this—there has to have been drama. I am going to do some homework."

Henry discussed this with Julia when he got back to the cottage.

"Henry, you have an almost childlike love of this place and all its beauty, why would you tempt fate and potentially contaminate your feelings if you discover real-life evil or tragedy that, right now, you're blissfully unaware of?" Julia was irritated. Henry reflected on her words, decided she was probably right, and got right back to enjoying the activities of summer.

The hot and dry summer flew by. The grass didn't need much cutting, yet the dandelions came up as always. Watering the vegetable patch was important, which Jim kindly did when Henry and Julia were in the city. Jim's green fingers were definitely superior to Henry's, and Jim had been harvesting vegetables from his own garden all summer.

One day, towards the end of the summer, Jim turned up at Henry's door, clearly a little upset. He had just found that many of his carrots and parsnips had been dug up. Henry went over with him to investigate.

The fence had been partly pushed over. There were some deer droppings around and the initial conclusion was that deer had pushed over the fence. There had been rain the night before and it would not have been difficult for the deer to pull out the carrots. Suddenly, Henry noticed a large footprint, clearly larger than Jim's.

"What do you think?" asked Jim.

"I think somebody dug your veggies up and pushed down the fence and then the deer finished off the rest."

"Who would do something like this?" Jim wondered.

"Somebody who's hungry and has no money and doesn't want to be seen," Henry replied.

"Cannot call anything your own in this day and age," Jim said a little despondently as he walked back to his house.

Henry hung around, inspecting the scene of the crime, and noticed a couple more footprints—unusually large ones, similar to ones Skip and Henry had seen on the quarry trail in the spring. *Looks like somebody is living rough on the island... but who? And where?* Henry's curiosity had been piqued.

CHAPTER SIX

Fall 2016

That fall was marvelous on the island. Lots of warm days and no storms which was unusual for the time of the year. *We're going to pay for this come the winter,* Henry thought, but for the moment he had every intention of enjoying the special time of the year.

He loved to read murder mysteries in the afternoon once he had completed his daily fall chores. Henry would often be found stretched out on his favourite couch in the lounge overlooking the ever-changing blues and greys of the water and the fall colours of the trees on the islands in the mid-distance. He had discovered an Icelandic murder-mystery writer by the name of Yrsa Sigurðardóttir and was binge reading a number of her books. He loved the sense of the place Yrsa managed to capture in her writing. He made a mental note to add "visit Iceland" to his bucket list.

Julia amused herself with her reading, books and scripts, along with cooking and her women's golf group that played twice a week and had done since the early summer. The mornings were getting cooler, but it looked likely that they would keep the local course open until the middle of October. She was meeting new folks every week and her social group, way exceeded Henry's.

Henry kayaked often. The crowds had gone, and the lake was a magical place in the early morning just as the sun came up. There was little wind most days, and the water was flat as a mirror.

Most of the time the only sound was the splashing of the paddles as they came in and out of the water. The exception were the regular sounds of squadrons of geese flying south, or the eerie, haunting cry of the loons.

The pelicans, ungainly in the water but beautiful in flight, had been gone for a short while.

It was cool, but Henry was dressed for the weather. Now that he was a more experienced kayaker, he had a circuit: south to the headland, round the back of Little Punk and Punk Islands, up to the northern headland of the main island, and then straight back across the bay. It was quite a distance, so this was the route he took when the wind was low. He had learned his lesson.

The last kilometre or so was a struggle, but Henry loved being on the water so much. He thought of getting a boat, but the convenience of storing and launching the kayak off his own property always trumped the hassle of a motorized vessel. Besides, kayaking was a great workout.

The green algae that filled the lake in August was gone by September and the water was clear and still mild in temperature. Every so often he would see a fish break the surface. *Not so smart*, he thought. Bald eagles drifted overhead, looking to fatten up for the winter.

The previous summer, Henry had witnessed a bald eagle swooping down and grabbing a large fish not five metres away from where he was paddling. Though amazing, it had been a little intimidating to see how large a fully grown eagle is, close up and personal.

This was the natural world that had been such a revelation to Henry during his midlife crisis. To see nature play out in front of him somehow put his life in perspective. He couldn't quite get his head around why these incidents were such joyful experiences. They just *were*, and that was enough.

The good weather continued into October, when Henry normally cleaned up and stored the kayaks back in the garage for the winter. But he didn't want to waste the mild weather and he decided to fulfill a little ambition: to paddle down to Kjartanson's Point to explore the spot where Hecla's Icelandic settlers had originally arrived and made their homes. Apparently, they didn't stay too long, a small number of years. The north side of the island was more exposed to the Arctic winds.

He wondered if there would be any evidence of the settlement. He had been told that after almost 150 years, everything had probably rotted back into the bush. But, *nothing ventured, nothing gained* he thought.

DEATH AT THE POINT

It was the end of the first week in October, and just as the sun came up, Henry set off across the bay. There was not a whisper of wind, and he made good progress, stopping off on a small beach just before the headland for a quick cup of tea from his thermos.

Henry had estimated it would take him a good eight hours, round trip, to paddle to the point. There would be no cellphone service on that side of the island, so he had been very clear to Julia that if he felt like he wasn't making the progress he needed he would turn back.

As he rounded the headland, a north west wind roughed up the water and a gentle rain steamed up his glasses, making it difficult to see. So he packed them away in his top pocket and continued to paddle close to the shore to protect himself from the wind. It was a longer ride, but paddling further out in the lake into the wind would have been really hard going. As it was, there was spray coming off the lake, stinging his eyes.

After about three hours of paddling, Henry realized he was running out of time. The wind had slowed his progress and although he saw the point in the distance, he knew it was farther than it looked. He wasn't equipped to camp, and he was a little concerned about bears, so the best thing to do was rest and then head back. In the time he had been on the island, Henry had rarely seen a bear, but he wasn't naive enough to think they were not around.

The thick growth of trees protected him a little from the wind as Henry attempted to get the kayak out of the water and up onto the stony beach. He ate his lunch, had another cup of tea, then finished off half a bar of chocolate.

When Henry made it back home, he was exhausted. Julia was both concerned and frustrated he had pushed himself so hard, especially considering his medical condition.

"Henry, you are not a thirty-year-old! What would have happened if you had had a heart attack, or your atrial fibrillation became problematic?" He just hunched his shoulders and apologized. Henry had always thought his wife was a pretty relaxed person most of the time, but could become a worry wart around her family. Henry also knew he sometimes could be impulsive with the tendency for the occasional recklessness so he appreciated and loved her for her "coaching moments." Although sore,

Henry was secretly exhilarated by his adventure and determined that after a couple of days of rest (and hopefully a day of little or no wind) he'd try again. The following week was "it's now or never" as the weather was perfect, a high of 13 degree was forecasted, with little or no wind. Henry started early and was on the water just as it was getting light. This time, he had decided to pace himself properly, taking a number of breaks. This time, he made it to the point in just under three and a half hours. A rocky and almost treeless protrusion into the lake, the point was a perfect place to beach the kayak.

Henry gazed down the point and into the densely treed bush. He really didn't know where to look, what he was likely to see, and he had no idea exactly where the settlement may have existed.

He assumed that the point itself would have been too exposed. As he explored, he didn't see any evidence of human habitation. Henry walked to the base of the point and started to push himself through a mixture of old- and new-growth forest. He had brought a machete and he needed it. The leaves on the trees and bushes had turned but very few had fallen, it was difficult to see too far into the forest.

Henry couldn't see anything to indicate any signs of human activity, past or present. He was about to turn around when something red caught his eye. He stopped and stared intensely into the bush for a while and eventually thought what he was seeing was a tent. After fighting his way through more bush and tree branches, Henry was standing in a small clearing. At the centre of it was a large tent with a burned-out fire pit in front of it. The remains of what looked like a rabbit were still on the spit over the fire. Close by was a clothesline, drawn between two trees, with a single, large pair of pants hanging by a couple of improvised wooden clothes pegs.

It was quiet in the clearing as Henry stood and looked around. He noticed a path cut in the bush, which he assumed followed the coastline north towards the old quarry. He made a mental note for the next time he walked to the quarry to look for evidence of a path. Henry had never ventured to the other side of the quarry.

Nearby was what looked like an old lime kiln, an effort in the days before cement supply to produce lime to use as mortar to build foundations for houses and barns, although in the immediate vicinity there was no evidence of any stone foundations.

The original settlement must be close by. However, Henry was feeling extremely uncomfortable, like he was trespassing in somebody's private space, and he was one hell of a long way from home if the occupant didn't take kindly to his presence. He fought the unsettling feeling that he was being watched, then made an instant decision to get back to his kayak and head home.

For some reason, Henry was on the edge of panic, constantly looking over his shoulder and stopping from time to time to listen for the sounds of anything behind him. There was complete silence except for the sounds he was making. At least following his route back, the trail was a little easier to traverse.

At first, Henry didn't see his kayak, and his feeling of panic escalated. It had come untethered from the rock he had secured it to, but fortunately it had only drifted off a short distance in the shallows. The rocks were slippery underfoot, but he quickly waded out and jumped in the boat. He didn't relax until he was safely offshore, and the point was far behind him. Henry was a little surprised by his emotion, as there was no direct threat and he had been in worse situations in the past. However he realized he wasn't young anymore and not in perfect health.

By the time he got home just before dark, he was exhausted. Julia once again, had been worried. She was thinking of sending out some kind of search party when he walked through the door. After an earful from Julia, Henry cracked opened a can of beer, sat down, and polished off a massive plate of shepherd's pie.

Any interest Julia may have had in what Henry may have seen was completely offset by the fear she had that her reckless husband almost hadn't made it home. She was not amused and all the hugs and apologies in the world were not going to help. Hopefully, a good sleep would reset things, Henry hoped.

They played a couple of games of cards and by the end of the evening, all was good between them.

The next morning, Henry awoke a little sore, with blistered hands but generally not too worse for wear. He made a lovely, cooked breakfast for

Julia and himself. Generally it was just cereal or an egg. Henry was pleased with himself for having concluded that the tall red-headed stranger had indeed been sleeping out rough. Henry needed to think through what he had seen and decide what his next steps should be.

After doing some chores, he reached for his coat. "I'm heading next door to see Jim."

"OK, see you later," Julia said. She was also heading out for one of the last golf games of the season.

Jim invited Henry in with a smile, happy for company. Ingrid, his wife, had headed back to the city for her father's medical appointment, so over a cup of coffee or three, Henry related the adventures of the past day. Jim, who had been a financial adviser for a big bank in a previous life, was a smart and practical guy with a great sense of humour—somebody Henry knew instinctively he could trust.

Jim interrupted Henry from time to time to poke fun at Henry's ability to create drama.

"So let me get this right," Jim said. "You paddled all the way to Kjartanson Point, pushed into the wood, found a campsite and not a heck of a lot more, got scared, and hightailed it home?"

"Jim, I for one was a little upset I didn't get a chance to explore more of the area. That was the whole intention behind me going all that way! Then there is the matter of somebody camping illegally in a provincial park. Aren't you a little intrigued as to who this character is and why he would be camping out in such a remote place?"

"Not really," Jim replied. "If the guy thinks he is going to survive all winter in a tent, he must be crazy—"

"I think he has already," Henry interrupted. "Remember in the spring I told you about the footprints and Skip's reaction when we were walking to the old quarry? I think he was around last winter or at least the end of it. We should keep this quiet for now."

"As far as we know, other than maybe stealing the odd carrot or parsnip, he hasn't caused any harm," Jim agreed.

The period up until Christmas kept Julia and Henry largely away from the lake. They were involved in a lot of volunteer activities and of course there were the various grandkid activities that they wanted to be part of as many as possible. James was playing the part of Joseph in his school's nativity play. Alex had swimming lessons and had reached Turtle Level, for which they were all very proud.

Thoughts of the person living rough on the island kept coming back to Henry. *Surely, he cannot be living in that tent all winter; it doesn't make any sense. Why would he be staying in such an out-of-the-way place, with minimal contact with the outside world?*

He decided to research the original community to see if there was some mystery this modern-day intruder could be connected with. Unlikely, but at least it would be an interesting winter project.

CHAPTER SEVEN

January 2017

Once Christmas was over, Henry resumed his interest in his project and rode out to Gimli. He thought a visit to the New Iceland Heritage Museum would be a good start. He studied all the text accompanying the artifacts on display, but there was little information on the original settlers of the north side of Hecla Island. They were definitely part of the second wave of settlers to New Iceland; the first settlers from Iceland had settled in the Gimli area. As more Icelanders arrived, the need for additional land for homesteading had continued. Those who made their homes on the island were probably fishers back home. The soil on the island was generally poor and there was limestone just below the surface. The island was named after the Mount Hekla volcano in Iceland, originally named "Mikley," which is Icelandic for "big island."

He learned the initials and surnames of the original settler families from a commemoration plaque on the west side of the island across from the church. According to the curator, the public archive in Winnipeg would have the original transit and immigration papers for each family, and he should be able to locate the names and ages of each member, their place of birth, and last address in Iceland.

Henry went to the public archives to find the documents. As the curator had suggested, their places of birth or last addresses were listed. Though the locations were basic, he was interested to see the general area they had come from, and it was no surprise that they immigrated from the same area in Iceland and were probably all related. They didn't seem to be remarkable in any particular way; they were probably poor fisher families trying to build a new start in a new and strange land.

He tried to imagine how challenging it must have been for the pioneering families to try to establish themselves in the short warmer season, build shelter, and to provide enough food to feed themselves—both immediately and to carry them over the winter. He wondered why they settled on the north side of the island. There was no substantive natural harbour for their boats. The forest would have come right down to the water and there was little soil to grow vegetables to supplement their fish-based diet.

The stranger kept entering Henry's mind. Was this stranger a fugitive? Was he possibly looking for something? He was certainly operating in secret for whatever reason. It seemed crazy that he would be sleeping out there all winter. What could he be doing?

Henry sensed that looking through the archives further would be a waste of time.

The next week, he drove up to the lake on his own. Chris, a neighbour who he didn't know so well, was out snow blowing his driveway. Henry stopped to exchange some pleasantries with him when he waved.

"Just a head's up Henry, you have a lot of snow on your driveway," Chris said. "Do you have a snow blower?"

"No, I don't, Chris."

"For a beer sometime, I'll snow blow your driveway when I am done here."

"Wow—that is kind of you Chris, thanks."

It was a milder day, and the sun was out, and they were standing out of the wind. They exchanged family news. Chris was a chatty guy, a big man with a craggy weather-beaten face. He had a deep gravelly voice. Henry didn't know him well but had made a late New Year's resolution to get to know his neighbours a little better.

Chris was quite the outdoorsman, and it wasn't long before they were talking snow shoeing and cross-country skiing. Henry promised to give Chris a call in the evening to set a time for the next day. The weather was looking to continue to be mild for the time of the year, and although the forecast showed a mixture of sun and cloud, there no wind was predicted.

DEATH AT THE POINT

Chris was a semi-retired RCMP officer who had served in the Canadian north most of his career and preferred the quiet life. At this time of year, he did plenty of ice fishing. He picked up the odd assignment, mainly in the north, providing coverage for officers on vacation. The money was good, and he could cherry-pick his assignments.

Chris, true to his word, cleared his driveway an hour or so later.

Relaxing over a cup of coffee and looking out at the lake, it suddenly occurred to Henry that he should take advantage of Chris's companionship and ski down to the point to see what was going on.

Other than Julia, Jim, and Ingrid, nobody was aware of the mysterious person out at the point and for whatever reason, Henry had kept it that way. The guy had not caused any issues and probably had his reasons for being there. Henry had a hunch that the person was likely the tall red-bearded stranger.

However, Henry's curiosity was getting the best of him and if he was planning to suggest they ski to the point, he should have the decency to open up to Chris about it. He mentioned it to Julia when he called her in Winnipeg that evening.

"Chris is your typical, tall, strong Mountie. You are going to have to battle to keep up to him Henry. No disrespect to you, but they build their police officers bigger here than they do in the UK," she smiled. "Oh, and I am sure he knows more than he's saying if he still works for the RCMP from time to time and is connected."

Henry phoned Chris that night. Initially, Chris was a little confused about his suggestion to go skiing on the lake. But once Henry had explained the background, Chris readily agreed to go.

Chris arrived early the next morning. They had breakfast together and Chris ensured they had all the kit they needed, including a spare set of warm clothes. They had food for lunch and a couple of thermoses of coffee and, just in case, dinner. They also had energy bars and the ability to make a fire if they got stuck outside for longer than planned. Chris also had a satellite phone as he knew there was no cell signal on that side of the island.

"You may need sunglasses," Chris said. "The sun will be in your face for at least part of the trip down there and the glare off the snow and the ice, can be tiring on the eyes."

It was barely light when they set out. There was almost no wind—a big blessing. They both had rucksacks on their backs and getting over the jumbled and jagged ice on the shoreline took some effort. There were also drifts that had built up against the ice on the foreshore.

Once they were past the drifts, there was not much snow on the ice. It had been very cold recently with little snow and the lake was frozen, well over a couple of feet, according to Chris.

They made OK progress on the way out. Chris, although older, was a strong skier and he had to slow down from time to time as Henry was struggling to keep up. Henry knew they had a long way to go and was trying to pace himself.

They picked a route that didn't follow the coastline, which turned out to be more direct and probably saved them a mile or two. Eventually, Henry fell into the rhythm of skiing, and it got a little easier. He was impressed by their progress compared to his kayaking efforts of the previous fall.

They approached the point cautiously. Taking off their skis, they stacked them in a landmark spot and proceeded to the area in the bush that Henry had seen the tent in the previous fall. It was still there, or what was left of it, barely visible, collapsed under the weight of the snow. The clothesline was still up, with a good number of frozen items dangling from the line. The fire pit was partly buried under the snow. There were a couple of animal prints, but no boot tracks in the snow. The place looked abandoned. Nobody had been around since the snows at the end of the previous year. The obvious thought occurred to Henry: if the stranger had left, why hadn't he taken his clothing with him? Generally, the camp looked very much like he had seen it the previous fall.

While they made a small fire and warmed up two tins of baked beans, they pondered what the stranger could have been up to. Chris suggested they do a search of the area after lunch.

They left their rucksacks by the fire and moved outside the clearing, Chris to the north, Henry to the south. Henry had never really identified where the original settlement had been and there was no obvious sign that it was where they were standing.

After five minutes or so, Henry heard Chris shouting. He followed the sound of his voice and found him standing among trees, many of which were growing oddly. It was an area vastly different from typical firs and birches that populated most of the island. The ground was uneven in places, and showed signs of having been disturbed. It was difficult to see because of the snow cover, but the regular forms in the snow represented some kind of stone foundation for small rectangular dwellings and a much larger structure, maybe a barn. Within these stone foundations were numerous, random mounds of snow. After removing some of the snow, they could see that the mounds were piles of soil and small rocks. "Somebody has been digging holes within the foundation of all of the structures," Chris said.

"Yes, this looks like what is left of the original settlement," Henry said.

"You're probably right, somebody has been excavating what would have been rough timber floors of the original buildings."

Henry tripped over something walking back from inspecting one of the spots, but Chris grabbed him before he fell. They looked down and realized something of a reasonable size was buried under the snow. Henry got down on his knees and swept away the snow. He was looking directly into a pair of snow-filled eye sockets.

Henry fell back in disbelief and horror. Chris was initially taken aback but regained his composure and laughed at Henry's reaction.

"Sorry, Henry. That was insensitive of me. I suppose I've seen too much of this in my RCMP career."

"Actually, me too, but I just wasn't expecting it here and now."

"Let's clear the rest of the snow and see what we're dealing with."

Given their backgrounds, Chris and Henry knew that disturbing the scene was not a great idea, but they were curious to see if they recognized the person. It was a man, face up, of average build, middle-aged, overweight, Caucasian, and wearing winter clothing. He was firmly frozen to the ground, both arms at his chest, indicating to Henry, at least, that he had died prior to the snowfall. It looked like he had fallen—or been laid—in a muddy, wet area. Other than a worn shovel and a pick, there was nothing close to the body that they could see.

There was no obvious cause of death. There was some evidence that crows had gotten to him. Chris didn't seem to recognize him, specifically. However, in spite of his frozen and blue-tinged face and the disfigured eyes and nose, there was something slightly familiar about him to Henry.

A quick search of his pockets didn't reveal a wallet or any personal effects. Just one receipt from a gas station in Gimli, dated October 31, which was a little odd.

Chris stood up. "Henry, can you cover him up again? I'm going to call the Riverton detachment to get investigative and forensic teams out here." Chris got on the sat phone. Henry could hear Chris talking in the clipped way police officers do, describing the location and the scene as well as giving the best description he could of the deceased person.

He could tell that they were being asked to sit tight and wait for a call back. It was starting to get late, the wind was coming up, and Henry was worried about being tied up at the scene and having to find their way back across the ice in the dark, particularly if there wasn't any moonlight.

The call came through a while later. Would they remain at the site overnight to secure the scene until a full team could be out early the next morning? Henry was not very happy, but Chris was practically revelling in the situation and assured Henry that they would be OK. He had slept out in far colder temperatures.

Reluctantly, Henry agreed. Chris rang the detachment back, then they both rang their wives on the satellite phone to explain. Julia said she would drive up from Winnipeg in the morning.

"The tent is toast," Chris said, back at the campsite. "There is plenty of snow, so we need to build a quinze. We will build it close to the firepit."

"What is a quinze?" Henry asked.

"You have been in Canada all these years and you don't know what a quinze is?" Chris said, laughing. "It is a shelter shaped from the loose snow. Not an igloo, if you are about to ask; that is made from harder snow."

They left the tools by the body as they would be part of the investigation. Finding a second old shovel adjacent to the tent, Henry set to work to build up the pile of snow, under Chris's guidance, while Chris started a fire. Luckily, there was a pile of logs that looked like it should last them the night.

It was dark by the time they completed the quinze, and the wind was blowing gently off the lake. The fire crackled and sparked. Chris's small cooking pot was only large enough for one portion at a time, so it was stew and a couple of protein bars for dinner.

"So who was this guy, Henry?" Chris asked. "You said the mysterious guy was a large chappie. Our victim was medium build at best, so clearly not the same guy."

"Good point, Chris, but just because we haven't seen him before doesn't mean the two of them weren't working together. Maybe they had a falling out?"

"But what were they looking for? There's no obvious thing of value lying around."

They were tired and headed into the quinze to get the best sleep they could. They shared the sleeping bag and the basic foam mattress they had recovered from beneath the collapsed tent.

Chris was a big guy and clearly suffered from sleep apnea; his snoring more or less kept Henry from deep sleep but at least he napped on and off and was surprisingly warm, considering how cold it was.

Henry was up first, and he loaded more wood onto the fire. He was so stiff—definitely not conditioned for skiing and sleeping outside. He melted some snow so they would be have a mug of steaming hot black coffee soon. Eventually, over Chris's snoring, Henry could hear the sound of vehicles.

"Looks like reinforcements are coming, Chris. Time to get up." Henry reached in to shake Chris from his cozy nest.

Sound travels long distance over the lake; it was a good fifteen minutes before the police vehicles appeared from the south. Henry walked out of the trees to the spit of rocks that had formed the original rough harbour and waved them in.

This most desolate place was now full of police officers and forensic investigators, all in white one-piece gear. *They're certainly putting good resources on it,* Henry thought. One of the police officers agreed to drive them back over the ice. A heck a lot easier than skiing, though Henry could see that Chris was a little disappointed to miss out on the adventure back. Henry was not a serious outdoorsman. He was tired, cold, and hungry and was looking forward to a nice hot bath and a home-cooked breakfast, thus a ride home sounded like a great idea.

Julia, who must have left early to drive up to the lake, opened the door, concern on her face.

"Aren't you getting a bit too old for these kinds of antics?" she asked, genuinely upset. "I knew this obsession with the tall red-bearded stranger was going to cause us some grief and look at you—" She realized Henry was too tired to take in what she was saying.

"Can you run a bath for me please—and make a couple of pieces of buttered toast, while I get my clothes off? It's been one hell of a last twenty-four hours."

Julia sat by the bath, holding the plate with the toast, while Henry related the details of their trek between bites of toast and sips of coffee.

"We found a body, but it's not the person I expected. The police are all over the scene right now and I'm sure they will be back in the spring, dependent on what they find. Difficult to see much in the snow."

Henry was now sitting in his favourite chair, looking out across the lake after his relaxing bath when there was a knock at the door. In walked Jim, relieved to see his friend looking good, and hungry to get caught up on the events of the previous day. Julia left the men with their coffees to talk everything through.

After Henry had finished, Jim asked, "So do you think the guy was murdered?"

"Don't know what to think," Henry replied. "I didn't see any obvious sign of injury. We'll have to wait and see what the pathologist finds. My guess is we will not be hearing anything specific, particularly if they find evidence of foul play."

A couple of days later, Chris popped over for coffee. "Any news about the investigation?" Henry asked.

"No, not directly, but do you remember that private investigator who disappeared in the fall? The pleas for any information from his family that was on the news a couple of times? Well, I'm pretty sure it's him. The police have just announced that they have found him 'in a location outside of Winnipeg'—from the pictures it looks like the same guy.

They were careful to not identify the location, but they did say he died of natural causes."

"What was he doing there? Who was he working for? How did he get there?" Henry asked. "Maybe we will have leads to go on," Henry said.

"We?" Chris said. "Henry, this is a police investigation."

"Yep, but where is it going to go? He died of 'natural causes. The police have more important things to do. We should attend the funeral service. I'll check out the Obituary page in the *Winnipeg Free Press*. Chris, aren't you curious?"

"Of course I'm curious, but I'm also curious about the fish under my ice hole so you can amuse yourself with all this and I'm going fishing." With that he stood up, put the mug on the kitchen counter, and walked to the door.

CHAPTER EIGHT

Late winter, early 2017

I suppose after a lifetime of police work, Chris is not interested, Henry thought. *Cannot blame him, really. However, this is close to home–I thought there would have been more enthusiasm to follow up.*

A couple of days later, the obituary for a David Einarson appeared in the *Winnipeg Free Press;* the funeral service was to be held in the Mennonite Church in East Kildonan the following Wednesday.

It was a relatively short obituary by Winnipeg standards. He was born in East Kildonan and had lived his whole life in Winnipeg. Prior to becoming a private investigator, he had worked for CP Rail, then spent five years with the Winnipeg Police Service. For a moment, Henry wondered whether their police service time overlapped but he thought not.

There was nothing really remarkable in the write-up, although it was a bit of a coincidence that he had an Icelandic surname and had died on an Icelandic-settled island. But many Winnipeggers were descendants of settlers from New Iceland.

Henry wanted to pay his respects. He had discovered his body, and so Julia was happy to drive home with Henry the Tuesday morning. Their eldest grandkid had been sick, and Christine was hoping Julia could spend some time with him, so she didn't have to take any more time off work.

They arrived home, unpacked, ate, then Henry cleaned up and opened up his iPad. He thought he would research David Einarson ahead of the funeral. A hundred pages appeared.

"That's not going to get me anywhere." He added "private investigator, Winnipeg." Up popped David Einarson's company website. It was well put together; a photo of him looking very suave and serious, graced the opening page. Clearly, it had been taken a number of years ago.

The site was general in nature. Of course, Einarson couldn't reference real cases he had successfully concluded, but it did make a statement about "references on request" and noted his twenty-five years in the business and the types of work he had been involved in. This included searches for long-lost relatives, surveillance of all kinds (including marital cases), and even tracking down lost pets.

Other than his website, there were no specific sites referencing this particular David Einarson—probably not unusual for a person who was quietly going about his business, not wanting to be particularly prominent in the community.

Henry went to the closet to ensure his suit was clean and presentable, selected a white shirt, pressed it, and hung it on a hanger for later.

He went downstairs, grabbed a can of Guinness from the fridge and a glass, flopped down on the sofa and spent the afternoon reading a book—a murder mystery of course. After a couple of hours, he turned on the evening news, cracked open another can, and slowly poured the beer into the glass. The latest political scandals were getting a little dull and he was about to change the channel when the photo from David Einarson's website showed up with a short update on the investigation. A typical news item, it didn't add much to the story, but it did say his car had been found. *I wonder where it was.*

Henry put a pizza in the microwave and minutes later was finishing eating when he heard the garage door opening. Julia came in, slamming the door as she always did.

"Hey! You don't have to close the door so hard," Henry shouted. Not that Julia took any notice. She was already giving Henry an update on their eldest grandson's condition as she took off her coat. Julia was a very nurturing person and just loved to help out where she could with the "boys"—her pet name for her Winnipeg grandkids.

Henry was a little sleepy, but it was not a good time to go to bed. Julia recognized the signals and was insistent that she update Henry on their kids' family drama.

DEATH AT THE POINT

"I haven't seen you all evening and you want to rush off to bed," she said with some enthusiasm. "A cup of tea?"

"Earl Grey, please."

"It's snowing like crazy," Julia said as she closed the lounge curtains, the mounds of white piled high on the deck. "You'll have to get out tomorrow and shovel, back and front."

"No problem," Henry replied. "I'll get it done before the funeral at eleven."

"So, you're still going?" Julia said.

"Yes. I'm very intrigued by what David Einarson was doing in such a remote spot." Julia just shook her head. "Once a police officer, always a police officer. I didn't retire to spend time watching you running around following up on an investigation that is no concern of yours." Henry just smiled.

He changed the subject and they chatted for a while—family drama to be shared—sipping their tea and then eventually proceeded to bed. Henry kissed Julia, turned over, and was asleep in a New York minute.

Henry got up at the crack of dawn; it was cold but clear and there was little to no wind. The snow was a couple of inches deep, and it didn't take Henry long to clear the driveway. By 9:00 a.m. when he stumbled back into the house, his balaclava heavy with ice and frost, he was greeted by a smiling Julia and a whistling kettle.

"Get upstairs and hop into the bath," Julia said. "I'll bring up a cuppa in a couple of minutes."

True to her word, Julia appeared at the door and placed a mug of tea on the side of the bath and settled on the closed toilet seat. As Henry sipped his tea, Julia asked, "So what do you think you are going to gain from attending a complete stranger's funeral?"

"Not sure," Henry replied. "I just know something is not right."

Julia didn't comment for a while, then said, "Well, if you're determined to find the answer to this mystery and you're going to continue to be obsessed by it, then I might as well come along and help you get to the bottom of this. The sooner we get your mystery solved, the sooner our life can get back to normal. Even the kids are talking about how distracted you are."

With that, she stood up. "I better see what I have to wear. I haven't been to a funeral for a good while; I assume you will be wearing your black suit?"

Henry nodded. Julia left the bathroom, an odd smirk on her face. *I think I have finally gotten Julia intrigued, too,* Henry thought.

They decided to get to the service early, as there would be a viewing and it would be a chance to observe the family a little. Traffic was lighter than expected, the streets were cleared of snow, and it was very cold but sunny. Henry felt sorry for the family, the burial a little later in the day would be no fun at these temperatures.

They walked into the church arm in arm and were greeted by the minister and encouraged to sign the book of remembrance, which they did, in their own names.

In the foyer was a table with a large display of photographs, and next to it, the body lying in the coffin. David Einarson laid out in a suit and tie looked at peace. His eyes were closed—a blessing considering what the crows had done—and he looked much better than when Henry had last seen him on the island. He looked good for his age: he had a healthy head of light-brown hair, and his face was barely lined.

They walked over to the table of photographs. There were pictures of him with his wife and children. There were older pictures, too, probably of him as a child, mostly taken in and around Winnipeg, although there were quite a few shot lakeside. Henry couldn't really tell which lake it was; there were no noticeable landmarks. There were older people as well, who he assumed were David's grandparents.

People were starting to arrive, so it was time to find a seat. Henry led the way. He wanted to get close to the reserved seating area so he could observe the funeral party. As they sat down, an organist started to play sombre music quietly.

It was past 11:00 a.m. and there was still no sign of the family. People were talking quietly. Henry estimated about a hundred people in the church. A lot of handshaking, hugs, and low-level whispering communicated to him that there were relatives and friends reacquainting themselves.

The music ceased and Julia touched Henry's arm as the funeral party, led by the minister, entered the church from a back room. The minister walked at a reverent speed, followed by David's wife, arm in hand with a slightly younger man. She was dressed in black, head held high. She was attractive, but her makeup could not cover up red-rimmed eyes. She carried a handkerchief in her hand, dabbing her eyes from time to time as they paraded to their seats at the front of the congregation. Their three children—Henry assumed—walked behind them. Henry guessed their ages as six through to about twelve.

The service was surprisingly upbeat—a celebration of his life. The man escorting the wife into the church turned out to be David's younger brother, Simon. He was the master of ceremony alongside the minister, and after an opening prayer, he got up to welcome the congregation on behalf of the family. He was an eloquent speaker and talked with respect and a little humour of growing up in East Kildonan with his big brother.

Simon was genuinely upset and hesitated from time to time to collect his thoughts. Henry noticed David's wife looking at him and often he looked directly back at her, rather than at the general congregation.

After a hymn and a song from David's two girls, his son joined them onstage, and they proceeded to share stories and special times about their father. They struggled to hold back tears as they read from their prepared notes. His wife was quietly weeping into her handkerchief as Simon hugged her. The children returned to their seats as the minister asked the congregation to stand for another hymn, gave a final prayer, and then issued an invitation to all to attend a small reception downstairs in the church basement.

The members of the funeral party rose from their seats and led the congregation past the open coffin and to the reception. As everybody filed downstairs, Henry asked Julia to hang around as he needed to use the washroom. Quietly minding his own business, he couldn't help but overhear the conversation between the two older gentlemen who had walked in.

"My condolences on the loss of your son, Arthur. I cannot imagine the impact on his wife and the family."

"Yes, it has been a terrible time—still so much we don't know," Arthur, the father, said.

"We still don't know where he was found, and why the police aren't saying anything?"

"All we really know is that he died of natural causes," Arthur said.

"It'll probably come out in due course," the other man said. "He was a private investigator, after all. He was probably working on a case when he died."

Henry rejoined Julia and they headed downstairs to enter the throng of people. "If anybody asks," Henry said, "we are friends from way back, just showing our respects." Julia nodded and smiled, enjoying the innocent subterfuge.

Henry took a cup of tea and proceeded to weave through the tight mass of people, trying not to spill his drink. He shuffled over and handed the cup to Julia, and she introduced her new acquaintances as a couple of David's aunts.

"Yes, as I was saying," the older of the two ladies said, "David was married before; his first wife is here. Lovely lady—married her far too young—neither one of them were ready for the responsibilities of marriage and kids. They had two kids; the eldest died very young of cancer and the second one immigrated to Australia some years ago. I feel sorry for Dorothy—that's the first wife's name—she never remarried, and her only son is living in Australia. David continued to be a good dad after the divorce, that was, until he married Emily, the second one.

"Yes," the other aunt continued. "I have never taken to her. She has always seemed a bit of a princess to me."

"I know Emily was very resentful of the childcare payments David continued to pay Dorothy. She didn't make it easy on him, particularly when they started to have kids of their own. Dorothy still lives in the neighbourhood, just down from my senior living place on Rothesay."

Henry looked around the room. The widow, surrounded by her three kids, was talking to a constant stream of people moving past and paying their condolences.

I wonder where Simon has gone, Henry thought. *He couldn't have been closer to his sister-in-law during the service if he tried.*

After scanning the room, Henry spotted Simon, talking in a rather agitated state to another man. They were both staring across the room.

At first, Henry couldn't see at what or who, then he locked in on Dorothy, who had her back turned to them, talking to an older lady. They were definitely staring at her. *I wonder what their issue is.*

People were starting to leave, and the room was thinning out a little. Henry was concerned about being asked too many questions and felt it was time to leave. However, Julia had other ideas and had made a beeline for Arthur, David's dad, after saying goodbye to the aunts, Doris, and Olive, her younger, quieter sister. It was clear from Julia's nodding head that David's dad was doing most of the talking. *Hopefully, she will reap some information*, Henry thought.

After another five minutes or so, she shook his hand, and Julia and Henry climbed the stairs, and retrieved their coats. The coffin was gone as was the table with the photographs, a missed opportunity.

They bundled up in the foyer as the wind had gotten up, evident from the snow blowing around the parking lot. They walked hurriedly to the car.

"So what did you manage to glean from your conversation with the family?" Julia didn't always have Henry's attention, but she sure did now.

"Well, I didn't get any answers as to what specifically David Einarson was doing in such a remote spot. It seems like the RCMP have not even shared his body's location with close family members. I got the idea that David's second wife was high maintenance and appears to have a slightly too intimate relationship with her brother-in-law. Other than that, not much. It would be nice to know if there was anything interesting with his will."

"Well, there has to be a connection with the big guy who was camping out at the point. Where did he go? Where was the car found? That may be very important to understanding what happened. I'll have to see if Chris has found that out—"

"Let's give it a rest, Henry. We have a cruise coming up and I need a break from this weather and a little warm sunshine on my back. Time to clear our heads is what we need."

CHAPTER NINE

Spring 2017

Julia loved cruises. Not that Henry didn't; he just winced at the cost. Now that they were both retired, they had to be more careful with their money. Unfortunately, Henry was struggling to turn off his investigative mind, which when "on" was irritating to Julia.

Henry and Julia generally had a great time, the weather was as advertised, the food was great, and they visited some wonderful places. Between the almost daily excursions, wine tastings, entertainment, and guest speakers, it was a relaxed and engaging time. The guest speaker was specifically interesting to Henry: an historian with specific knowledge of piracy in the Caribbean during the seventeenth and eighteen centuries.

Fascinating stuff. Blackbeard featured quite prominently in his talks and Julia and Henry got to visit Blackbeard's "castle" on the island of St. Thomas. Apparently, he buried his treasure on a remote spot off the coast of the US, and it has never been found, or so the legend goes.

Of course, Henry's mind couldn't help but go back to the piles of dirt and rock that littered the original Icelandic settlement on Hecla. If "they" were not looking for treasure, what were they looking for? Henry spent a lot of time thinking about this during the balance of the trip, which didn't thrill Julia. She was happy not to give home a moment's thought.

When they returned home, Henry spent some time at the New Iceland Heritage Museum. From the records, it was clear that the first settlement on the north side of the island struggled, and it was only a small number of year before they joined other Icelandic settlers who were establishing themselves on the east side of the island in the area where the village is today.

From an early map Henry could see that a road made around that time, just wide enough for horse and cart connected the original and new settlement. Prior to that, the first families at Kjartanson Point had probably cut a trail through the forest along the edge of the island to the marsh area. Initially, they were isolated on the point but could access the mainland by boat and sail to Riverton to sell their catch.

Henry reasoned that the road or what was left of it, linking the original and later settlement on the east side of the island must cross the modern highway at some point.

Henry took a copy of the map and drove up to the island. While Julia was in Winnipeg babysitting the grandkids, he was going to attempt to find the original trail.

The late-winter weather had been an adjustment after the Caribbean. As often happens, Henry managed to catch a nasty cold, and he wasn't much fun to be around when he was sick, so Julia didn't have any problem with him running up to the island.

It was surprisingly warm for the time of the year, but there were still icy patches on the road, so in spite of Henry's relaxed drive, he couldn't be complacent. The snow became deeper as he drove north over the causeway and onto the island, past the still-closed park office, past the turn-off for the village, a couple of kilometres further he turned off onto the shoulder to consult his map. He was pretty sure he was in the right spot.

A couple of stags were standing close to the road in a clump of trees. They made no attempt to move away when he got out of his car. They looked a little thin and hungry. *It's been a hard winter with lots of snow*, Henry thought. *Not the best survival conditions for deer.*

Henry had estimated that the trail ran close to where he was standing. Grabbing a machete from the back of his vehicle, he struggled through the snow and walked a line—initially south—but when he couldn't find any evidence of a trail, he cut north. He was almost at the point of calling it a day when he noticed the trees where he was standing were different from the ones in the general area. Henry knew that the whole island's old growth trees had been cut down from the 1870s onwards and it was likely that any original trails would have been cut even earlier and used as haul roads to get the timber out.

It was probably a walk of a number of kilometres from this spot to the point. He noticed that somebody had cleared a narrow slot through the bush. It must have been quite a challenge. There was still snow between the trees and it was not particularly easy to walk. Henry eventually emerged into the camp area he had kayaked to and first seen the tent and later found David's body with Chris. The perimeter was still marked by yellow police tape.

Interesting, thought Henry. *There's clearly a path from the camp to the quarry because that was the area that first alerted Skip and I to the stranger in the woods. However, that would have been a far longer walk. Then there's this newly discovered trail and then there's also the possibility of access by boat or over the ice in the winter. I wonder which way David Einarson managed to get here. Is that significant?*

Henry sat on trunk of a downed tree and opened his bag for something to eat. It was so still that he could hear the distant caw of crows and the sound of the odd squirrel calling out. Other than that, silence. Not even the rustle of the wind in the trees. It seemed a sombre place, abandoned so long ago, and with an obvious mystery attached to the area, it didn't seem at peace.

From his position, Henry could see the flags marking the position of David Einarson's body and within the original foundations of each of the buildings were mounds of soil and rock fragments. There was no way that David could have dug this number of holes in the short period between the time he had disappeared and the snow fall and resulting freezing ground that occurred a week or so later. Henry surmised they were dug during the summer months by the tall red-headed guy who had been camping out in the area.

The stranger was obviously looking for something buried in the ground, but what had David Einarson been doing there? There didn't seem to be any fresh excavations since Henry and Chris had been there and no evidence of anybody being around. Did he and David know each other? Were they working together? Where had he gone?

When Henry got back to Winnipeg, the grandkids had gone, and Julia looked exhausted.

"That will teach you to volunteer to look after the two boys for the whole day," Henry said.

"Fat lot of help you were," she replied with grin.

"So what are we having for dinner?"

"Whatever you want to make."

Henry got right to work; he wasn't a great cook, but he could do the basics and he enjoyed it. He glanced at the TV as David Einarson's name showed up on the news ticker at the bottom of the screen.

"Hey, did you see what it said about David Einarson?"

"No," Julia replied, "I'll wait to see it come round again."

After a couple of minutes, the ticker update read, "David Einarson, whose body was recently found, had likely passed away around the time he was reported to have disappeared. RCMP continue to investigate—any persons with information are to contact the Winnipeg detachment of the RCMP."

"Well that's not news to us, but it is interesting that they say they are continuing to investigate," said Henry. "Chris was thinking as there was no foul play suspected that they would not be following up."

"Surely the family needs closure and would want to know what he was doing up there, assuming they now know," Julia replied.

"You're probably right. He had to be working for someone. How could we get his client files?"

"We'd have to find a way to befriend the family. The wife seems to have moved on, judging from her body language with David's brother, so I wonder if she is even interested in finding out what he was doing there."

"Hey, Julia; you got on very well with the older aunt—any chance you could bump into her and encourage her curiosity? Didn't she say she lived on Rothesay?"

"Yes, she did," Julia replied with a smile.

"That's just up the road. Why don't you change your walking route and see if you can 'accidentally' bump into her."

"Henry, I don't know what you are getting me into. I'll think about it." Those were her final words on the subject.

DEATH AT THE POINT

Julia walked alone every day except Wednesdays when she joined friends and they stopped off for coffee at the Tim Hortons on Henderson Highway—not her favourite coffee, but the companionship was good. It was easy to persuade her friends to reroute themselves that week and instead head to the Starbucks on Leila Avenue. It was Julia's birthday and they had offered to buy her a coffee and a little cake.

As she walked into the coffee shop, she bumped into Doris and Olive.

"You're a little way from Rothesay Street, Doris," Julia said as she shook her hand.

"It's my birthday, so Olive is treating me to a coffee," Doris replied. Julia laughed.

"What a coincidence! It's my birthday, too!" The aunts had a little chuckle.

"Hope to see you around sometime," Julia added as she rejoined her group.

A couple of weeks later, Julia was walking down Rothesay Street when she saw Doris on the other side of the road and crossed to greet her.

"How are you?" Julia asked.

"Fine, thanks for asking. So, whereabouts do you actually live?" Doris asked.

"Down on Longsmore, just south of here. We've lived in the area for a long time."

"I was on my way to Tim Hortons—can I buy you a coffee?" Doris asked.

"Sure, thanks," said Julia. They chattered their way to the coffee shop and were soon seated with two large black coffees.

"Did you see the recent news on my nephew?" said Doris. "Apparently, he died soon after he disappeared last fall."

"Yes, I did," Julia replied, still don't know where they found him," she continued.

"No, but it clearly wasn't in Winnipeg. I am pretty sure his widow knows," Doris said. "They must have asked her questions; nobody else in the family knows anything. All I know is the widow seemed confused about where he was found. Her only comment was, 'He was clearly not having an affair,', which I thought was a strange thing to say."

"Do you think it's connected with his work?" Julia added. "Why else would he be out of town?"

"Good point," Doris replied. "It's a pity they took my computer and his files."

"Why would they take your computer, Doris?" Julia's heart was speeding up.

"Because I did David's accounting and administrative work. I have four invoices left to send out so we can collect the outstanding balances. The police said the information on the computer may be useful in their enquiries."

"How many of those account addresses are out of town?" Julia asked.

"Well, if you don't tell anyone… To the best of my recollection, there was a Jessica Bird, a missing wife case out in the Arborg area, and some research work for a Kristian Kjartanson, a small property developer in Riverton."

Interesting, thought Julia, *Arborg and Riverton are close to Hecla. There has to be some kind of connection. Surely, the police would be following up on these leads.*

When Julia got home, Henry had been out in the garden and he was tired and thirsty when he came inside. He poured himself a glass of cold water from the jug in the fridge and slumped down next to Julia.

"My back is killing me."

"You always go at everything like a bull at a gate—you need to pace yourself better; you're still recovering from a cold, and you are not getting any younger."

Eventually, Julia shared what she had learned from Doris.

"Kristian Kjartanson is the guy who was trying to secure the original Icelandic settlement area on the island for some kind of development!" Henry said excitedly. "More than a coincidence, wouldn't you say?"

"Yes," Julia replied, "I think we're onto something. Having said that, the developer's interest in the area was common knowledge, as he had made application to the Provincial Park's Department. It wasn't as if he were sneaking around, so I wonder what he was using Dave Einarson for."

"This may be the break we're looking for—"

"I'm quite sure Mr. Kjartanson is being interviewed by the police," Julia interrupted as she got up from the sofa. "Let's sit tight and see what floats to the surface."

Julia and Henry complemented each other well and were still deeply in love after nearly forty years of marriage. At the end of the day, they had spats like any other couple, but they were content in each other's company and were very aware of each other's strengths and weaknesses. As it turned out, these were proving to make them an effective investigative team, much to their amusement.

CHAPTER TEN

Julia and Henry were busy in the city for a week or so and didn't get back up to Hecla until the following Friday.

While up there, they had decided to pop into Riverton, visit the Co-op for some groceries, and stake out the developer's office. It was in an older building on the Main Street; a weather-beaten sign over the front read, "Kjartanson Builders."

"I thought he was a developer," Julia said.

"I suppose he could be a developer and a builder. Maybe this is somebody else? There are probably a lot of Kjartansons in this area," Henry suggested. "The place looks closed up—a little strange for a Friday."

They walked around the building; there was a fenced-in yard area at the back with piles of timber and other building materials and a couple of older half-ton trucks with company logos. They drove around the small town but couldn't see any other buildings that held a sign with the Kjartanson name.

"Let's pop into the coffee shop on the Main Street and ask some questions," Julia suggested.

"Seems like a plan," said Henry, reversing into a parking space.

There was a lineup at the counter, and they eavesdropped over a little town gossip. An old man was talking to a younger provincial park worker wearing his uniform.

"So, Kristian Kjartanson had no luck persuading the parks department to develop that area on the north side of the island and now he wants to build a subdivision at the end of our quiet road. I am not happy, Ned," said the older man. Clearly agitated, he continued. "What can I do?"

"My suggestion," the younger guy replied, "is to draw up a petition, get your neighbours to sign it, and present your objections at the next Rural Municipality Planning Meeting. That land is not designated as part of Riverton town area."

The older man nodded and picked up his coffee. "Thanks, Ned," he said as he put a couple of coins down on the counter. "I might just take your advice." The old man nodded to others in the line as he left the shop.

"So where is Mr. Kjartanson planning to develop?" Julia asked, not intending to waste the opportunity. The young man did not disappoint her.

"On the east side of the river. It's over the bridge, adjacent to the existing subdivision on the agricultural land owned by the Wilson family. The locals are not for it, but I know Mr. Kjartanson has some influence on the rural municipality, so we'll have to see what happens."

He ordered a coffee and a bagel. "What is your interest, if I may ask?"

"We have a place at Hecla, and we were not happy about his proposed development up on the northwest side of the island, so frankly, we were glad to hear he's turning his attention elsewhere, although it's unfortunate that his plans are upsetting other people," Julia replied.

"A lot of people are not for change and development, and I get that. However, the park budget is so stretched, we barely have enough money to fill the potholes; it's very frustrating. We've even considered converting the roads back to gravel because we have a grader and a water truck to maintain the existing gravel roads on the island."

"Why don't you develop timeshares or smaller cottage units around the existing hotel? It would be a way to increase the tax base without creating sprawl—like what was done on the edge of Clearwater Lake," Julia suggested.

"I know it has been suggested, but the new owners of the hotel are still trying to understand the seasonality of the business. Until they have grown the business to be more sustainable year-round, I don't know if any further investment will be contemplated between the province and the operators of the property," Ned replied.

After they had introduced themselves, the server appeared with their orders. Before Ned had a chance to reach into his pocket, Julia had handed a twenty to the server.

"Keep the change," she said. "Would you like to sit with us? We are interested in what you know about Mr. Kjartanson's proposal if you don't mind speaking about it. I had assumed it was a development proposal for more cottages."

He nodded and they found a round table by the window and sat down.

"So what was the logic behind Kristian Kjartanson setting up a totally separate development on the original settlement area at Hecla?" Julia asked. Henry felt a little emasculated, but Julia was on a roll. She had a real talent for developing rapport with people.

"His relatives on his mother's side were one of the original families to settle on the north shore. That's where the Kjartanson Point name comes from. The intention was not to build a cottage community. He was interested in rebuilding the original settlement and operating like a theme village. He envisioned volunteers dressed in settler's original clothing, engaging in the day-to-day activities like the farming and fishing practices as they would have done in the 1870s. The park staff thought it was a great idea.

"He's proud of his heritage and wanted to give back to the community but he wanted financial support from the province which was not forthcoming—there was also so much resistance from the current cottagers. Particularly, those of Icelandic background who just wanted things left alone."

"I have to say, we were not aware of all this; we thought it was just a new cottage development," Henry said. "I've actually been to the site; there is nothing really to see other than the foundations—I assume everything except the foundations were built out of timber and rotted away years ago. I'm told the place was totally abandoned by the 1890s."

"Yes, some years ago, the University of Manitoba wanted to do an archeological dig at the site, but the original descendants had a problem with that as well. It is as if they want that original community to be left alone… very strange," Ned said.

"Thanks—really interesting," Julia interjected. "I actually think Mr. Kjartanson's idea is a good one; we were not aware of those details. It would be an attraction to draw tourist dollars and would help to keep the

Icelandic traditions alive. I see there is a Kjartanson Builder sign up in the Main Street. Is that the Mr. Kjartanson we're talking about?"

"No," Ned replied. "That's his brother, Karl. Kristian operates from the family farm just south of here. You cannot miss it; it's on the west side of the road, immediately north of the Icelandic River. There is an old tractor by the road with a flagpole. It's always flying the Icelandic flag."

"Thanks. Good to know," Julia replied, and stood up.

"Good talking to you," Henry said as they shook his hand and left the shop.

Henry was met with Julia's broad smile as they got into the car. "What are you smiling about?" Henry chuckled.

"It's amazing what you can find out by just talking to people—look what information we gleaned. It only cost us a cup of coffee and a bagel."

"You're right, Julia," Henry replied. He had to acknowledge Julia was an expert when it came to extracting information from people. She was so charming that people did it willingly. "So we know Kristian Kjartanson employed David Einarson, but don't know what for. How are we going to find that out? It has to be the key to the mystery."

"Maybe Chris has heard something," Julia replied. "It's worth following up, you can go see him when we get back to Hecla."

"Makes sense; we could call," Henry said.

"In person is always best."

CHAPTER ELEVEN

It was hot, and Henry opened the sunroof. It took forty minutes to drive to the cottage from Riverton. They parked the car in the garage, put their groceries inside, and immediately walked over to Chris's place.

"Looks like his boat is gone," Henry said after peeking at the dock when no one came to the door. "Let's go back to the cottage for now."

Chris was still not back when Henry and Julia returned from their evening walk.

"We'll have to try again in the morning," Henry said. "He seldom goes out fishing two days in a row."

The next morning, Henry stopped in at Chris's house on his way back from Skip's walk. He could see him sitting with a cup of coffee at the kitchen table as he knocked on the door. Chris opened it with a broad smile.

"So how are things with you, Julia, and the family, Henry?" Chris asked, as Henry removed his shoes.

"Pretty good, Chris. It's been a while."

"Fancy a cup of coffee?"

"Is the Pope a Catholic?" Henry replied.

Chris smiled as he poured the coffee. "The expressions you come up with Henry, never cease to amaze me."

"So let me guess: we're going to be talking about the investigation into the David Einarson death?" Chris said.

"Well, Julia and I have been busy."

"So you've suckered Julia into your project as well now? I didn't think she was interested at all in what you were doing."

"Well, she is now," Henry replied. "Ever since we went to the funeral—it triggered her interest."

"So what have you folks found out?" Chris asked, looking strangely uncomfortable.

"Well, not a heck of a lot, but enough to be interesting. We met some of David's family and got to know them a little. It seems the property developer, Kristian Kjartanson, employed David, but it's not clear why. Maybe connected with the proposed development at the site of the original Icelandic settlement on the island? It turned out that he was really up against it with the other original settler's descendants. They really had no interest in allowing the site to be disturbed and even rejected a request for a University of Manitoba archeological dig. It's strange, because Mr. Kjartanson was planning to build an interpretive centre on the foundations of the original buildings. Surely, that would be honouring their memory and the culture?"

"Agreed," Chris replied. "There has to be more to this."

"How about you? Have you heard anything from the RCMP investigation?"

"I know a Kristian Kjartanson was interviewed but from what I gathered, he had had acts of vandalism perpetrated against some of his properties and had employed David Einarson to do some digging. Apparently, he thought there was a connection with his proposed development on Hecla. Once his application was rejected the vandalism stopped."

"A bit too much of a coincidence, I would say," Henry replied. Chris nodded in agreement. "Did Mr. Kjartanson ever report the vandalism?"

"He did—he needed to for the insurance claim. But I don't think they found any evidence. No fingerprints, no camera footage, no witnesses. There was no violence so it would not be a top priority unfortunately for the local, overworked RCMP, and that is why Mr. Kjartanson would have employed a private investigator, I guess. His insurance premiums would be heading in the wrong direction, and he could not just sit idly by."

After a few moments, Chris diverted the conversation to his favourite subject: fishing. "So, what is your fishing experience Henry?" he asked, genuinely curious, as he poured two more mugs of hot coffee and sat down.

"Fishing never really interested me," Henry began. "In my childhood, we lived close to rivers, and I had a fishing rod. I have no good recollections of my first efforts. I was squeamish around putting live bait on the hook and managed to lose the hook and half the rod on the way home one day. That would be the end of my fishing story, if it wasn't for a friend a couple of years ago persuading me to go on a fishing trip off the coast of British Columbia to make up the numbers."

"God, I'm jealous Henry. Never managed to afford that type of experience; must have been amazing," Chris said in awe.

"It was just before I retired. I got what, for most people, would have been a trip of a lifetime. A salmon fishing trip off the most northerly island of the Haida Gwaii archipelago, north of Vancouver Island. In fact, closer to Alaska.

"It was a quite a trek to get there. A flight to Vancouver, a small plane to the regional capital of the islands and then a helicopter ride to the island resort—beautiful place set high up, overlooking the water—wet and cold, or at least cool, year-round. The accommodation, food, and service were five-star. The only problem was the actual fishing trip. I have a tendency to be seasick, especially in small boats. I took Gravol and this fixed any potential nausea, but I felt so drowsy, at times I could barely keep my head up. I caught a lot of salmon but was always glad to get back on firm soil."

Henry, aware that Chris was an avid fisher, blurted out an apology. "Sorry, Chris. It is the only fishing adventure I've really had. As you can tell, I am really a city guy." They both laughed.

"I don't believe you," Chris said. "I've skied with you and camped in the snow with you—few city folk would do that! You really should come fishing with me sometime, Henry. I know you don't get seasick on the lake; I've seen you out kayaking!" Chris was nothing if not persistent.

"Sometime," was Henry's smiling reply as he got up, put his coffee mug in the sink, then put on his boots.

"Henry, to be honest, I don't think the RCMP is going to be doing much more investigation unless something new crops up," Chris said. "After all, there was no foul play."

"Clearly somebody was looking for something, but nothing criminal appeared to be going on. I'm sure digging holes on provincial land without permission is an offence, but it doesn't really warrant further RCMP resources."

"Sorry Henry. I don't think you're going to hear anything further from me or the RCMP on this matter."

Henry walked home, wondering about Chris's final comment, but he let it go as he entered the cottage and Skip joyously rushed to the door to welcome him. That, and the smell of a nice beef stew was emulating from the kitchen.

"Hey luv," he shouted out as he unlaced his boots.

"Hi," Julia shouted back from the kitchen. "How did it go with Chris?"

"David Einarson was investigating a spate of vandalism on some of Kristian Kjartanson's properties in the area," Henry said, "that apparently stopped once Mr. Kjartanson's application for the development on the island was declined."

Henry could see Julia was lost in thought. Finally, she broke the silence.

"Henry, it's pretty clear to me that we need to get to know the descendants of the original settlers. Are they an organization or a loose group of individuals?"

"Not sure."

"Either way, it would be good to get to know these people." Henry was pleased; he had piqued Julia's curiosity.

CHAPTER TWELVE

It was only a matter of time before Julia would bump into Jantie Bjornson, a local fisher and chair of the Descendants of the Original Settlement Association.

She was in the village general store, buying some basics one morning when he came in. An enormous guy with a weather-beaten, tanned face, greying blood-red hair and piercing blue eyes, they locked onto Julia as he entered the store and closed the door.

"Morning," he said, temporarily taking them off of Julia as he glanced down at Janice, smiling at him from behind the counter.

"Haven't seen you for a while, Jantie," Janice said as she bagged Julia's purchases.

"Visiting the grandkids for a week in BC was exhausting, so came back to Hecla for a rest," he said, laughing. "Forgot how tiring little kids can be."

He looked down at Julia, who was smiling in a knowing way. "I know what you mean," she chuckled. "We have a couple in Winnipeg."

"Don't think we've met," Jantie said as he reached out with his paw-sized hand to shake Julia's.

"I'm Julia Trevellyn. We have a place on Lakeside Road." His demeanor immediately changed, and the smile was gone. "You're the people poking your noses around at Kjartanson Point."

"I suppose we are," Julia replied, her face open and innocent.

"We don't appreciate you and others digging around up at the point. Leave the place alone," he barked aggressively, exiting the store empty-handed, and slamming the door closed behind him.

"Well, that went well," Julia said, smiling at Janice.

"Don't mind him, Julia," Janice replied. "He has a hot temper, but he's a good guy and passionate about his ancestors, who apparently he counts as some of the original descendants who settled on the north side of the island. The Descendants of the Original Settlement Association, for which he is currently board chair, represents all the original settler's descendants, not just those who settled on the north side of the island. They formed after the creation of the provincial park here and the de-population of the island in the 1960s. The Association was the principal negotiating group that fought for proper compensation for what they said was a land grab by the provincial government to set up the provincial park.

"They later won a legal settlement that negotiated for better compensation for those that lost their land and for those that wanted their land ownership back. Where the land fell outside the provincial park borders, the land was restored to them, for those whose land fell within the park, they were offered land elsewhere on the island. None of this would have been possible without the lobbying efforts of the group."

"What do you know about the original settlers, Janice?" Julia asked.

"I'm actually a descendent myself, but I grew up in Arborg. My dad's family was Ukrainian, and we tended to celebrate more of their traditions growing up. I don't know much about Hecla and the people from Kjartanson Point. I do know people who probably do though. Marisa Jones; she lives at the bottom end of the village. Her maiden name was Helguson and as far as I know, she was born and grew up on the island. She is in frail health, but her mind is still sharp, and she is a no-nonsense person. She keeps to herself and rarely leaves her house. Her neighbour fetches her groceries, and her neighbour's husband drives her off the island for her regular doctor's appointment. I think they are relatives. She lives in the last cottage on the lake side before the bend in the road that leads back to the main road off the island."

"Thanks Janice, maybe I'll pay her a visit. See you again," Julia said, smiling as she picked up her groceries and headed for the door.

"Oh, by the way, Julia—Marisa is a past chair of the Hecla Village Resident's Association. This organization is not connected with the Descendants of the Original Settlement Association; it represents all the property owners on the east side of the island. There is very little about this island and its people that she doesn't know about," Janice said.

Julia reflected on that as she closed the store door.

It was warm outside for the time of the year, and the car was a hot box. The seat was almost too warm to sit on. Fortunately, there was a little breeze and after a couple of minutes the temperature became bearable. Julia decided to run down to the other end of the village to check out Marisa's place. She had not really noticed the house before. They had no reason for going down to that end of the village.

There were almost no cars on the road on the other side of the village, in spite of it being tourist season. Most of the original village was closer to the general store. A flock of geese was aimlessly wandering across the road, the goslings, now teens, were a couple of paces behind. Nobody was rushing on this hot and humid day.

The house was set back from the road. It was quite small but quaint. It looked like an original house from the early years of the last century, except for the replaced windows and front door. The exterior was painted a matte yellow with white trim. Flower boxes in bloom were hanging on the front veranda and the lawn was well cared for. Behind the house was the lake. With no trees or foliage, there would be no protection from a storm coming from the south. There was an old garage on the side of the house, built in the same style and colour as the house and was probably a similar vintage—early 1920s she guessed.

An old '90s Chevy was parked in front. *Maybe she has a visitor*, Julia wondered. She assumed Marisa was not driving anymore, from what Janice had said. Julia parked in the driveway close to the garage, managing to find a little shade. She left the car and air conditioning running while she contemplated what she was going to say. She decided the direct approach was the right way to go.

Standing at the front door, Julia could see through the lounge window. A pastor was sitting on the sofa next to a woman who must be Marisa, and it looked like they were praying together.

Julia turned away respectfully and waited a few minutes. Just as she was about to turn tail, the pastor got up. It looked like he was saying his goodbyes.

Julia decided it was now or never and knocked on the door.

"OK, Mrs. Jones, thanks for the coffee and cake. I'll see you same time next week. God bless," he said with a smile, nodding to Julia as he stepped out of the house and proceeded down the path to the Chevy.

"Good afternoon, Mrs. Jones. My name is Julia Trevellyn and I live on Lakeside Road. I was hoping we could have a chat if you have the time," Julia said respectfully.

"Well, young lady, please call me Marisa! I am a little tired, but it is always good to have company. You're welcome to stay for a while, particularly if you would put the kettle on and make some tea for the two of us."

"Only too happy to oblige," Julia said as she closed the door and walked towards the kitchen. Mrs. Jones hobbled after Julia, using her cane for support.

The kettle was whistling, and within minutes the ladies were sitting opposite each other at the kitchen table with a teapot, two mugs, and a small jug of milk between them.

"So, what is on your mind?" Marisa asked in a blunt but not unfriendly manner.

"Well, I really don't know where to begin, to be honest," Julia said, embarrassed.

"Well, I am in no hurry. I'm not going anywhere, and it is always good to meet new people. I don't get out much these days. Why don't you start off by telling me about yourself? You are from England; I can tell from your accent you are from the west country I would say?"

"Correct," Julia replied, a little surprised. "Not originally, though. My Dad is actually Italian—we moved to London when I was a teenager. My mum comes from Chudleigh, a small village near Exeter in Devon, and we lived in the village."

"Thought as much," Marisa replied with a smile. "My husband was from Tavistock, a town on the edge of Dartmoor. You probably know it."

"Actually, I do! It isn't that far from Chudleigh."

Marisa was clearly enjoying finding that they already had something in common. "Will you pour the tea now, dear? I don't like it too strong." Julia did as she asked, then reached over and lifted the milk jug. "Milk?"

"Yes, just a splash."

"So how did a girl from Hecla meet a guy from Tavistock, England? They're worlds apart," asked Julia.

"It is a long story. I was in London at the start of the Second World War. I was still a teenager and when the war broke out—I was effectively stuck in the UK. All passenger ships were co-opted by the navy. When the blitz started, I was staying with a family. As I was still under eighteen, I was evacuated out with the rest of the family's kids to a large house on the edge of Dartmoor.

"That was where I met Jim. He was four years older than me and worked on the family farm next door. He would regularly pop in to deliver milk and eggs. I loved his thick west country accent, although it was a little hard to understand him at first. Jim was carefree and fun, but hardworking, too. I suppose that goes with the responsibilities of a family farm—not much to like—"

"I feel a romance brewing," Julia interjected.

"Yes, you are right Julia," Marisa said smiling. "Sweet memories. We spent time together and developed feelings for each other. Unfortunately, he was one of the first to be drafted for the army. I was barely eighteen when he left. Except for two periods when he came home on leave, I didn't see him for four years. We wrote regularly. I still have all the letters in my study area over there." Marisa pointed to a leather case the size of a shoe box.

"I volunteered for the Women's Royal Naval Service and initially worked in Air Defence for the Plymouth Naval Base. I couldn't get home and Jim was away. Everybody's life was on hold until the war was over."

"Yes, I can imagine it was a difficult time, Julia replied.

"It was, Julia, but as a young person it was exciting, too. Growing up in Hecla, which at that time was such an isolated place, you can imagine the culture shock and life experiences I had in England. It really grew me as a person.

"Jim, in the four years he was away, suffered the loss of many of his comrades but most tragic and ironic of all was the loss of his mum, dad, and siblings when the farm suffered a direct hit from a stray German V-1 flying bomb, just before the end of the war."

"Oh, no! What a tragic story," Julia said, genuinely shocked by Marisa words. "I cannot imagine how that would have impacted Jim, particularly after surviving the war with barely a scratch."

"Well it did really affect him, Julia, as you suggest, in a very significant way. When Jim was released from the military at the end of the war, he couldn't stand to be on the farm and rebuilding it was beyond his resources. He quickly sold it and encouraged us to leave for Canada as soon as we could. He wanted a new start, and I was happy to come home.

"We settled in Winnipeg. I went to teacher's college and Jim got a job selling feed and fertilizer in the farming industry. He used to travel a lot, but I was studying hard, so it all worked out. I got a teaching job in the south end of the city after I graduated, and we purchased a small place in Fort Gary in Winnipeg. By then Jim was a sales manager and he was not travelling quite so much.

"Can you put the kettle back on Julia? Seems like it is going to be at least a two-tea story," Marisa said, laughing.

Julia got up and took care of the kettle, then ducked into the washroom. By the time she returned, there were two full mugs of tea sitting in the middle of the table.

"Now, where was I...?" Marisa said, smiling at Julia, clearly enjoying telling her story. "Oh, yes. We tried to have kids. Jim particularly wanted kids, but it wasn't to be. We were a good aunt and uncle to one of my siblings' children, so we have had the joy of spending time with kids and—as they stayed in Winnipeg—we got to see a lot of them growing up.

"We used to get up to Hecla quite a lot. Jim and I loved it here. Jim really got on with my mother and father. I had an older brother who fished with my father. My two sisters had moved off the island and one settled in Winnipeg. Jim used to help out with the fishing when he could. This is my parents' house. You cannot believe they brought up four kids in this tiny house, but they did."

"So what was your early life like growing up on Hecla?" Julia asked.

"Julia, I should tell you, I don't get a lot of visitors, and when I do, I can talk the hind leg off a donkey, which I believe is one of those ridiculous English expression I picked up. So just tell me when it's time for you to go and I won't be offended.

DEATH AT THE POINT

"No problem, Marisa. I am loving your story." Julia was always fascinated by other people's life experiences.

"I was born in 1922, actually in this house. Dad and his family built it a couple of years before my brother was born. My two younger sisters were born a couple of years later. The original settlers came here in 1876—just a few families at first, and as you might know, they made their homes on the other side of the island. Life was extremely tough for our people, initially. However, they had left worse behind and had to make a success of their lives in their new country, there was no turning back.

"By the time I came along fifty years later, much had been achieved and the community was settled. The Great Depression was a number of years off, fishing prices were reasonably good, and my early years, from what I can remember, were happy.

"My grandfather, Erik Larson, arrived with his parents in 1880 when he was only about fifteen years old. His father secured a section of land a little further south of here, cleared it, and built a house and barn. He used to tell me how close everybody was and how the other slightly more established settlers came and helped with the building for which they were forever grateful. Getting proper shelter before winter was important in such an extreme climate. Fish were plentiful back then, and soon my great-grandfather was fishing and supporting his family, like he had been in Iceland. Of course, fishing in Lake Winnipeg is quite different to the Atlantic Ocean and it took a while for him to be able to read the weather and find the fish.

"My grandfather continued the fishing tradition when he grew up, he was a short stocky man. He was a prolific reader like many Icelanders were, and he wanted to encourage me to be a better one, too. We spent a lot of time together, special times. Although schooling was limited, reading and writing was emphasized. Of course, I learned Icelandic first. I have always loved the Icelandic classics—I have to say my Icelandic is pretty rough these days, though. He died when I was fifteen. I remember his funeral; it was an incredibly sad day for me.

"My grandma was from the original settlement of the island. She was a spirited lady, almost ageless, they had five children. My dad, a Helguson, another fisher family who was born in 1900 married one of the larson girls He was out on the boat at a young age. He, like his father before him, spent his life on the water.

"It was an isolated community, and everybody spoke Icelandic. The younger people picked up English and some of them found work on farms and in the small towns, and some even worked in Winnipeg where, of course, they had to know English or French.

"My father insisted I learn English. I picked it up quickly, although as you can hear, I have always spoken English with a strong Icelandic accent. Unfortunately, I didn't get much opportunity on Hecla to practice as I didn't get off the island much.

"Traditions were kept alive by the elders, and I grew up with a strong sense of community. I have wonderful memories of grandmother and grandfather coming over to the house. I would run to the door when I heard his big feet crunching down the crushed-limestone path. He would give me a hearty squeeze, and I would always beg for a story from the old country. Sometimes he would tell me and my siblings stories with happy endings; often they would be scary stories, but I loved them all.

"We have a big family as Father's siblings were all fishers and married with kids. Christmas was an epic party time that continued unabated until New Year's.

"Hecla became a close community and people were generally distrusting of strangers, whether that was travelling salespeople or government officials. There was no real crime in the community and the small amount of burglary or thieving was most always outsiders. As I said, life was good—until the Great Depression when fish prices plummeted. We could at least feed ourselves, and with everybody sticking together, we got through the next number of years as a community. It was tough for outside communities, and we helped with what we could.

"I was sad to leave my family, friends, and community but the island began to feel isolating to me, and reading had made me curious of the world outside of Hecla and so, when an English acquaintance of father's offered me a chance to travel to England to get some teacher training, I jumped at it. Little did I know that a world war was about to happen."

"Yes, I can imagine the culture shock you must have gone through when you landed in England," Julia said.

"Yes, it was," said Marisa. "But at least thanks to my dad, I spoke a little English. Although I must say I struggled with the various dialects I encountered. I was always amused how such a small country had so many accents to adjust to."

Julia laughed. She was a bit of a mimic, and as part of her drama training had discovered she could imitate most of the UK accents, but she decided this wasn't the right time to perform. She didn't want to slow Marisa's momentum.

"My parents passed away just prior to Jim and me retiring. The sixties had been hard on them. The lake had been over-fished, and the community was losing all its young people. Hecla was dying and the old life was gone. The provincial government took over the island for an insulting amount of money in compensation to the villagers.

"My mother and father moved into Riverton to be closer to services, and that is where they saw out their time."

The kettle was whistling again, and Julia got up and made another pot of tea.

"If you look in the larder in the corner you will find muffins and the plates are to the left of the sink," Marisa said.

"Thanks, Marisa. I am just going to pop to the loo and then call Henry my husband to let him know I will be a while longer. Then, I will be back."

When Julia returned, she poured the tea, picked out two nice-looking muffins, and put them on the plates. Marisa continued, picking up the story without missing a beat.

"We used to go regularly to see my parents. Most of the community ended up in Winnipeg and my parents felt isolated and alone, but they were not interested in moving in with us and starting a new life; it was a sad time for them. Once they became ill, mercifully, they passed away reasonably quickly.

"We eventually retired and decided to move here—back up to the old family place at Hecla. It was not in good repair and technically it wasn't our land anymore, but for nominal rent we got to live here. We spent some money and sweat equity fixing it up and making it our home. Eventually, through the land settlement, we acquired the property back again. I negotiated with my siblings to buy out their share.

"We kept an apartment in Winnipeg but spent most of the summers here at the cottage. They were happy years. We had two lounge chairs parked out back with a table between, facing the lake, and we would have a sundowner every evening—our tradition.

"About ten years ago, Jim quietly passed away in his chair, looking out across the lake, his eyes wide open and a smile on his face. I was devastated for a while, but to be honest, I still feel Jim around and I talk to him all the time. Hecla is my home, and it became Jim's home, too. He is buried in the cemetery at the church, and I'll be buried next to him when it is my turn."

"Wow, what a story," Julia said. "Thank you for sharing it with me. You have had a full life. I should probably be getting along; my guess Henry's stomach will be growling about now."

"Well, you haven't told me much about yourself. Please come again and let me get to know you a little," Marisa said. "I'm sorry I rattled on a little. I'm a little starved for company."

"Of course I will. It has been a lovely time. We do have a lot in common and I would be glad to tell our story, maybe not as dramatic as yours, but it is still a good story. I will call you and I hope we can get together again soon."

Marisa grabbed her cane and came to the door to say goodbye. Julia, shook Marisa's hand, smiling. "Thanks again, Marisa, I have really enjoyed our time together." Marisa stayed at the door and waved as she left the driveway and headed back on the road through the village.

What a wonderful woman, Julia thought as she drove back through the village. *She has seen Hecla at its best, worst, and like a phoenix, it has come back in a new form. Maybe not as vibrant as it was but at least providing a livelihood for some residents although it is unlikely that there will be enough kids to reopen the school anytime soon.*

CHAPTER THIRTEEN

It was bucketing down; Henry could barely see Little Punk Island through the rain. It was running over the gutters and drumming on the deck. *Obviously, the drainpipes are blocked,* he thought. It was a real fireworks show, lightening of all types illuminating the late afternoon sky. For a while, the thunderclaps and lightening were simultaneous, and so loud the windows would vibrate.

Henry could never get tired of the view out the window. As he sat, his mind drifted off to the lonely spot at Kjartanson Point. For some reason, it continued to be unfinished business for him. He needed to find out more about the original settlers. He made his mind up that he would go to the museum in Gimli to research the founding families.

Over the next couple of days, he had other chores to do. Julia was heading back to Winnipeg for a medical appointment on the Wednesday that week, so she agreed to drop Henry at the museum on the way there, then pick him up later in the afternoon on the way back.

Henry was known to the museum staff, and he was hopeful that he would find something on the founding families. Susie, at the enquiry desk, was always helpful. In fact, she was always enthusiastic in assisting and that Wednesday was no exception. When Henry enquired about the families at Kjartanson Point, she beamed back at him with a wonderful smile.

"Mr. Trevellyn, you are going to be very pleased," she said excitedly. "A package was donated to us recently. Inside was a small journal. It's written in Icelandic, but from the name on the inside front page, we know it to be the eldest daughter of the Kjartanson's from Kjartanson Point— one of the four original families. The pages are dated as well, so we know exactly the time period and it appears to be the year following their initial arrival early the previous summer."

"Can we get it translated?" Henry asked.

"We are already on that," Susie replied. "We've sent it through to the Department of Icelandic Language and Literature at the University of Manitoba. We expect it back in less than a month. I can give you a bit of background on the families, though. We know where they came from in Iceland. They were related to each other. The two Kjartanson families were headed by two brothers, Jacob and Jon, who had teenage kids. The younger sister of Jon's wife Elva, her husband, and their three younger children made up the third. The fourth family was headed by a cousin of the two brothers with four teenage kids who all survived into adulthood.

"What we know from previous research," Susie continued, "is that Elva's family lost two of their kids. Smallpox hit New Iceland hard and only the sister's female child recovered. They were devastated by the loss of their babies and decided to abandon Kjartanson Point, relocate across the border, and join other relatives in a thriving community in North Dakota.

"The two Kjartanson brothers' families and the cousin and his family stayed for a while but eventually relocated to the southeast side of the island where a growing number of settlers were becoming established."

"Wow, thanks Susie. That was a good brain dump—useful background," Henry said.

"There's more," Susie said, smiling, obviously enjoying the big reveal. "So the girl's name was Greta, and she was the eldest daughter of Jacob's family and was about fourteen when the family started their adventure in 1877. They arrived early in the summer after a rough crossing from Iceland, and I am not sure how they ended up at Hecla, but I assume it was a wild scramble to secure land. Particularly land close to the lake."

"Thanks, Susie. I really appreciate you sharing this with me," Henry said.

"I'll give you a call when it comes in. It will make interesting reading."

"Goodbye, Susie," Henry said. "Better go—I can see Julia in the car outside."

"Henry, it has arrived," Susie said, assuming quite rightly that Henry knew exactly what she was talking about, even though quite a time had passed. "You're welcome to come down anytime to read the translated version, but you cannot remove it from the museum library."

"Thanks. I'll be there first thing tomorrow if that's OK," Henry replied. "I am excited to get a better sense of those early days."

Henry had emigrated in modern times and things had been tough enough, but nothing like what those early settlers experienced, and he had a real fascination and curiosity to understand their adventure and there was nothing better than a first-hand account. It seemed to Henry that any connection with the death of David Einarson and the journey of a young girl from more than 150 years ago would likely be remote, but one never knew.

The next morning, the drive down to Gimli took about an hour. He wasn't in a hurry as he knew the museum opened at 9:00 a.m., and he was planning to have a coffee and a bagel at Robin's Coffee House first. All went as planned.

Henry was at the door of the museum just as it opened. Susie's smile widened when she saw that Henry had not come empty-handed: he had brought coffee and doughnuts.

"That's what I like about you, Henry; you never come empty-handed," Susie said as she winked at her assistant, Debbie.

"Debbie, can you manage the desk for ten minutes? I need to talk to Henry for awhile."

She quietly closed the door to the kitchenette they had entered and pulled a chair up to the small table, suddenly looking a little serious. Henry pulled the remaining two coffees from the carry crate and offered Susie a doughnut.

"Just to let you know, Henry, a couple of visitors turned up here last Wednesday. They both had strong accents. They also expressed an interest in the original settlement on Hecla. They said they were looking for a lost relative. I gave them some information on the original settler families, but I didn't share anything else with them. To be honest, I didn't get a good feeling about them."

"You probably did the right thing, Susie. No need to get involved," Henry said.

"They had a photograph of him," she continued. "A tall guy with a red head of hair and a long beard. I reached out to get a better look, but they would not let me hold onto the photo."

"Can you describe these guys to me, Susie."

"I would say they had Eastern European accents. Caucasians for sure. They were well dressed. The older one was short and stocky, the younger one, unusually tall. They were dressed in dark trousers and white shirts and jackets—they almost looked like the Mormon lads you see going house to house. One was probably early twenties, the other, in his forties. Like I said, I didn't get a good feeling. They weren't very friendly. Oh, and they were driving a dark blue Ford F150 truck," Susie continued.

"Thanks for the heads up, Susie," Henry replied. "So, do you have the translated version of the diary?"

"Of course! Sorry, Henry. Come with me and I'll get it for you," Susie said, still a little flustered from telling her story about the strangers.

She walked him to the back of the museum where there was a small archive room with a table and a couple of chairs and left him for a moment. He had just pulled out a notepad and a pen when Susie returned with a copy of Greta's diary.

"Well, this is going to be fascinating, Susie," Henry said, smiling with excitement. He just loved this kind of stuff.

"I can only imagine," Susie replied. "Best of luck! Do you want me to bring you a coffee in a couple of hours?"

"That'll be great. Thanks, Susie." With that, she stepped out, closing the door behind her.

The diary of a young girl from 1878 through 1879 living at the edge of civilization was a compelling read. It started as a reader would imagine, with an entry on January 1. From the page, Greta's voice spoke to him in English with an Icelandic accent.

January 1

I got up early, unlike my sleeping family. It was cold out of the bed, which I shared with my sister; she fussed a bit as I slipped out from under the blankets. I was shivering immediately and grabbed a shawl that was hanging over a chair. I could see my own breath it was that cold in the bedroom.

Stepping into the main room of the house, it was just getting light, the fire was embers only and I threw on a couple of logs from the pile next to the hearth to keep things going. It was vital to keep the fire alive; it was bitterly cold outside, and we had to protect our underfloor root store from freezing.

Our four families celebrated New Year's Eve last night. We used the barn for our party as our houses were too small for everyone. We sang traditional songs, feasted on salted fish, and the small number of vegetables we had. The men had some liquor left over from Christmas and had several drinks.

When midnight came, a couple of the fathers had things to say. A mix of good humour and sadness, I would say, but expressed well the emotions we all felt about surviving the voyage over and the mad scramble to find land and secure shelter for the winter that we had no idea of how difficult it would be to survive.

We toasted the year in, and I had my first taste of liquor, I cannot say I enjoyed it much, but it was good to give it a try. After all I am fourteen. I coughed and spluttered a little, much to everybody else's amusement.

As I look through the trees, I can see the frozen expanse of the lake. The sun just starting to light up the snow out on the ice. Father's ice hole and tent are just visible offshore.

I am excited by the possibilities of our new life but feel very isolated where we are. It is good to have family close and I have much to be grateful for, but I know we are *barely getting by right now. There is just enough food for now. Every day is filled with chores. I miss the school and my friends, but we do have enough firewood on this island to keep us warm forever, and right now I know I need to be patient. Dad keeps on reminding us how much we have achieved in the very short time we have been here.*

Henry was drawn into Greta's life. He had always had a strong imagination and he could easily picture the scene and life she was describing.

January 2

Back to the regular chores. My first job in the morning was to feed the chickens, ensure the cow has some fodder and fetch some ice from the lake, for washing and cooking. Breaking the ice up is always hard work, but at least the effort warmed me up. Once we finished breakfast, the three of us were home schooled as always by Mother. Father was already out on the lake with the other men fishing.

After lunch, my mother asked me to go out and help my father. He needed wood to keep the small fire going in the fishing hut. It was bitterly cold, and the wind was blowing in my face as I dragged a sled of wood across the bumpy ice. I covered my face as best I could with a scarf, but Father said my face was blue when I got into the hut, and he was a little concerned that I may have exposed myself to frostbite on my nose. Much to my relief, a little while in front of the fire and the colour returned to my face. I need to cover myself more careful when I am out on the ice.

I always love my time with Father. He has taught me a lot about ice fishing something he had to learn in a hurry but looks to have a knack for it. So many new things we have to adapt to. Surviving in this extreme climate is not easy. Too hot or too cold. So different to Iceland.

Father had already caught a good supply of fish. So he was happy and relaxed enough to let me have a go. He got up from the stool and gestured for me to sit down. He handed the rod over and sat on the logs next to me.

I love my father and I know I am the apple of his eye. My younger brothers are always sniggering around me, so I like my time with Father alone.

I also did well today, caught three reasonably sized fish. It was starting to get dark. Father said it was time to go. So we put some extra logs on the fire, loaded up the sled with the fish, and headed home.

We packed most of the fish in the icehouse and brought two fish outside for gutting, prepping, and washing down before going inside. Fried fish today, as always.

The day-to-day routine continued all winter. The daily entries slowly brought to light who Greta was, and the interactions with the other families. It was clear that they worked together closely, and the skills of all family members were used for the survival of all. They were God-fearing and they had a service of sorts every Sunday morning led by her father. He was older than the other men and had at one time thought of entering the ministry. There was no Communion, but there were prayers and hymns to sing. Greta had a good voice and proudly wrote about the solos she occasionally did.

That first winter, Greta only left the settlement once and that was to go with her father and another man to Riverton. The two options were by sled across the ice or by cart across the ice and then over the rough track to the town. There had been far too much snow that first winter, and it was decided that the sled was the only real option.

February 15

Today, we left with two small sleds to fetch supplies from the nearest settlement, Riverton. Things like flour, tea, sugar, rice, butter, tinned vegetables, and laundry and cleaning supplies, were all running low.

It was cold and clear and there was little wind. Looking like a cold and sunny day, perfect for a sledding.

We loaded up one of the sleds with salted fish that we hoped to trade for supplies. We made good progress and stopped after a couple of hours for a break. A little bannock and some reheated tea on a small kerosene stove. We were all quite warm, with little wind and a sunny sky and a little exertion, it was not difficult to maintain body temperature.

For me, it was good to get away from the settlement and I was excited to go to Riverton, meet some new people, and see the place that we barely saw when we came up from Gimli just over six months ago.

In all, it took us six hours to reach Riverton. I was exhausted. Father managed to find a couple of rooms in a small Inn in town and traded off some fish for some board and lodge for the three of us. The men shared a room, and I had a bed all to myself. Total luxury. I even got to have a bath! I slept like a baby.

February 16

Today, we got up early had a fantastic breakfast of bacon, eggs and sausage, and piles of toast, washed down with tea.

We packed up our belongings and headed out to the sleds that were stored at the back of the inn. There was a wind blowing gently and it was overcast. It felt a lot colder than yesterday.

DEATH AT THE POINT

We got to the general store just as it opened. For me, it was like an Aladdin's cave, it was full of everything you could ever want. I was assigned to find the laundry and cleaning articles, whilst my father and uncle found the food and cooking items. In half an hour, everything was purchased. Father was disappointed with the price he got for the salted fish, but he didn't really have much choice, and the two men had to pay partly with the small amount of cash that they had. It took another fifteen minutes to load everything securely on the sleds and then it was time to leave.

Father told me to pull down my hat over my ears and to cover my face as best I could. If that wind came up anymore, it would be a cold and difficult sled ride home.

Father was not joking the first couple of miles were OK but then a northwest wind blew up, stirring up the snow off the ice and blowing it right in our faces.

We did think about turning back, but my uncle wanted to push on, so we did. It was almost a serious mistake. After another hour or so, the visibility started to disappear. We couldn't risk the shortest straight-line distance across the lake as there was every likelihood we would lose our way; it was decided the longer but safer route along the shoreline was the way to go. That added at least an hour to our journey.

It was a real struggle; the sleds were fully loaded, and the wind was in our faces. We really needed two people per sled, and I got so tired halfway along it was all I could do to keep up.

Eventually, we saw the island and we knew we were no more than an hour away.

> It was a real relief; I could hear in my father's voice he had been worried, and the sight of the island brought a smile back to his face.
>
> He kept on saying, "Not long now." I couldn't feel my feet or my hands.
>
> Our families were worried about us. Fortunately, the other two men, had walked back towards us. I can tell you, it couldn't have been a more welcome sight. To have the two extra people pulling really helped and we were home in no time.
>
> The sleds were dragged into the barn.
>
> Mother pulled us in and put all of us in front of the fire. It was agony getting the feeling back into our hands and feet, but mother poured us each a shot of liquor. I felt proud to share a drink with the men, in spite of the fact that I probably didn't really do my full share.
>
> Whilst we told our story, mother served us bowls of fish soup, which tasted like heaven. We were so hungry. The kids wanted to know everything about the trip, but I was just too tired. Once I warmed up, I hugged Mother and Father and went straight to bed. I was so very tired.

The journal continued in the same vein. There was a certain routine to their lives during that first winter, tough, isolating, and monotonous. That first year was a battle for survival but they did survive, and Henry could feel Greta's pent-up excitement for the spring and warmer weather.

He stopped for a washroom break and Susie arrived with coffee.

"How is it going, Henry?"

"Fascinating, Susie. You really get a sense of what it was like back in the day. My goodness, they were tough, God-fearing people."

"No doubt," Susie replied. "Their faith carried them through. I'll let you get back to your reading." She smiled and left the room. Henry continued to read, and time stood still as he got lost in the diary.

April 15

Will spring ever come? The days are much longer now and much of the snow has melted in areas exposed to the sun, there is still snow among the trees. The lake remains stubbornly frozen over and it is below zero at night.

But I can see green grass starting to show and the leaves are almost about to burst out on the trees. You can hear the drip, drip sound everywhere as the ice and snow starts to melt. The sounds of the crows cawing seems louder than ever. I hate those birds.

The fathers have been building a fishing boat all winter and have been busy recently rigging it out with a mast and sail. Spring cannot come quick enough now. Supplies are low, as are our savings. Father says it is imperative to get out on the water soon.

The ice has been very slow to thaw.

May 16

Today was a special day. The day we launched our first fishing boat! It took all of us to haul the boat from the barn to the water. There was still quite a lot of ice on the water but there was enough open water to give the boat a run. The men had cut rollers from the smaller trees cut down last winter and lined them up along the ground. Two long haul ropes were tied to each side of the boat and all of us pulled as if our life depended on it... which it did.

> It took us half the morning, but we finally got the boat down and onto the lake. The men were pleased that the leakage was small and survived the process of hauling it into the water. As there was no pier built, the boat would have to be hauled up onto the beach every night and tied to trees in the case of a wild storm during the night. This boat was critical to the survival of our families.
>
> May 30
>
> A fisherman came up from Riverton to help educate our men in the ways of lake fishing. The species of fish, the prices they fetched, and where to find them and catch them. Most of all, how to watch the weather and avoid getting caught out on the lake in a storm. The fisherman explained that the lake was relatively shallow and when the wind blew the water would rise up quickly and a storm on this lake was a terrible thing.
>
> He said we would be able to make a good living right now. Winnipeg was growing fast and needed food supply and certain species of fish were sought after further afield. He said he would put the men in touch with fish buyers. Which was important if they want to grow their livelihood past a subsistence level.
>
> Things were looking up.

Greta appeared to be a positive, mature-for-her-age girl. He couldn't believe two hours had passed when he looked up to the knock on the door as Susie walked in.

"OK if I sit down?" Susie asked as she put two coffees down on the table. "I'm curious to know what you are discovering."

Henry nodded with a smile and pulled out the chair next to his. "Of course, Susie. It's been a fascinating read." Susie listened without saying a word. Henry, like Julia, had a talent for telling stories, and this was a good one.

Henry concluded by saying, "I cannot imagine how tough it was for those first settlers in 1878, but I think we as a species are very resilient, and what choice did they have but to persist and make a go of the cards they were dealt. They did have the basic skills to make a living."

Susie nodded in agreement. "Henry, an idea has suddenly occurred to me. You probably know we occasionally have special events at our museum? Would you be prepared to talk about this diary once you have read and digested its significance? I know you are not an historian or anything, but there would be many people with an interest in this very personal document."

"No problem, Susie. I would be happy to do it."

"Thanks, Henry; that would be great." With that Susie pushed back the chair and grabbed the now-empty mugs. "Well, I better let you get straight to it—I have an event to plan," she said laughing. "Oh by the way, Henry, during my break, I went for a walk and saw that Ford truck again, parked up the street at the Tergesen general store, still asking questions it would appear." Susie said as she left the room.

These guys are nothing if not persistent, Henry thought as he packed his bag and put on his jacket.

CHAPTER FOURTEEN

The next morning, Julia headed down to Gimli to do a couple of chores and planned to drop Henry off at the museum so he could continue to read the diary.

Julia pulled up outside the coffee shop in Gimli at just about 9:00 a.m. Henry popped in and purchased four coffees and some doughnuts, returned to the car, and leaned into the window.

"Here's your coffee, Julia. Have a good day." He kissed her gently through the window. "I'll walk down to the museum."

Almost half-way through the diary–should make some more progress today, Henry thought as he stepped into the museum and greeted Debbie and Susie.

"Hi, ladies. It will be a short read today. Julia brought me down. She's doing some chores and wants to leave by lunchtime."

"No problem; the museum library is free, and the diary is on the table," Susie said smiling.

After a short chat with the ladies, he headed down the hall, got comfortable, and continued to read the diary.

> July 1
>
> The fishers name was Jake. He wasn't Icelandic, but he did speak a little of the language which was helpful as our English had not improved too much in spite of our best efforts at home schooling. I suppose being so isolated all winter with just our families hasn't helped to learn the language.

July 7

Jake ended up staying for a week. He ate at our house and slept in our main room. I could hear his snores through the bedroom door at night. I don't know how his wife could stand it.

I spent a lot of time practising my English with him when he wasn't out with the men orientating them to lake fishing.

After dinner, Jake and Father sat down with me and to my excitement proposed that I go back with Jake. Earn my keep helping his wife with chores and in return they would continue to build on my basic English skills.

Father told me that it was important that we all learned English, that I had a bit of a knack for picking it up, and if I worked hard and listened well during the summer and early fall, I could make a lot of progress.

The intention being to spend the winter teaching all the families enough conversational English for everybody to get by.

It was a little intimidating. I had never lived with strangers, but I was still feeling very isolated, and I wanted to explore my new country a little.

All was agreed, I spent the evening packing a bag with the few clothes and possessions I had and saying goodbye to the other families.

July 8

Struggled to sleep last night, I was so excited. I think I drove my sister crazy, tossing and turning.

DEATH AT THE POINT

I got up just as it was getting light. Jake was buried under blankets, snoring, of course. I filled the kettle and loaded the stove with more wood.

I cut up some bread and butter and found some jam in the pantry, a quick breakfast before an early departure. I was sad to leave my family after everything we have been through, but I didn't want to drag out the goodbyes. Father suddenly appeared at the door, and he came over and gave me a big hug. "I am going to miss you so much Greta," he whispered into my ear.

Father then reached down and shook Jake. Jake opened his eyes, nodded, and slowly got up from the mattress on the floor, clearly stiff as the mattress was not the best.

He looked up at me and smiled. "Big day," he said. He wasn't joking, it was now very real. I was leaving home for the first time.

Just then, the kettle started whistling. I quickly removed it from the stove. I didn't want to awake the whole family right now. The three of us had breakfast and then Jake went outside to hitch the horse to the cart.

Father woke the rest of the family. While I packed the last of my stuff, he went outside to help Jake and I said goodbye to my sleepy and sad family. My mother was tearful, but I could tell she was excited for me and gave me a small little purse to put in my bag.

Jake helped me up into the cart as the family gathered outside. Mum handed me up a shawl and scarf. "You'll need these, Greta. As you go through the marshlands, the insects will be bad, so cover yourself up the best you can."

I didn't stop waving to my family until I was out of sight.

The track was in reasonable condition, and we made good progress. I think Jake was anxious to get home and see his own family.

The insects were very bad through the marshland, sitting like a halo over our heads. Once we were through the area, things got a little easier. We loaded up the rope ferry to get across the short stretch of water to the mainland. Once across, the cart path was in good condition, and we were in Riverton by the afternoon.

Jake's wife was outside gardening when we arrived. As she walked out to the street, I could see the bowl of tomatoes and beans she had just picked. Her garden was full of vegetables. No wonder they looked so healthy.

Jake jumped down from the cart and gave his wife Kate a big hug. He introduced me to her, and I was encouraged to call Kate by name.

While Jake took the cart round the back, I took my bag and followed Kate into the house. She was much younger than her husband and to me she felt like an older sister. She took me through to a small bedroom at the back of the house.

It had a small bed, a dresser, and a wardrobe. A bright rug covered part of the wooden floor.

It was exciting for me, my own bed for the first time in my life.

I went downstairs and helped Kate finish preparing dinner. Jake came in after sorting out the horse, and we all sat down for dinner.

We said grace. I was going to be reciting this every day. My first prayer in English I know I'll learn quickly.

Kate gave me a couple of children's books that she had picked up and told me we would be starting English lessons tomorrow, in between doing the chores.

As I lay in bed contemplating the hours that had passed, I imagined how my family's day had gone, the first without me.

July 9

I was a little tired when waking up, probably recovering from the long ride the day before. I walked downstairs. Kate gave me a concerned look. Apparently, my face was quite swollen with bug bites. It was the only place really exposed during our ride through the marshland!

Kate reached into a kitchen cupboard and took out a small glass jar. With a small rag, she applied the white lotion to each of the bites. She told me to leave the bites alone and not rub them in spite of the itch I was feeling.

Jake was long gone fishing and the two of us had a small breakfast and set about the day's chores.

Kate spoke slowly to help me hear the words properly and she encouraged me to repeat them. I had a good memory, and I was quickly building up a vocabulary of words. The grammar was going to take longer and, of course, I would also have to learn the written words.

The day went quickly, and I have started to meet some of the neighbours, who are very nice.

The entries continued along the same lines every day. It was clear that Greta was enjoying her time with Jake and Kate and village life, and her English was coming along quickly. She wrote that she had contemplated trying to write her journal in English but had decided against it as she wanted to keep a record of her time here that her family could read.

August 21

Every Sunday, we have been going to church and I have met many people in the village. The service is a little different to what I am used to in Iceland, but I am starting to learn when to stand up, sit down, and kneel down to pray.

Today was a special day as Kate had asked the vicar if I could recite the Lord's Prayer when it comes up in the service. The vicar happily agreed.

I had been learning it by heart, so I didn't even need the prayer book, although I had it with me just in case the nerves got the best of me.

As it turned out, at least according to Jake, I recited the prayer perfectly. This was a big confidence booster for me as I continued to master the language and customs of the English people.

The entries continued, but it was clear Greta was missing her family terribly. She discussed this with Jake and Kate and it was agreed that he would take her home in the middle of September.

September 21

My father had come out for supplies twice, and both times, I have been away. Once to the bigger community of Gimli and the second time visiting one of Kate's relatives on a farm a little west of Riverton.

Each time, father had left letters from the family. Which I have read and re-read.

October 1

It was a difficult day today. Leaving the special place that had been my home for the last three months.

DEATH AT THE POINT

Kate had recently got pregnant and was struggling with morning sickness. I decided I had to stay with her a while longer and support her. She had been feeling better recently so it was time to leave.

We both had tears in our eyes when we hugged, and I promised her I would be back for the birth which she estimated would be around the end of May. I quietly handed Kate the small purse and an envelope. I had written Kate and Jake a letter of thanks and gratitude, which of course was in English, and I referenced the purse that contained the money my mother had given me months before and asked that she should buy something nice for the baby.

Jake helped me up into the cart, and I waved to Kate until she was out of sight.

I have to say, I was quiet and reflective and not particularly good company for Jake, but I sensed he understood.

It was colder now. No bugs to contend with in the marshland and it was gently raining.

By the time we got to my family's place, we were both drenched and cold.

Everybody was out of the house to welcome us; they obviously had heard the cart coming down the track.

I was so excited to see everyone, and everybody was excited to see me.

Jake stayed the night and joined in the celebration of my return. I had missed my family so much and it was good to be home.

CHAPTER FIFTEEN

Henry was so engrossed in the diary that he didn't even notice Julia had walked into the room. Feeling a gentle touch on his shoulder, he turned and gave her a smile.

"Sorry! This journal is a fascinating slice of life so long ago—I was totally absorbed. I suppose it is time to go."

Henry said as he handed the translated journal to Susie on their way out. "Thanks so much, Susie. "I'll be back. It's so interesting."

"No problem, Henry. We always have coffee on for you," Susie replied with a smile.

"I'm good for the doughnuts," Henry shouted over his shoulder as he and Julia walked out the door of the museum.

The ride home consisted of updates from Julia on her time in Gimli and the calls she got from family while she was wandering around.

By the time Henry and Julia got home, the trees in the driveway were straining hard against the northwest wind. Henry walked around to the lake side of the property and could see that the white caps were an awesome and fearful sight.

He suddenly thought of the kayaks and rushed down the stairs. The water was crashing hard against the rocks, but to Henry's relief, somebody had brought the boats up to safer ground.

That Jim is a good man, Henry thought as he braced himself against the wind and stared at the spectacular sight in front of him. The lake could turn dangerous in the blink of an eye, but it was a magnificent scene. The spray was blowing so high up the rocks, it was stinging his eyes. He turned away and walked back to the house.

His cellphone was vibrating on the dining room table.

"Are you going to get that?" Julia shouted from somewhere in the house.

"On my way," Henry replied as he closed the sliding door behind him.

"Hey, Jim. How are you doing? Thanks for pulling the kayaks up on the lawn. I appreciate it. They'd be gone by now in this wind."

"No problem, Henry. I know you normally leave them on the beach, and I was down by the water fixing my steps. I hope we don't get any trees down. We typically lose a few in this kind of storm. Actually, the reason for my call is to share something I overhead at the general store this morning."

"Go on," Henry said.

"Two well-dressed guys were at the counter. They had very strong accents. Anyway, they were enquiring whether there were any cottages for rent. Janice gave them Jantie Bjornson's number. He has lived here his whole life and seems to know most of the cottage owners and probably knew if anybody wanted to rent out their property."

"Makes sense," Henry replied. "What makes you share this story, Jim?"

"Apparently, they were also looking for somebody and showed Janice a photograph. I saw her shake her head. They seemed frustrated but said goodbye politely and drove off to the north in a good-looking truck."

"It wasn't a blue Ford F150, was it Jim?" Henry asked.

"Actually, I think it was. What's going on, Henry?" Jim asked, sounding a little concerned.

"I was at the museum doing research on a recently translated journal of a young girl who came to the island with her family, some of the very first settlers to the island. Anyway, I have gotten to know the curator of the museum and she was telling me about a couple of well-dressed men with foreign accents that had shown her a picture of someone they were looking for—she had assumed it was a family member—a tall red-headed guy with a bushy beard. From her description, it made me think of that mysterious stranger who I think was camping out at the point. I think we can assume it was the same photograph that was shown to Janice.

"So… what happened to this guy? We know he was around; we know now that people are looking for him. We know somehow David Einarson was involved—or at least he was in the same remote spot."

"Not a clue," Jim replied. "Hey, got to rush Henry. My dog is scratching at the door—time for his walk. Stay in touch." With that, Jim rang off.

"What did Jim have to say, Henry?" Julia asked.

"Apparently, those two guys that were looking for somebody were also up at the general store showing the same photo and enquiring about places to rent."

"Why would they want to rent here now? It's the end of the season, and it's an isolated place—makes no sense," Julia wondered aloud.

The next day, Henry travelled back down to Gimli and was at the door when Susie arrived at the museum.

"How are you doing, Henry?" Susie said as she fumbled around for the keys in her bag.

"Let me grab those."

"Thanks, Henry. I always seem to have my arms full."

Henry balanced the box of doughnuts on top of the pile of books he took from her arms as she unlocked the door and let them in.

"I assume you're still working on the journal, Henry?" Susie asked.

"Yes, I am hooked," he replied. "I'd like to see if I can finish reading it today."

"I'll put the coffee on," Susie said as she hung up her coat.

Debbie brought the journal in as Henry was removing his coat and hanging it on the chair in the archive room.

"Thanks, Debbie. You two ladies always make me feel so welcome here." Henry sat and turned to the next page in the diary.

October 5

It's so good to be back with the family; I didn't realize how much I have missed them. My younger siblings laugh at my "Canadian accent." Which apparently, I have developed in my months at Riverton. Father says I have grown up and matured. I had presents for everyone and it was fun to hand them out. They were only small items, but I did put a lot of thought into every gift and I was thrilled how everybody appreciated them.

October 6

We are now back in the old routine, schooling in the morning, chores in the afternoon. With a small difference, I am now an English teacher to the children for one hour a day. I am really enjoying sharing my knowledge with the other children. In the evening, we spend one hour over dinner as a family speaking English. My Mother is struggling but my siblings and father are doing well.

October 25

There are big storms on the lake; it is too dangerous to fish until the storm dies down.

The men are maintaining the boats and the women are repairing the nets. It is getting colder now. Even had a little snow a couple of days ago.

Most of the family had gone to bed, and father and I were up at the kitchen table. He was attempting to read a newspaper article from a newspaper I had brought back from Riverton.

It was an article on the Icelandic settlers, giving some background to the English readers on the history of our country and the reason for the immigration of the Icelandic people to New Iceland and other parts of North America.

I didn't realize that Iceland had the oldest parliament in the world, nearly one thousand years old.

A little-known fact my father told me, but it's true. He looked at me and said he was encouraged by my enthusiasm; he then told me that he wanted to show me some things that I would find interesting.

He pulled up the trapdoor to the root cellar and jumped down with the lamp. I peered into the cellar as he opened a metal chest with a key and started to remove a number of articles that he handed up to me.

He laid a number of items on the table, lying on top of the kitchen table was an object, covered in an oily fabric. Father slowly removed the wrapping and to my amazement, shiny as the day it was probably made was a dagger. It had an ornate handle decorated with bronze infill. I picked it up. I was surprised by its weight.

In addition, there was a Bible. He opened it to the inside page. There was a handwritten note in beautiful old Icelandic script that was difficult to read but appeared to be addressed to a Jan Kjartanson, I guessed a coming-of-age gift and a date, 1 April 1599. Signed apparently by his father. The Bible was bound in leather and was in excellent condition for its age.

Father explained that it was a precious family heirloom and that someday I would inherit it. With the responsibility to hand it on eventually to my first born. I was speechless I really didn't know what to say.

I was curious about the other items in the chest. Father picked up another package. It was also covered in a thick, oiled fabric, which was tied up with string. He unknotted the string, gently unwrapped the covering, and showed me what was a much larger and older book. The leather cover was faded and a little tatty on the edges, and I could see even before he opened the book there was staining on the exposed edges of the pages.

It was truly an ancient book. Handwritten on parchment, detailing the proceedings of one of the parliaments held during the 13th century. The summer of 1285 AD."

> I was stunned. I had never seen anything so old.
>
> There were a number of old artifacts made of bronze that were also protected with oily cloth.
>
> I asked how they came to be in our family. He told me other than the family Bible, which belongs to our family, the other items were entrusted to him by the government, at a time just prior to our departure from Iceland when things were very chaotic in the country, and they wanted to safeguard these and other national treasures.
>
> "Surely, the government will want them back," I asked. "Of course," he replied, "There will be a time when they will be returned; for now we need to keep this to ourselves."
>
> Father packed everything away and made me promise to keep this a secret. I was proud that he felt I was old enough to be entrusted with this knowledge.
>
> I went to bed that night, excited by what I had seen and a little fearful I may say something in my sleep my sister may hear.

Henry sat back in his chair, stunned. *What an incredible moment for Greta to be trusted by her father with this knowledge,* he thought.

Henry read through the rest of the entries. There was no further mention of the chest or its contents. The rest of the entries spoke of a young girl starting to assert herself through her English classes and the special relationship and trust she had with her father.

CHAPTER SIXTEEN

Henry drove home with mixed emotions. The revelation of a horde of priceless artifacts was both exciting and fascinating, but he was also saddened to know he had completed the readings, and this was likely to be the only real insight he would probably ever have into Greta, whom he had gotten to know through her words.

When he got back to the house, he shared the latest entries of the diary with Julia, who was amazed. Always capable of asking the obvious, Julia said, "So what do you think happened to those artifacts? They could be worth a lot of money or at least have a lot of historical value to some people."

Henry nodded, but he was not really listening. He suddenly saw the two strangers in a new light.

"Henry! You didn't hear a word I said, did you?"

"No, Julia," he replied honestly. "I was considering the two strangers and whether or not there is a link between them and the artifacts. Could the tall stranger I thought was camping at Kjartanson's Point, David Einarson's death, and the two new strangers all be linked to these artifacts? I wonder—who donated the journal? I never thought to ask Susie. I need to find out; I'll call her in the morning."

"Oh, by the way, Chris popped in earlier today, looking for you. He said the RCMP were planning to return to the site at Kjartanson's Point before the snow falls."

"Well, that's interesting. Do they have new leads?"

"I don't know. Speak to Chris."

"I'll do that after dinner."

Julia had made shepherd's pie for dinner—simple food, but Henry's favourite. They talked about the grandkids while they ate, but Henry was distracted.

Once he had done the washing up, he was out the door.

"How long are you going to be?" Julia shouted as Henry was putting on his coat.

"Not too long." He was tired, and it wouldn't take long to extract the small amount of information that Chris probably had. He was aware the RCMP would not give too much away even though Chris was a retired part time officer.

It was a pitch-black night, overcast, and no moon. It was a short walk, but Henry stumbled a couple of times before his eyes adjusted to the dark. *Doesn't get any easier to see in the dark as you get older,* he thought as he walked along the gravel road.

He walked down Chris and Jane's driveway to the sound of barking from inside the house. *Great guard dogs,* Henry thought as he pressed the doorbell.

Chris opened the door with a smile. "Henry, you always ring the doorbell, which I never understand—you must know from the dogs barking that we're aware somebody is paying us a visit."

"Sorry, Chris. I always think it's the polite thing to do," Henry replied with a sarcastic smirk.

As Henry removed his boots, Jane came to the door to say hi.

"You guys up for a coffee?"

"Is the Pope a Catholic?" was Henry's standard reply.

"I assume that means 'yes,'" Jane replied with a wry smile. "You and your expressions Henry—you are full of it."

Henry and Chris sat in front of a wonderful open fire.

"A little nippy out there," Henry said as he rubbed his hands together. "Should've put on my gloves."

The men chatted for a while. Jane appeared from the kitchen with a tray and three coffees. Two black, cream for Henry, and to his excitement, some homemade ricotta cookies.

"Enjoy!" Jane said as she grabbed one of the black coffees and retreated to the bedroom.

"How is the investigation going? I know you haven't managed to put David Einarson's death behind you," Chris said after a moment of silence.

"The more I dig, the more intriguing it gets. Although I must say, it is difficult to make sense of it all," Henry said, and laid out what he knew or at least what he thought he knew.

"Somebody had been living out rough at Kjartanson's Point. He had obviously been looking for something, judging from the piles of soil and rock that littered the area of the original homestead. David Einarson was working for Kristian Kjartanson, a local property developer who was suffering a number of vandalism and arson attacks to his properties. David was hired to try to identify the perpetrators of these criminal acts. Mr. Kjartanson had submitted a proposal to develop a living museum at the Point that was largely opposed by the Descendants of the Original Settlement Association.

"Why David was actually at the Point is a mystery, as it is unclear what he hoped to uncover at that site for his employer, Mr. Kjartanson. The fact that he appeared to have died of natural causes leaves me confused about why he was found with a pick and shovel by his side and, of course, dead men tell no tales.

"Next is, what happened to the tall red-headed stranger I've seen, and who are the foreign gentlemen who are claiming they are looking for somebody that may be this person—possibly a family member of theirs?

"Finally, does Marisa Jones—maiden name, Helguson—who Julia spent some time with recently, know anything about the past that may be impacting recent events?" Henry went on to share the contents of Greta Kjartanson's diary with Chris.

"So... the cache of ancient artifacts could be what everybody is looking for?" Chris wondered.

"Maybe. But what are the chances that those artifacts would still be buried in the remains of the house after almost 150 years?" Henry replied.

"From what you said, the responsibility for the artifacts would have been carried down by the eldest child," Chris said, thinking aloud. "That would be how many generations?"

"Greta was a teenager. Life was precarious in those days, and life expectancy is not what it is like today. But assuming Greta did acquire the artifacts upon the death of her father, and assuming she got married and had kids and lived to say, sixty-five, then the artifacts would have been transferred to the next generation around the late 1920s. So, assuming that her eldest child was in his or her 40s when Greta died, that 'child' would have had kids in the early years of the last century, say 1905. Now if that person had lived seventy years, that would place that person's death and life within living memory of others with an estimated time of death around the 1970s. Assuming that he or she would have had kids. They would have been born in the 1920s early 1930s. That person may still be alive. A bit of a long shot but possible."

"I think you need to check births and deaths," Chris suggested.

"I don't think that information is available to anybody outside the family for up to 100 years," Henry replied.

"Is that the same for census records?" Chris asked.

"Yes," Henry replied. "It would be fascinating to find out what happened to Greta's descendants—and are there still old timers around who may know something? Oh, I almost forgot why I came here," Henry said. "Why are the police visiting the site again?"

"From what I heard, they are testing out some equipment that can see what's under the ground, called ground penetrating radar. Not sure what they are looking for, but I know the inspector was suspicious about the site of David Einarson's death and the coincidental piles of earth and rocks. Somebody was definitely looking for something. Apparently, they have spare resources right now; I believe they are starting tomorrow."

"Thanks, Chris," Henry said as he got up. "It's going to be an interesting day."

"Don't get your hopes up, Henry. They are going to cordon off the site so there is no point going up there. Whatever—if anything—they find, they'll probably keep to themselves... at least for a while."

Henry hurried home in the black of the night, overwhelmingly excited by the discussion and the news that the police were not done quite yet with the site.

CHAPTER SEVENTEEN

That night, the wind howled, and the weather forecast predicted a late-fall storm coming up from the US. It was already snowing hard. At some point, the storm had changed direction, and the eye of the storm that was originally staying south of the border was now heading in a more northerly path.

"Julia, what do you think? If we don't leave now, we could be snowbound on the island for at least a couple of days—looking like at least six inches of snow."

"Well, we have a lot of food, and lots of firewood in case we lose power. If we attempt to get home now and run off the road we could be in big trouble. I think it's better we stay."

"OK. Let's ring the family quickly and let them know where we are. Cell reception is always bad in a storm."

Julia called their daughter in Winnipeg, but the line was bad, and the signal dropped more than once. Eventually, they managed to let their family know that they may be snowed in for a little while, but they would be fine. The internet—never good on the island—got worse in a storm. They would likely be cut off for a day or two.

They filled some large plastic containers with water before they headed to bed that night, just in case the power went out and they couldn't pump water. Though they had a forced-air electric furnace, the woodstove with hot plate was excellent backup.

Henry got up a couple of times during the night. The wind did not let up. He walked to the front of the house. The driveway was fast disappearing under a thick blanket of snow. *Tomorrow's problem,* he thought as he hopped back into bed. He was asleep again in minutes.

Unusually for Henry, he slept late, and it was already light when he woke up. He put on slippers and a dressing gown, walked to the lounge, and raised the blinds. The wind was still howling, and he could see some trees were down. The lake was rough with icy white caps, the water was a dark green colour, and it was ominously overcast.

He quickly realized it was cool in the house.

"Dammit," he thought as he checked the thermostat. "Eleven degrees—the power must be out." He checked the fuse box, and as nothing was tripped, knew the power was definitely down. He picked up his cellphone and tried to make a call. Though it was charged, he couldn't get service, so he knew he wouldn't even be able to ring Manitoba Hydro to confirm the power status or when to expect it back on.

He opened the door. There was a pile of snow against the door that was so frozen, it didn't collapse when he opened it.

Wow, so much for the forecasters! There has to be at least eight inches of drifting snow on the ground–nobody is moving on or off the island anytime soon, Henry thought.

The wind continued to blow, and the snow continued to fall off and on.

Henry built a fire in the woodstove, and in about twenty minutes it was loaded with larger logs and was putting out some good heat.

He put a kettle on the hot plate and scooped some ground coffee into a French press. In a couple of minutes when the kettle was squealing, Henry poured the boiling water and waited for the coffee to steep.

Looking at the scene outside made him suddenly realize that the RCMP would not be coming up to the island anytime soon. He was disappointed but hopeful that this early snow would melt quickly and the RCMP would make their return to continue their investigation.

He poured two mugs of coffee and gently opened the bedroom door. To his surprise, Julia was sitting up in the bed, playing on her phone. "Hey Julia, you should try to preserve power on your phone. The power's out—almost certainly a tree falling on the power line."

"I didn't know. I suppose our body heat has kept this room a little warmer. You have the wood stove going?"

"Yes. I hope this storm dies down soon," Henry said, "I'm sure this is a widespread problem. Hydro will prioritize the larger populations first, so we could be without power for a number of days."

"It's going to be a fun experience, Henry," Julia said, smiling. She was always game for a little adventure. "We need water to flush the toilets and wash. We can always bring in buckets of snow to melt, and we can cook simple food on the stove top. It will be like camping—at least we are out of the weather." Julia's said, her cup was always half full. That was something that Henry had found attractive about her. She also still had the bright-eyed smile that captured him the first time they met, and she was smiling that same smile now.

"You're right, Julia. We have gotten into a bit of a rut recently with the DVDs we've been watching. We should play cards and some of our word games to pass away the time."

"I wonder how our neighbours are doing. I know Jim and Ingrid are in Winnipeg. The Krugers on the other side aren't around. I am pretty sure there are not too many people about."

For the next twenty-four hours, the wind and snow continued. By the time the storm passed Hecla, eighteen inches of snow had accumulated. Finally, the sky cleared, it was now bitterly cold. The sun was shining, and Henry was out early, listening to the sound of someone powering up and utilizing their snow blower. The sound of the wind had been replaced by the sound of snow blowers and what he assumed was a power saw. Tree branches were likely to be down with all the relatively wet snow.

Henry got out his snow shovel. It took him over three hours to clear a third of the driveway. He had never seen so much snow. He was exhausted. At times like these, he regretted not having a snow blower. He would clear the rest with Julia's help the next morning; there was no point having a heart attack. His feet and fingers were suffering from the cold, although the rest of his body was fine.

Their driveway would be clean by tomorrow, but the provincial snow-plough had not made its way up the island yet. They would be stuck for a while longer. At least the cellphones had service again, although they decided to keep calls short to save the batteries. Julia rang the family and learned that Winnipeg had received almost as much snow. Schools and businesses were closed—something that had not happened since 1986. This was a rare weather event.

By late in the afternoon, the snowplough had cleared the main road on the island, but it would be a while until they cleared the cottage roads. Finally, the power came back on for good. If nothing else, having power again made them appreciate the creature comforts of the modern age anew!

That night, Henry went to bed early, exhausted from his show shovelling. He had a vivid dream and remembered it in the morning for once. He got the clear sense that the tall red-headed stranger was dead and not lying far away.

The next morning, Henry heard the sound of a snowblower close by and he peered out the front window to see Chris working his way down his driveway. *That is a sight for sore eyes!* Henry thought. *No shovelling today. What a relief.*

They invited Chris in for a coffee to warm up when he had finished. When he came inside, he was completely frosted up: his hair, eyebrows, and stubble were all white. He was barely recognizable.

"A little cool out there," he said, with a wry smile on his face.

"Coffee is just brewing," Julia said, "Come in and warm up."

"The worst part of winter is getting in and out of the layers of clothes," Chris said, struggling to remove his gear.

Julia and Henry laughed. "You aren't joking—that was a real pain in the you-know-where," Henry said as they walked into the dining room area.

"Grab a chair, Chris," Henry said.

"Yum! I love your coffee cake, Julia," Chris said, appreciative of his first bite.

"Plenty more where that came from, Chris," Julia replied, always happy when her baking was appreciated.

"Do you think the RCMP will be back before spring now that we've had this horrendous amount of snow?" Henry got right to the point.

"If this bitter weather keeps up, I would say no," Chris replied, looking a little serious. "However, if we get a warm patch and the snow melts, it's a possibility—we'll have to wait and see."

DEATH AT THE POINT

After another mug of coffee and two more pieces of coffee cake, Chris headed out as he had one more neighbour's driveway to clear.

"Many thanks, Chris—very kind of you. I wasn't looking forward to clearing the rest of the driveway," Henry said.

"No problem, Henry. As long as Julia's coffee cake's around, my snowblower will not be far away."

"Chris is a great neighbour, Julia. I'm glad he has decided to befriend us," Henry said as they walked back to the lounge.

"Yes, he is a good guy, Henry, and I know you appreciate his snow blowing and his wife's ricotta cookies, but you do need to be careful. He is still an RCMP officer, at least on contract, and you need to ensure in our enthusiasm to get to the bottom of the mystery at Kjartanson's point we are not doing anything illegal."

"You are right Julia, but I am an ex-police officer you remember."

I know that, but you have to admit you have a bit of an obsession with, dare I say it, this case."

"Julia, I am concerned, my spider senses are telling me that there is more to this mystery than we are seeing right now. I love this island and our life here. I want the innocence and tranquility back. And I am not feeling it right now."

"I know." Julia reached out to hug Henry. "I'm sure we will get to the bottom of things."

CHAPTER EIGHTEEN

More snow came a couple of days later. Chris called to say the RCMP were abandoning any work at Kjartanson Point until the spring. Henry was disappointed, but it was already a pretty inaccessible spot and the deep snow made searching for clues next to impossible.

Henry and Julia put up a Christmas tree and spent a full Saturday decorating the cottage and stringing lights outside.

"Henry, you have to admit it looks lovely," Julia said as they stood in the yard in the darkness, gazing at the outside lights and the beautifully dressed tree, sparkling through the window. I just love Christmas, Henry. It's the most beautiful time of the year."

Julia had managed to persuade the rest of the family to come up for Christmas Day—something they had never done before. The normal tradition was to come up a couple of days after Christmas and stay for New Year's Eve. Not this year, apparently.

Julia and Henry attended a craft sale at the community hall the following Saturday afternoon. It was a fundraiser to support maintenance of the church. Provincial funding was scarce and the money they did receive was not enough for all the basic upkeep required.

Julia baked some English Christmas Cakes—fruit cake with marzipan and royal icing—to donate for this worthy cause. She had also made two dozen mince pies. They arrived early to help set up refreshments and to position their donations among the other tasty treats. The hall was wonderfully decorated. Outside, there were lights around the door and inside, lights and streamers hung from the ceiling. A beautiful large Christmas tree had been positioned between the trestle tables of food. Everywhere there were tables loaded with things for sale. There was also a wide array of handcrafted articles, practical items carved from wood, plus an assortment of homemade candles, soaps, and jewelry.

It was such a popular event that folks came from all over to partake. It wasn't long before there was a host of customers struggling to get to the tables to check the merchandise.

Julia had volunteered to serve hot drinks and was quickly pressed into service. It was cold outside, and they were doing a roaring trade, particularly with Icelandic hot chocolate. A little like Irish coffee, but instead of whisky, it contained Brennivin, an Icelandic spirit distilled from fermented grain mash and flavoured with caraway.

There were chairs in the middle of the room to accommodate those who wanted to eat and drink sitting down.

It smelled of Christmas. Henry was not quite sure what the smell was, but his mind immediately went back to his childhood and simpler times. He was not interested in what was for sale, as Julia did most of the Christmas shopping, so he grabbed a coffee and found a seat next to an older lady. She smiled as he seated himself and stuck out his hand.

"How do you do? I am Henry Trevellyn,"

"I'm Marisa Jones. I live in the village," she replied.

"Oh! You know my wife, Julia. She visited you a while ago."

"Yes, that's right. She comes from Chudleigh in Devon—we had a good chat. Are you the gentleman who found the body on the north side of the island? It must have been quite a shock."

"I have to admit, it *was* quite a shock, and to be honest, I don't want to see another one anytime soon, particularly in such circumstances." Henry's mind flashed back to the black eye sockets staring up at him—something he would never get out of his mind. He shuddered. "Actually, I was hoping to visit you too, as I am trying to draw up a family tree of the first settlers and their descendants," Henry said gently.

"More than happy to do that, young man. Bring Julia with you—she promised to come back and visit anyway," Marisa said, a smile on her face. "I only buy tea, so if you want anything else, you will have to bring it a long." She looked up and noticed a man, a pastor, walking in the door, scanning the room for somebody.

"It's been good to meet you, Henry. Please bring Julia along. Wednesdays are good days, any time," she said as Henry reached out to assist her to her feet. She smiled back at Henry as she made her way slowly over to the pastor, using her cane for support. She put on her coat and her hat as he opened the door for her and followed her outside.

The tables were almost bare within the hour, and every seat was taken as customers were busy consuming their Icelandic coffees now that their buying frenzy was complete.

When a man appeared at the door, Julia elbowed Henry and whispered, "That's Jantie Bjornson, that rude guy I met at the general store. I wonder what he's doing here. He doesn't look like a gift-shop type."

"Well, this is a Hecla Village Resident's Association fundraising event, and he is chairperson," Henry replied. "He is also Chairperson of the Descendents of the Original Settlement Association as you know", Henry continued.

As if he had heard them, Jante walked towards Julia and Henry, making them feel a little uncomfortable. One of the women Julia was working with was his wife, and he had brought some additional milk supplies for the coffee production. He said a few words to his wife before turning to address Julia.

"How are you doing, Mrs. Trevellyn?" he asked politely.

"Good, thank you, Mr. Bjornson. It has been a busy and I would guess profitable afternoon for the Resident's Association."

"Yes, I think it has, thank you for helping out." Looking at Henry he said, "I assume this is your husband." Henry reached out his hand. "Yes, I am Henry Trevellyn. Good to meet you."

Jantie grabbed his hand in a vicelike grip and shook it firmly. "So Mr. Trevellyn, what do you think is going on at the original settlement?"

"Not sure, to be honest, but something is, going on." From the look on his face, Jantie clearly thought that Henry knew more than he was saying.

Jantie replied, obviously a little irritated. "I believe the police are planning to continue a search there. Not sure why; the guy died of natural causes. They should just leave things as they are. People are buried there; it is a sacred site." If he was looking for support for his position with Henry, he had clearly misjudged him.

"It's the digging around the site that has the police curious, not necessarily David Einarson's body," Henry said. "You have to admit it's obvious that somebody had been looking for something."

"Irrelevant to me. Some of my ancestors died of smallpox and are buried there and should be left in peace. Stay away." With that, he wandered off and worked the room with the old timers.

Eventually, it grew quieter, and Henry and Julia hung around to help clear the tables, fold the tablecloths, and put away the mugs and spoons from the hot drinks station.

"Seems to have been quite a success, Henry," Julia said, watching the cash being counted by two ladies. "The taller of the two is the organizer," she continued. "Apparently, she's been involved in this event for thirty-five years. That is dedication!"

It had grown dark, and the wind was whipping up the snow when they eventually left the building. Fortunately, they had arrived early, so the car was close by and, for once, Henry had remembered to use the remote starter.

"Volunteering feels good, Henry. I should do this again," Julia said. Henry nodded. "You were talking to Marisa Jones—what's up?"

"I told her I was trying to establish the family tree of the original descendants and asked for her help," Henry said. "She told me that she would be happy to help but she would love it if you would come along, too. I told her that you would be happy to. I hope that was OK."

"No problem, Henry. She is an interesting person to talk to."

Henry followed up with Marisa Jones the next day and she agreed to meet them at 2:00 p.m. the next Wednesday.

Wednesday was a cold and windy day. The snow had blown up against the garage door and it took Henry fifteen minutes to clear it.

"Why don't you get a snow blower Henry? It won't be getting any easier for us," Julia said, a wry smile on her face, as she stepped into the car. She had said the same thing a thousand times, but Henry enjoyed the workout. He enjoyed spending money on passions and holidays but was a bit of a skinflint when it came to practical things. Although he had to admit after the recent snow fall, the snow blowing purchase was not far away.

Henry patiently waited in the car, as he always did for Julia—totally a mystery to him why it always took her so long to get ready.

When stopped at the T junction with the main road, Henry was just about to pull out when the large blue Ford F150 appeared out of the swirling, blowing snow, and sped through the intersection.

"That's the same vehicle that was around in the summer. Maybe those foreign guys found a place to rent on the island," Henry said.

"Must be on the village side—we would have noticed the truck if they were around our area," Julia replied. "Good job you didn't pull out."

With that, Henry cautiously turned and continued down the main road towards the village.

CHAPTER NINETEEN

Henry turned left towards the lakeshore and the village. Visibility was low, the snow blowing over the road. There was nobody around and the heritage part of the village was closed for the season. The only lights were the Christmas lights on the community hall, which should have been on a timer to conserve the electrical costs. This had clearly not been given any thought, but it was a cheery scene on this miserable day.

The snow in Marisa's driveway was quite deep and Henry parked at the end so they wouldn't get stuck. Walking even the short distance to the house was not a popular idea with Julia.

"Just make sure you have the remote start on for a while before we leave, Henry. I'm not dressed for this." She was a little grumpy. *Best to say nothing other than 'yes, Dear,'* Henry thought.

"Yes, Dear!" he shouted as they got out of the car and raced for the relative shelter of the front porch.

"Wow; that was painful," Julia said, panting.

They rang the doorbell and waited until Marisa's smiling face appeared and the door opened.

"Come in, come in! You folks must be freezing," she said as she ushered them in, quickly closing the door behind them. Bending over in the confined space on the mat by the door, Henry and Julia unzipped their boots and then hung up their coats.

"Wicked day today. That wind has been blowing hard since last night," Marisa said. "A nice cup of tea will warm us up. Ah! There goes the whistle—water's boiled."

They followed Marisa into the kitchen.

"OK to sit anywhere, Marisa?" Julia asked.

"I would prefer you sit on the right side of the table," Marisa said. "I am going deaf in my left ear and my hearing aid isn't working for some reason." She put the teapot on the table and seated herself.

"So why your interest in the first settlers on the north side of the island?" Marisa asked, looking directly at Henry.

"A number of reasons. But first, it looks as if the stranger or strangers had been digging within the foundations of the original dwellings."

"Why would they be doing that?" Marisa asked innocently.

"Looking for something, I assume," Henry replied.

Marisa nodded. "The tea is steeped and ready to be poured. Do you take milk in your tea?"

"Black for us both," Julia replied. Marisa put a mug in front of each of them and then offered a plate of various dainties.

"Homemade. Please, eat up—they were freshly baked today. Please, carry on, Henry. I'm getting intrigued," Marisa said after they'd enjoyed some treats.

"Well, I also got my hands on a fascinating diary by a young girl named Greta Kjartanson. It was incredibly interesting to read a year in the life of a young person living in the very early settlement days when life was a battle for survival. I read the translated version from cover to cover."

"Must have been interesting," Marisa said with a sly smile. "The original would have been written in Icelandic."

"Correct," Henry replied. "The New Iceland Heritage Museum hired the Icelandic Department of the University of Manitoba to undertake the translation to English."

"Well, Henry—Greta was my grandmother. She married my grandfather and became Greta Larson. She was a little older than my grandfather but outlived him by quite a bit. She died in the early 1930s. As far as I know, she only left the province once and that was for a trip back to Iceland in the 1920s. She was the only one of her family to actually stay on the island. Her dad died young, and her mother moved in with one of her younger brothers. All her siblings moved down to Winnipeg. She kept in touch mainly by letter as Winnipeg was quite a trip in those early days. She loved the island and worked hard to maintain the Icelandic traditions. They had four children and their eldest daughter, Elisabet, married my dad and became Elisabet Helguson. It is good she didn't live long enough to see what happened to the community in the 1960s like my poor mother and father."

"Are you OK, Henry?" Julia asked. "You look a little stunned."

"It never occurred to me that somebody alive on the island could be Greta's granddaughter! I feel I know her now. What else can you tell me, Marisa?" Henry asked.

"Not sure, Henry. "I cannot read or write more than the odd word in Icelandic now, and I was the one who donated the diary to the museum. It wasn't much practical use to me. I was concerned that it would be thrown away when I pass, and I wanted to make sure it was kept in a safe place. I never got around to getting it translated, but I would love to read it."

"I can definitely arrange that, Marisa. The original is kept in the archives of the museum, but the English translation is available to be read any time. It cannot be removed, but if you are interested, we could do a day trip to the museum. What do you say?"

"I would love that, Henry! Thank you. I look forward to it."

"Actually," Henry said, "the museum has asked me to speak at a meeting to promote the Icelandic culture and the discovery of Greta's journal. Maybe we can kill two birds with one stone so to speak."

"I have some old photo albums you could look through, Henry, while Julia and I have a good chat and another cup of tea, and maybe another dainty," Marisa said, smiling at Julia as she got up and invited her to sit on the large and rather ancient sofa in the lounge. It was now bathed in sunshine as the skies had cleared and the low sun was now shining directly through the main window in the room.

"The albums are over there, on the bookshelf, bottom right," Marisa pointed to the books that populated an entire wall of the lounge. "I think there are two of them."

Henry crouched down and pulled out the two old albums. One was plainly more time-worn than the other. "Just to let you know," Marisa called out, "the older one is my parents' and the newer one is mine and Jim's."

Henry decided the older one would likely be of the most interest. He opened it gently; the front of the album was almost completely separated from the rest. Many of the photographs were loose; the gummed corner mountings had come away from the pages of the album.

As Henry scanned each photo, he thought to himself how silly it was that nobody had identified the individuals in each snap. *I suppose it's because the person who assembled the album knows all the people and nobody really considers the albums being a valuable source of family history for the next generation.*

CHAPTER TWENTY

The photographs were mainly black and white and some of them had yellowed a little. But generally, they were in good condition.

There were lots of family group pictures, particularly from the 1920s and the 1930s. There were birthdays, Christmases, and other family gatherings. There was one photograph in particular that caught his eye: Marisa was standing with an older lady. Marisa was about two years old so that would date the picture at around 1924. If this older woman was Greta, she would have been about sixty at the time. She was an attractive lady with a pretty smile, wearing a nice hat.

Henry got up and showed Marisa the picture.

"Is that your Grandma Greta?" Henry asked.

"Yes, it is Henry. She was an attractive woman—widowed relatively early. She had many admirers but never remarried. Although, there were rumours that she had met somebody special when she went to Iceland."

Henry returned to the table and reviewed all the pictures in the album. There were lots of Greta as she got older. She was always in good shape and nicely dressed, even when playing with her grandkids, the same beautiful smile in every picture. She must have been blessed with good health into her old age. *Clean living.*

There were a group of photos taken in Iceland—Henry assumed from Greta's trip in the 1920s. They were mainly of landscapes, although there were a couple of Greta dressed formally, involved in some kind of ritual or presentation. Henry was going to ask Marisa about it, but she was completely engaged in conversation with Julia, and he didn't want to keep interrupting her. It could wait.

He checked his watch, then closed the album and put both of them back on the bookshelf. Julia looked up.

"Time to go?" she asked.

"Yep, my tummy's rumbling," Henry replied with a smile.

"I suppose all good things have to come to an end, unfortunately," Marisa said. "It has been such a nice afternoon. Thank you so much for coming."

As they were putting on their coats, Marisa said, "Henry, I'll find the letters and newspaper cuttings I promised you and give you a call—we didn't really speak about other descendants other than my own."

"No problem. You dropped a couple of bombshells: you being related to Greta and having had the diary all these years, which gives me much food for thought. I wonder what else you know that may be of interest in trying to solve the reasons for the strange activity on the north side of the island."

Henry had remembered to use the remote start. The lights on the car, were somehow warm and comforting in the twilight.

"Marisa, I'll let you know when the museum organizes the meeting I talked about," Henry said, struggling with his boots.

They said goodbye and could see Marisa waving from the lounge window.

"What a nice lady," Julia said above the hum of the heater fan that Henry had turned up full blast.

"Yes, I like her. She has grace and class just like I imagine her grandmother had."

The ride home didn't take long; the wind had actually blown most of the snow off the road, except in areas that were heavily treed. A large vehicle followed them home before continuing down Lakeside Road as they turned into their driveway. Henry was not really paying attention as his stomach was growling.

"Bangers and mash for dinner?" Julia asked.

"Fantastic, Julia. I would love a couple of brats. I'll give you a hand peeling the potatoes."

Julia uncorked a bottle of red wine and pulled a couple of glasses from the cupboard as Henry started to peel the potatoes.

"Do you think the tall red-headed stranger and the two foreign guys in the Ford truck were looking for what Greta's father showed her under the floor in their house? If they haven't read the diary, how would they know about these artifacts? In all these months, I have not discovered any other reason for why somebody would be digging in the areas they were."

"Maybe you're right, Henry, but we need to be careful. Those two guys in the truck scare me and they are still hanging around."

Henry was also concerned about the two strangers and what they were up to. He needed to find out where they were holed up.

He called Jantie Bjornson, who was not friendly at all.

"Yes, I have met the two people you mentioned. Although I don't think it is any of your business, I believe they are renting an old place right at the end of the village near Marisa Jones's place. That's all I know—goodnight." He slammed down the phone.

Henry was a little shocked at his rudeness, especially after his relative politeness the previous week at the community hall. However, he was glad he had gained a valuable piece of information. It was too much of a coincidence he thought, that they had found a place so close to Marisa's.

Henry rang the museum early the next week and asked Susie whether or not anybody else had asked to see the journal.

"No. They are going to make its availability known at the speaking event coming up." Apparently, a social media campaign had been put together and Susie was hoping Henry would be available the following Saturday night to participate.

"Happy to speak, Susie, as we agreed. A recent acquaintance on the island, Marisa Jones, is Greta's granddaughter and would also like to be part of the evening."

"Wow! That would be fabulous. Would she be willing to speak as well?" Susie asked.

"Quite sure she would. She has some recollection of Greta from her childhood days. Where and what time, Susie?"

"In our meeting room at the museum library starting at 6:30 p.m. There are only twenty-five seats available."

"OK, Susie. I wonder if you could do us a favour? Mrs. Jones is interested in reading some of the English translation of the journal. Could we come a little early?"

"Of course, Henry. That is no trouble."

Henry called Marisa.

"Yes, I would be thrilled to come to the event and more than happy to speak, although my memories are not extensive," Marisa said. "Looking forward to getting out Henry. Thank you."

Henry said goodbye and turned to Julia. "It will be interesting to see who turns up for the event." Julia just gave a wry smile in reply.

Henry and Julia picked Marisa up promptly at 4:00 p.m. Saturday afternoon. They were in Gimli in fifty minutes. He parked the car across the road from the museum and they slowly made their way into the museum.

Susie was escorting out the day's final visitors. She locked the door behind them and flipped the sign on the door to closed.

"Hi, Mrs. Jones. What a pleasure to meet you. I am so glad you could attend our event this evening," Susie said reaching out to shake Marisa's hand.

"Well thank you, Susie. My *amma* was a special lady and she will be smiling down on all of us, thrilled to know we are making a fuss of her tonight."

"Come along, Mrs. Jones. I have the English translation laid out in the archive room. There's a cozy chair and good lighting. I hope you will be comfortable."

After a couple of minutes, Susie returned to the foyer where Henry and Julia waited for her. She smiled at them. "She is so excited to be reading her grandma's diary. She told me she has been in possession of it ever since her parents passed away but has never read it. This is a big deal to her."

Julia and Henry followed Susie down the passage to the meeting room. Sectional tables were laid out like a boardroom table. There were chairs around it and additional chairs around the edges of the room. Within forty-five minutes they had transformed it into a more classroom style: a lectern set up in front of rows of chairs.

Susie then went to make some coffee and returned with a tray, the coffee, and some dainties and cookies.

"We've received a strong response to our social media campaign and decided to squeeze in a few more people. There will be thirty here tonight."

"Packing the place," Henry said, laughing.

When it was time, Henry went to the archive room and knocked on the door. Marisa was sitting in front of the journal— Kleenex in hand— and had obviously been weeping.

"Are you OK, Marisa?" Henry asked gently.

"Yes, of course Henry. It is just a little emotional connecting with Grandma as a child from so long ago. Feels really strange as I only knew her as an old lady."

"I can only imagine, Marisa," Henry replied. "But we need to get ready for this evening, if you're feeling up to it."

"Of course, Henry. This is important to her memory. I would not want to be anywhere else."

She carefully got out of her seat, grabbed her cane, and followed Henry down the passage. Marisa was in remarkably good shape for a ninety-five-year-old.

Susie opened the front door and people slowly flowed in. Henry greeted them as they entered the meeting room. To his surprise, there was a wide age range; he'd jumped to the conclusion that it would just be older people attending.

By the time everybody had arrived, and Susie had ticked off the list of names and closed the door, the room was full. Jantie Bjornson was present with his wife. There was no sign of the two strangers and nobody else he recognized.

Susie opened the meeting with a welcome and introduced the guest speakers and provided a little background on the donation of the journal and the translation process and its availability to the general public in the future.

Henry gave a short history of the settlement of the island, particularly on the first settlers on the north shore. He paraphrased from the journal and described the year in Greta's life—the details were clear in Henry's mind, and the challenges, difficulties, and joys came through in his speech. He didn't mention the treasures from the old country as he didn't want to put it out there until he had raised it with Marisa.

Marisa, having just read sections of the diary, filled in the details about the later part of her life. At the end of the evening there was a question-and-answer session, a round of applause, and then coffee, dainties and cookies.

Julia worked the room as always; Henry was always amazed at the way she could pick up a conversation with anyone—a wonderful life skill. At the heart of it was her genuine interest in people.

A tall, attractive lady was in conversation with Marisa who was smiling and nodding intensely.

Marisa introduced Henry to her new acquaintance.

"Henry, please meet Sophie Dubois, a journalist with the Manitoba French newspaper *La Liberté*. Henry smiled and shook Sophie's hand.

"Pleased to meet you, Sophie. Thank you for coming. Are you on official business?"

"Actually, yes. My editor and I were intrigued by the discovery of the diary. I saw the notice of the meeting and thought I would come along to see if there's a story here."

"What do you think, Sophie? Is there a story to write about?" Marisa asked.

"Yes. I think the diary of a young settler girl is always fascinating. Hopefully, I'll get the chance to read the diary itself and interview you, Marisa. Maybe we can arrange a time and date to meet?"

"Sophie, it would be a pleasure. She was such an extraordinary woman and to celebrate her story with an article would be fabulous."

"Actually, with the museum's permission, we were considering serializing the diary in our Saturday book section with some commentary regarding historical context and your recollections if you are interested. Also, how would I get to read the diary?"

"As we said earlier, the translated version is available to read here at the museum. Apparently, it cannot leave the museum," Marisa said. "I think you will have to speak to the museum management in order to get permission to reproduce it in your newspaper. I know they paid a fair sum to get it translated from the Icelandic original," Marisa added.

"OK. I'll follow that up with them," Sophie said smiling, excited by the possibility of having something to run with. "Can I have a contact number to reach you two folks if I have questions?"

"No problem," Henry said, handing Sophie an old business card, with his old title and email lined out and personal contact details added.

"Oh, so you were head of the Major Crime Unit in Winnipeg at one time. I have to say Henry Trevellyn sounded familiar—thanks Henry." She wrote Marisa's phone number down in her book, thanked the two of them, and headed off to replenish her coffee.

Everybody seemed to have enjoyed the evening, especially Marisa, who was animated and looked twenty years younger.

Sophie found Henry alone a few minutes later and he could tell she had something on her mind. He asked if she had more questions.

"Actually, I do," she said, speaking deliberately softly. "As an ex-officer, what theories do you have regarding the discovery of David Einarson's body at the original settlement at Hecla?"

Henry was taken a little aback at the question and surprised she knew or had guessed the site of death.

"Well, I really don't know what to say, Sophie. I am a little intrigued where you would have gotten the idea he died up at Hecla."

"Come on, Henry. Don't be so coy. All newspapers have their sources," Sophie said staring directly into Henry's eyes.

Henry was uncomfortable; he was more familiar being the interrogator. "With respect, Sophie, this isn't the time or place for that conversation. Happy to talk more, once it is out in the public domain. I have my sources, too, that I need to protect," he said smiling.

"No problem, Henry. Thought it was worth a try and your body language gave you away anyway. Talk soon."

Sophie waved to Marisa, put on her coat, and left.

After fifteen minutes or so, people started to leave. This had truly been a successful event.

Jantie and his wife thanked Marisa and said goodbye to Henry and Julia. They were obviously glad to see the island getting some positive exposure. *Jantie is an odd bird,* Henry thought. He never knew how to take him. *Rude one moment and polite the next.* Henry drove as close to Marisa's front door as he could and stopped the car.

"Let me help you out," Henry said.

"Thanks to the two of you. This has been a special day for me and my family. I hope to see you both here again soon." There was a tear in Marisa's eye as she stepped out of the car. She unlocked her front door, turned, and waved, and in a moment the door closed, and Henry was reversing back down the driveway.

"Who was that tall attractive lady you were obviously taken with, Henry?" Julia asked with a wry smile on her face as they drove through the village. Henry, a little awkward that he was so transparent, smiled back and said, "Her name is Sophie Dubois, and she is a journalist with the only French newspaper in Manitoba. She said was here to research a story around Greta's diary."

"Well, that's good. Marisa must be pleased," Julia replied.

"Yes, apparently she will be coming up to Hecla soon—she wants to interview the two of us," Henry said.

CHAPTER TWENTY-ONE

That night as Julia gently purred in her sleep, Henry laid on his back, reflecting on the evening; he had a lot on his mind. The journalist, Sophie Dubois, was now a consideration—he knew her interest in Hecla was not solely about Greta's diary. *Is she going to be an ally, or something else? Something to park for now.*

His mind kept going back to the two gentlemen in the Ford pickup and how they fit into the story. He couldn't imagine Marisa letting those two unsavoury characters into her home. How else would they know about what had been buried under the floor, if that was what they were looking for? Was that why they were still hanging around? According to Susie, nobody else had read Greta's diary.

It had been snowing hard since they got back from Marisa's. Though Henry struggled to sleep, eventually he dozed off, only to be awoken by a banging noise outside. He put on his dressing gown and boots, went out to the front of the house, and looked up. Part of the fascia had worked loose and was banging every time the wind gusted.

He looked down the driveway, noting that the snow was quite deep. To his surprise, he saw some wide tire tracks. They definitely were not tracks from Henry's vehicle, and they definitely were recent, like in the last hour or two. Henry checked his watch. It was 2:00 a.m. Who would be coming down their driveway in the middle of the night? Henry got the uncomfortable feeling it had been the strangers' truck. He went back inside the cottage and locked the front door. He was sure he had locked the front door that evening. *That's strange,* he thought. *The mat at the front door is a little wet. Nobody had used that door all day.*

He turned off the light and struggled to get back to sleep but, eventually, he did.

While making coffee the next morning, Henry made up his mind that he wasn't going to worry Julia by saying anything about last night. He looked out at the fresh snow: no tire tracks. It was like a dream, but any sense he had imagined it was dashed as a gust of wind blew against the house and the section of fascia started to bang again. Fortunately, the damaged section was on the lower part of the roof, and it didn't take Henry long to repair it.

Over the next couple of days, the weather warmed up, like it often does that time of the year for short periods. There were even a number of unseasonably warm days above zero. The skies were blue, and the sun was up as high as it gets in December.

Julia and Henry were walking Skip down their road; it was wet and slushy. Suddenly, a procession of RCMP vehicles were moving up towards the turnaround section at the entrance through the forest and the trail to the quarry. "Seems like they are taking advantage of the break in the weather, to continue their search of the original settlement," Henry said to Julia.

"Give your RCMP buddy a call. Maybe he knows something," Julia replied.

Jane answered the phone. "Oh, hi, Henry. No, he's not here. Actually, he's been contracted by the RCMP to be part of what you are seeing going past your place. He hasn't and probably will not tell me what it is about."

"Thanks Jane, I appreciate the heads up," Henry said. "I suppose we will have to just wait and see."

Sounds like the RCMP are taking advantage of this strange warmer weather to continue their search, Henry thought. The snow was almost gone, at least for a while, and he wondered if something specific had triggered this renewed effort. *They seem to be putting a lot of resources into this investigation.*

A couple of days went by, the warmer weather continued and judging from the activity, the search for something or someone was continuing. The quarry path had been closed off with police tape.

"Why do you think they're using our road, Henry?" Julia asked.

"Don't know for sure, but the lake has not safely frozen over, and the path from Highway 8, although shorter, is not wide enough for the size of vehicles they have; it is the practical way to access the site."

At the end of the week, Henry walked up to the top of the road; it was late in the day and starting to get dark. Two uniformed RCMP officers were carrying a stretcher with what looked like a body in a black bag on it, bringing it to a white truck. A third officer hurried to open the door and helped to slide the stretcher into the vehicle. The body was so long it was almost overhanging the stretcher. Henry immediately assumed it was the tall red-bearded stranger that had been hanging around a year or so ago. *So he has been around all this time? Crazy.*

He was about to turn around when two more officers, carrying a second stretcher and another black bag, appeared from the quarry path. *A second body bag–wow–I wasn't expecting that.* The second body bag was much smaller, and Henry concluded it was probably a much more decomposed body.

As he turned, he noticed the blue Ford F150 reversing and heading back down the road. They had obviously seen what Henry had seen and had seen him, too. He was very concerned that he was not as alert as he should be and had been unaware of his surroundings. Henry was starting to feel uncomfortable.

When he got home, he shared the latest development with Julia.

"Henry, somebody dying of natural causes in strange circumstances is one thing. A second and then a *third* body—this is starting to freak me out," Julia said, not amused by the news.

"I've got a feeling the second body is not related," Henry said. It was cold comfort to Julia, who felt no reassurance from Henry's words.

A couple of days went by and there was a news story on TV of a second body found, probably connected with the natural death of David Einarson. There were still few details shared but there was an artist's rendition of the deceased person as no form of identity had been found. The report stated that the person's death was "suspicious." The police were requesting anyone that may recognize the person to come forward. There was no mention of a second body.

A couple of days later, Henry bumped into Chris on their road.

"Cannot say anything Henry—you know how it is," Chris said anticipating the questions that would be coming from his neighbour. Henry shrugged his shoulders, disappointed but not surprised.

"I'll tell you he is not from around here," Chris shouted as he walked away back down his driveway. "Not Canadian, not Icelandic, if that was going to be your next question. See you around." Then he disappeared into his garage.

Henry understood: the post-retirement income from the RCMP was important to Chris and he obviously didn't want to jeopardize that. *I didn't even get a chance to ask about the second body.*

Henry was full of the latest information when he walked in the door. Julia's demeanor was not good.

"Henry, I have to say, I am sick and tired of talking about all this. We have Christmas coming and I need you to focus on the family for once." Julia had actually raised her voice. Henry knew he obsessed.

"Julia you are right—giving it a break is important, to focus on the family is important and besides, leaving it alone for a while may create some out-of-the-box thinking which is what this case needs."

"I'm fit to be tied," Julia said. "This investigation is not yours. You are retired! When are you going to get that into your head? See those boxes over there? They are the outdoor Christmas lights. I need you to start stringing them up in time for Christmas. Now would be a very good time. Oh, and by the way, Diane rang earlier. She seems really settled now in the UK since her big move from Montreal and she wants to bring her boyfriend over for Christmas. I told her we were OK with that."

"OK, Dear. That's fine with me. It will be good to meet him." Henry realized that giving Julia a little space and getting those lights up would put a smile on her face. He grabbed the boxes and opened the door to the garage to fetch the step ladder.

When he was done, he called Julia outside to inspect his Christmas light installation. He had also lit up a small fir tree in the yard and put up lights around their house number sign on the front of the road.

"Wow, you've been busy, Henry. I am impressed." He gave his wife a squeeze, relieved he had put a smile back on her face.

As they walked back to the house, Julia told him he had a number of calls. "I let them go to voicemail."

"OK. I'll put the ladder and tools away and check to see who called. Thanks," Henry said.

"It was the Dubois lady," Julia said. "As she's coming up to interview the two of you, this latest news is likely an added incentive."

Henry knew Julia well— she was suspicious that Sophie Dubois was at least as interested in the current goings on as she was in following up on the Greta diary. "She is just doing her job Julia."

Henry slumped down in his favourite cozy chair, looking out onto the lake. He put his coffee down on his side table and reached for his phone. Finding his calls, he checked the two messages—both from Sophie—the second a little more insistent than the first.

"Hi, Henry. Please give me a call. I'm trying to coordinate a time to get together with you and Marisa. I've spoken to her, and she can make this coming Wednesday morning at 11:00 a.m. I hope that works for you. Please call back and let me know. I'm staying over for the night, so an alternative time later in the day will still work. Thanks."

He dialled Sophie's number. "Hi, Henry. How are you?"

"Good, thanks, Sophie, and you?"

"Great, thanks. Looking forward to getting out of Winnipeg. I haven't been to Hecla in years."

"Not the best time of the year to visit, Sophie, but it will be good to get going on your feature for the newspaper. It is important publicity for the island. 11:00 a.m. works for me. Shall we meet at Marisa's place?"

"Yes. I'll drive up in the morning. Weather willing, I'll be on time. Marisa says it's a two-hour drive from Winnipeg."

Wednesday came quickly—Henry thought he would find the time passing a little more slowly once he had retired, but time, rather alarmingly, was going by faster.

Henry, always punctual, pulled up at Marisa's a couple of minutes before 11:00 a.m. and there was a small, red compact car in the spot where he normally parked. *Sophie's car.* He pulled up alongside and walked to the door. Just as it opened, and an older woman stepped out.

"OK, Marisa—should be back in a couple of hours. I have your shopping list," the woman said, "The first of your visitors have arrived; goodbye!" She hurried off, acknowledging Henry with a nod and a smile as she passed by.

"Hi, Marisa. How are you doing?"

"Good, thank you, Henry. Any sign of Sophie?"

"No, not yet. I thought the car parked outside was hers."

"No, that's my neighbour. She kindly does my grocery shopping once a week."

After a couple of minutes of idle chit chat at the kitchen table, a car pulled up outside.

Henry walked to the front window and looked out. "It's Sophie."

"Can you let her in Henry, please? My legs are playing up a little today."

He opened the front. Sophie's long, auburn-brown hair caught the sun. Henry smiled and shielded his eyes from the brilliant sunlight.

"Hi, Sophie. Good to see you. Let me take your coat. Did you have a good drive?"

"It was excellent, the roads were fine, and once past Gimli, almost no traffic. Your directions on the island were excellent, Marisa—found the place, no problem."

Sophie removed her coat and proceeded to greet Marisa and Henry with a kiss on each check. Henry smelled just the slightest hint of a very agreeable perfume.

"Can I just use your washroom, Marisa? I had a couple of cups of coffee before driving. Not one of my smartest moves," she said, grinning at Marisa.

"I assume tea will be OK, Sophie? I don't actually keep coffee in the house."

"No problem, Marisa. I'll be right back."

By the time Sophie settled at the table, three mugs, a teapot, milk and sugar, and a plate of dainties graced the table.

"How do you like your tea, Sophie?" Marisa asked.

"White, no sugar, please."

"Black is good; thanks Marisa," Henry said, smiling.

Sophie pulled out a notebook and pen from her bag and opened it to a blank page.

Looking up at Henry and Marisa, she said, "Where shall we start? Oh, yes. Well, I have travelled to Gimli a couple of times now and have read the diary through. It is a great memoir of life at that time and my editor has also negotiated the rights to reproduce the work for a sum that will be donated to the museum library, if you are OK with that, Marisa?"

"Completely. How much did you negotiate?" Marisa asked.

"$5,000. I know the museum library said the infusion of that kind of cash will be invaluable for them," Sophie replied. "What I am interested in are your anecdotes, memories, and photographs of Greta."

"Henry, can you grab that older album, please?" Marisa asked pointing to the album on the bookshelf. "If you sit next to me, Sophie, I can take you through the album and you can borrow any photos that you think would support your story." Placing the album between the two of them, Henry resumed his position on the other side of the table.

"Do you mind if I record this? I want to capture the stories as well as I can, without getting writer's cramp." Marisa nodded in agreement and Sophie placed a small recorder on the table.

Hours later, Sophie turned off the recorder and put it and the notebook in her bag. Marisa had found Sophie a small box for the stack of photos she was loaning the newspaper.

"How about a late lunch, folks? It's on me. I assume we can eat at the hotel?" Sophie asked.

"Sounds marvellous. Sophie, I cannot remember the last time I went out to lunch," Marisa said, excitement in her voice.

"I'll drive you, Marisa," Sophie said, "and bring you home after lunch. Just need a couple of minutes to check in when we arrive."

"Better still, Sophie, I'll drive Marisa and the two of us can find a table while you check in," Henry said.

"OK with me," Sophie said in reply.

Twenty minutes later, Marisa, Henry, and Sophie were sitting around a table, looking at the menus.

"Hi, folks. My name is Justin. I am going to be your waiter. What can I get you for drinks?" Sophie took the lead. "Marisa, I think you said tea—milk and sugar. Henry what would you like?"

"A coffee with cream would be good," Henry said, looking up at the waiter.

"And I'll have a coffee, black please. I'm taking care of the bill." Henry and Marisa nodded in appreciation to Sophie.

"Thank you, madam. I'll be right back to take your food orders."

They were relaxed with each other, and Henry welcomed the uncomplicated conversations.

The waiter arrived with the tea and coffee and took their food orders.

"So, Sophie, we don't really know too much about you," Henry said, a little curious.

"Well, I am from St. Boniface—a Franco-Manitoban, as you know. I live close to Provencher Boulevard with my partner Cecile and our two labradoodles, Chloe and Esme. My ex-husband and two children live close by. I have worked in Manitoba my whole life, except for a couple of years in Lyon in France, where I did a master's degree in journalism and stayed for a couple of years after that to get some international working experience. I love my job and travel quite a bit, which I like, and have a busy, full life."

The conversation then turned to the hotel and its amenities, and the things to do on the island at that time of the year.

"It's a little early to be on the lake, for ice fishing," Henry said, "but cross-country skiing is quite popular, as is Ski-Dooing and snowshoeing when we have a little more snow. The hotel has a spa facility, indoor and outdoor pools, and a toboggan hill, if you are so inclined. There are lots of walking trails."

"Wow, I didn't know there was so much to do here. If this place is dog-friendly, I know my partner and I would enjoy a weekend here," Sophie said, looking genuinely excited.

The food arrived quickly, and the conversation toned down as everybody was hungry. Sophie's demeanour returned to a business-like mode as soon as lunch was finished.

"Marisa, I think I have all I need. I have already coordinated with the New Icelandic Heritage Museum and have an electronic copy of the translation of Greta's diary, and I have both of your input into her life and background in Hecla and its history. I think I am good to go and will keep you up to date on our publishing dates."

"Happy to drive you home now, if that is OK, Marisa," Sophie said smiling.

"It's been a lovely lunch, Sophie. Thank you," Marisa said.

Henry helped Marisa out of her chair, handed her cane, and helped her into her coat. They walked to the front entrance.

"Henry, thank you," Sophie said. "May I call you a little later? I have something to discuss with you."

"No problem, Sophie. You have my number. I am heading home now—I just live up the road on Lakeside Road."

As Henry drove away, he tried to guess what was on Sophie's mind and he speculated it was questions regarding the bodies slowly piling up at the point.

An hour later, Sophie rang and confirmed his suspicions.

"Hi, Henry. I didn't want to talk in front of Marisa and confuse her, but as a journalist, I am obviously very interested in what is going on at the original settlement. I read the entire diary and I am wondering if there is a link between the old relics her father was protecting and what has been going on in recent months at the site. What are your thoughts?"

"It is clear that somebody has been looking for something at the site and people have died—one person for sure under suspicious circumstances. I think you need to be careful, Sophie, as something is going on and the police are continuing to investigate," Henry said.

"Thank you for your concern, Henry, but I am primarily an investigative journalist. This is what I do for a living," Sophie said, with a slight edge in her voice for emphasis. "I have been in a lot of tight scrapes. I know how to look after myself." She didn't seem to appreciate his efforts to be protective of her.

"I know you have an interest in this investigation, Henry. Don't deny it. Why don't we work together?"

"I do have an interest in resolving this. The tranquility of the island has been negatively impacted and Julia and I don't like it."

"No need to be so defensive, Henry. I can do this alone. I just thought it would make sense to pool knowledge and resources."

The working Sophie Dubois is much more assertive than the charming Sophie I first met, Henry thought, reflecting on her words.

"How about you take me out to the site tomorrow morning? That's all I ask," Sophie pleaded.

"OK," Henry said with a smile. He liked Sophie's get up and go and wanted to retain a cordial relationship with her.

"I will meet you at the hotel at 8am and you can follow me down the highway. It's quite a difficult walk: a narrow trail, partly overgrown, and of course there will be ice and snow," Henry continued.

They said goodbye and Henry put down his phone.

Julia was a little negative regarding Henry giving any assistance to Sophie in regard to the original settlement but took his assurances that they would not be working together.

"You find Sophie attractive, don't you Henry?"

"Actually, I do Julia," Henry replied grinning. "But don't worry; I only have eyes for you… besides, she's gay."

"You mean 'a lesbian," Julia said. "Yes, she was sharing her background with Marisa and me at lunchtime. She has a partner, two dogs, and seems to have a settled life."

Henry reached out and gave Julia a big hug. "You are the only gal for me, Julia."

The next morning, Henry arrived a little early. It was cold and a light wind was blowing through the trees when he stepped out of the car. Sophie drove up exactly on time and waved and smiled as she parked next to Henry's vehicle.

"Hi, Henry. Ready for a hike?"

"Always, Sophie." He was smiling as he looked at her. She always dressed the part and was wearing some nice gear and boots, which accentuated her tall willowy figure. He thought about making a compliment but decided against it. He got the impression she probably got a lot of them anyway.

"We go this way," Henry pointed to a gap between two large trees. He quickly realized she was in great shape.

Eventually, they approached the yellow police tape moving in the breeze through the trees. The ground was still snow covered, but the piles of earth and rocks were evident, pushing out of the partly melted snow

"Wow. Looks like moles have been working the ground over," she said, amazed at the amount of excavation that was evident.

They ducked under the police tape and looked around. They did not speak. Dead leaves, still clinging to the branches of a few trees, were rattling in the breeze. It was definitely colder on this side of the island.

"If you look carefully, you can see that the excavations are limited to the area of the five foundations—four dwellings and a large barn."

"Yes, I can see. Somebody must have been busy for a good while," Sophie said pulling a camera from her rucksack.

"Hey, Sophie, you need to be careful. We are within the police cordon, and we shouldn't be taking photos of an investigative crime scene—certainly not publishing them."

"There doesn't seem to be much to see," Sophie said, disappointed.

"The original buildings have long since rotted back into the earth and only the weather-worn stone foundations remain," Henry replied. "Those two holes are obviously where they found the bodies." He immediately knew he had said too much. There was a moment of silence and then Sophie said, "Which bodies are we talking about Henry? I thought David Einarson was found by you on the ground, having fallen after a deadly heart attack—so he wasn't buried. The second body of a very tall man was discovered recently. Who was the third person?" Sophie asked with inquisitive eyes.

"You got me. When they searched the site recently, they found two bodies—they only publicly reported one of them. I think the other body was much older and probably has nothing to do with the case or the body reported, or that's what I assume—I don't know for sure. That's all I can tell you, Sophie—for all I know, the other body could have been one of the original settlers."

Thirty minutes later, Sophie had seen enough.

"Thanks, Henry. It's really good as a reporter to get a sense of the place and I have that now. Next, I will be focusing on getting Greta's diary out with the interviews. We are planning to start publishing the diary starting immediately after Christmas. The articles will run for quite a few weeks."

They walked back to the road

"My offer still stands, you know," Sophie said.

"Sorry—what offer?" Henry was distracted, looking for his keys.

"To work together—remember?" Sophie said.

"I'll tell you what: let's talk after Christmas," Henry said. "This has to be for our mutual advantage."

"Agreed, Henry. Thanks for showing me around. Have a great Christmas and say hi to Julia."

After the customary kiss on both cheeks, she got into her car, waved, smiled, and then turned left towards the village. *Strange,* Henry thought, *where is she off to now?*

CHAPTER TWENTY-TWO

It was almost Christmas, and the entire family was about to arrive in Hecla.

Julia was in her element as she had been planning the Christmas retreat for months and she wanted it to be perfect. Henry was exhausted from all the planning activities, but he had to admit to himself that the distraction was good. Preparing enough firewood, sourcing out temporary mattresses and additional sheets and blankets, and putting up a couple of trees plus decorations all took time and effort.

They began to arrive a few days before Christmas. Johnny and Christine and the two boys showed up first. Christine would help Julia with some final baking, while Henry and Johnny attempted to keep the boys amused. The good news was that although it was still relatively mild, it had snowed hard over the previous couple of days, making it the perfect time to be outside. Making snowmen and tobogganing down the one hill on the island was a huge hit with the boys.

Henry loved Christmas. He loved his grandkids and seeing the look of excitement on their faces on Christmas Eve as they put up their stockings and set out carrots for the reindeer and milk and cookies for Santa in front of the tree. It was only a couple of days away now. The four-inch chimney from the firebox in the lounge wasn't going to faze the skinny Santa who would be visiting the cottage.

Julia and Christine did a fine job in the kitchen. The amount of baking was amazing: mincemeat pies aplenty (Henry's favourite), cookies of all flavours, and a number of cakes. Harry and Karen and the girls arrived on December 23. Blowing snow and poor visibility had slowed them down. They texted when they got off the main road, so Henry and Julia went to front door to greet them. They lived in Toronto now, so Henry and Julia didn't get to see their little girls too often.

The girls were screaming with excitement as they leaped into Julia and Henry's arms. That was, until they heard their cousins. Then they were furiously removing their boots, coats, and hats, leaving a trail of discarded winter clothing through the house to the lounge, where the boys were playing in front of the fire.

Diane and Rob's plane was late, so they arrived on the morning of Christmas Eve. This was the first time anybody had met Rob. Diane had met him soon after she arrived in the UK for a medical research job. They got a taxi to Henry's and Julia's Winnipeg house, then drove Julia's car up to Hecla. They arrived at lunchtime, a little jet-lagged and needed an hour's snooze to recover so they would have the energy to enjoy reuniting with their siblings and nephews and nieces that evening.

Julia and Christine made finger foods for Christmas Eve dinner: there were cheeses of all types, cold meats, mini sausages, chicken and beef on sticks with delicious dipping sauces, pickled onions, guacamole dip and chips, sausage rolls, and sushi. Just when it looked like the food was all gone, Julia would pull out more treats. It was a real feast and a great party, the sound of voices getting louder and louder as everyone competed to be heard.

Christmas music played in the background. Wine corks were popping, and beer cans were cracking. The fragrance of pine from the tree was mixing with the smell of the food and the scented candles that were distributed around the room. It was a jolly scene. Johnny had a hilarious laugh and sense of humour and when he started off, his laughter was infectious.

Diane and Rob appeared after their nap and worked the room. Rob had never been to Canada before—and hadn't met any of the family—but didn't seem fazed at all by the madness going on. His booming voice added to the volume and happiness of the evening.

Henry and Julia were right in the middle of everything. It was a blessing to have the whole family together and they were making the very best of it.

Henry noticed the attentiveness that Diane and Rob showed each other as they worked the room. They clearly were very fond of each other.

As if Diane had read her dad's mind, she walked up to him and gave him a hug.

"So good to be home, Dad. You don't have to worry about us eloping," she said mysteriously. Henry laughed. "I know what you were thinking," she continued, "…that you need to start saving to pay for the wedding! I'm hoping for a ring under the tree."

"That's exciting! Have you told Mum?" Henry replied.

"No, I want it to be a surprise," she said almost whispering. Henry hugged his youngest daughter, and quietly whispered into her ear, "Congratulations. I love you so much." Henry released his grip.

"Dad you are weeping? Don't give the game away," Diane said softly.

CHAPTER TWENTY-THREE

Christmas Day was special. The grandkids were excited to be opening their stockings, and Henry recorded everything with his video camera. He loved capturing his special people having so much fun and joy in his favourite place in the world. The highlight of the gift opening for the adults was, of course, the little box that Rob had carefully placed under the tree.

When the moment came, he couldn't have been more romantic. Presenting the small package to Diane while down on one knee was a dead giveaway. Nobody was surprised that it was indeed an engagement ring when Diane opened the little box—and he then proposed, which she joyfully accepted. A bottle of sparkling wine appeared, and everybody toasted the newly engaged couple. Even the grandkids got to toast—with orange juice, of course.

After Christmas lunch, it was time to head to the toboggan slope and have some crazy fun on the hill and burn off some calories. All manner of things were piled up in the garage to be used on the slope. There was an individual sled, a tandem sled, some slip slides, and a couple of round sliders.

It was a sunny, cold, but windless day and everybody had a lot of fun, including Julia and Henry. Eventually, the youngsters were feeling the cold, and it was time to get them home and into a hot bath.

As Henry was loading the last of the sleds into the back of their car, the blue Ford F150 drove past.

"There they are again!" Henry burst out.

"Not now, Henry. You promised," Julia said, trying to shut him down immediately.

Everybody went to bed early. It had been a lovely day and the time outside had exhausted them. The kids drifted off quickly and the adults were not far behind.

The parents with children headed home on the 28th. It was a sad to see them go, but everybody had had a good time, and nobody had gotten sick—not even a hangover.

Henry and Julia appreciated the extra time to get to know Rob a little more and for him to continue to experience the Canadian outdoors. The next morning, Diane and Rob grabbed the snowshoes and headed out. They came back just in time for leftovers from Christmas for lunch. After lunch, Julia announced she was going into Arborg for supplies. Rob happily agreed to go with her. After they left, Diane asked, "Dad, do you want a coffee?"

"Would love one," was Henry's reply.

When the coffee had brewed, Diane poured a couple of mugs and carried them to the lounge where Henry was sitting in his favourite chair. Henry sipped his coffee.

"So Dad, what was the blue truck conversation a couple of days ago all about?" Diane asked.

"Not sure if I want to burden you with the whole story."

"Go on, Dad. We have the time. Mum and Rob are going to be out for a while."

With no further encouragement, Henry related the whole story right from the beginning. He could see Diane getting more engaged the longer he spoke.

"Dad, this is fascinating—no wonder it has captured your imagination! What are your next steps?"

"Spend some more time with Marisa Jones. She has some newspaper clippings and some old letters. I could give her a call. Would you want to come along?"

"Sure; would love to, Dad."

Much to Julia's annoyance when she came home, Henry had already rung Marisa, who agreed that he and Diane could visit her the following morning.

CHAPTER TWENTY-FOUR

The village was picture perfect. It was dusted with snow, the sun was shining, and the roofs were almost overloaded with the white stuff. It was overhanging the roofs of homes in odd shapes, curved by the wind. A random distribution of colourful ice-fishing huts dotted the bay as they drove past. Fishers were getting busy for the day and Henry and Diane could see that there was a lot of activity, even though the huts were little off in the distance. There were hundreds of gulls, looking for an easy meal.

Thankfully, Marisa's driveway and front step were clear when they arrived. She was waiting for them, door wide open.

"Come in, come in," she said with a smile, obviously happy to see them. "Well, this must be Diane!"

"How do you do?" Diane replied as they took off their boots and coats. "I have heard so much about you from my dad."

The ladies walked into the kitchen. There was an instant rapport between them, just as Henry had expected.

"Dad," Diane called, "tea or tea?"

"Tea would be nice!" he called back, smiling, but a little distracted. He was in the lounge with many old photos spread over the coffee table—one in particular had caught his eye. It was a picture of Greta, probably in the early 1920s, and she was holding a large and heavy-looking leather-bound book. She was surrounded by people dressed in the formal clothes of the day and she was the centre of attention.

After a couple of minutes, Marisa and Diane appeared.

"Can you push those photos to the side, Henry?" Marisa asked. "We need some space to put the tray down."

"Of course," Henry carefully moved the photos, placing the photo of Greta and the book on top of the pile.

"Sorry about the mess," Marisa said. "I was going through some drawers and found more photos of Gran and her family that I had forgotten about."

"No problem. One caught my eye and I'd love to talk about it later," Henry said.

"By the way Henry, over there on the sideboard is a series of letters she kept," Marisa said. "One is even from the prime minister of Iceland! Makes for interesting reading."

"I'm intrigued," Henry smiled, feeling more than a little excited but wanting to be patient and polite.

"OK. Diane, I assume you are black tea like your dad—no milk?"

"Actually I was, but now I that live in England, I have developed a taste for it with milk and sugar," Diane replied.

"A girl after my own heart," Marisa said, pouring a little milk in Diane's cup. "Here's the sugar bowl," she continued, handing it to Diane. Marisa was always the perfect host.

"Henry, here is a black for you—not sure how an Englishman got to drinking black, no milk and sugar, a story for another day no doubt," she said grinning at her own humour.

Diane was chatting up a storm with Marisa and Henry was finding it difficult to pay attention to the conversation. Marisa looked fascinated, hearing about what life was like in England today. Diane had clearly come to love it there. The two really seemed to be connecting, so Henry quietly scanned the photos as he stacked them neatly. He saw photos of a visit to what he assumed was Iceland and it was clear Greta was enjoying an elevated level of hospitality and staying in some high-end places, almost like she was being treated like a VIP.

After their second cup, Diane and Marisa's animated conversation slowed down a little, and Diane managed to steer the conversation back to the island, its history, and eventually to Marisa's grandma.

Henry passed a few of the photos that interested him to Marisa. She glanced at them, then hobbled to the sideboard, and took out a pile of letters. Returning to her seat, she untied the string around them and eventually pulled a letter out.

"Henry, come sit next to your daughter so you can both read the letter," Marisa said.

Henry carefully opened the envelope and unfolded the page, which was in a remarkably good state considering it was almost one hundred years old. The paper was quite thick, had a crest embossed at the top of the page, and was dated 17th November 1922. It was addressed to Greta Kjartanson/Larson, and it referenced an earlier letter that Greta herself had written. It requested that the relics—mentioned in the diary that Greta had written—in Greta's possession should be repatriated to Iceland and her father would receive acknowledgement of his contribution to preserving the relics at a time of great uncertainty for the nation. The relics would then be formally housed in Iceland's national museum.

"So, Henry, now you understand the context of the photos of Greta in Iceland," Marisa said. "She was there for a month, engaged in activities around the ceremony to commemorate the safe return of the relics, then had a tour of the island, meeting relatives who hadn't left. She was treated as a bit of a celebrity and had a wonderful time. Years later, she was still talking about it to anyone who would listen. Other than her marriage, kids, and grandkids, it was the biggest thing that ever happened to her."

"Wow! So much history, and what a great connection story between Iceland and Hecla Island. Things must have been really bad to make it OK to take those kinds of historical relics away from the island," Diane said, fascinated.

"Yes, it was a really bad time, Diane," Marisa replied. "Her father had been a trusted senior civil servant as well as a part-time fisher and the government was worried about the security of these and other national treasures. It took years for the country to get back on its feet and after Greta's father passed away, Greta was entrusted with keeping them safe and returning them when the time was right."

Henry was quietly mulling over what the possible connection might be to what had happened at the original settlement site. *We have folks searching and killing for relics that are not even on the island anymore–or were they all looking for something else?* For the first time, he was seriously considering that maybe the relics were *not* at the centre of the mystery.

He couldn't resist asking, "Marisa, have you had two strangers call on you recently? One older and short, the other unusually tall, both with Eastern European accents? They have been hanging around the island and have apparently rented a cottage close to here."

"No," Marisa replied. "Nobody has called recently. The only thing I have noticed lately has been a new large truck driving by frequently."

Two hours had passed in a flash, and it was time to leave. Diane and Henry said thanks and goodbye and hurried to the car that was now half-buried in a drift of snow. Henry had to climb in from the passenger's side as the driver's side was buried almost up to the roof. Of course, he had not put the remote starter on ahead of time. A cold wind was blowing from the north and it was chilling. The car had barely warmed up by the time they got home.

Julia and Rob had dinner on the go. The place settings were laid, and within ten minutes everybody was seated and discussing the afternoon's activities.

"The ride back from Arborg was pretty scary. I haven't experienced weather like that in my life. I am glad Julia was driving," Rob said with a relieved smile, still recovering from the trauma of it all.

"We were so engaged with Marisa, I didn't even look out of the window," Diane said. "Couldn't believe how the snow had drifted against dad's car. Something I am not missing in England," she said with a chuckle.

Henry decided to be in the moment and not dwell on what Marisa's revelation meant to what was going on. He didn't get to see Diane that often and it looked like the next subject of conversation would be wedding plans, so he would have to pay attention.

CHAPTER TWENTY-FIVE

The wedding conversation made for a happy time. The kids wanted a destination wedding and decided on Barbados. They didn't want a big affair, just family and close friends.

Rob's parents had already agreed to pay half of the costs of the ceremony, venue, pastor, reception, photographer, and so forth, which was a nice surprise for Henry, who always looked after the pennies. They chose a date for the last weekend in April the coming spring—only a few months away.

After clearing up the dinner, the girls retired to the lounge to make up a list of things to do and the guys grabbed a couple of beers and sat down in the TV room. Henry didn't know much about Rob and his family, and all Rob really knew about Henry was what Diane would have told him.

Rob's parents were Ukrainian and had immigrated to the UK when Rob and his siblings were small. Rob said he and his siblings had picked up English quickly, as did his father, but his mother struggled for years as she was quite shy, and it led to a lot of homesickness and unhappiness when he was younger. The need for more money meant she had to find a job and was forced to learn the language. Eventually became quite proficient and was happy in her new country. They were ethnic Ukrainians who lived in the east of the country and grateful they left when they did, what with all the Russians interfering in their affairs.

Rob was a police officer working in the Major Crimes Unit for the London Metropolitan Police. Apparently, his knowledge of Ukrainian and Russian affairs was an advantage as Russian gangs were operating in the UK, particularly in London. He had done fieldwork and was undercover at one time, but his cover had eventually gotten blown, so he was mainly office-based now.

"A little safer," he said, looking a little relieved. Diane was much happier with that arrangement.

Rob asked what Henry did. Henry was happy to share his working history and share stories about his time working for the Metropolitan police before he left England after taking the policing position in Winnipeg.

"So what keeps you in Winnipeg? I was thinking you would have come back to retire to the UK," Rob said.

"No, Rob. Much as I love the UK and all my family's there, Canada is definitely home. We finally got our citizenship some years ago and all our kids and grandkids with the exception of Diane are here. As cold as Winnipeg is, it does feel like home. Besides, our money would not go very far buying a place in the UK. No; we are happy here and will go back regularly. We watch BritBox on television; that will be it."

Rob laughed. "Shame you won't see our future kids so often, but I like Canada and hope we can come over on a more regular basis. Once kids come along, it would be better if you and Julia come over to see us."

"Don't worry; Julia has already mentioned that," Henry said, grinning.

"Time for me to hit the bed Rob—it's been a good day, and good to know a little more about you," Henry said. "I suppose we will meet all your immediate family in Barbados for the wedding?"

"That's the plan, Henry," Rob said as he got up and grabbed his glass.

"Seems like the ladies are still at it. I'll see if Diane is ready for bed." Henry loaded the dishwasher as the other three chatted and said their goodnights. The evening was at an end. Diane gave her dad a hug and everybody headed for bed. Henry could see that Julia was tired but elated. As they climbed into bed, the light was out in an instant.

"I'm excited, Henry," Julia said, whispering. "He seems like a really nice guy. I am so happy Diane has finally found somebody mature and settled. I have never seen her so happy."

"I agree," Henry said, before kissing Julia gently and turning over to his side of the bed. They were asleep in minutes.

DEATH AT THE POINT

The next day was cold but sunny and Diane and Rob announced over breakfast they would wrap up and go for a hike on the Blackwolf Trail on the other side of the island.

After they had left, Henry and Julia cleared up the breakfast things. "I am going to really miss Diane after this visit, Henry," she said, a little emotionally. "It's such a pity they live so far away."

"Yes, it's really been a lovely Christmas—the first time we've all gotten together in years," Henry said. "But let's just enjoy the last couple of days as much as we can. Tears can come later." Julia gave Henry the look, nodding her head.

Henry had always been emotionally tough and sometimes lacked the sensitivity to do the right thing when Julia was upset. To Julia's surprise, he hugged her.

"I know you are so upset that Diane will be gone in a couple of days and I am too—but let's be excited for her and we will see her again in just over three months and have a very special time."

Henry wiped her tears away with his thumbs and kissed her on the lips. Julia's smile grew on her face. She stared at him.

"You have tears too," she said. "I think Mr. Henry Trevellyn is getting a little more emotional in his old age."

Henry released his hug and checked his face with his fingers. "You know Julia, you are right." He could feel the tears that had spontaneously appeared. "I actually noticed a couple of times recently that tears were welling up in me. I suppose this has been a special and happy time for me, too."

A number of hours later, Diane and Rob returned. They looked relatively defrosted, probably due to the fifteen-minute car ride home from the trail with the heater on full blast. Diane was carrying a shopping bag.

"We went to Riverton before coming back to the island to walk the trail. I saw we were low on bread and milk, so we picked them up, along with a little chocolate for tonight." She handed Julia the bag as they struggled to remove their boots and ski pants and other cold weather paraphernalia.

"Didn't know you had Ukrainians up here, Henry," Rob said.

"What do you mean, Rob?" Henry asked.

"Diane has told me about the bodies found at the original settlement and the excavations that had been going on there. When we were at the store in Riverton," Rob continued, "There were two well-dressed foreigners, shopping, I guess. I initiated a conversation with the younger of the two guys and we got chatting. He lost interest quickly when we said we were just visitors. They were talking quietly to each other, and they were definitely conversing in Ukrainian. The younger one sounded frustrated and impatient. He was clearly bored and not particularly respectful to the older one who I thought was his father, or at least an older member of the family.

"They talked about the police returning to the settlement, and the finding of a relative's body. They mentioned the name Andriy, the frustration that they cannot identify themselves as family and claim the body—that's all I could really pick up."

"Wow, well that solves a bit of a mystery," Henry said, "Those guys have been hanging around for a while—they had apparently been looking for somebody that appears was one of the other bodies found at the original Icelandic site. Not sure why they are uncomfortable identifying themselves as family members unless they are up to no good."

"One thing that was a little strange—if they truly are close relatives—is that the younger one was also Ukrainian speaking but oddly, I detected a British accent when he spoke in English. The older spoke Ukrainian mainly and little or no English."

Julia, not interested in them spending any more time on the subject, quickly changed it—there was so little time left with Diane and Rob.

They spent the afternoon taking it easy. Snow squalls blew in off the lake, continuing into the evening, and the wind grew stronger.

After dinner, they played cards. Rob was a whiz at gin rummy and won almost every game. He certainly had a fun but competitive streak in him.

Everybody seemed tired; it was an early night. Henry lay in bed, listening to the wind. No doubt there would be drifting snow to contend with in the morning.

He struggled to sleep. He couldn't get the two foreigners out of his mind. Something didn't make sense. The key had to be the original settlement on the point. Maybe there was a Ukrainian connection, not an

Icelandic one. That got him thinking that when Diane and Rob had gone, he would go to the museum and follow up on any potential links between the Icelandic and Ukrainian settlers.

The next day, they headed back to Winnipeg. Diane was going to spend most of the remaining time they had visiting some of her many friends, and Rob planned to go along for the ride.

Their last evening together was spent enjoying a roast-beef dinner, with roast potatoes and Yorkshire pudding—Diane's favourite. It was a lovely evening, but as they had an early flight in the morning, Diane and Rob headed upstairs around 9:00 p.m. to finish packing and Julia and Henry distracted themselves with a little BritBox entertainment, then headed to bed.

Everybody was up early the next morning. After breakfast, the rest of the family popped over to say their goodbyes, then Henry loaded the suitcases in the back of the car. Julia, Diane, and Rob climbed in for the drive to the airport.

The airport was a zoo—mainly people heading home after the holidays. Henry gave Diane a huge hug. At one stage, Diane whispered in his ear, "Daddy please be careful with that whole Hecla thing; I have a bad feeling and I don't want your curiosity to get you and Mum hurt." Henry nodded

"Sure, I'll be careful Diane. The next time I see you I'll be walking you down the aisle."

"You better be," Diane replied, laughing, relieved that her dad had taken her seriously.

It was a tearful goodbye and Diane and Rob disappeared through security and after a final wave, they were gone.

CHAPTER TWENTY-SIX

After Christmas, the weather turned frigid. It was a period of bitterly cold days when the smallest breeze sends the windchill plunging. Even Canadians disliked temperatures that were too cold for even cross-country skiing.

Eventually, the deep freeze let up a little, hitting minus twenty-five degrees at night, warming up to minus twelve to fifteen during the day. Even the wind had died down for a couple of days.

Henry rang the museum and spoke to Susie. He updated her on the mysterious strangers, their suspected nationality, and the body of the person who apparently was the individual in the photograph that the two strangers had showed her last summer.

"So, what do you know about the history of the Ukrainians in the Interlake area and their interaction with the Icelandic people?" Henry asked.

"They came after the Icelanders, the first wave arriving in the 1890s. As settlers in a foreign country, they had many of the same challenges that Icelandic and other non-British people experienced. The language and culture were an adjustment and they had to put up with the arrogance and prejudices of the system.

"It was not easy; folks of a common culture and language tended to stick together and rely on each other. Even in the growing community of Winnipeg this was the case, although there was probably more exposure to different nationalities, particularly among the children who may not have experienced the old country and grew up in this multi-cultural environment. By the early 1900s, Winnipeg was truly a melting pot. Hecla Island and its inhabitants had by then gone through an epidemic and an early break-up of the community due to religious differences. It was out of the way and still largely homogenous."

"So what would a Ukrainian family be doing hanging around New Iceland?" Henry asked.

"I really cannot say. There would have been some inter-marrying after a time. The original community history is well known: the original immigrants' settlement on the north side of the island was abandoned not too many years after they arrived. And as you know, there was the smallpox outbreak and a good number of the settlers moved away quite a time before the Ukrainians even arrived, so I really don't understand why there would be a Ukrainian connection with the area."

"Thanks, Susie. This is really a strange story. I feel like it must be connected to the past in some way and definitely has a Ukrainian connection."

"Why don't you ask the two strangers yourself, or better still, the police?" Susie suggested.

"I have to say, the strangers scare me a little."

"Then let the police do their job. Don't get sucked into this anymore," Susie said, evidently nervous about Henry's continued interest.

"You are probably right—will stay in touch." Henry rang off, disappointed, though he hadn't really had any expectations that Susie would have had any key, useful knowledge but it had been worth a try.

Chris rang a couple of days later and they discussed the latest news. He was initially cagey as always in sharing information that he had gained through the sources he still had at the RCMP.

"I probably shouldn't be sharing this, but the RCMP did briefly interview those two Ukrainians a couple of days ago. Apparently, they initially denied any connection with the tall red-headed stranger's body but later admitted they were looking for the brother of the older of the two of them, and they did eventually identify the body."

"Surely the police asked what they were doing on Hecla."

"They said they were searching for a relative and suspected he was on Hecla Island in Manitoba. They had no explanation as to why a Ukrainian national would be living rough on a very isolated part of the island. The police didn't hold them, as judging from their entries in their passports; they only entered the country *after* the deaths of David Einarson and their relative in the previous fall. Apparently, they have secured working visas and are doing maintenance at the local hotel," Chris said.

"So they are hanging around—they have to be looking for something else," Henry said, frustrated.

"If they plan to search the site, they won't be doing it again until after the thaw, the frost is out of the ground, and the police have cleared out," Chris suggested.

"You're right, Chris. We should keep an eye on the site, come the spring. My guess is they will park their truck in the clearing we discovered off the road, and walk in."

Henry hung up and briefed Julia on the latest on the case. She was checking out hotels in Barbados and general travel arrangements and was distracted while he spoke with her. But it didn't matter; his phone rang. This time, it was Sophie.

"Hey, Henry! Happy New Year. I hope you have been reading our articles in *La Liberté?*"

"You know I don't speak French, Sophie," Henry replied, laughing.

"Well it's about time you learned. I have been sending the articles to Marisa. I hope she is getting them. I am planning to go to see Marisa tomorrow to make sure she is OK with the way we are telling the story. I was hoping we could get together and catch up—maybe just after lunch sometime?" Sophie asked persuasively.

"Yes, that would be fine, Sophie. Come to the house—twenty-one Lakeside Road."

"OK. See you around 1:30 p.m.—bye for now."

Henry had barely put down the phone when it rang again. Julia just shook her head.

"Hi, Henry. It's Jan at number twenty-five. Stephen is turning fifty this weekend and I wanted to know if you and Julia would like to come to a surprise party I am arranging for this Saturday."

"Sounds great, Jan. I'll check with Julia and get back to you. I don't think we have any other plans. What should we bring?"

"Just a bottle of wine—I've got the rest covered. I have to say, Stephen is finding hitting the big five-O a little overwhelming."

"I remember the feeling," Henry said sympathetically.

Julia was always up for a party and was excited to go so he rang Jan back to confirm.

Sophie showed up the next afternoon and Henry briefed her on the two new items of news: that the bombshell for his line of investigation—the relics—had turned out to be an unlikely target for treasure hunters and murderers as they had been returned to the authorities in Iceland, and second, the two Ukrainians were relatives, had been looking for someone, and had identified the older guy's brother as the deceased person.

"What do you think now, Henry?" Sophie asked.

"Well, either our tall red-headed stranger friend—now we think Ukrainian—was looking for the relics and never even knew they had been returned to Iceland, or else this isn't about the original Icelanders at all, which now seems to me more than likely. It's a bit of a dead end for now."

"I'm driving home tonight, so I should leave before it starts to get dark," Sophie said. "We need to research Ukrainians in Manitoba and see what comes up. Having their surnames sure would help."

It snowed over the next couple of days—fine, cold pellets of snow drifted in the wind. Everything was pristine white again. The walk over to number twenty-five was quite a challenge. It was pitch black and Henry and Julia, having forgotten a flashlight, could see lights as other neighbours with better equipment were finding their way to the party.

It turned out to be quite an event, like many on the lake were. The wine and beer flowed generously and there were many neighbours as well as family and old friends of Jan and Stephen.

While Julia was introducing herself and enjoying mingling with the others, Henry looked around the room for Chris and Jane or Jim and Ingrid, but there was no sign of any of them.

He approached a small group of men who were deep in conversation. As it happened, they were talking about Henry's favourite subject. The birthday boy, Stephen who was just on the edge of being drunk, was sharing his theories on what was going on at the original settlement on the point.

"It's got to be drug-related. Drugs, not treasure; that's where the money is."

"No way," said Derek from number twenty-seven. "Why would anybody bury drugs in such an isolated spot, when there are a million of other, more convenient and safer places to hide a relatively small million-dollar package."

Derek turned to Henry. "What is your theory? We all know you have been a little obsessed about the goings on."

There were a lot of encouraging nods. For some strange reason, Henry was more than a little surprised that so many people knew about his interest in what was going on.

"Well, the body count is officially at two right now," he said, deciding not to mention the older body, "and I don't think the authorities have the faintest idea about what is going on. I thought I had a theory, but that recently got blown out of the water, so I am back at square one."

"So you don't think it was drug-related?" Stephen asked.

"To be honest, I am at a loss—there does seem to be something buried up there," Henry replied. "Or at least that's what I think—something that somebody may or may not have found." Henry left the conversation at that. Nobody mentioned the two Ukrainian foreigners.

For most people in Hecla, whatever was going on at the original settlement was a side story in their lives. It hadn't affected them, as it has been isolated to one remote spot. "Let sleeping dogs lie" seemed to be the sentiment of most of the neighbours.

Henry had a couple more beers and got to know a lot more of his neighbours. Many were from Winnipeg and came up the island for the weekends. A few couples had retired up to Hecla or tended to come up for the whole summer.

The hotel golf club was a strong pull for a lot of the cottagers, and it would appear that people talked about golf until it was actually warm enough to play. Henry enjoyed the odd game, but was definitely not on par with the level of enthusiasm of many of the people at the party.

Henry and Julia had a wonderful time then wandered home, a little late and worse for wear as they discovered the next morning.

Henry laid in the next morning—almost totally unheard of. Julia woke up later, too, and it was apparent she had more than a small headache.

"That Stephen is a good guy," Henry whispered. "He has snow-blown our driveway at least twice this winter. There are some good people up here. We need to do a better job of being more open and friendly—maybe we should have a party of our own." He turned over and looked at Julia.

"Cannot think of anything that could involve alcohol," Julia said as she rolled over and went back to sleep.

It was still cold, but the ice had broken up and there was a lot of open water, so Chris and Henry kayaked down the coast to the point later that day. The cool air worked wonders for Henry's sore head.

Somebody had obviously been on the site as there were fresh piles of dirt.

"Chris, I assume that this is the Ukrainian's efforts not the police—darn hard work—the frost is barely out of the ground," Henry said.

"Yes, I believe that is the case: the larger excavation over there is where they found we found David Einarson's body but, ironically, it was also the spot where they found the body of the Ukrainian. The RCMP's current theory is that they suspect that David succumbed to a heart attack on completion of the burial of the Ukrainian. Whether or not David killed him is not known for sure, but it is likely, as he had been hit over the head with what could have been a shovel or similar object—like the one that David had used to bury him. There was no DNA evidence on this shovel, but that doesn't mean it wasn't the murder weapon."

"Well, if the Ukrainians are still looking, it obviously means they haven't found anything," Henry noted as Chris inspected some of the piles.

"I think they have been using metal-detecting equipment. See the odd rusty old metal objects lying near the holes?"

"You're right," Henry said. "That's exciting! So they're looking for something metal or contained in something metal."

"Maybe they *have* found something," Chris said. "It's difficult to tell."

"The only way to know is if they come back," Henry replied, then pointed to a larger excavation, a little way from the patchwork of smaller holes. "Chris, look at that."

"Yes, that was the site of the second body—much older, almost completely decomposed—just a pile of bones and some rags of clothing, from what I heard," Chris said. "Not sure where that investigation is going. It's probably not connected to the other two bodies. Maybe they're a deceased family member from the original settlement? Strange thing is, it wasn't buried deep, like you would expect a body for a regular burial would be, so it is a bit of mystery."

The sun was starting to go down and the wind was coming up—time to leave. It was a long paddle home, and they were exhausted before they were an hour or so from home. They took a short rest and Henry called Julia to give her their ETA. By the time they pulled the kayaks up on shore and got into the house, Julia and Jane were setting the table.

"Dinner—just what we needed," Henry said, relieved to be home. He went to the fridge.

"Fancy a beer, Chris?" Henry asked rhetorically. Chris smiled and nodded.

Once they all had food and drink in front of them, the men described what they saw at the site, but soon the conversation turned to other things. The girls were not interested in talking about Icelanders or Ukrainians. The upcoming wedding became the main subject of conversation.

It was a nice evening, but not a late one. Chris and his wife said goodbye, then Henry and Julia cleaned up the dishes and headed for bed. Henry was asleep in minutes.

Over coffee the next morning, Julia told Henry how restless he'd been all night. His subconscious mind was obviously ruminating over the case.

CHAPTER TWENTY-SEVEN

It was a warm start to the day, and Henry decided to do the quarry walk with Skip. There was quite a breeze and he knew that would keep down the insects that were starting to appear. Henry was in a thoughtful mood. Who knew if the Ukrainians had found anything? He was convinced that as long as they were still hanging around, they more than likely hadn't.

What is the link to the original settlement site? Maybe a connection with Ukrainians in Canada? Maybe they're relatives of Ukrainian Canadians who had lived here at some time in the past.

After breakfast, he booted up his computer and started to search. He tried "Ukrainians, Hecla Island, Manitoba." The sites that came up were mainly the Manitoba government, promoting the provincial park. There was a brief mention of Ukrainian and Anishinaabe heritage on Hecla, but the focus was on the Icelanders who had settled there from the 1870s onwards. He then widened the search to "Ukrainians, Manitoba" and was dismayed to see the number of sites that popped up. The University of Manitoba's site had a reference to Ukrainian surnames in Canada. On top of all of those, there were the Canadianized versions of Ukrainian surnames. As there were dozens of names, Henry decided it would be a nightmare to look further without something to go on.

He decided to pop around to see if Jim and his wife were back. Jim always seemed to have practical suggestions for most situations. They normally drove to their place in Texas after Christmas and returned once it had warmed, sometimes as early as June. Jim normally worked at the hotel part-time in the warmer months. To Henry's surprise, their truck was parked in front of the garage and Jim and his wife were unpacking. *A lucky coincidence*, Henry thought. They looked tired.

"It was a long drive," Jim said, shaking Henry's hand, "but it's good to be home. So Henry, how are you doing? Have I missed anything?"

"Actually, you have. You have a couple of new workmates, and you won't believe who they are."

"Let me guess: the two Ukrainian foreigners?"

"How did you know, Jim?" Henry said, laughing.

"Simple," Jim responded. "Rang the supervisor to confirm my shift this week and he told me. Not rocket science, really." He chuckled.

Henry's heart began to pound in excitement. "Chris and I visited the original settlement site a while ago and it was obvious that somebody had continued digging and they had clearly been using a metal detector. We suspected it was the two foreigners. I think the fact that they have signed up for work at the hotel confirms that they haven't found what they're looking for yet, so they are hanging around for a while.

"Any chance you can find out what their surnames are, particularly the older one? Maybe there is a Ukrainian connection to the original settlement site." Henry couldn't believe his good luck that Jim might be able to help him find a piece of the puzzle.

"Couldn't imagine what that connection would be—Marisa told me she thought the site was abandoned before the beginning of the 1900s."

"OK, Henry. I will see what I can do," Jim replied.

Ingrid gave him the look. Henry knew the look. "OK, Jim—will leave you to get on with getting in the house and unpacking. Let's stay in touch."

Jim popped around Saturday morning for a coffee. He was in good form and back to his normal jovial self after a couple nights of good sleep in his own bed.

"So, I've found that piece of information you were looking for." He pulled a small, folded piece of paper out of his pocket. Henry could hardly sit still.

"I glanced at their timecard stamps. The older guy's name is Vladimir Krafchenko. I assume it's his real name. The younger guy's name is Dmitry Melnyk, which I think is a more common Ukrainian surname. Nobody could invent a surname like that." Jim, always the joker, sniggered at his own humour.

Not father and son—maybe uncle and nephew? Henry thought.

DEATH AT THE POINT

After another coffee and some of Julia's home cooking, Jim stood to leave.

"Hope the names help, Henry. Catch up again soon," he said as stepped out the front door and headed across the grass to his place.

Henry could barely contain his excitement. Julia was intrigued, too. "Let's clean up here Henry and I'll sit with you and see what we can find."

With the dishes taken care of, Henry booted up the computer and Julia grabbed a second chair. Henry typed "K-r-a-f-c-h-e-n-k-o," slowly using his two-finger typing technique that drove Julia crazy with impatience.

"When are you going to learn to type with all your fingers?"

"Never," Henry replied. "It's good enough for me."

He pressed enter and in a second, the results popped up. The first was a reference to a Victor Kravchenko, a Soviet diplomat who had defected to the west. Henry wrote the site down in his notebook. The next site was titled "Manitoba History: The Story of 'Bloody Jack' Krafchenko." It read, "The execution of John 'Bloody Jack' Krafchenko in Winnipeg on 9 July 1914 brought to an end the 'most dramatic episode in the history of Manitoba up to that time.'"

"Julia, look!"

She leaned over and read the section of the article his finger was pointing to. "You really have finally found something!" Julia exclaimed, seeing the broad grin on Henry's face and could not help feeling a little excited herself.

They continued to read through a number of references to John Bloody Jack Krafchenko.

"He wasn't even Ukrainian—he was Romanian," Henry said, a little stunned. He continued to quote the article, "...born in 1881 but of Ukrainian parents... that made him by definition a Ruthenian—an ethnic Ukrainian minority that lived in the Carpathian Mountains."

"So was he John or Jack?" Julia was confused. "I think his given name is John," Henry replied, still reading. "Krafchenko's family had emigrated to south-western Manitoba in 1888. His father was the local blacksmith. As a young boy, Krafchenko was smart and friendly but would fly into violent rages and had an aggressive mean streak. By the age of eleven, he was already in trouble with the law and by fifteen was jailed for stealing a bicycle." *Maybe living with some kind of mental illness,* Henry thought.

The family eventually moved to Winnipeg, where his mother passed away and his father married a German woman. Krafchenko had a talent for languages and could speak Ukrainian, Russian, German, and English.

He toured Canada as a boxer as a late teenager. He also wrestled in both Australia and the US. He was a well-built man but his unmarked face didn't match with this legend so who knew how much of it was true—and there was more.

His life of crime really began to unfold in 1902 when he returned to southern Manitoba and toured as a temperance lecturer. During this time, he passed numerous bad cheques and was eventually caught in Regina and was sentenced to eighteen months in the Prince Albert Penitentiary.

"A piece of work for sure," Henry said, clearly fascinated by the article.

"No doubt about that, a larger-than-life character for sure," Julia said, nodding.

He tried to escape when they were transporting him to jail. He was assigned to painting the outside walls of the penitentiary and he escaped with three other inmates. The other three were recaptured but not Krafchenko. He then held up a shipment of cash at gun point and escaped over the American border with $25,000.

He worked his way over to New York where he held up more banks before stowing away on a freighter heading for Europe. Once there, his crime spree continued, and he robbed banks in England, Germany, and Italy.

From there, he travelled to Russia and married a local girl in 1905. In 1906, he returned to Canada with his new wife, Fanica, and settled in Plum Coulee, where he robbed a nearby bank. He slipped back across the US border, remaining at large until 1908, when he appeared as a witness for a person tried for murdering someone in the CP Rail yards in Winnipeg. He was not incriminated for this murder but was arrested for the 1906 bank robbery and sentenced to three years in Stony Mountain Penitentiary.

After his release, Krafchenko and his wife moved to Graham, a small community across the border in Ontario, where he worked as a blacksmith and ultimately became a boiler-maker foreman for the National Transcontinental Railway.

But eventually his temper got the better of him again, he was demoted from his foreman position in 1913, and so he quit. He returned to Winnipeg and gambled and drank with his old criminal associates. He travelled between Winnipeg and Plum Coulee a lot during the November of that year. Krafchenko and three of his cronies, one of whom was Icelandic, made plans to rob the bank in the town. The robbery took place on December 4, 1913.

The bank manager was the only employee in the bank over lunch time. Armed with a gun, he pursued them after they left the building and was shot dead by one of the robbers. They hijacked a car parked nearby, commanding the driver to drive southeast, close to the US border.

A large manhunt was initiated and Krafchenko was the prime suspect.

The criminals went underground for a while. He eventually sneaked back into Winnipeg and was arrested initially on a minor charge after an informant had tipped off the police.

Krafchenko was charged with murder and robbery once enough evidence had been collected. He then made it his business to escape his police station cell and started informing the guards of all the jewelry, diamonds, and money he had stashed away. His lawyer also saw the opportunity for gain and a constable, and that lawyer started plotting Krafchenko's escape. Two former employees of the lawyer were also brought into the plot and one of these gentlemen secured rope and a revolver and smuggled them into Krafchenko's cell via the constable.

He escaped, but the rope was too short, and he fell thirty feet to the ground. He strained his back and both knees, but somehow didn't break anything. He crossed the road and, seeing him injured, a crowd of joyriders stopped their car to give him a ride to one of his former employee's apartments, where he went into hiding.

Meanwhile, there was an inquiry into the escape and the constable, after extensive interrogation, admitted his involvement. One of the former employees turned state witness and all the others received prison sentences.

Krafchenko was eventually rearrested and properly secured. He was tried in Morden. More than seventy witnesses testified, and he was found guilty. In spite of a petition for clemency, the judgment was upheld.

He was executed a few seconds before 7:00 a.m. on July 9, 1914.

Henry looked up from the computer. "Julia, I think we have been chasing shadows all along. This is a Ukrainian story."

"There is no link with Hecla. I am not really sure why you are so excited, Henry."

"There is something buried in the original settlement that the two strangers and others have been looking for. There must be a link—one of his accomplices was Icelandic."

CHAPTER TWENTY-EIGHT

"So, what is your plan today?" Julia asked, having just arisen from under the covers after the smell of steaming coffee filled the room and aroused her senses.

"Not sure," Henry replied. "Need to walk Skip. I was a little late getting up this morning."

"Yes, you were a little restless last night," Julia said. "Thinking about your Ruthenian, no doubt," she said, a little amused.

Henry sipped his coffee quietly. He had decided to pay Chris a visit, share his new information, and see what he suggested for next steps.

"Lost in thought again, Henry? You aren't much of a conversationalist these days. It will be a good day when we get this mystery behind us. We need to get back to our normal life."

"I'm sorry it's turned into a bit of an obsession, Julia, but people have died and Hecla is our special place. Its innocence and beauty has been desecrated and I need to get that special feeling we have had about this place back."

"Life and death have always been part of the island, Henry. You are such a romantic sometimes."

"And that's a bad thing?" Henry said with a wry smile.

Julia grinned, resigned to the fact that her husband was going to be distracted for a while longer. They had been married for thirty-seven years; she could be a little more patient.

After breakfast, Henry put on a light jacket. Before he had a chance to pick up the leash, the dog was already at the door.

"Ready for a good walk, Skip?" He pawed the door with excitement.

"We'll walk up to the quarry and on the way back, pop in on Chris," Henry said in his doggie voice. "See you later, Julia," he called as he opened the front door.

It was humid and a fine rain was gently falling. The odd truck passed them as they walked down the gravel road. *At least it isn't dusty*, Henry thought. *Just enough dampness to slate the dust.*

Henry had to encourage Skip to keep moving as he was in a "smell everything" mood and Henry wanted to maximize his time with Chris. The round trip normally took about an hour, but today it was looking like fifty minutes. By the time they got back on the gravel road, the rain had stopped, and the sun was appearing between breaks in the clouds. When they arrived at Chris's place, the clouds had drifted away and it was a nice, sunny, if slightly humid, warm spring day.

Chris's dogs started barking as soon as they entered the property, and they could see that Chris was sitting out on the front porch.

"Hey, Henry! How're you doing?" Chris shouted down from the deck.

"Good, Chris. A little thirsty maybe," Henry said. "It's got suddenly hot humid."

"No problem, I'll get us some coffee and some water for Skip. Scotty and Tiger are thirsty too."

By the time Henry had made it up to the porch, the dogs had happily greeted one another, and Chris had reappeared through the screen door with two coffees and three bowls. The dogs emptied their bowls, settled down next to the table, and closed their eyes.

Chris handed Henry a coffee. Henry happily inhaled the smell of the steaming brew.

"Henry, what's on your mind?" Chris asked after giving his friend a couple of seconds to appreciate his latest favourite coffee bean.

"You're going to enjoy this one, Chris," Henry said excitedly. "The two strangers are Ukrainian-speaking—they may be Ruthenian, and I think this mystery is about a Ruthenian immigrant who came out to Canada in the late 1800s as a child. He turned to a life of crime, carried out numerous, reckless robberies, and eventually ended up murdering somebody. After a life on the run under an assumed name, and eventually after a brazen escape, he was finally re-captured and executed in 1914.

His surname, "Krafchenko," is the *same as the older of the two foreigners* who now, strangely enough, are working in maintenance at the hotel. As far as I am concerned, it is all too much of a coincidence," Henry said, barely taking a breath.

"It *is* an unusual Ukrainian surname," Chris said.

"Well, it's pretty obvious they're looking for something and if that logic is right, that's why they're digging at the old settlement. They certainly haven't found anything yet, or else they would be gone."

"You need to be careful Henry—you don't know what or who you're messing with," Chris said. "I suppose the good news is they have been interviewed by the police as you know and couldn't have been involved in either death as they occurred before these two men had even entered the country. They have work permits and are legally allowed to be here, and to not be harassed by the police or anybody else," said Chris.

"But Chris, they don't have the right to be digging around at the old settlement."

"Probably not," Chris said, "but it's not harming anybody and there is almost nothing of the site left for them to desecrate if we are being honest."

"Right. And if they're this guy's descendants, whatever property they find is probably theirs," Henry said.

"Not if it's the proceeds from a crime," Chris added.

Henry thanked Chris for the coffee and headed off the deck and up Chris's driveway with Skip by his side. He felt deflated that Chris didn't appear to be overly interested—something Henry found difficult to fathom. *Where is his curiosity?* he thought. But it certainly didn't mean he was giving up.

Maybe Sophie could do some more digging. The newspaper must have an archive. It is the oldest publication in Manitoba and preceded the exploits of John "Bloody Jack" Krafchenko, Henry thought, picking up his cell once he got home.

"Hi, Henry. Always good to hear from you." Henry couldn't help but find her slight French accent quite attractive.

"What's happening up there?" Sophie asked.

"Actually, a breakthrough we think, and I would appreciate your help," Henry said excitedly. "We have discovered an incredible coincidence. The older of the two Ukrainian strangers has the surname Krafchenko. In the early years of the last century, Krafchenko ran loose around Manitoba and other places, stealing, robbing banks, and eventually killing someone. He was eventually hanged in Winnipeg in 1914. What do you think?"

"I think you are on to something," Sophie excitedly replied. "I'll go through our archives and see if there is any link between Krafchenko and Hecla Island, though I cannot imagine what it could be. His execution would have been newsworthy as well as any criminal exploits like robbing a bank, so I can search those by keywords. I'll get back to you in a couple of days."

Henry contemplated the current status of things. *Background research could be useful, but it's frustrating that the guys that probably have the key to this story are living right here on the island,* he thought. *Maybe I could get a job in the hotel for few hours a week. They are always looking for staff.*

He floated this idea to Julia. As he expected, she was less than enthusiastic. "I know your motivation for getting to the bottom of this mystery however, in my mind, you should be staying the maximum distance away from these men."

He struggled to sleep that night, so he got up and turned on the lamp in the lounge and read a book. Something was bugging him. For some reason, his mind went back to the stormy night when the fascia was banging and he had gotten up and found that the front mat was damp.

Nothing seemed to have been taken… Then it occurred to him, *maybe somebody had left something behind.* He checked the house, focusing his search on the lounge and kitchen where he and Julia spent most of their time together.

Sure enough, Henry's training as a police officer led him to what he was looking for. A surveillance bug had very carefully been hidden in the lampshade above the kitchen table. He found another one in the lounge in a similar position. *Things are getting curiouser and curiouser.*

Now he had a dilemma: if he left them there, whoever had placed them would continue to be privy to their conversations. If he removed them, they'd know their game was up. If he told Julia, either way, she would freak out. Henry couldn't blame her. Things were escalating. He tried to remember what conversations had occurred in the house and he realized that "they" probably knew everything he knew anyway.

Assuming it was the two Ukrainians, maybe he could turn this to his advantage. Like with the tire tracks and wet mat, he decided not to tell Julia. He would try to manage their conversations as best as he could and ensure that more sensitive conversations occurred in other parts of the house. A sweep of the rest of the house revealed, as he hoped, no further bugs.

Time flew by. The next week was the trip to Barbados for Rob and Diane's wedding. Henry prudently put thoughts of the case on the back burner. He loved his youngest daughter and was thrilled she had found the special person in her life, even if it meant she would be putting even deeper roots down in the UK.

It was a small wedding but included all the kids and grandkids as well as Rob's immediate family and his best man. The weather was fabulous, and the wedding was wonderful. Henry eyes filled with tears as he walked his beautiful daughter down the aisle, but he didn't care; this was another great moment in his and Julia's life and he was going to savour it.

The week went far too quickly and soon they were heading home. The weather was cold and windy when they arrived back in Winnipeg, a typical, disappointing, grey spring day. The weather was always so unpredictable at this time of the year.

CHAPTER TWENTY-NINE

Henry caught a stinker of a cold, as he often did when he returned from a hot holiday location back to a cool Winnipeg.

He shifted his thoughts back to the reality of the moment. He realized that if he were to get close to the two Ukrainians, he would have to have something they wanted, some information or insight that would be valuable to them.

Although he didn't really have a clue what that would be, he decided in the meantime to apply for a part-time job in maintenance at the hotel to see if he could, at the very least, overhear one or two of their conversations. The interview with the maintenance supervisor was very informal and with Jim's personal reference, he found he had a job with little difficulty. The hotel always had a problem recruiting and retaining staff as the location was relatively remote.

The supervisor gave him an early shift a couple of days a week and an occasional weekend. There was a "handing over" period between the night and day shifts, so Henry would get to meet the two Ukrainians shortly.

When Henry arrived one morning, the men were changing in the locker room. They looked tired after their all-night shift, and they were talking quietly in their language. *Overhearing this conversation certainly won't help me* he thought, then stuck out his hand and introduced himself.

"How do you do? I'm Henry Trevellyn, new on the job," Henry smiled as he shook the older one's hand. He was intimidated by the strength of his grip and bear-like hands.

"Hi. My name is Vlad," the older one said in a very strong accent. "My English, no good.

Henry reached out a hand to the younger guy.

"I'm Dmitry, Vladimir's nephew. I speak OK English. I lived in London for a couple of years. You are wasting your time talking with Vlad—he is making no effort to learn English. So, I am stuck with the job of translating all the time," Dmitry said, obviously a little frustrated. His accent was strong, too. But, as Rob had observed, when shopping with Julia in Arborg, it had an English twang. *Nephew!* Henry thought. *I wonder.*

"We were told you were starting today," Dmitry said in a friendly manner, smiling at Henry. "Do I detect an English accent?" he asked.

"We've been in Canada for more than twenty years, but it's still there," Henry replied. *An innocent question.* But Henry sensed that they knew more about him than they were saying. "I have been retired awhile and we spend a lot of time here at the cottage. We have a place on Lakeside Road, but our main place is in Winnipeg."

"Oh, another part-time Hecla islander," Dmitry said.

"Yep, the best of both worlds."

"You think so? In this polar wilderness? I don't think I agree," Dmitry replied, laughing.

Vlad looked to be in his later fifties, had a short, almost military-style haircut, a large scar across his left cheek, and tattoos on both arms—a pair of serpents. Dmitry looked like he was in his thirties, had the same short haircut, and slightly darker complexion than Vlad. Their haircuts, the clothes they wore, and their language were the only things they really had in common. Henry couldn't see any family likeness. Vlad was tall and well built, Dmitry average height and slender. Neither were particularly friendly. They were constantly talking in their languages between Dmitry's replies in English and translating back in Ukrainian for Vlad. Henry realized quickly that forming a relationship with these two guys would not be easy. Henry was a pretty friendly guy and got along with most people. *Maybe learning a couple of words in Ukrainian would help me build some kind of rapport with them,* he thought as he headed home that day.

After supper that night, he found a website that explained simple greetings like good morning, hello, and goodbye in Ukrainian with an audio guide for their pronunciation.

"I am not impressed by your Ukrainian or your reason for doing this," was Julia's reply when he tried out his basic vocabulary with her later in the evening. "This is going too far, Henry. I am really uncomfortable encouraging you anymore. I'm going to bed." She managed a kiss before heading to the bedroom.

Henry sat up for a while, contemplating his next move. *I need to be patient and not be too hasty–I need them to come to me,* he thought. He decided to stay up; he was restless and didn't feel tired. It was 2:00 a.m., 8:00 a.m. in England, so he decided on a whim to ring Rob. Couldn't do any harm to get his insight, now that he knew Vlad and Dmitry. Rob picked up the phone immediately.

"Hi, Henry! How are you doing?"

"Good, thanks, Rob. I know you're probably just off to work, but I have an update on the two Ukrainians and would like your advice."

"Sure, Henry. Fire away."

"They say they are related—the younger one, Dmitry, says he is the older one's nephew. They don't look related. That is my first concern. Secondly, the younger one speaks English well, almost with a London accent, and said he lived in England for a while."

"Well, I wouldn't be surprised if they weren't related," Rob said. "They looked a couple of shady characters and the younger one's English accent made me think of East European criminal gangs in London. Maybe a little unfair but you wanted my opinion. I could do a search of the younger guy, Dmitry, in our system if you have a photo."

"They're pretty secretive. I wouldn't imagine they would pose for a photograph, Rob," Henry said, a little frustrated.

"Well, I can't really help you unless you have a photo."

"Wouldn't their names help?" Henry asked.

"Maybe," Rob replied, "but if they are here for nefarious reasons, they would likely be using false names and passports—give them to me anyway."

"Vladimir Krafchenko and Dmitry Melnyk." Henry spelled them out slowly. "Thanks Rob. I appreciate any help."

"No problem," Rob said. They said goodbye and hung up.

The next morning, Henry tried out his rudimentary language skills on the two men, who were a little surprised but amused and impressed by his efforts.

Although remaining guarded, they opened up a little. Conversation was still awkward. It was obvious to Henry that Dmitry really did have a commanding understanding and use of English, even better than he was admitting. *No great surprise. They are keeping a lot to themselves, really not talking about their background at all.*

A week later, Henry was asked to work a Saturday afternoon shift. He was waiting when Vladimir and Dmitry arrived—dirty and breathless—a little late for the handover.

"Sorry, Henry," Dmitry said, looking a little stressed.

"No problem." Henry smiled to show "no harm done" and proceeded to share the outstanding work on a couple of projects that would form their work for the night.

"Why do you look like you've put in a day's work already?" Henry asked. The men looked at each other, hesitating. Vlad nodded to Dmitry.

"We are searching for something that belongs to our family," Dmitry said, "and we are struggling to find it. It involves a lot of digging."

It was clear for whatever reason the two men had decided to bring Henry into their confidence. Henry tried to look innocent and asked the obvious question. "Where are you digging?"

"Let's talk tomorrow after your shift—don't want to speak here," Dmitry said. "Come round to our house and we will talk over coffee." Their attitude had changed considerably, and it appeared they wanted his help in some way. Maybe they had gotten desperate due to lack of progress.

They undressed and stepped into the shower. Henry saw his opportunity: their company ID cards lay on top of their clothes, and he snapped photos of them with his cell. He left them to clean the dirt from themselves and headed to his car, where he quickly emailed the pictures to Rob.

Henry went home, excited. Of course, Julia was very concerned.

"You don't know them; you shouldn't be trusting them—they may be criminals!"

"I sent their photos to Rob to see if they are in the system there," Henry replied.

"Henry, you are relentless," Julia said, more than a little frustrated.

The next morning, Dmitry handed him their address on a piece of paper that Henry tucked into his pocket.

"We are going home to sleep now and will see you when your shift is finished around 2:00 p.m. We will have the coffee on," he said with a smile.

Henry worked his shift, hung up his overalls, and dressed for his visit. The cottage they had rented was at the extreme south end of the village, close to Marisa Jones's place.

He saw the house number on a sign hanging on an old wooden frame attached to a pole, close to the road. The driveway was gravel, but you would hardly know it—it was full of weeds as was the property as a whole. It was a small house, built long ago, about the size of Marisa's place but not half as pretty or well maintained.

The blue F150 was parked by the house and Henry pulled up just behind it.

He approached the front door and knocked. The paint was peeling off of it and the siding and fascia boards looked rotten. There were grey net curtains on the window and Henry could see a pale light shining from the dark interior.

He knocked again. Finally, Dmitry cracked open the door, squinting in the sunlight and looking like he had just woken up.

Yawning, he said, "Come in and find a seat. I'll wake Vladimir." Vlad finally appeared and the coffee smelled like it was on the go. Moments later, they sat at the kitchen table, coffee cups in hand.

"You won't be writing down anything we will be saying, Henry," Dmitry said assertively, looking pointedly at the pen and notebook on the table beside Henry's coffee. He nodded and closed the notebook.

"How do you think I can help you guys? Where have you have been digging?" Henry asked, trying not to overplay the innocent tone in his voice.

"I think you know," Dmitry said, menace in his voice. He looked at Vlad, who said something in Ukrainian and Dmitry nodded.

Dmitry went into the bedroom and came out with what looked like a very old envelope. He carefully removed the single folded piece of paper, put it on the table, and turned it towards Henry.

Henry smiled. "I don't know Ukrainian," he said, looking up at Dmitry, confused and still processing the hint of menace around them.

"This is a copy of an original letter that Vlad's brother had. It is dated July 9, 1914. It is a letter that has been handed down in the family for generations. It was written by a relative who immigrated to Canada well over a hundred years ago. We have read it hundreds of times and haven't found what we are looking for. The letter mentions Mickley, the Icelandic name for Hecla and the original settlement—it also mentions a metal box and says it's 'not buried deep.' It says the metal box is located 'where the two boys lie.' It is a curious statement and we assumed it would be inside one of the houses, under a bedroom where the kids had slept, but we have found nothing. We have used state of the art metal detectors and found nothing. What do you think Henry?"

Henry thought for a couple of minutes—the pressure of their gazes on him.

"The only two logical explanations I can think of are that the box has already been found by someone else or you have misinterpreted the clues and it isn't within the body of the houses. Let me give this some thought and I'll get back to you," Henry said.

Dmitry nodded, his demeanor once again friendly. "Thanks, Henry. We appreciate any ideas. Please don't share this with anyone," he said, making direct eye contact with Henry. "We just want what is ours and we will be gone. We think Vlad's brother was killed looking for this box and we could be at risk, too," he added.

They don't seem so menacing now–they actually seem a little vulnerable. "So the tall red-headed guy who was hanging around before you folks arrived was your brother?" Henry asked Vlad, then looked to Dmitry.

"Yes, he was Vlad's older brother Andriy," Dmitry said. "As the eldest brother, he was handed the letter when his father died. He was the smart one in the family, a university professor. He shared the letter with Vlad a number of years ago. Vlad was intrigued but not sufficiently curious to do anything about it. Andriy was the eldest sibling and fascinated by our family tree. He was aware we had a relative that immigrated to Canada in the late 1880s. He was the one who connected the rather cryptic letter with Hecla Island and decided to come investigate."

Henry didn't let on that he knew who this family member was—it was clear to him that Bloody Jack was that relative and that the Ukrainians were not going to share the backstory.

"Vlad lost contact with Andriy and asked if I would go to Canada with him to try and find him," Dmitry added.

Dmitry and Vlad looked a little dejected as Henry put his jacket on and walked to the door.

"Don't worry, guys; we will find it. We'll have to put ourselves back in the time and space of the early 1900s when the letter was written to understand the context of the clues." Henry already had an idea brewing as he headed home. He would need to look back at his notes and follow up on something.

Later that afternoon, Henry got a call from Rob.

"Hi, Henry. Just to let you know, I got some feedback on the photographs. The older guy, Vlad, is not known to us, but Dmitry is. He's been in the UK about five years—he is in a gang that we suspect specializes in robbing wealthy people of things like significant works of art. We've never managed to apprehend him. We do have a number of warrants for his arrest. Real name: Yuri Melnyk. He is a thief but no specific evidence of involvement in any violent crime as far as we know."

"That a relief," Henry said, a little jest about Rob's last sentence. "Thanks Rob. I'll keep you posted."

CHAPTER THIRTY

Henry came home to an empty house—Julia was out shopping. Henry got out of his work clothes and showered. As the hot water cascaded over his body, his mind swirled with questions and thoughts about the conversation he'd just had with Vlad and Dmitry. He tried to imagine what the properties would have looked like in the early 1900s. If the roofs had not collapsed, the places may still have been habitable—certainly very out of the way and a perfect place to lay low for a period of time.

Anything of value would have been stripped out of the places when the original inhabitants left but everything else would have been left as is. *Marginally better than living in a tent*, he thought.

If Krafchenko, the relative he was sure Dmitry and Vlad were referring to, had been holed up in one of the old settlement buildings back when they still stood, what did he see and why had he not buried his metal box under the floor of one the buildings? They would be easy to identify at that time. *What else would have stood out as an identifiable landmark? Clearly, the guy was planning to go back and retrieve the box.*

He was grappling with this dilemma when there was a knock on the bathroom door.

"Hi, Henry!" Julia shouted over the noise of the shower. "Just got back from Riverton. I'll put the coffee on."

"OK!" Henry shouted back, his train of thought lost. He turned off the shower, dried himself, and headed for coffee.

Dressed in a pair of shorts, a golf shirt, and flip-flops, he headed out the patio door where Julia was already seated and nibbling cookies. There was a cool breeze blowing from the north and the lake was full of white caps. The umbrella was flapping as the wind gusted from time to time.

"Great—I needed a decent cup of coffee—didn't think much of Vlad's coffee earlier."

"So how did it go?" Julia asked, seeming genuinely interested in Henry's answer.

Henry was happy to talk outside, away from the bugs in the house that were quietly monitoring their conversations.

"They definitely want my help. I think they are running out of ideas. They have been searching for a while and found almost nothing and certainly don't have any sense at all of making progress. They know—I am not sure from whom—of my interest in the original settlement and they think I might know something that will help with their search."

"Drink your coffee, Henry. It's getting cold," Julia said.

Henry picked up his cup and sipped his drink thoughtfully.

"They have searched within the foundation walls of all the original dwellings with a metal detector and have found nothing. According to a family heirloom-type letter they have, some metal box is apparently 'where the two boys lie.' We know there were four original families on Kjartanson Point, but they had long moved away or to the south side of the island before Jack sought refuge there. So how would he know where 'the boys lie'?"

"Simple," Julia said. "Didn't you say there was a major smallpox epidemic in the Icelandic community? Greta's journal mentions a number of her close male relatives dying. I think Jack buried his box in the grave of the boys that succumbed to smallpox."

"Brilliant, Julia! That is the only explanation. I was planning to revisit that diary and check, but I think you are right."

"Now where would a grieving family, living in such a remote place, bury their children?" Julia asked.

"Good question," Henry replied. "I would imagine not in the middle of the forest, not right by their homes. I would say in a prominent place, maybe overlooking the lake?"

"Good idea. If you're right, that explains why they have not found anything—because they have been looking in the wrong place."

"I tell you one thing that is troubling me, Julia," Henry said. "What kind of valuables would Krafchenko have hoarded away that would be worth anything today?" Henry said. "Early 1900s cash would have no value today."

"Maybe jewellery?"

"A long way to come to pick up a couple of diamond rings," Henry thought out loud.

"You are right—and to *die* for them."

"When I see the guys tomorrow, I'll share our thoughts on a gravesite and see what happens."

"Hopefully, they find what they are looking for and leave the island and we can get back to our regular life," Julia said with feeling.

Henry nodded, looking down at his empty mug. "Another cup of coffee?"

"Sure."

Henry was stretching his imagination as to what could possibly be in that metal box that would have attracted so much attention.

Once the coffee had brewed, he poured black for Julia, added a touch of cream to his, and headed back out to the patio. The wind had died down and some early season mosquitos were nipping. After about five minutes, they decided to finish their coffees inside, away from the pesky insects.

Julia began dinner, and Henry prepared the veggies. She was a good cook but often asked for Henry's assistance, particularly with a new recipe. Tonight, it was pork loin with a rather tasty marinade made with marmalade and French mustard. He was getting hungry, so he hoped the marinating wasn't going to take too long. Julia was very slavish to what the quantities and times stated in the recipe.

"Shall I open a bottle of wine, Julia?" Henry asked with a smile. "Always helps to cook with a glass of wine in hand, especially when the prep work is basically done."

"We'll give the marinade an hour, the veggies for roasting are covered and ready to go, and the potatoes are cleaned and ready for the microwave. Perfect timing for a glass, thanks Henry."

Henry had already uncorked the wine and poured two glasses.

"Wow, that was fast, Henry! You obviously need a drink," Julia said, clinking glasses with him.

"I think you are really onto something, Julia, and that is exciting," Henry said, clearly in a positive mood. "One thing I'm thinking—surely folks would be buried in the same area. That third body was found on the edge of the settlement. Maybe it's in that same general area."

"Do me a favour—can we talk about anything else, just for tonight? I want to live in the here and now, and not be constantly trying to imagine what a criminal was or was not doing and thinking over a hundred years ago."

He decided that when it came up in conversation with Vlad and Dmitry, he wasn't going to engage in any speculation. Instead, he'd merely suggest that the box could be in the general area where the third body had been buried and found recently—maybe it was a gravesite?

"OK, I get the message, loud and clear. Fancy a game of gin rummy?"

"Sure, I'll get the cards."

Henry reached for a pen and a pad of paper, and it was game on.

Once the marinating time was up, they temporarily halted the game to roast the meat and vegetables. It was a close game—they had competitive streaks and were having fun. There wasn't much of the bottle of wine left when the game ended and Henry admitted defeat.

"Well done, Julia. That was a tight game."

She smiled at him a little too smugly for Henry's liking. As she got up, she couldn't resist a shot.

"That's what happens when you hang onto high-points cards too long."

In a couple of minutes, the gravy and the microwaved potatoes were made. It was quite a feast and Henry was very complimentary.

"That marinade is a hit, Julia. This meal knocks it out of the park."

There was one thing about Henry: he loved his wife's cooking.

Henry took the next day off to go with Julia back to the city. The grandkids had a day off school, and they were going to take the boys to the zoo and have a sleepover. Of course, the lawn needed to be cut at the house and a few other things taken care of. It was a chore having two properties to look after, particularly in the warmer weather, but they loved the place at the lake and if they each did their share, it was manageable.

If things got tougher when they got older and they still had the money, they would pay for help. Selling the property at Hecla was going to be at a much later stage of their life, health willing, of course.

CHAPTER THIRTY-ONE

The next day was windy and overcast. Henry loaded the car—they were travelling light as they would be back in a day or so. He paced around as he often did while Julia went through her daily ritual of a bath and then makeup—"patch, prime, and paint" as he would often rather ungenerously describe it.

The two and a quarter-hour ride home was never his favourite. He much preferred the ride up. Henry always drove, as he didn't mind, and Julia preferred not to. Just past Gimli, Henry's phone rang.

"Hi, Sophie, how are you doing?"

"Not too bad, Henry. I may have some information for you. Not sure if it has any value, but from the newspaper clippings, it was clear that Krafchenko had a number of accomplices, a couple of them of Icelandic descent. I am trying to find their names to see if there is any link to Hecla Island."

"That's very interesting. I thought there had to be a link with his possible presence on the island. It would make sense if one of his accomplices was an Icelander who had just immigrated to Hecla. Maybe one of the sons or grandsons of the original four families?" Henry wondered.

"OK, that's all I have for now. I'll keep digging—say hi to Julia. Bye for now." Sophie rang off.

When they arrived at their daughter's house, her kids were waiting excitedly on the porch. The kids loved spending time with Grandma and Grandpa and enjoyed the little bit of spoiling they always got: at a minimum, a nice lunch, and if they were good, ice cream.

James, the eldest, was six and was a fun chatterbox. His poor younger brother struggled to get a word in edgewise sometimes; he was three and a much quieter child than his brother. He had a close relationship with Grandma.

They arrived at the zoo early afternoon and the boys were hungry, so that was the priority on arrival. They ordered hamburgers and fries and washed it all down with apple juice. They were not normally big eaters, but they made short work of their lunch. Henry and Julia settled for a ham and cheese sandwich and a cup of tea.

The sun came out and it turned out to be a warm day. Around 3:00 p.m., it was time for a break and, apparently, ice cream. Henry purchased a couple of cones for them, and a popsicle for himself; just as he was about to start licking it, his phone rang. He pulled it off his belt and checked the number.

"It's Dmitry."

Julia just gave him the look.

"OK, I'll let it go to voice mail," Henry said. "I'll call him when we get home." He put the phone on vibrate.

After another hour, the boys were tired, and it was time to take them home.

Johnny and Christine had invited Henry and Julia for a barbecue. Though his phone vibrated a couple more times throughout the meal, Henry left it alone. Even after years of retirement, he was still hotwired to check his phone immediately, but he realized this was important family time.

He waited until they got home—all the calls were from Dmitry. There was even a text, which was unlike Dmitry as he didn't like to leave messages. It simply said, "call me, urgently."

Henry took advantage of Julia's trip to the bathroom to call him back.

"Hey, what's up?" Henry asked in his normal jovial way.

"Henry, we have been trying to call you all afternoon! Where are you?" Dmitry was abrupt, upset, and sounded panicky. Before Henry could respond, he continued.

"Jantie Bjornason has been attacked and killed in our house. When we came home from our shift, we found that somebody had broken into the house and trashed it. Jantie had been stabbed a number of times. There was blood everywhere. He must have put up a real fight. We reported it to the police immediately, and now it looks like they are going to be taking us into custody—we are not sure why—to the Gimli police station. Vlad and I didn't know who else to ring. We *didn't do it* Henry. Honestly, the last thing we wanted to do was call attention to ourselves."

"I believe you Dmitry. If you have an alibi, you will be OK. It will just take a little time for the police to establish the time of death. I know a criminal lawyer in Winnipeg who speaks Ukrainian. I'll call him and explain the situation to get you some representation. Sit tight; we'll sort this out."

"Just so you know, Henry," Dmitry said, "the letter is gone. Somebody must've completely trashed the house to find it. We have competition."

"I hope you didn't touch anything," Henry said, "Maybe the police can find evidence of who this assailant was."

"Of course we didn't, Henry. The front room had been turned upside down and when we got to the bedroom, we saw Jantie, checked his vitals, and called 911. We checked where we had hidden the letter in the bedroom, and it wasn't there. We then just sat on the sofa and waited for emergency services."

"OK. I'll get the lawyer to contact you as soon as possible."

As Julia emerged from the washroom, she was livid. "So they were burgled and Jantie has been murdered. I told you nothing good will come from these guys. I am so mad with at you Henry," Julia was practically shouting, which was very unlike her. "They clearly attract trouble! How do we know that Jantie wasn't snooping around—they caught him and killed him, and now are trying to pin it on an accomplice of Jantie's or somebody else?" She was so seething mad, now she was ranting.

"You could be right, Julia." Henry nodded in acceptance. "But they say they were at work. Nothing I can do from here."

"Nothing you are *going* to do," Julia stated assertively. "Make that call to the lawyer and leave it at that."

Henry made the call, then they decided to stay in Winnipeg for the night and drive back to the lake in the morning.

What was Jantie doing in the house? Who killed him and what did he or she know what to be looking for? This is getting more complicated. Henry had a restless night and wrestled with his thoughts as he tried to get some sleep.

As Henry and Julia headed back to the lake the next morning, his phone rang.

"Hi, Henry. It's Jamie Horenko. I followed up with the two individuals, and I have the permission of my clients to talk to you. They wanted to keep you informed of the latest situation. The time of Jantie's death has been established approximately, as around 7:00 a.m. yesterday morning. This still needs to be confirmed by the formal autopsy. There is no sign of the murder weapon. My two clients have clear alibis, as there is sufficient video camera evidence to place them at work for their entire shift. They will not be charged with the murder, but they are going to be held for further interviews and they have had to surrender their passports. The police are very curious as to why the house was so methodically searched and want to know what the intruders or murderers were looking for."

Henry noted that Vlad and Dmitry had not taken the lawyer fully into their confidence regarding the letter; they were getting into dangerous territory.

"What was Jantie doing there?" Henry asked.

"That is the only thing I *can* answer with confidence," Jamie replied. "He went the same time every month to pick up the rent cheque from the kitchen table if Vlad and Dmitry weren't home. Jantie managed quite a few properties in the area—as a sideline to his main fishing business. Dmitry and Vlad's place was just one of many he helped maintain.

"He must have walked in while the burglary was in progress—classic wrong place, wrong time situation—or he was searching the house and was silenced by an accomplice or somebody else. He had told his wife he would be out for a while, collecting cheques and checking out a number of properties, then he was going into Riverton for supplies. That is why she wasn't alarmed or concerned by his absence. She is obviously absolutely devastated.

"Also, from talking to the police, I gathered Jantie Bjornason was a pillar of society and had an unblemished reputation and no criminal record. It seems most likely, therefore, that he interrupted someone who was searching the house."

CHAPTER THIRTY-TWO

There was a clear blue sky and no breeze as Henry and Skip went for their early morning walk. Plenty of deer were around, eating the new shoots of grass growing on the side of the road. They moved away as Henry and Skip approached, gently stepping back into the bush. It was wet and sticky underfoot, a little above zero, and the frost was slowly melting from the ground. The peace and quiet of nature provided Henry a strange contrast to the violence happening on Hecla—it was still a beautiful, unspoiled part of the world.

Henry tried calling Dmitry's cell later in the morning.

"So, how did it go with the police? I am sure you were relieved to be taken off the suspect's list," Henry asked.

"Yes," Dmitry said, "but they were relentless Henry, asking questions about why somebody would want to take the place apart. They even got a Ukrainian translator to interview Vlad. We were consistent in our story. We said we had nothing to hide, no information to give, and no idea what our relative was doing in the original settlement area. The police obviously think there is a link though, and don't believe us."

"Are you surprised, Dmitry? Experienced interrogators are good at spotting liars. My guess is they will be keeping a watch on you two."

"The concern now is, we have a person or persons unknown who now knows what we know. We have to work fast to find that burial site and recover that box," Dmitry added.

Julia was not happy at all when Henry told her they were going to hire a boat the next morning to search out a possible grave site.

"You should not be trusting these guys—you don't really know anything about them or even what it is they hope to find."

"I think we both want this sorted once and for all, Julia. I'm getting a little worried about what's going on, too."

"A little worried. *A little worried?* I don't want you going anywhere with these guys," Julia said, frustrated by Henry's commitment to what she thought was a reckless course of action.

"We're going to leave early and should hopefully be done by lunch time," he said, looking a little guilty. "We have a much better idea of where to look now, thanks to you." The compliment did little to ease her concerns.

The next morning, it was barely light when Henry reached the harbour.

He cycled as he didn't want to leave his vehicle in plain sight as a clue to where they were going. Vlad and Dmitry were already waiting. Henry didn't see their truck, either—they had obviously had the same thought.

"Did you see anybody around, Dmitry?" Henry whispered.

"No, you?"

"Nope. This was a good plan to leave really early."

Jake, the harbour manager, had given Henry the key to the boat the afternoon before and promised he would fill the tank with gas for him. Jake had kept his promise.

Vlad and Dmitry carefully stepped into the boat. They were wearing rucksacks and had brought a shovel, a pick, a scythe, a branch lopper, and a metal detector they carefully stowed on the boat.

Henry started the engine, adjusted the throttle, and they were off, leaving the harbour with no lights on—a little dangerous but necessary.

As Henry glanced back as the lights of a vehicle was clearing the trees and entering the harbour parking lot. He couldn't recognize it in the dark, but he hoped and assumed it was a fisher, preparing for his day's work. For once, he wasn't worried about it being a blue F150.

The boat was small, and the lake was a little rough once they cleared the north tip of the island and headed southwest, hugging the coastline to minimize the chance of being seen and to shelter a little from the wind that was blowing moderately enough to slow their progress.

They reached their destination an hour later and they searched for a place to hide the boat between the rocks to minimize the chance of being

DEATH AT THE POINT

spotted from the water. It was light now and overcast, a little drizzle in the air.

"So where is this spot you were thinking is the place we should be looking, Henry?" Dmitry asked.

"About thirty metres south of here, where the land is a little elevated. It's just a hunch remember—no promises."

"It's the best we've got, Henry," Dmitry said, smiling at Vlad.

"Let's try the metal detector in the area between the tree line and the elevated shoreline, before the beach," Henry suggested. "Dmitry, can you ask Vlad to use the scythe? We are going to have to remove the bushes in this area."

It took an hour of work to clear a site, then Vlad started to work the area with his metal detector. Henry stopped abruptly—the mosquitoes were becoming a real nuisance. He was frustrated they had not thought to bring insect repellent.

"Hey guys, what is this?" Henry reached down and pointed to a regular-shaped flat piece of rock lying on the ground, partly overgrown with grass. "Look! That thin piece of rock has been cut into a rectangle—no way that would have formed naturally. I bet it was the boys' headstone."

Henry scraped away at the soil that covered part of the stone, looking for any markings. "If they had painted anything on the rock, it would have been erased by the weather after all this time. No, cannot see anything, but we should scan this area."

Dmitry spoke to Vlad in Ukrainian. Vlad started the metal detector, walked the area, and within minutes, had picked up a signal. He was smiling strangely and looking at Dmitry. He then scanned the area from a different angle to pinpoint the spot.

"Henry, can you grab the pick? Let's open up the ground a little and see what we can find."

Henry worked to break up the ground, then Dmitry grabbed the spade and removed the soil. Everybody was excited. Henry lifted the pick and brought it down. A clang echoed in the stillness. Metal. Henry got down on his knees and carefully pushed away the loose soil and small stones. The corner of what looked like a rusty black box poked out of the hole.

Vlad reached in and wriggled it loose from the soil's grip. It was badly corroded with sharp edges, and he was cautious not to cut himself.

They could see it wasn't much bigger than a shoe box as Dmitry lifted it out with reverence and tried to unlatch the clasp. Of course, it was rusted to the wall of the box.

"It feels quite heavy," Dmitry said smiling with expectation.

"I've got a knife," Henry said and used it to pry it open and lift the lid of the box as Dmitry held it.

The contents were packed to the brim: bank notes rolled up in wads, jewellery, and something wrapped in a cloth bag. Vlad and Dmitry smiled at each other, visibly satisfied with what they had found. Dmitry lifted what looked like an egg out the cloth bag. Although dusty, it was an astoundingly beautiful piece.

"Is it a Fabergé egg?" Henry asked, amazed.

"Correct, Henry," Dmitry said. "It's from Tsar Nicolas II's collection. It's probably one given to his wife Alexandra or to his mother, the Dowager Empress Maria Feodorovna. Many eggs were lost during the Russian Revolution, but this was obviously 'lost' before. Jack must have stolen it in 1911 when he was in the service of the Tsar and Tsarina. It's worth probably up to ten million at auction and a little less if sold to a private collector."

Henry was a little taken aback by the conversation. "You folks seem to know a lot about Fabergé eggs. I somehow thought it would be larger," Henry said.

"My brother, Andriy, had done his research and he had his suspicions that an egg that went missing at the time could be connected with Jack Krafchenko within the community that values these particular works of art. There were no newspaper reports about it, just rumours. Krafchenko and his girlfriend did not cut and run after it was reported missing. My guess: they didn't want to attract attention as he was a foreigner and would have been suspected and no doubt interrogated, like all the staff."

"So, this belongs to the late Tsar's descendants, right?" Henry said naively.

"Yes, technically," Dmitry said, smiling at Vlad. "Our private buyer isn't worried about that—he's a friend of higher-ups in Moscow." While Dmitry was speaking, Vlad had been placing the items in their rucksacks.

For the first time, Henry realized for certain that these people were not messing around—this was a high-stakes game, and he was right in the middle of it. He also realized that they needed to get away as quickly as possible to avoid whoever was chasing them. He now considered seriously whether or not his life was in danger. Henry's head was spinning as he considered his options. It became all too clear: he had been taken for a ride.

Dmitry must have suspected that Henry had eventually cottoned on to his predicament, suddenly revealing that he was armed, by just placing his hand against an object under his jacket. Henry stood up, now seriously contemplating his mortality.

Vlad carefully packed the metal box in his rucksack. "Thanks, Henry," Dmitry said. "We appreciate your help but, unfortunately, we cannot trust you to not alert the police, so we are going to take your phone and we are going to tie you to this tree. When you don't turn up at home, your wife will alert the police and they'll find you—a little hungry and thirsty—but fine, and we'll be long gone."

Henry accepted his fate without protest and walked to the tree—he really didn't have any other options. *Julia will be saying "I told you so," when they eventually find me*, he thought as he sat down, his back to a pine.

Vlad pulled a rope from his rucksack and carefully tied Henry up tightly enough that he couldn't easily shake himself loose but not so tight that he couldn't breathe.

Dmitry checked Vlad's handiwork and smiled. "Trussed up like a turkey," he said, looking at Vlad and laughing. "So long, Henry. Thanks for everything." They spoke to each other in Ukrainian as they put on their rucksacks and got ready to leave.

Suddenly there was a *crack!*

A splinter blew off the tree just above Henry's head Somebody was shooting at them. The two men turned and ran through the trees towards the boat. Another *crack!* Henry heard one of them scream.

He wriggled, trying to reach for the knife in his pocket. Henry managed to get his left hand into it and with difficulty got the knife out and opened it up. His hand was seriously constrained, but as long as he didn't drop it, he had a chance to cut himself loose. He realized that he was in mortal danger from whoever had fired the shots.

He heard Vlad and Dmitry clambering into the boat and then the outboard starting up. There were a couple more shots. Henry hoped this would be a distraction to the shooter and give him a little time—he knew he had seconds at the most to get himself free. He finally cut through the rope and crawled into the bush, praying that he had not been spotted and the shooter was concentrating his attention on the others. Once confident he had enough cover, Henry scrambled with all the speed he could find and kept moving until he found a spot in the deep bush to hide out. He hunkered down and tried to slow his breathing. Not moving was a challenge as the insects started to find him.

He guessed that the shooter would try to intercept them at the harbour before they had a chance to get to their rented place and their vehicle. There was only one way off the island—the causeway—so they were in a tight spot. Henry even felt a little sorry for their predicament.

The insects were brutal, but Henry had no choice but to lie completely still. In a funny way, he was relieved that this would now be all out in the open and hopefully resolved in the near future.

CHAPTER THIRTY-THREE

After a couple of hours frozen in fear and tortured by the incessant mosquitoes dive-bombing any exposed skin, Henry tried to assess exactly where he was. He had run inland through the bush and could hear the distant sound of vehicles on the main road—he guessed he was less than half a mile from it. Eventually, he convinced himself that if he could stop a car coming onto the island, he could make it home and get some police support.

Henry struggled through the thick bush that tore at his clothes and his body, but the motivation to get the farthest distance from the shooter as possible was very powerful and soon he had found a place where he could see up and down the road and waited for an incoming car. It didn't take long. The first car Henry flagged down stopped and he sprinted to it. The driver was cautious as Henry approached as his face and upper chest were a mass of swollen bites and his clothes were badly torn.

"Who are you?" the driver called through his half-cracked open window, nervous.

"Henry Trevellyn is my name—I need to talk to a police officer immediately."

"There is a police roadblock on the causeway. What's going on?" the driver said.

"Thank goodness can you take me back to the police," Henry said. "I have something important to tell them."

They were on the causeway and at the roadblock in minutes. Henry leaped out of the car, thanking the driver over his shoulder. He was vaguely aware of his rescuer asking the police whether or not proceeding up the island was a good idea. Henry gave his full name to the first officer he saw and reported the basics of what had happened.

"Your wife reported you missing just over an hour ago. There are officers on the way to the original settlement. They have just co-opted a fishing boat from the harbour to ferry our folks out to the site."

"They took my phone. Can I call my wife?" Henry asked impatiently.

"Sure, sir. Just need to speak to the senior officer on the boat, let him know you've turned up, and then you can talk to your wife. Don't worry; they have a satellite radio, and the reception is good," the police officer said kindly.

"I have Henry Trevellyn with me, sir! A little shaken up but otherwise, he's OK," the officer said.

"Put him on the line, please," the senior officer shouted over the engine of the boat.

"Trevellyn here!"

"Mr. Trevellyn, we are on the way to the site—what can you tell me?"

"I left with two Ukrainian nationals very early this morning to do an excavation for a metal box at the original settlement site on Kjartanson Point. We found it and then they tied me up. I'm not injured. As they left, someone started shooting at us. I think one of them was hit, as I heard a scream. I think they were heading north to their getaway vehicle parked somewhere close to the harbour—they didn't tell me where."

"OK, OK, sir. Just calm down. The boat was a fourteen-footer, painted blue?" the officer asked.

"Yes, it was," Henry replied.

"Well, the boat went south. Not north, to just past the causeway. We assume that was where their getaway vehicle was parked, and we assume they are off the island now. Do you have a description of their vehicle?"

"Yes," Henry replied, "a blue Ford F150 with Manitoba license plates. I am pretty sure it was a rental."

"Thanks. We'll follow up with the rental companies in the area and get a registration number. We'll also put out an all-points bulletin to our patrol cars to be on the lookout."

"Thanks, officer," Henry said. "Can I speak to my wife now, please?"

"Of course", the senior officer said.

"Henry! Are you OK?" He could hear the panic in Julia's voice.

"Yes, I am—there were some scary moments, but I am OK."

"Thank goodness," Julia said. "I am so mad at you! I told you it wasn't a good idea to go with those men."

"You were right. I was wrong," Henry said, rather sheepishly.

"Get your rear end home soon," Julia said. "I am coming home to meet you now. We're having something stronger than a cup of coffee today."

That night, there were reports of the incident on all the local TV and radio channels. Descriptions of the two people of interest were given, as well as the make, model, colour, and registration of the truck they were driving. There was no discussion of the unknown shooter.

Sophie rang that night, alarmed at what she had heard over the news, and was relieved to know Henry and Julia were OK.

"Henry, looks like things have come to a head," Sophie said. "By the way, one of the criminals working alongside Krafchenko was a Daniel Sigurdson, an Icelander who hailed from Hecla Island. Do you think it is a possibility the other badly decomposed body that nobody is talking about could be him?"

"I suppose it could," Henry replied. "It was a very shallow grave, which would rule out the body having been formally buried. He could have been murdered to protect the secret of the cache's location. Maybe Daniel caught Jack in the act of burying his metal box. This may be just an old side story, or it may be relevant and significant."

"You know what, Henry? I'll go to the Manitoba archives downtown tomorrow and see what I can find out about Daniel Sigurdson."

"Thanks, Sophie. That would be great."

"Looks like we're working together whether you like it or not," Sophie replied, laughing.

"Sophie, please be careful. The person shooting at us was not messing around. Even with Vlad and Dmitry out of the picture, there is still a person or persons, armed and dangerous, with an unknown interest in what is going on, who is still out there."

CHAPTER THIRTY-FOUR

The RCMP interviewed Henry a couple of times over the next week. They made it clear that they didn't think much of Henry's obsession with the case, his interference, his direct involvement with two people of interest, or the desecration of a grave, or graves. They were not, at this stage, going to press any charges. He was just cautioned to avoid any further involvement.

"So Vlad and Dmitry got what they came for and we can all relax, and hopefully you can focus on things a little more positive," Julia said. Henry had decided not to tell her the whole story as he described it to the police, she had been upset enough.

Henry nodded, saw the relief in Julia's face, and realized he had been very lucky. He had never really felt that the two Ukrainians were killers, but clearly somebody was, and as far as he was concerned, they were still on the loose. Not that he felt he was in harm's way now that the other two had made their getaway. Over the next few days, there were a couple more speculative reports and then media interest died down. Life eventually got back to normal, and Henry had to admit that it was good to no longer have the obsession in the back of his mind.

That Friday, there was a knock at the door. To Henry's surprise, it was two RCMP officers. They requested that he accompany them to the Gimli detachment. He rang Julia, who was in Winnipeg, and told her where he was going.

"No, I'm not arrested or anything like that. They just want to ask me more questions. I'll be going in my own car."

"OK, Henry. I'll be driving up this afternoon. See you later," Julia said.

"Drive carefully," Henry said. "Love you."

He parked outside of the station, walked into the building, and was escorted by one of the officers to an interview room. "Coffee?" he asked.

"Milk, no sugar, please," Henry said as he sat down at the table. A couple minutes later, the officer returned with the coffee and sat across from Henry. A senior officer entered the room, identified himself and the others, stated the date, and sat down next to the other police officer.

"Interview—commencing at 13:05 hours," the senior officer said.

"Mr. Trevellyn, I know you were a senior officer with the Winnipeg Police Service, so we can dispense with some of the formalities. There has been a development in the case that has taken things to a new level."

Henry was taken aback. He'd expect this to be a formality, an interview to tie up loose ends connected with the case.

"A local farmer found a blue Ford F150 in a wooded area close to the US border. It had been burned out. Our forensic people said it was as a result of a controlled incendiary device planted in the vehicle. Two deceased occupants were found close to the vehicle. Both had been shot at close range. They have been identified by DNA recovered from their rented house as the two Ukrainians.

"Although the vehicle had been burned out, there was evidence it had been ransacked and intensively searched. The seating has been slashed and anywhere a small object could be concealed has been exposed. We think the killer or killers were searching for the metal box and its contents, and they probably found what they were looking for. This case is far from closed. Do you have any idea who this killer or killers could be?" the officer asked.

"No idea, really," Henry said. "I told the other officers that my theory was that the last letter Krafchenko ever wrote was stolen from Vlad and Dmitry's rented place—the person who broke into their house and killed Jantie could possibly be involved in the killing and truck-burning."

The officer didn't seem to be particularly impressed by Henry's answer.

"Not exactly rocket science, Mr. Trevellyn," he said. It was true. Henry didn't have any idea how anybody else other than the person who had stolen the letter could have worked out what the Ukrainians were looking for.

The interview wrapped up, and as he walked to the car, Henry had a very uncomfortable feeling that everyone was missing something that would identify the murderous person still lurking in the shadows.

DEATH AT THE POINT

Henry called Julia from the car to let her know all was OK. In reality, he was worried. It was raining so hard, the spray from larger oncoming vehicles was blinding him and he really needed to concentrate.

Henry arrived back at Hecla just after 3:00 p.m. It was still raining hard, the wind had come up, and the lake looked dark and stormy with whitecaps on every wave. He was relieved to be home. Julia had made coffee and they sat in front of the cathedral window, facing the lake, their cups warming their hands. It had become so dark they needed the lights on to see.

"Well, there is still a murderer or murderers out there, so I don't feel particularly at ease," Henry said, relating the latest news about Vlad and Dmitry's deaths, which went down like a lead balloon.

"Is this ever going to end, Henry? Is this all really about a Fabergé egg?" Julia asked angrily.

"It's worth a heck of a lot of money, so yes, it probably is."

Henry had one concern that was aching at him: he had not seen the shooter, but maybe the shooter didn't know that. He could still be a target.

Sophie rang that evening.

"Hi, Henry. I managed to spend some time in the archives. Apparently, the disappearance of Daniel was a cold case, investigated on more than one occasion over the years. There are a number of files on Daniel Sigurdson as part of the case against Krafchenko as well some subsequent investigations after his execution. It was suspected that Daniel came to a sticky end, possibly at the hands of Krafchenko, but there was no body. He was an accomplice in Jack's final bank robbery, which resulted in his murder conviction and eventually, his execution. It is more than conceivable that Daniel Sigurdson suggested the abandoned original settlement as a hideout if Krafchenko was looking for someplace remote. Maybe there was a falling out between the two criminals.

"I'm not sure what this means, but it is all one hell of a coincidence. I suppose DNA testing to track down relatives will probably not be that hard," Sophie suggested.

"Good work, Sophie. Let's contemplate what this could mean for the case," Henry said. "Call you tomorrow."

CHAPTER THIRTY-FIVE

Henry mulled the situation over again—the Fabergé egg was probably in the hands of the murderer now, and he or she would now be satisfied so he shouldn't be any threat to anyone. He hadn't seen who was shooting and hopefully the shooter who was probably well camouflaged knew that. As far as Henry figured, there were no loose ends.

Except maybe… one. It suddenly occurred to him that nobody was talking about the older third body found when the tall red-haired man was discovered, the one he and Sophia thought might be Jack's old buddy, Daniel Sigurdson. It probably dated back to much earlier times, but maybe there was another connection to this story that hadn't been explored.

Henry decided to be his normal persistent self and he rang the officer at the Gimli detachment and offered up this snippet of information in an effort to draw more information and it kind of worked—to a point.

"Well, thanks, Mr. Trevellyn; we decided to do the DNA testing on the older body, and we have concluded from our investigation that this individual was a relatively young male. DNA test results show he's of Icelandic background, and there is a chance that he could be the Daniel Sigurdson you mentioned. His death wasn't due to natural causes. Jack Krafchenko was present at the original settlement. His accomplice or accomplices could have been holed up there, too. We will be attempting to contact descendants at some time to match DNA and make a final identification, but the priority is to find the murderer or murderers of the two Ukrainians and Mr. Bjornson who are still at large."

A few weeks later, when Julia got home from a trip to Arborg, he suggested they go out to the Harbour Inn Restaurant to grab something to eat and drink. Julia always liked a treat night, and it would be a distraction for Henry. It was a nice evening and they stayed for a couple extra drinks before walking home. They talked about everything and anything and it felt like things were getting back to their regular routine.

Over the past few weeks, Julia had returned to her normal self. It seemed that for the others on the island, the recent drama had quickly faded from the conversation.

Julia had suggested spending an extended period in the UK for a vacation and Henry was up for that. Since they had immigrated, they had not returned to England for more than a couple of weeks at a time. They planned to go later in the fall and were engrossed in a conversation about that trip as they walked home.

It was a mild evening—dark, cloudy, with only a little light from the moon. Neither of them noticed a dark-coloured truck parked at the entrance of the campground on the opposite side of the road. Its lights were dimmed, and its engine was gently idling as they walked by. They were halfway to the turnoff to Lakeside Road when they turned to the sound of a vehicle accelerating alarmingly right behind them. They were stunned, surprised, like deer caught in the headlights.

Henry awoke, blinded by the overhead lights as Julia coincidentally limped into his room on a crutch, doing her best to carry a cup of coffee.

A nurse held Henry's hand and smiled as she turned to Julia. "I told you he would come around."

Julia burst into tears as she put down the coffee and manoeuvred herself to his bedside.

Henry, still dazed and confused, looked around the room. He was propped up in a hospital bed and could see that his leg was in plaster, his arm was in a cast, and he was incapable of turning his head due to a neck brace. He noticed tears were running down his face and felt almost hypnotized by the blinking lights and bleeps of the numerous monitors surrounding his bed. His throat felt dry, and he struggled to speak.

"Where am I, Julia?" he croaked, his voice barely audible. "What happened?"

"You're in the Health Sciences Centre in Winnipeg. We were struck by a hit-and-run driver up at the lake when we were walking home from the restaurant two weeks ago."

"I've been lying here for two weeks? I can't believe it," Henry said, staring in shock at Julia.

"You've been sedated for most of that time—you had some brain swelling as a result of the accident," Julia said, squeezing his hand and kissing his forehead. "You got the worse of it. You pushed me out of the way, then you bounced off the front of the vehicle when it hit you, and you flew into a road sign. I got away with just a broken ankle and some cuts and bruises, thanks to you." Her relief was obvious. "You've been in protective custody while you've been here, as have I at home. Somebody was out to get us."

"What's happened to me?" Henry asked, bewildered.

"Your right leg is broken in two places, as is your right arm," the nurse said. "You have damaged a couple of vertebrae in your neck, and you have had brain trauma due to a fractured skull. You were in a medically induced coma for a while to give time for the brain swelling to go down."

"You've had other emergencies, as well—all of which the team here has handled, thankfully." Julia smiled gratefully at the nurse, then leaned over the bed and gave Henry a kiss. "So glad you are going to be OK." Her warm tears fell onto Henry's upturned face as he smiled back at her. Only now was Henry aware of how lucky they both had been.

The doctor appeared and asked everybody to leave while he examined Henry.

"Henry is doing well," the doctor said as Julia came back into the room. "He will have to stay for a least a couple more days before he can go home. We'll organize some home care while both of you are still recovering. You have suffered considerable muscle wasting and will need to rebuild your strength on top of recovering from your other injuries. Nurse, let's chat outside and update his prescriptions for the next couple of days."

Julia remained at Henry's bedside over the next few days. There was a police guard stationed outside his room, and another at the end of the passage—something Henry discovered when the nurse gave him a short wheelchair ride, Julia in tow. Late in the afternoon, a senior RCMP officer arrived for a confidential meeting with Henry and Julia.

The nurse closed the door and pulled the curtain around the bed after Henry got settled, Julia and the officer on either side of him. The officer deliberately spoke quietly to reduce the possibility of being overheard.

"My name is Inspector Smit, and I am a senior officer with an investigation unit, specializing in international crime. We have been shadowing the goings on at Hecla ever since our border authorities alerted us to the presence of the two Ukrainians crossing from the US into Canada.

"What we have confirmed is that Vlad is the brother of Andriy, both now deceased. Dmitry Melnyk, also deceased, was no relation to either of them. Vlad and Dmitry were members of a Russian crime organization specializing in precious works of art, which may or may not be connected to the higher-ups in Moscow.

"They have had a rival or rivals competing to find Krafchenko's hidden egg who could be the men's criminal bosses, or somebody else. Our guess is that Vlad and Dmitry's killer probably set a tracking device on their truck, followed them, cornered them, then killed them. Whoever it was tore the vehicle apart in an effort to find the egg, which I think we can assume was successful. We have alerted our international network to the existence of the found Fabergé egg and the likelihood that somebody will be looking for a buyer. No word of any development in that area at the moment.

"I can tell you now we received intelligence from somebody you know—your son-in-law, Rob. He has been collaborating with us all along. When Rob was out at your place at Christmas time, he recognized Melnyk from his former under-cover days. Imagine a UK police officer randomly running into Eastern European criminals in a tiny place north of Winnipeg! An incredible coincidence, but a lucky break for us.

"After some digging, he found out that Vlad and Dmitry were not here working for their criminal gangs but were apparently on holiday. The chase is now on to identify the individual or individuals who have murdered Jantie Bjornson, our two Ukrainians and attacked you and your wife. They are clearly still at large and for whatever reason, still see you two as a threat. We will continue to provide police protection. Your son-in law was uncomfortable keeping this from you, but we didn't believe these gentlemen were killers or a direct threat to you, and we didn't want to jeopardize our investigation.

"If anybody else from the RCMP contacts you for any reason, please let me know. I will leave my card. Wishing you both all the best on a speedy recovery." The inspector said his goodbyes and left the room.

Henry and Julia looked at each other, wide-eyed in disbelief.

"This is crazy. Sounds like we are still involved whether we like it or not," Henry said.

"Unfortunately, I think you're right."

Sophie called that evening. She had visited Henry during his recovery a couple of times, but he had been unconscious at the time.

"Doing much better, thanks, Sophie," he said when she asked. "I am sure our Hecla story is still making the news from time to time."

"Yes! After the series we ran, and my subsequent research, my editor told me to keep an eye on things up at Hecla as we all know this isn't over."

"You're not kidding, Sophie. I cannot reveal everything, but we are hoping the police have a plan to catch whoever is at large and finally put this matter to bed before anybody else gets killed."

"Anything I can do, Henry?"

"Keep yourself out of harm's way, Sophie. You don't want to get in this person or persons' way, they are clearly ruthless."

"I hear you, Henry. I hope we can get together once everything is concluded."

"It's a promise," Henry said, chuckling over the phone.

CHAPTER THIRTY-SIX

The next couple of weeks were tough on both Julia and Henry. After getting released from the hospital, they endured constant rounds of physio appointments and trips back to the hospital. Henry still had recurring headaches the neurologist said would probably continue for quite a while. The physio sessions were tough and painful at first. After a couple of weeks of home care, Henry became less reliant on Julia, and she finally managed to claim her house back. Much as it was a relief that they were both feeling better, the anxiety of the threat to their lives had not gone away, at least for now.

Henry was mystified how he could possibly be a threat to anyone. He didn't know who the shooter was, so what could the motivation have been to try to run them over?

Eventually, they got a call from Inspector Smit who told them that they had started to track down relatives of Daniel Sigurdson and that from their intelligence, there had been no evidence of any efforts to sell the Fabergé egg.

A month or so later, Henry and Julia decided they needed to go up to the lake in spite of the fact that Jim was looking after the grass and keeping an eye on the property.

They kept in touch with Inspector Smit, and they had a plainclothes officer with them at all times, which was proving to be painful. The RCMP, Henry, and Julia all knew this wasn't a good long-term plan. Henry and Julia indicated that they were ready to cooperate to get this whole affair resolved as soon as possible.

Bit by bit, their life returned to normal.

By late summer, the morning coolness of the season had crept in. By the end of the first week of September there would be frost. There were still some warm days ahead, but the die had been cast that the best days of the year were behind them. The trees were turning a myriad of colours—a sight to behold; it was Henry and Julia's favourite time of the year.

After a hot and dry August, the grass had had its final growing spurt of the year. Although it took them two days, Julia and Henry managed to cut it themselves, a sure sign their rehabilitation was continuing.

One Saturday morning, Henry got a call from Sophie who told him that she, Cecile, and their dogs, Chloe and Esme, were staying at the hotel in Hecla for the long weekend.

"Hi, Henry. How is the recovery going for you and Julia?"

"Pretty good, Sophie, thanks for asking. We managed to cut the grass ourselves over the last couple of days, so we must be on the mend. Popping over sometime?" Henry asked.

"Would love to—we are having dinner with Marisa tonight, but Sunday and Monday nights are open. We've been spending the days hiking the trails—this place is beautiful in the fall Henry, absolutely amazing."

"Let's make it Monday night."

"Fine with us. What should we bring?"

"The dogs if you like and a bottle of red is always good. Will 6:30 p.m. work for you?"

"Great, thanks. Looking forward to it. See you soon."

Henry called out to Julia on the deck and told her they were coming.

"No problem," Julia replied, "as I am assuming you're doing a barbecue."

Jim, who had been around helping out with odd jobs, popped by with some of Ingrid's dainties and stayed for coffee. They sat together out on the deck, overlooking the lake.

"It's been a magnificent September so far," Jim said.

"You're right, Jim. After the cold, long spring, it's a nice consolation prize," Julia said smiling as she presented the plate of dainties to Jim.

"Actually, no thank you—Ingrid is saying I am getting a little plump and has me on a bit of a diet right now—she sent those over for you two."

"More for us then," Julia said, putting the plate down in front of Henry. Henry took another one, although he already had two on his plate.

"No dieting going on here," Julia said, grinning at Jim.

"Fishing is good right now," Jim said, looking encouragingly at Henry.

"I didn't know you were a fisher, Jim," Henry said. "Chris has asked me numerous times and I've never really been interested."

"So what is it going to be Henry: yes or no?"

Henry thought for a second. "Yes, thanks Jim. It would be a good experience. Just don't let Chris know," Henry said, laughing. "One thing I have learned recently is how precious life is and now is the time to say yes to new experiences."

"Wow, I never thought you would say those words, Henry. Great. How about tomorrow? Let's not let the opportunity slip through your fingers," Jim said, grinning.

It was agreed, there and then, that they would get an early start at 7:00 a.m.

"So, do we have to bring your minder with you?" Jim said.

"Mike goes everywhere with me Jim—you know that," Henry replied.

"OK, I'll pack him a lunch, too," Jim said as he stepped out the front door to head up Henry's driveway. "See you tomorrow—leaving promptly at 7:00 a.m.," he shouted.

Henry closed the front door and headed to the kitchen where Julia was putting the plates and cups in the sink.

"So we are having fish for dinner tomorrow night?" Julia asked a little mockingly.

"No, I wouldn't bank on it. Not sure what kind of fisherman I am going to turn out to be."

"Okey dokey," Julia said as Henry gave her a squeeze.

Later that evening, Henry shared his plan with Mike, who then reported it up the line. Mike insisted that their route be agreed upon ahead of time, so Henry confirmed with Jim that they would be fishing in the channel between the two islands. Henry was actually looking forward to his fishing experience. He checked the weather forecast. It would be five degrees overnight but it was to be a sunny day tomorrow and up to eighteen degrees with little or no wind. That helped him to select appropriate clothing from his wardrobe.

Julia was propped up reading a book—it was romantic fiction, a change from the murder mysteries she normally chose.

"Good book?" Henry asked.

Julia replied, "Yes," clearly engrossed in her book, "recent events have rather soured me to murder mysteries."

Henry decided that saying nothing was probably the prudent thing to do. He grabbed a book of crosswords from the side of the bed and flipped to a clean page. For some reason he felt at peace, maybe due to Mike being in the other bedroom. To ease some aches and pains, he adjusted himself in the bed. It wasn't long before it was lights out and both of them drifted off to sleep.

CHAPTER THIRTY-SEVEN

There was just a hint of light when Henry got up. He was surprised he hadn't needed the alarm clock; he was obviously looking forward to his day.

He could hear Mike using the main washroom.

Henry was up quickly—a cup of coffee and cereal was on the menu. A second protection officer was just arriving to keep an eye on Julia while Mike and Henry were out.

He checked his phone; Sophie must have called late the night before as there was a message. He decided he would check it when he got back from fishing.

Henry could hear Jim's truck starting up next door—headed to the harbour of course, to get everything sorted with the boat and the fishing equipment.

Henry and the Mike arrived just after 7:00 a.m., parked the car, and headed down into the area where the pleasure boats were moored. Jim raised his arm in greeting. Henry waved back.

"There he is, Mike." Henry was pointing to the back of the harbour.

The boat was gently idling when they arrived. Henry carefully climbed in with Mike just behind him.

"Hi Jim, meet Mike, my protection officer." The two guys briefly shook hands.

"OK, guys. Coffee is in the thermoses over there," Jim said and pointed to a canvas bag at the back of the boat. Mugs are in the bag, too. Sorry, I've only got black coffee."

"That works," Mike said as he shuffled down the boat to the bag.

"Anybody else?"

"I'll have a mug," Jim said.

"The bucket at the back is for peeing in, gentlemen. Standing over the side is probably not an option with the swells we'll have today. The water is cold, and I don't want to be fishing either of you out. Much safer to pee into the bucket on your knees."

"Your life jackets are in front of you. Please put them on: safety first," Jim said. It was a comfort to Henry that Jim was safety conscious.

"We're going to head north around the headland and then west to the area between Punk and Little Punk islands. Should take about twenty minutes—this engine is not the fastest," Jim said.

"Mike, can you step out and untie the mooring rope please?" In seconds, Jim was cautiously backing out of the mooring spot and then they were heading into the main channel of the harbour.

As they exited the harbour, Jim accelerated the boat and headed north. It was a fairly bumpy ride; the wind was blowing from the northwest. It was a cold wind, and everybody hunkered down as best as they could to stay out of the breeze, which was not easy in an open boat. After an exhilarating ride, they arrived in the relatively calmer spot between the two islands.

"Right. Here we are, boys," Jim said. "I'm going to throw the anchor in to stabilize our position, so we don't have to use the trolling motor too much."

Jim handed each of them a rod. "Not sure what you guys know about fishing?"

"I'm pretty experienced," Mike said, grabbing his rod and a small container of live bait that were wriggling around. "I'm good to go."

"I'm going to need some coaching," Henry said. "I'm almost a complete novice."

Jim explained the workings of the rod and reel, as well as how to load his hook with bait.

"Yuck, these things are still alive," Henry said in disgust.

"It's better if the bait is wriggling around," Henry. "That's how the fish like it."

"Maybe so, but it takes a little to get used to it," Henry said, still uncomfortable.

After a while, he got the hang of things. Mike caught a small pike early on and he was definitely getting into it.

To his surprise, even Henry got a bite and with Jim's help pulled in what turned out to be the biggest fish of the day, an eight-pound pickerel. Henry was pretty self-satisfied with this effort.

After a couple of hours, the weather had warmed up and the wind had really died down. The boat had drifted a little in spite of the anchor and was now closer to Little Punk Island. They were also obscured from Henry and Julia's cottage now—Julia was likely looking out for them.

There didn't appear at first to be another boat on the water. Then, Jim was saying something about a boat moored on the north side of Little Punk Island, when there was a *crack!* Mike let out a cry, jerked, and tumbled off the back of the boat into the lake with a splash. Henry, momentarily stunned, quickly reached down, and attempted to grab Mike by his life jacket to stop him drifting away—a concerning red cloud was spreading out around Mike's body.

"Get down! Get down! There's a shooter on Little Punk Island," Mike shouted once he felt shielded by the boat. "I've been hit."

Another shot was fired, Henry released his grip on Mike, and he and Jim did as Mike had commanded, pressing themselves as tightly to the floor of the small boat as they could.

"The shooter is an excellent shot—we have to get out of here fast—he's aiming to finish us all off," Mike gasped. "Grab my radio! Press the 'transmit' button and say, 'Mayday! Under fire!'"

Henry scrambled around in the bottom of the boat and did as he was told.

What seemed like minutes later, but was likely only seconds, a voice responded, "Received. Understood. How many shooters? Anybody injured?"

"Officer down—think there is one shooter," Henry shouted into the radio

"Help is on its way—"

The rain of bullets continued. There was no way Jim could safely lift himself out of the bottom of the boat to start the engine. They were like rats in a trap. Maybe the shooter had heard the radio and assumed help was on its way and wanted to finish things quickly. Henry suddenly realized he had been shot, and Jim too—adrenaline was pumping, and he was on the edge of panic. It was not looking hopeful. Mike had now drifted a few feet away and appeared to be unconscious. Thank God he had his life jacket on. Jim, looking terrified, was curled in the fetal position, holding his left thigh, blood flowing between his fingers.

With the sound of an approaching aircraft, the firing stopped. From his perspective from the bottom of the boat, Henry could see a helicopter approaching from the direction of Hecla Island. It was heading low and fast across the water to their location. Henry knew they wouldn't have survived much longer without some kind of intervention. He bravely peeked over the side and saw a large police speedboat heading in their direction from the northside of the island. As it pulled up beside them, a paramedic pulled Mike from the water and began to assess him. Henry was vaguely aware that someone from the helicopter was feeding information to the officers on the boat, so they knew where to shoot towards the gunman. Their fire had alarmed the shooter, as shots from his direction had ceased.

"Call for the Star air ambulance helicopter while I check the other two," the paramedic shouted to the officer in charge, he clambered into the fishing boat, and performed a quick assessment of Jim, then Henry. He spoke quickly and efficiently. "I have a superficial bullet wound to an arm, bleeding under control, and what looks like a more serious thigh wound. Stabilizing his bleeding as priority." An officer relayed that information to dispatch then they were all quickly loaded onto the speedboat. Within seconds, they were headed for the harbour.

Apparently the Stars ambulance helicopter had been dispatched to meet the vehicle that was whisking Mike, Jim and Henry down the highway back to Gimli and winnipeg.

Henry was told that he had lost a little blood and the wound need to be cleaned out and stitched, but his injury was not serious.

Back on shore, Julia had already arrived with Ingrid and drove to Winnipeg and the Health Science Centre. While Henry got his treatment, Julia and Ingrid went to find out the status of Jim and the officer.

Mike had been shot in the abdomen and required extensive surgery, but the bullet had fortunately missed all his major organs. He was expected to make a full recovery.

Jim's injury turned out to be extensive; the bullet needed to be removed and there was vascular damage to be repaired, on top of all the blood loss.

After thirty minutes or so, Henry returned to the waiting room after his treatment. Julia and Ingrid were sitting together at the back of the room chatting quietly.

"So what is the latest ladies?" Henry said, walking up to them, his arm bandaged and in a sling.

"Mike and Jim are both in surgery, so we won't know anything for a while," Julia said. "Thank God you're OK! You are far too old for active duty, Henry." Julia reached up to hug him. "I don't know what to do with you." She was smiling but had tears running down her face.

They realized that Ingrid was living with the uncertainty of what was going on with Jim and quickly turned to support her. She was stoic and just smiled. "Waiting is difficult," was all she would say.

"So what is happening up at Hecla—is this nightmare over?" Henry asked.

"No idea," Julia said. "You folks were our first priority."

A nurse approached and asked Julia and Henry to go with her.

CHAPTER THIRTY-EIGHT

The nurse escorted Henry and Julia into a small room where Inspector Smit was already sitting, He rose to greet them.

"Sit down, folks," he said indicating the two chairs in front of him.

They did, with Julia assertively made it clear that she was extremely angry and disappointed with the RCMP for putting both her, her husband, and their friend in mortal danger. Smit remained quiet and composed as Julia let off steam. When he was sure she had finished, he nodded in a resigned manner.

"Yes, we are sorry Henry and Jim ended up in harm's way, but we needed a method to draw the murderer out. We succeeded—"

"Yes, but Jim was not in on it, and he is seriously injured, and it could have been worse," Henry interrupted.

"Yes, you are right Henry," said Inspector Smit. "Most unfortunate. We still have not managed to apprehend the suspect. He abandoned a boat on the mainland, stolen from the harbour, and disappeared into the forest, where we assume he is hiding now. We unfortunately did not have enough feet on the ground to do a ground search to flush him out, but we have secured the causeway—his only escape route—until more resources arrive. We'll keep you posted."

As they left the office, Henry said to Julia. "I don't have a good feeling about this. I think the assailant is going to slip away."

"I really hope you are wrong, Henry. I'm not so sure how much more of this nightmare I can take."

They returned to the waiting area and sat again with Ingrid. "Apparently Jim is out of surgery," Ingrid said. "A nurse just spoke to me. He is doing well but is still unconscious."

"That's great news, Ingrid," Julia said, giving her neighbour a hug.

Henry turned on his almost-dead phone. He had just remembered that Sophie had left a message. In fact, she had rang again recently, but Henry had been getting treated for his gunshot wound.

He stepped outside and called her.

"Henry! How are you? We heard that you'd all been shot." There was obvious concern in her voice.

"This time I got away relatively unscathed," Henry said, "which is more than I can say for my neighbour, Jim, and Mike, the police officer, who are both seriously injured but at least out of danger."

"Well that's a relief."

"Thanks Sophie. What's happening there?"

"The police are looking for the shooter—nobody can leave the hotel for our own safety."

"Good advice Sophie—advice you should both take. You called last night, Sophie; what was on your mind?"

"Oh, yes. This is important. Last night we were with Marisa, and we got talking about the case and the discovery of who I think was Daniel Sigurdson—you know, the remains? Marisa has the genealogy of all the all the descendants of the original settlers, created in the early 1960s, which she inherited when her mother and father passed away. It turns out that Daniel Sigurdson was Greta's nephew, the son of her younger sister, Alda. She had married a Sigurdson from the village and gave birth to Daniel in 1887. Marisa said she would look down in the basement she says she knows it is there."

After two days, the search was called off, and it seemed the murderer had melted into the woods. The police embarrassingly admitting the suspect was probably long gone. After interviews, the guests at the hotel were allowed to go home.

Sophie had more news when she contacted Henry.

"Hi, Henry. It's Sophie. I have just gotten home from dropping off Cecile and the dogs, but I am coming back up. Apparently, Marisa has found that genealogical document I told you about. Can you meet me at her house in about two and a half hours?"

"Of course I'll be there, Sophie."

DEATH AT THE POINT

"OK, great. See you soon."

Two and a half hours later, Marisa, Sophie, Henry, and Julia were sitting around the kitchen table, trying to make sense of the rather faded document spread out in front of them. Their police protection was outside—sadly, Mike was not with them—sitting on the deck and watching the occasional vehicle go by.

Sophie scanned the document and quickly located Daniel Sigurdson's name.

"There he is," Sophie said, pointing to a section of the document. Daniel Sigurdson although he died or disappeared young, had a child named Elisabet who was born just before he disappeared. Elisabet had married a local fisher from the island, Gunnar Einarson, and they had a daughter, Anna, and two boys, Jon and Ari. The youngest, Ari, left the island and found work in Winnipeg, marrying Anita Arnason, a local girl with an Icelandic background. They had three boys, Chris, David and Simon.

"Is the David Einarson who died of a heart attack on the island the same person?" Henry asked, looking at Marisa, stunned.

"Sorry, Henry. I don't have a clue. After the first generation, families tend to veer off in all directions."

"Julia, you got to know David's aunt at his funeral. I'm sure if you contacted her, she could confirm or deny these connections very quickly," Henry excitedly. "Can you call her now?"

"Sure, I have Doris's number." Julia put the phone on speaker as it dialled.

"Hi Doris, it's Julia Trevellyn. We met at David's funeral and a couple of times afterwards. How are you doing?"

"Pretty good, Julia. How are you?"

"Crazy, if I am honest. You've probably heard about all the drama on Hecla."

"Actually, I have heard, and I was meaning to call you," Doris replied.

"The suspect the police have been searching for has probably escaped but there is a possibility that David may have been in cahoots with someone else, in addition to working for his client, Kristian Kjartanson. We know David has a younger r brother Simon but aonther brother Chris?"

245

"Yes, Simon was at the funeral. Chris, the older one, was away on assignment for his job and couldn't make it back in time. He is not close to his younger brothers; they had a falling out years ago."

"Great," Julia replied, very encouraged. "That means there may be a direct family connection between David and a body that was exhumed at the same time the tall Ukrainian's body was discovered; we are guessing it is Daniel Sigurdson. So Doris, where was Chris working that he couldn't come home for the funeral?"

"He is retired but works for the RCMP up north from time to time, in some remote Arctic locations. He lives on Hecla—you probably know him."

"We do know a Chris who works for the RCMP—a neighbour of ours who lives a couple of houses down—but we never knew his last name!"

Julia and Henry looked at one another in total shock. "This is too much of a coincidence Julia," Henry. Sophie and Marisa could see the looks of astonishment on their faces and wanted to ask about the source of it but sat silently so Doris wasn't aware of Julia's entourage.

"So the police think they have found Daniel Sigurdson's body," Doris said. "That is amazing; it was always suspected that one of his fellow criminals killed him. It's a bit of a family legend. He was the black sheep in the family and—"

Julia interrupted her. "Doris, the police have not fully identified the body yet. We are still awaiting the DNA results from willing potential family members. It was just Henry and I coming up with possibilities. Please don't assume we are right at this stage—let's wait for an official police announcement. Apparently, they will be matching the deceased with family members."

"OK, Julia. I'll wait. Next time you are in town, let's meet for coffee. I've enjoyed our chats."

"Will do Doris. Take care. Speak to you soon."

"Something is not right here," Henry said. "Chris never said a word that he was related to anyone or anything to do with all of this. He must have been devastated when we uncovered David's body, but he didn't let on or say a word that it was his brother, and I was standing right next to him. Now that I think about it, he's always appeared a little oddly disinterested. But how is he involved? What would be his motivation?" Henry asked himself, confused.

"My guess is he was involved with his brother, David, in some way," Julia suggested.

"Why would he hide that?" Sophie asked.

"My guess? They were both up to something." Henry added, "I cannot think of any other explanation. At the time we discovered David, the other body had not been found—and he died of natural causes. Chris probably hoped that everything would die down. He was probably aware of the tall red-bearded stranger. He probably didn't expect Vlad and Dmitry to show up or the police to go back in and undertake the extensive search of the site that they did."

"So why was David there?" Marisa asked.

"He probably went to the site originally as part of his investigation into the issues that Kristian Kjartanson was having with his properties, maybe to get a sense of what Mr. Kjartanson was proposing and then stumbled onto what Andriy Krafchenko, the tall, red-headed Ukrainian, was doing," Henry suggested.

"We know in the Einarson family lore, from Doris, that they had long suspected that one of his criminal buddies had probably killed their great-grandfather Daniel Einarson and the most likely site was the original settlement, Hecla Island or on the way there or back from Winnipeg."

"I think David and Chris must have done some research and discovered the fact that no money or valuables were discovered when Krafchenko was arrested and he never revealed, at the time to the police anyway, where the loot was."

"There was never any hard proof that the original settlement was a definite hideout for the two criminals, but the recovery of Daniel Sigurdson's body and the metal box, if that's who it is, proves they were there," Sophie said out loud what everybody was thinking.

"My guess," Henry suggested, "was that David Einarson visited the site, was probably suspicious of why the tall red-bearded stranger was digging holes all over the property, and confronted him. At that stage, David didn't have the letter and was probably acting on a hunch that something valuable was hidden there. Maybe not getting a straight answer, he and Andriy had an altercation? Somehow, David ended up killing him, and dying of a heart attack after burying him. He couldn't have called Chris, as there is no cell service on the point."

"Seems like a plausible story," Julia mused. "Clearly, David didn't get any real information from Andriy, or if he did, it died with him," Julia said. "Chris was probably concerned when he heard David went missing but may not have even known that David was working on an investigation that involved the original settlement. Maybe he had nothing to do with what went on until after his brother died? Henry, now it makes some sense why he was so happy to accompany you on your ski trip over to the original settlement—maybe he wanted to see if his brother was there.

"Likely, Chris was on his own," Julia continued the logic. "So now he's on the hunt for more information, the two Ukrainians turn up out of the blue, and Chris must have seen that as too much of a coincidence, hence the burglary at the rented place and the killing of Jantie who likely interrupted Chris while he was searching the bedroom for some clue and found the letter. Nobody in the RCMP had linked him to David or his death and Chris made a point of staying away from his funeral and not advertising they were brothers. Any attempt by Chris to survey and dig the site himself was complicated by continual police investigations and the arrival of Vlad and Dmitry."

Henry continued the thought process, "So Chris became confident that there had to be something of value hidden there somewhere, and this was reinforced when, as he must have suspected, the third body, potentially his great-grandfather, Daniel Einarson, was discovered at the same time as Andriy's."

Julia chimed in again. "But what was his motivation for killing the Ukrainians, running us over, and shooting you, Jim, and Mike? Revenge for Daniel Einarson's murder? For the murder of his great-grandfather? Doesn't make any sense."

"Greed maybe—" suggested Marisa.

"They didn't even know how much," Henry interrupted. "Surely that was a pretty reckless thing to be doing. What I don't understand is that if Chris suspected I had seen him or in any way suspected he was involved, then surely I would have told the police and he would have been interviewed, right?"

"From Chris's perspective, you are the only loose end," Sophie suggested. "As far as we know, there is no direct evidence to connect Chris with the break-in and Jantie's murder, the attack on you and Julia, the killing and truck-burning, or the shooting incidents. You can guarantee that he has alibis for these periods or time—remember he's been a cop for a long time."

"Well, it is going to get interesting if the police have the DNA proof that the old body found was Daniel Sigurdson's. We'll know that once the current-day relatives' DNA tests are collated. It also won't be long before the link with David will lead them to the coincidental proximity of Chris," Henry said.

"Henry, we need to alert the police, right now," Julia said.

"We can do that, but without any evidence, they cannot hold him," Henry said. "We still don't have confirmation that the dead guy is Daniel Sigurdson."

"I don't like the idea of living a couple of cottages away from a man we called a friend, who may have tried to kill us on more than one occasion," Julia said. "The guy is a total menace; he has to be arrested. I'm ringing the police and sharing what we know. I'm not sitting on my hands anymore."

Julia took out her phone and put it on speaker. "Inspector Smit, this is the Trevellyns ringing you to share information you may or may not be aware of. I know you have not confirmed the DNA of the older body found at the original settlement, but we are convinced that it is Daniel Sigurdson who is the great-grandfather of Chris Einarson, one of your semi-retired police officers who lives up here at Hecla and is a friend and neighbour of ours. David Einarson was his brother. We are convinced that Chris is the primary suspect in the murders and injuries that have occurred."

"Stupidly, I've been confiding in him all along," Henry said, "never thinking he was involved in this at all."

"But what was his motive?" Inspector Smit asked.

"We thought maybe it's revenge for the death of their great-grandfather. But it makes no sense to go on this rampage to avenge a relative that died over a hundred years ago, when the culprit was probably a guy by the name of Krafchenko who is long dead. We think it was plain greed—that while with me, Chris discovered the excavations being done by Andrij at the original settlement, and the body of his brother. Somehow he started to get suspicious without any real proof at that time that it involved his family in some way," Henry offered.

"The discovery of the body, still yet to be positively identified, of his great-grandfather Daniel confirmed in his own mind that he and another criminal, likely Krafchenko, probably buried something in the area. Of course, Chris didn't have a clue where it could be, but was probably convinced Vlad and Dmitry knew something and that is why Chris broke in and searched their place. Once he found that letter and had it translated, it all came together. Then, all he had to do was stake out the site, let Vlad and Dmitry—and, stupidly, me— do all the work. When we uncovered the metal box, he made his move. Dmitry told me the egg was worth more than ten million dollars at auction."

"OK. I have heard enough, folks," Inspector Smit said. "Let me follow up on the DNA testing to see if we can at least confirm any family link between David and Chris Einarson and Daniel Sigurdson. We will also go over all the evidence we have to see if we can build a case now that we have a potential suspect in the frame. Please sit tight—go home to Winnipeg—we'll continue to ensure police protection and will put Chris Einarson under surveillance before we bring him in for questioning." With that, he said goodbye.

Henry pressed "end" on Julia's phone. "Some hope at last this nightmare could be over," Julia said as he handed it back to her.

"Yes, but I am going to have a great story to tell when this is all over," Sophie said.

"*When it's all over*, Sophie," Henry said." We don't want to spook Chris before the police are ready to make their move."

The police were sufficiently worried about the threat to Julia and Henry's safety that they were relocated to a safe house out of town while preparations were made to complete their case and prepare to make the arrest.

DEATH AT THE POINT

Chris was clearly a dangerous man and they wanted to avoid more loss of life. They had no evidence to suggest that Jane was an accomplice, so she was potentially a hostage in the making and they decided to make the arrest away from his house. They also planned to lure Chris to the RCMP offices in Gimli for a briefing of another temporary assignment up north. The trap was laid and a contingent of fully armed officers were waiting for him the moment he stepped out of his car. He was arrested peacefully and charged with the second-degree murders of Jantie Bjornason, and first-degree murder of Vladimir Krafchenko, and Yuri "Dmitry: Melnyk. He was also charged with the attempted murders of Henry Trevellyn—twice—Julia Trevellyn, Jim Briar, and Mike Bridges.

Inspector Smit had called to say Chris was safely in custody.

"Hi, Henry. We have enough circumstantial evidence to charge him. We found a copy of the letter and the English translation, hidden in his mattress. We are working on finding the translator to confirm the date Chris requested the work to be done. From the blood found in the bathroom sink at the Ukrainian's house, a sample matched Chris's. Jantie Bjornason must have injured him in a scuffle, so he likely cleaned up in their bathroom—not quite carefully enough. His alibis are weak and although nothing placed him specifically at the scenes where criminal activities occurred, it didn't rule him out, either.

"We also investigated both Chris and his brother a little more. It turns out they both had financial problems. David was having an affair and spending all his money on his young lover, according to his wife, and Chris has a serious online-gambling addiction. It seems clear to us this whole case was driven by the opportunity or at least the possibility to make some serious money. Oh, and it is a very high level of probability that the old body is that of Daniel Sigurdson—we were successfully able to test a number of people who are now confirmed relatives."

"Well this is a serious relief, Inspector Smit. I'll tell Julia. Thank you," Henry said.

"No problem. Thanks for all your help, Henry."

Henry headed to the garden where Julia was cleaning up some old flowers in a bed by the fence.

"You will never guess," Henry said.

"What?" Julia said, smiling.

"Inspector Smit says they arrested Chris Einarson this morning. Apparently, they had enough evidence to make the arrest and hopefully a conviction comes of this."

"Oh, what a relief!" Julia reached out to Henry, and they hugged for a good couple of minutes. Both of them felt the stress of the last couple of years, if not melt away, at least fade a little. It would take time for normal to be normal again.

The story of the arrest made front-page news and, of course, Sophie had a little more information than the other journalists, which she shamelessly exploited like all good news people did.

The island's resident, shocked by the revelation that it was one of their own, took a couple of days to process the news but soon afterward, the weather and other normal things filled people's conversations again, life goes on.

CHAPTER THIRTY-NINE

It was clear that Jane knew nothing of Chris's criminal behaviour. Though it was a second marriage for both of them, they had been together for twenty-five years, so she was understandably shocked.

Julia and Henry paid her a visit. It was important to both of them that Jane knew there was no malice or bad feelings towards her. In fact, there was only sympathy. Despite the support she received from Henry, Julia, and the other neighbours, she decided to sell the property and move back to Winnipeg.

"I like it here, but it was really Chris who loved the great outdoors and Hecla Island," she said. "His roots are here, and he's passionate about the place. Now he's going to be spending the rest of his life in prison—the recent bad experiences have completely wiped out all the good times we had, and I feel like I need to make a clean break. I feel betrayed," she had said the last time they spoke. Henry and Julia had told Christine and Johnny about the sale. They quickly put in an offer on the cottage, and it was accepted.

Henry was struggling to process all that had happened. In all the years he was in the police force, he had had some scrapes and near misses, but it was inconceivable to him that in his retirement years he and Julia had come so close to a violent death—in Henry's case, not once but twice—in such a short period of time and at the hand of somebody he considered a friend.

Henry reflected and contemplated all in the aftermath of the events and rationalized that the violence and greed of the past had, in a strange way, metamorphized to the present. It was shocking and would shake any right-minded person to one's foundation—but bad things do happen.

However, the natural life on Hecla continued, in spite of the evil things that men did. That had always been the attraction of the place: the peace and quiet that had originally lured them to the island would return, physically and emotionally.

In spite of an intensive investigation, the Fabergé egg was never located.

"Maybe it's in the hands of a private collector, but not likely. Chris is not confessing and there is no evidence that he has ever benefited financially from his crimes," Inspector Smit had said the last time they spoke.

EPILOGUE

The Descendants of the Original Settlement Association reflected again on Kristian Kjartanson's original proposal for the original settlement development on Kjartanson Point and decided to support his concept. Of course, he agreed that any further graves found would be marked with respect.

Greta's diary was the main resource for the rebuilding project. The University of Manitoba completed the necessary archeological work and digs prior to the redevelopment. After a lengthy consultative planning stage, construction was planned to begin in the spring of 2022. Kristian and a number of benefactors provided fifty per cent of the cash and the province the other half. A charitable foundation was set up with a board of directors from the community and the funding agencies, which would oversee the operation and maintenance of the hamlet. With the municipality's permission, Daniel Sigurdson was reburied close to the spot where the two boys who had died of smallpox so long ago were interred.

A gravel road was cut to the project along the footprint of the original track and a small parking area was laid out among the trees a little way off from the development, so it didn't feel quite so isolated anymore.

However, in the winter, the gate on the main road would be locked. Julia and Henry would occasionally walk the road to the site, any road noise fading away as they entered the forest and disappeared into history—back into a harsh, tough time when people needed to work together to survive each day.

Henry, although in no way wishing to live in those tough times, reflected on how society seemed to have lost some of that sense of community. It had been replaced with a level of selfishness that ultimately could lead to the slippery slope of anarchy and criminality, when the challenges of the future may be staring Manitobans starkly in the face.

As Henry and Julia walked the original settlement grounds, they stared out across the lake, arm-in-arm, grateful to have each other and to be able to enjoy the peace of this special place: a testament to the persistence and courage of the first Icelandic settlers and those nameless people who came before.

The wind was a little cool; the only sound was the gentle rustling of the leaves and the far away sound of a woodpecker going about his business. Julia shivered and Henry pulled her close.

Henry had an uncomfortable feeling that they were not alone. Was it the spirits of the people from the past and recent past who had died at this spot? Or somebody else in the here and now?

Henry took a deep breath and pulled Julia even closer.

Printed in the USA
CPSIA information can be obtained
at www.ICGtesting.com
LVHW091353151223
766505LV00002B/162

9 781039 166998

Also By the Author

The Menmenet Series
The Jackal of Inpu
The Lion of Bastet
The Bull of Mentju

The Founding Fathers Mysteries
Murder at Mount Vernon

The Pirates of Khonoë
Hyperkill

Death of a Golden State

THE BLOCKCHAIN KILLING

A Technothriller

Robert J. Muller

POESYS ASSOCIATES
San Francisco

Copyright © 2025 Robert J. Muller, all rights reserved.

Published in the United States of America by Poesys Associates, San Francisco.

www.poesys.com

ISBN: 978-1-939386-17-5 (print)
ISBN: 978-1-939386-18-2 (ebook)

Library of Congress Control Number: 2025901067

Library of Congress Subject Headings:
Thrillers (Fiction)
Political fiction
Human rights—Fiction
Social justice—Fiction
Espionage—Fiction
Cyberterrorism—Fiction
Suspense fiction, American
Blockchain (Technology)—Fiction
Cryptocurrencies—Fiction
Bitcoin—Fiction
Electronic funds transfers—Fiction
Digital currencies—Fiction
Cryptography—Fiction

This is a work of fiction. Names, characters, businesses, places, events, locales, and incidents are either the products of the author's imagination or used in a fictitious manner. Any resemblance to actual persons, living or dead, or actual events is purely coincidental.

Cover Design by Brandi Doane McCann
https://www.ebook-coverdesigns.com

Published February 1, 2025
First Edition

To M'Linn and Theo

Between the idea

And the reality

Between the motion

And the act

Falls the shadow.
> T. S. Eliot, The Hollow Men

Right and wrong are so 20th century.
> Nick Galifianakis in The Washington Post 11/18/2022

To be a rock, and not to roll….
> Jimmy Page and Robert Plant, "Stairway to Heaven"

CHAPTER ONE
Alec's Ideals

Every aspect of the day captivated Alec Chenais, from when he entered McGill University's computer center until he and his mother departed late at night. The global impact and criminal intent behind the cyberattack on the university stunned him, but the security technology and the people wielding it impressed him even more.

Mary Bethune Chenais, PhD, a full professor of computer science, had brought sixteen-year-old Alec in as a kind of "bring your precocious and naïve youth into work day." She'd told Alec that she wanted him to learn what McGill had to offer to an undergraduate. His mother, as usual, pleaded urgent work as she led him into the big room where the systems and network engineers hung out doing whatever it was they did. Alec assumed she'd turn him over to some guy who'd bore him to death, then she'd leave and come back in eight hours, annoyed at having to find him.

They halted at the door and peered into the room. It was a madhouse. People yelling at each other. Engineers typing furiously at their workstations. His mother looked around and spotted the supervisor.

"Hey, Ralph. What's going on?" She patted Alec on the shoulder. "I brought Alec in for you to show him the real world of computers. For college."

"Oh, Professor Chenais. Oh, my God. No. It's." Ralph, eyes popping, stuttered into silence.

Mary grew a little impatient. "I can see things are out of control, Ralph. Here, you take Alec and show him how you do your job, cleaning up all this mess. All right?" Without waiting for an answer, she pushed Alec toward Ralph with a gentle nudge, turned, and walked out.

Alec gave Ralph a big smile. Why not get on his good side? His mother's attitude toward chaos was that of a firm teacher toward unruly ADHD students. Her leaving so abruptly told him that she had no formal authority over Ralph or his engineers.

Ralph's mouth dropped open in dismay as he looked Alec over. Alec stiffened, trying to look like a college student, although it would be two years before he actually was one.

Ralph closed his mouth and looked a little wild. He burst out in Quebecois French. "Look, kid. I have a crisis on my hands. Your mother —well, you know what she's like. If you want to stay, shut up and watch."

"What's going on? Should I call you Ralph?"

"Call me any damn thing you want, kid. What's your name again?"

"Alec."

"*Bien*. What's going on, Alec, is a massive distributed denial of service attack on this data center."

"Someone's overloading your sites with a huge number of requests, right?" Alec had had a computer nearby since he was six, and he'd learned a lot from social media. That was one reason he agreed to come to the computer center with his mother. He wanted to check out the pros, and to learn about some real technology.

Ralph half smiled. "*Oui, c'est vrai.*" He patted Alec on the shoulder and switched to English. "OK, you can stay. Follow me around. You got questions, ask. If we're too busy, we'll ignore you. Have fun!"

Alec asked, "Who's attacking?"

Ralph pointed to a web browser open on a nearby workstation. "It's happening all over the world. The network security engineers think it's some government doing a cyberwar test-run on random sites. We got lucky," he said sarcastically. "They haven't been able to trace it back to whoever's responsible. Too many layers of anonymous servers and botnets. *Vous comprenez?*"

"*Oui,*" Alec said with another smile.

The DDoS attack lasted all day, with no rest for the weary engineers. Alec spent a lot of time with the security team, awed by their wizardry and arcane knowledge. It was like watching Gandalf at work, holding back the legions of Mordor. Alec itched to pitch in and help, but he quickly realized that he didn't know enough. He had to get those skills. At university. It wasn't fair to attack a university just to test some kind of criminal software. All the people and research the denial of service hurt. And all the time the security team had to spend containing it.

This was what he wanted to do with his life. With the right skills, he could help fight things like this cyberattack. Just…not at McGill. Not in Montreal. Not near his parents.

His mother came to pick him up at midnight, later than expected and clearly annoyed. She was more understanding of Ralph. She and the other professors had swiftly grasped the problem as their research websites crashed. The security team had reinforced their firewalls and worked like dogs to contain the attack, which was petering out by midnight.

"Well, I hope you learned a lot, Alec. That's not what computer science is all about, it's just a big pain in the ass. You'll see once we get the quantum computer up and running. I'll show you."

Alec rolled his eyes in the dark night. In the year of our Lord 2006, quantum computing was just a few months off. Sure it was. On paper. So were fusion and artificial intelligence. But quantum computing was his mother's field, and she was a leading expert, so she must know, right? Alec shook his head. Wizards came in all shapes and sizes, and they weren't always right.

But most of the time they were. He'd seen that today. He wanted to be one of them, the real wizards.

"Here, *ti-cul,* take this and show these bastards what hell is!"

Alec Chenais involuntarily grabbed the bottle the masked Mohawk protester forced on him. He stepped back, the bottle cool in his hand but the flame at the top making his heart pound. Time slowed, his thoughts raced. The peaceful protest in downtown Montreal he'd joined with his high-school friends had gone wrong so quickly. The shouting and chaos enveloped him. He'd lost sight of the friends he'd so passionately convinced to come. It wasn't what he had imagined.

From an early age, his father had taken him to protests all over Canada, some in the States. The photo trip earlier in the year to the railroad blockades on the 2007 Aboriginal Day of Action had really fired him up. The poverty, the land grabs, the poor quality health care, the government betrayals; all of it made him shout slogans along with the Mohawks. His own white privilege, the generations of white injustice toward the Indians, snapped at his heels. But his father pulled him away, annoyed at his son's upstaging of his organization's support of the protestors.

Alec's hand closed around the bottle. Time stood still. Hell? He wasn't ready for hell. He...held his future in his hand. Hell? Or help? Wasn't that what he'd told his friends? We'll be there to support them, to *help* them protest the injustices. Add our voices. But not with *explosives*. That wasn't right. Wasn't what he believed in. His stomach ached at the thought of it. These thoughts took under a second. He took another step back.

Alec tripped on the curb and fell to the Crescent Street sidewalk, landing on his ass and scraping his back on the rough concrete. The bottle flamed through the air and smashed into the wall of a store. The glass shattered, igniting a sheet of flame that spread across the concrete wall, radiating intense heat and light before fading into nothingness.

Someone reached down to help him. But no, it was a gloved hand. It was a cop. The cop, his face anonymous behind the shield of his riot helmet, grabbed Alec's flailing arm and jerked him to his feet. The cop shouted, but the surrounding din meant Alec heard only the sound, not the meaning. He got the gist, though; it wasn't hard. Fury coursed through his 17-year-old brain as the cop pinned him against the very wall he had just attacked, his hands secured behind his back with plastic restraints. Alec struggled, defying the injustice of it all. Just as he'd struggled when his father had pulled him away from the blockade. Was this his Oka moment, the protest that would change things forever?

But as the cop pressed his face into the blackened concrete, rationality kicked in. The rage and defiance died as quickly as the flames. His life had turned upside down. The wall's harsh, stony reality crushed his idealism, at least for that day. He wasn't prepared for all this. The cop's hand pushing against his back, pinning him to the wall, drove the zipper pull of his jacket into his chest in a painful hint of humiliation to come.

Paul Chenais forcefully pushed Alec inside their house and slammed the front door. Stumbling, Alec fell against the hallway wall, leaving a black mark as his soot-smeared face slid against the white-painted plaster.

"I'll get your mother. This is…." Whatever it was, it was too much for his father to articulate. Alec slouched through to the living room and sat on the couch. His butt hurt. His wrists hurt more, from the cuffs. But his pride was unsalvageable. He unzipped his jacket and took it off. It, too, was unsalvageable, marked all over by the blackened remnants of the Molotov cocktail explosion.

"I don't have time for this," said Mary Chenais, following his father into the room. "I have to get my paper off to the journal tomorrow, and it won't write itself."

"Mary, we need to fix this," said Paul. "Sit."

His mother lowered herself stiffly into the armchair. She inspected Alec's appearance, making only one comment. "Get that filthy jacket off our clean couch, Alec. Now." Alec lifted the jacket and held it on his lap.

"What were you thinking, Alec?" asked his father, a rough edge to his voice. The edge came from the earlier shouting and from lingering anger. Alec considered the best approach to getting through this without utterly humiliating himself. Explain that it was a mistake. Explain that his pacifist views would never allow him to throw a Molotov cocktail intentionally. Plead for mercy. Turn things around and justify his supposed anarchistic action by his support for indigenous rights. So many possibilities. None would change his father's fiery anger or his mother's icy irritation.

"Well?" demanded his father belligerently.

Alec strove for a cool, rational explanation. "Here's what happened, Dad. My friends and I headed down Crescent Street in the protest, and this Mohawk guy came up to us. He pushed this bottle at me, I tripped, and the bottle flew out of my hand and into the building. Then—"

"Oh, Christ. This is the story? The best you've got?"

"Paul, can we get to the part where you tell the boy what will happen to him? I need to return to my paper."

Alec eyed his mother. He approved the demand, if not the level of support. But he knew his father too well.

"This is not how you help the cause of human rights, Alec." And there it was. The Paul Chenais lecture.

Paul Chenais was the executive director of a human-rights NGO based in Montreal. He cared deeply about every kind of human rights violation, including indigenous rights. Alec had absorbed this concern for justice all his life. It was why he'd gone to the protest. The Mohawks had endured such a long history of oppressive tyranny. His father's organization supported them with funds and publicity. Alec had handed out flyers at school, and his friends were afire with support for them. But his father believed collective action at the global level was far more important than local protests. He said so. Often.

And again. "You know that these tiny protests result only in arrests, not in progress, Alec. You are damn lucky to escape with only a fine. But I have to pay it. $700, Alec. Your allowance for six months. Of which you won't see a penny. Alec: serious action for human rights costs money. Lots of money. You won't get anywhere just pounding the streets. Or, God forbid, throwing Molotov cocktails. This is unacceptable. You're grounded for six months, no allowance. Jesus. It's unbelievable. How the hell did we get such a stupid kid?"

Serious money. Alec, having absorbed his dose of reality with more to come, considered it ironic that his human-rights-champion father was now punishing him for standing up for what he believed in. Now he grasped the truth: it was all about money. Lots of it. Human rights work was more than street protests. His father wasn't wrong. It needed to go beyond flyers and handouts for indigenous warriors. More effective, and more complicated. His mind turned from empathy with Mohawks to how to get the money to do something real, big, to have a serious impact on the world. His resulting abstraction and reawakening idealism did nothing to improve his father's anger. But this punishment would not deter him, not in the long run.

"Is that it, Paul? May I get back to my paper now?" asked his mother.

"Yes, Mary, you may. Thank you so much for your help," said Paul, voice now dripping with sarcasm.

"You're very welcome," said his mother icily. She got up and left. Alec sighed with relief and thanked the journal's editors for the deadline. He'd expected his mother to bring her icy and deadly disdain into play to make his punishment even worse. But the paper had spared him that. Not his father's ire, though.

"I ought to ground you for life. Go to your room," said his father. "And take that filthy damn jacket with you."

Alec sighed and headed to his room. He stopped at his door, considering whether to slam it. But his mind filled with ideas and the means to bring them to life. He needed to prepare. Figure out what to learn. To get ready for his future. So, first up: college. Slamming doors was juvenile.

The isolation Alec had earned with his flaming cocktail forced him to understand where his skills and talents lay and what kind of college education he needed. His mother, a full professor of computer science at McGill University, had encouraged his software development skills. The intricacies of puzzling out a program fascinated him. He excelled at ripping out code. His mother bought him a series of high-throughput computers and then ignored him, which was just as well for her peace of mind, or so Alec judged. His father just ignored him, not being the least bit interested in software. "People, Alec. That's what's important." No doubt that's why he'd grounded Alec for six months, to make sure he spent enough time with people instead of computers. More irony.

During the 2008 college acceptance season, Alec eagerly grabbed the mail before anyone else in the household. His mother had taken advantage of the McGill staff benefit that waived tuition and got him in with ease. The letter from MIT had come next, its crisp paper and fancy modern logo impressive, but not good enough for him. MIT was great for hardware, electrical engineering, and chimerical fantasies like artificial intelligence.

He needed serious software engineering and systems skills, deep ones, to make his mark in the software industry. The dot-com bust hit rock bottom, leaving only anticipation of massive growth in the software industry. With the skills and contacts he'd acquire in college, he'd take concrete steps to become a multimillionaire before the age of thirty, and he'd put those millions to good use. Effective use. A monumental change in human rights that would reshape the world. No more street protests, no more jail time, no more leafletting. Something big. But first, college.

The MIT letter preceded a desultory stream of Canadian and American schools his parents deemed worthy—not of him, but of them. All acceptances, no rejections, a testament to Alec's outstanding grades and achievements. These were fine, very satisfying to Alec's ego. But his parents favored McGill, rooted in their attachment to Montreal. Of course, his mother praised McGill because it had shaped her career over the years, while his father loved it because it was free. But Alec needed certain things from college, and with today's mail, they were within reach. Regardless of his parents' wishes, he would make his own life's choices.

And there it was: Carnegie Mellon University. There were no fancy scrolls, ornate logos, or Latin mottos, just the name on the envelope's return address. Founded by a dour Scots industrialist to encourage young men like Alec, CMU promised growth and opportunity, not fantasy. He savored the envelope, certain it contained his acceptance to the university he knew he had to attend. He weighed the envelope in the palm of his hand, feeling the heavy, high-quality paper that held the key to his aspirations.

No other institution offered the software expertise he needed, not even MIT, especially in operating systems and network programming. Alec had meticulously researched the professors he would study with. He'd read and understood all of their journal articles. He'd even learned the names of most of the computer science graduate students because they'd be his competition for coveted mentorship opportunities. CMU offered everything he wanted to achieve his future goals, his life of altruism. And he'd go, regardless of what his parents wanted.

Alec brought the mail in and unceremoniously dumped the mess on the table. He took the letter into his room and closed the door. Sitting at his small desk, he held the envelope in front of him and savored it. He smoothed his hand over the high-quality envelope and its embossed, name-only logo, his fingertips tingling with pleasure. This letter would expand his world.

His letter opener slit open the envelope with a soft whisper. He unfolded the letter. "We are happy…."

No happier than he.

With sharp, precise movements, Alec refolded the letter and slid it back into its envelope. He was eager to embrace every challenge and opportunity on his way. The CMU letter had lit a fire in him. That fire would carry him through the rough road ahead in pursuit of his vision.

"Think about it, Alec," insisted Paul Chenais. He was at the kitchen table with a cup of tea, while Alec sipped his *café au lait*. The aroma of the freshly brewed beverages wafted through the kitchen, establishing an illusory sense of truce between the negotiating parties. Paul's hands wrapped around his mug as though to absorb as much warmth as he could to support his argument. Alec paid more attention to the coffee than to his father. Paul continued, "Your mom went to a lot of trouble getting you into McGill. She'd be sitting here telling you the same if it weren't for the Chicago conference. And the damn place is free, for God's sake."

Alec's gaze shifted to the unfolded letter on the table between them. He had deliberately brought only that acceptance letter, so as not to give his father any material leverage in the argument. He'd tossed the others into his wastebasket. And he didn't need to pay any attention to his absent mother. The crisp edges of the letter only strengthened his resolve. He said, "CMU, Dad. Got to be. Nowhere else has—"

"We don't have the money, Alec," Paul countered, frustration coloring his voice.

"I've got a scholarship that covers half. They want me, Dad. My acceptance is due at the end of the month." Alec remained composed and kept his voice persuasive rather than expressing his own frustration. He remained resolute. He stretched out his hand and placed a tapping finger on the paragraph about financial aid in the letter.

Paul's voice rose. "I don't give a shit about half. We don't have the money. I run a nonprofit, for the love of God. And we have a mortgage. Montreal is not cheap. Attending McGill lets you work part-time for my NGO and make an impact. You've interned already. I'll pay you a per-hour wage." Paul drank the last of his tea and paced the floor, a scowl on his patrician features. Alec saw the anger growing on his face. "And whether they want you is irrelevant. Though why anyone would want you, I can't imagine."

Alec ignored his father's angry dig in favor of his own point. "I can get loans to cover the rest, live cheap, get a job." Alec switched to French to hammer home the point. French had more fire to it than Canadian English. It might blunt his father's anger, or it might let him express the emotion more elegantly, but it would certainly raise the tone of their conversation. "I must attend CMU to achieve everything I want for myself, for the world. The world is a dreadful place. Your organization publishes reams of paper about the people in jail, the people in refugee camps, the genocides, the wars. CMU will give me the knowledge and skills I need to excel in the software world. Once I am successful there, I can do something about human rights."

Paul responded in English, unwilling to yield to Alec's emotion. "Software?" he said, the word taking on connotations of incredulity. He modulated into persuasion. "Work for me for a year, Alec, if you want to help human rights. Learn how human rights work is really done. Take a gap year. Then decide about college. I surely need the help. Just…no street protests, OK?"

Alec couldn't contain his frustration. The aroma of the coffee had dissipated, and the *café au lait* had grown cold while the argument warmed. He told his father the truth he'd learned interning at his nonprofit. "You need more than my help, Dad. It's 2008. When have you busted someone out of jail in some rotten country? Maybe 1995? Or the guy who died from a hunger strike in Russia in 1989? All you do is generate campaigns asking for money, then use that money to generate more campaigns." The kitchen table, with its contested terrain around the letter, had become a battleground of conflicting means and ends.

The force and weight of Alec's attack stung his father. Offended, he tightened his lips and resumed his seat with finality. "No CMU, Alec. That's final."

But it wasn't. Alec needed to win this battle at all costs. For his future.

A year later, Alec sat at his usual corner table in the CMU student dining hall. He was slowly consuming the poutine he'd persuaded one of the kindly cooks to prepare for him. He'd given her the recipe he'd found on the web and argued her out of her objections to the nutritional disaster the dish represented. He'd OK'd mozzarella in place of cheese curds after a trial run. It was food therapy. The intense work for his class projects needed some relief. And some other things. The hacking.

A voice broke into his reverie. "Hey Alec, can I join you?"

Alec looked up and swallowed the bite of cheesy, gravy-covered chips. Stevie Tobin, the guy he'd met in the system programming class, carrying a tray of food.

"Sure, Stevie."

Stevie stared at the gooey mess on Alec's plate. "What the hell is that?" he asked.

"Poutine. Canadian specialty."

"Jesus. French fries? Gravy? What's the white stuff?"

"Cheese."

"Jesus."

"It's food therapy. Makes me less homesick." Not true; he wasn't homesick at all. The poutine just satisfied something deep within him in response to his freshman's frustration with CMU.

"This is about the hacking. Isn't it?" Stevie said with a smile.

Alec gave him a half smile. He'd told Stevie about some perverse upperclassman pranking him and having to redo six term papers. Stevie had just nodded knowingly and said, "I'll check it out."

Stevie folded his arms and relaxed in his chair. Smirking, he said, "Tracked down your hacker, dude."

Alec forked another chip and chewed and swallowed. "Yeah? And?"

Steve grinned and said, "Hacked him back. Anonymous ransomware hack. I extorted a promise to never hack a fresher again. He signed the agreement, and I unlocked his data. White hat stuff."

"Thanks? I guess?"

Stevie gave Alec a hard look. "You don't sound that grateful, dude. Anyway, you got to get up to speed on hacking, Alec. Woeful deficiency in your education so far."

"I don't have time, Stevie. And I don't really give a shit about hacking." Alec ate another forkful of potato and considered. "But I'd love to learn how to stop it. Network security, HTTPS, server security; stuff like that."

"Can do, bro. You won't get anything useful in class, so come by the house and we'll take you through our cybersuite. The entire stack of tools." He grinned and gestured toward Alec's plate. "Let me try some of that stuff."

A small price to pay for invaluable knowledge. Alec had learned that classroom knowledge was not enough for a great software developer. He'd also learned that everybody liked poutine. Who wouldn't?

He grinned. "Sure, grab a plate and fork. And a napkin. Plenty for all."

CHAPTER TWO
Aamna's Choice

"B.I.S.E HSSC (INTERMEDIATE PART II) ANNUAL EXAMINATION 2008 RESULT WILL BE DECLARED ON AUGUST 08, 2008."

Aamna Jaffrey was among the anxious students on that humid August 8th in Islamabad, Pakistan. Her best friend, Reema Kathia, was with her. The girls had rearranged their busy social schedules on that Friday to await the results that would decide their futures. They waited in the computer room at the school, along with the other intermediate college students. Aamna found a corner of the harshly lit concrete classroom away from the others to keep her conversation with Reema confidential, so it wouldn't get back to their parents. The echoing din of the crowd of restless girls awaiting their results helped to mask their conversation but did nothing to ease her apprehension.

Although the examination results would be available online, that didn't help Aamna or Reema. Neither girl had the luxury of her own laptop, even though they'd gone through the sheer hell of two years of studying computers. Why? Their parents felt that too much computer time would burn up their brains. At least, that was Aamna's theory. Reema, being the more reasonable of the two, suggested it reflected their families' Islamic traditions. Tradition had little room for modernity. Their parents thus refused to buy laptops for them. They had to use the computers at school for everything. And the attitude of their parents toward computers did not bode well for their future educational plans.

"Have you told your parents yet, Aamna?" asked Reema.

"Why, no, Reema. Have you?" Aamna, always the cool one, deflected her friend's probe into her family life with ease. Underneath her bravado, she trembled for her future. The tension within her made it hard for her to breathe. The world often threw fairness and justice out of the window to its death. School exams were no exception to this. Doubting, Aamna put up a cool front. But Reema refused to accept Aamna's deflection, sensing her inner turmoil. Aamna had told her too much about her plans and about her parents. Reema had always been a worrier.

She pressed Aamna on her plans. "I will stay in Pakistan, Aamna. You must fly to America. How will you do that unless your parents pay for it? How will you make them pay for it without telling them you are attending MIT? And how will you get them to pay for MIT itself? None of this is free, Aamna."

As Aamna could not form any answers to such questions, she shrugged. "I will find a way, Reema. And I am receiving a scholarship." One that would cover about 10% of her tuition.

"A scholarship will not give you an airline ticket to Boston, Aamna. What are you going to do? Hike across Afghanistan, Iran, Iraq, and Turkey, then take a boat?" Reema understood the geography of refugee life well. Her plans involved working with NGOs to help refugees, something her parents would never approve. Not really of much help. Also, Reema could be too sarcastic. But Aamna knew that she understood her dilemma. And her best friend was always there to give her solace and support. The need to confront her parents and convince them to support her filled her with dread. Her aspirations depended on so many things, exam results included. She took her friend's hands in hers and squeezed her appreciation for Reema's concern.

"Aamna!" The shrill scream came from a friend over by the computer. "You got a first! Aamna!"

Still not ready to believe in her success, Aamna trudged across the linoleum floor to the computer and inspected the posting. Yes, undoubtedly that was her picture and her roll number: "**FIRST POSITION NAME AAMNA JAFFREY MARKS 1061.**" It didn't really matter. MIT wanted her regardless. And she wanted MIT. She wanted the freedom of America and the joy of controlling her own destiny. The joy was there anyway, filling her up to the brim. Now she had affirmation of her hard work and capabilities. She could breathe again. And surely this first would influence her parents when she told them she was moving to Cambridge in a month. The first made everything possible.

Reema hugged her, then searched for her own name. MARKS 875. She had told Aamna she expected a 750, humble as always. Aamna hugged her friend back, and the pair went home to celebrate their success with their families.

Reema Kathia walked up the three flights to her family's small apartment, thinking only of Aamna and her first. Was she disappointed in not getting a first from the college herself? Why was she even asking the question? There had never been the slightest chance of such a thing. No, the tight feeling in her heart wasn't disappointment, it was fear. Fear for Aamna's future. The woman simply didn't see the walls, the barriers that society would place in her path. Reema shook her head. Aamna was about to discover she was not as cool and collected as she thought. Reality would soon break down her walls. Her parent's reality.

Her own father was at work, and her mother had gone shopping, so she had the apartment to herself. She walked into the bathroom and eased off her *dupatta*. She looked in the mirror. Smiling, she compared herself to Aamna. Beauty and the beast. Well, not quite that bad. But Aamna's face had a clear complexion, a beautiful color, a classic nose, and lovely eyes. Reema stroked her own cheek. The acne had left a few pits but was mostly gone now, but her eyes were a little lopsided and her nose was larger than it had any reason to be. Aamna's lips invited kissing, while hers were thin and plain. And her hair was hopelessly frizzy.

Reema averted her mind from Aamna's lips, knowing the pit of darkness to which such thoughts must lead. No.

Now that she had her degree from intermediate college, it was time to persuade her parents that she must find a profession. She'd already put out feelers to the local office of a Canadian NGO, and they'd offered her an assistant's position for a pittance. It was a start. And she need only tell her parents it was an administrative job, very white collar, helping the poor children of the country find educational opportunities. It was an income, and her parents needed that income. They would look the other way as Reema moved from administration to field work to whatever she could find that could best address the ills of the world.

By the time her parents realized what she was doing, it would be done.

Reema's thoughts again turned to her friend. Aamna's wealthy parents would not accept her decision to go to America. Too traditional. Too status oriented. Entirely too, too, what—too rich? The rich never wanted to lose control of things. Look at Aamna herself. Never having to worry about a job, about bringing money into the family. Never questioning her own right to do whatever she wanted. Never considering the barriers to her ambitions. What was the word? Entitled. Aamna was entitled. In a *good* way. But entitlement only took you so far in Pakistan. It was not a blank check, not for unmarried young women of good families. Even if you were too rich.

Exasperated with herself, with Aamna, and with the world, Reema changed her clothes and got out the vacuum cleaner.

On her return from the college, Aamna found her parents in their living room. Tea things on the low table filled the room with the aroma of the freshly brewed beverage. The cool room eased the strain of the humid weather outside.

A young man, a stranger, sat on one of the large tapestry chairs, legs spread like a dolt. He grinned a lazy grin, at home in a house not his own. His companion, an older woman dressed in traditional *sari* and *dupatta,* sat straight-backed on a smaller wood chair and eyed Aamna warily.

"And who are these people?" asked Aamna.

Her father rose from the large, modern-design couch, smiled, and said, "Aamna, this is Farazman Syed. He is to be your husband. And this is the matchmaker, Begum Rabia Safdar."

Farazman got up and said, "My word. No one told me she was this beautiful." He stepped toward Aamna, who stepped back in alarm, backing up against a giant decorative pot that sat against one wall of the room.

Aamna struggled to regain her composure, her jaw having dropped and bounced off the floor. She had rushed home with the joyous news of her first, only to find her life had moved on. She darted her eyes from this interloper Farazman to her parents to the matchmaker. There was absolutely nothing to be done, no way to ease her parents into the truth, no way to recover from this imposition of the weight of tradition. She felt the heat rise into her face, but she understood that anger would not help this situation. This was a battle she must not lose if she were to live a reasonable life.

She declared in a firm voice, "I am going to MIT. In a month."

Her father smiled pleasantly, not comprehending her response. His mind was on other things. Those things involved traditions she wanted no part of. He must listen to her.

"MIT, papa. In Cambridge, Massachusetts. In America."

Her mother rose from the couch, her face etched with sorrow at her daughter's words. Her father made restraining motions to tell his wife that he would handle this unaccountable situation.

Farazman grinned an even wider grin and said, "You have no need for further education now you are to marry me, Aamna. Your father's generous dowry and my participation in my family's business ensure you a wonderful and fruitful life raising our family."

The anger overwhelmed her, and she spat out her response loaded with venom. "Fuck you, you silly buffoon."

"Aamna!" Her father finally grasped that his plans for her life had run into a ravine, an unexpected and unwelcome obstinacy in the daughter he had raised with such care.

Begum Rabia, whose interest in the matter was both a matter of reputation and cash flow, leapt into the fray.

"Miss Jaffrey, you really must be more polite to your family and to my client. But clearly your family has not sufficiently prepared the ground for this announcement, despite my advice." She glared at Aamna's father, whose face turned from anger to helpless consternation. "Simply announcing the marriage is inadequate in this day and age. One must ease into it and develop the relationship between the parties in a civilized way. Perhaps we could start over? Surely we can find satisfying compromises."

Aamna, by the end of this exhortation, had stifled her anger, gathered her resources, organized her thoughts, and reasoned through to logical conclusions. She said, "Fuck you too, you meddling old biddy."

Mahmoud Jaffrey, his voice resonant with authority, declared, "Compromise, Aamna, is what makes our society possible."

Aamna understood her father well. She loved him and her mother and wanted to please them. But such feelings only go so far. Her life plans were at stake. And she knew her father's authority was only a facade, a mask he wore to conceal his love and understanding when he considered discipline to be in order. His compromises started as diktats but always slid sideways into real compromise, at least with her.

The buffoonish dolt and the wizened old hag matchmaker had left for whatever dens they inhabited. Her mother and father corralled their recalcitrant daughter in the living room. The subtle browns and reds of the tapestry decor softened the tension that filled the room. The parents deemed her brothers too young to understand the conflict to come and banished the two of them from the family council to the local cricket field. They departed with joy.

Once they'd gone, Aamna summoned a Gandhi quote she'd learned in school. "Your compromise, papa, is all give and no take. I'm doing all the giving." But she had no intention of giving on this one. Marry that buffoon? Not a chance.

Aamna got her way with her father by playing on his emotions. This tactic never worked on her mother, so her strategy was to get her father alone and work on him until he broke. She ignored his words, focusing only on his delivery. She sought the warmth in his eyes that reflected his loving heart.

But now, her mother took charge of the situation. She unleashed her tears and protestations the instant the family was alone and the boys were safely outdoors.

"You are eighteen now, daughter," wailed Asya Jaffrey. "You will not get any younger. There will be no children. You will be too old. Where will the family be? Where will *you* be? Oh, Aamna...."

"Aamna, Aamna," said her father mournfully, "how can you be so unreasonable? We didn't raise you to become a professor. Nonsense!"

"I have no intention of being a professor, papa," replied Aamna, crossing her legs, stretching her back up very straight in the wooden chair, and looking him in the eye. "I intend to be a software developer."

Her mother and father stared at each other in dismay. Aamna wondered whether they even knew what a software developer was. But her father brought her down to earth. "Men do that job, not silly women like you, Aamna."

She exclaimed, "I am not silly." Her father's words stung. How could he have such outdated beliefs, modern business person that he was?

"But, Aamna, my dear one!" Her mother's tears trickled down her face. "What will everyone think? What will befall us when our family and friends hear of your behavior? I cannot bear it, Mahmoud!"

Aamna kept cool. "You are *not* responsible for my behavior. I am."

"Speak to her, Mahmoud. Explain to her. I cannot." Her mother, overcome, pulled up her *dupatta* over her face to wipe up the tears.

Her father cleared his throat. "Aamna, my dear one. Society has certain norms, certain values that all must observe if society is to succeed. Arranged marriage is a tradition as old as time. It honors your parents as elders of the family. It honors me as head of the family. Our family does not take this lightly, Aamna."

Aamna had nothing but contempt for these out-of-date family traditions but did not wish to terrify her parents with her opinions. She shifted uncomfortably in her chair as a charged silence developed. The room smelled faintly of the furniture polish the maid used on the expensive wood. The house, once her sanctuary, now suffocated her with unmet expectations.

She explained, "Papa, I need money to go to America and learn about software. You have reserved money for our university educations. Even for me. I simply want to use those funds wisely, papa. To build a successful life."

He drew back in surprise. "Those monies are for university here, or Oxford, to learn how to behave in our advanced society, Aamna. Not to, to *work*."

Advanced society? How far behind had her parents fallen? "I know you intend for my brothers Babur and Sohail to work. In your company." Aamna smiled without humor. "You insisted they learn to read and do maths to prepare for university to learn what they must learn to help you build your empires. Am I not right?"

"Mahmoud, explain to her. Make her see," her mother cried, dropping her *dupatta* in her desperation. "She must not damage her brother's lives in this way. Do not let her bludgeon your morals this way! Do not let her corrupt your sons!"

"Now that's enough of that," said her father, impatient and annoyed at this defense of his honor that left him so little of it. He said to Aamna, "We must find a compromise on this, Aamna. Here is my offer. I can use those funds, instead of sending you to university, to give an extra dowry to the Syeds. That will establish you as a valued member of their family, both as the bride of Farazman and as a major contributor to Syed family wealth."

Aamna leaned forward a little. "I have no wish to become a valued member of their family. I thought I was a valued member of *your* family, papa. And that my value did not depend on selling me as a slave to some bunch of fools." She rethought the metaphor and felt tears coming. "Papa, you are not even selling me, you are paying them to take me away, like garbage." She allowed her anger to squeeze some tears from her eyes. Her voice broke as she exclaimed, "*Garbage,* papa! Trash for them to display on their family landfill. Is that all I am to you?"

Her mother threw up her hands. Her father, appalled by the images she painted, shook his head in sorrow.

Aamna gathered herself together and moved on to a determined response. "Very well, papa. You want a compromise. Here is my compromise. When you send me to MIT, I shall come back with my Master's degree and then, only then, shall I consider marrying Farazman. I am sure he can wait a few years, as he will never attract a reasonable woman. MIT will challenge me, but I have a first in maths and science, papa. It will be but a short time. With or without Farazman, I can be a valuable member of Pakistani society. And I shall be someone you can be proud of, like my brothers."

Privately, Aamna believed her brothers would be lucky to get out of secondary school. Neither of them showed the least interest in learning anything other than the tactics of football and cricket. But then, the Prime Minister was an Oxford Blue and a retired cricket hero. In Pakistan, anything was possible. Even for her brothers. With her MIT degree, she could achieve anything, anywhere in the world.

The room in the basement of MIT Building 32, the newish and very modern Stata Center, was dark and uninviting.

"Hello?" said Aamna, cautiously easing her way inside, holding her shiny new MacBook. She had purchased it using the money she had finally extorted from her parents by badgering them until they gave in. She took advantage of the Apple educational discount over the web from Islamabad even before she bought her airline ticket. Aamna clutched the laptop tightly against her breasts with her left arm as she strained to make out the shadowy figures illuminated solely by dark-background monitor screens. The air carried a hint of mildew, strong coffee, and a faint odor of what she now called "weed," having learned the word only a few weeks before.

"Hi! Who're you?" asked a pimply-faced kid. He leaned back in a seriously damaged office chair cadged from some junk pile. He looked too young even for MIT.

"Aamna Jaffrey. Ricardo said I could find some people here who would show me...." Aamna's voice trailed off as she looked around and found six undergrads observing her with big eyes and pale faces.

"Show you what, AJ?" asked the biggest of the six, broad-shouldered, thick around the middle, and sporting a medium brown beard to complement his long brown hair. He stepped forward and grabbed her hand in a double-handed handshake. "Great to have you here, darlin'. I'm Jeff." His accent was what Aamna associated with country, a musical form she had just learned about from a girl in her dorm. A southern accent. Hard-edged, not whiny or soft. Texas? New Orleans? AJ? She liked the sound of that and grinned. She lowered the laptop to her side, her grip not so tight.

"Hacking."

"Well, shit, AJ. We can do that. Can't we, fellas?" The boy brushed his long brown hair back and grinned widely, looking around at the crew of which he was clearly the leader.

"Sure, Jeff." The pimply kid looked uncertain. "But we've never had a girl here."

The crew's snickers prompted Aamna—AJ—to set boundaries.

She smiled and said, "I'll learn whatever I can from you, but I'm not here to fuck, and I'm not here to suck up to a bunch of weirdo toads that can't write a program on their best day. If you chaps have it, I want to learn it. Otherwise, tell me now, and I'm gone."

AJ's first few weeks doing the social rounds at MIT had formed her opinion of MIT undergraduates: sex-crazed maniacs all. College life in the United States was not as she expected. Perhaps Oxford and Cambridge were different. More mannered. She had her doubts about that.

The western world was indeed a corrupt place. She loved it. But she had things to accomplish, and sex would distract her.

"God *damn*, I love that Brit talk," said Jeff. "Have a seat, AJ. Tell me why you want to get into this stuff." He pulled a chair around for her to sit in, which she did, gingerly. She held her laptop across her knees. Jeff sat facing her in another chair, backwards, arms over the chair back, grinning at her.

"It's a challenge," she said.

"So's physics or mechanical engineering. Why us?" asked Jeff.

AJ had never really considered why she wanted to learn to hack. She didn't care about joining the club. She wasn't rebelling against society. She didn't think hacking was a way to challenge global power structures, or even local ones. She didn't want to steal large amounts of money—at least, not yet. Nobody was pressuring her; her roommate was a heads-down aerospace engineer uninterested in anything but rocket engines. So, why them?

"I just know, Jeff. I'm determined to learn and do this well. And I want the challenge. The way you can challenge me. Will you do it?"

Jeff laughed. "AJ, we will teach you everything we got! Which is way more than you want to learn. Anyway, hacking is a lot more fun than fucking."

"Speak for yourself, dickhead." The speaker was a reasonable-looking undergrad about twenty with socks that didn't match and a bizarre accent. New York? "But, AJ, we're all woke, you're safe with us. Why, this is the safest space on campus for a beautiful woman such as yourself. My advice, though. Stay away from the robot folks upstairs, they're incapable of restraining themselves. Artificially intelligent, if you get me." This smooth response was marred by signs that the man used his T-shirt as a pizza napkin. This was another American innovation she had lately discovered—pizza, not the lack of personal hygiene. Her brothers had excelled at the latter.

"I'm software, not hardware," she asserted.

"And if that ain't a come-on line, I don't know what is," said Jeff. "Well, come *on,* darlin', let me show you the tools." He got up and pushed his chair toward a laptop in front of a huge monitor, screen dark with white letters and dense with graphs. Pimple-face turned and put big headphones on.

AJ stepped forward into her new world.

CHAPTER THREE

Liberty or Death

Elliot Perry reviewed with pleasure the sale contract his corporate attorney had given him an hour earlier. He sat on a comfortable vintage leather sofa, hunched forward with the mass of paper on his lap. The lawyer, Tim Shorter, sat across from him in a chair, awaiting Elliot's verdict. The faint aroma of Kenyan coffee served at their breakfast meeting filled the room. Shorter's chair was an antique, Federal-era armchair that had once belonged to Thomas Jefferson, Elliot's libertarian hero. It creaked under Shorter's medium weight. Have to get rid of that soon. Jefferson had fallen from Elliot's grace when the scientists proved he'd fathered children with a Black slave, Sally Hemings. That was a little too much for Elliot to stomach. Could there be such a thing as too much liberty?

Elliot finished reading the contract. He knew he would sign it, but he gazed out the window. It was a second-floor window in an office building that fronted a park in downtown Palo Alto. A nanny with a baby stroller sat in the park, soaking up the sun. An illegal? Perhaps the nanny possessed a green card. Way too many of those out there, too.

"Elliot?" Shorter's medium baritone voice was soft in the quiet room.

He brought his gaze down to his lawyer's questioning face. Shorter was a medium man. Medium height, medium brown hair, gray eyes, a medium nose and chin, and a medium paunch. Middle-aged, somewhere between 40 and 50, with a touch of medium gray at the sides of his head. Elliot wouldn't tolerate mediocrity in his employees. But Tim, medium though he might be, was the best damn corporate attorney Elliot had ever hired. Tim did a magnificent job convincing Chairman Mao and his team that Elliot's financial software firm was worth billions.

"Chairman Mao" was Elliot's private name for the Chinese executive the Communist Party had allowed to buy the company. Chairman Mao and the Party craved a foothold in the American software industry. Elliot had the cash to prove it. Tim had sewn up every loose end imaginable, and some unimaginable, satisfying Chairman Mao and his team. Now that Elliot had read the contract, Tim had satisfied him, too. More than satisfied him.

"Is there a problem, Elliot?" Shorter checked his watch. "Their lawyer is expecting—"

"No, Tim. I'm just considering what to do with—" He flipped three pages over and did some quick arithmetic. "Thirty-two point six billion dollars." He smiled.

His attorney returned the smile, saying, "I'm sure you'll find something, Elliot. There are plenty of rescue dog shelters out there. Or you could buy Madagascar. Or run for President."

Power was great, and money was power. But real estate created liquidity problems, and money often vanished into the political ether with negligible return on investment. Elliot chuckled. "I hate dogs. Greenland is for sale, though, I hear. No, I don't believe I'll dabble in real estate. Mr. Trump has that scam locked up." He chuckled again. "And I hate politicians worse than dogs. No, private equity is the only career left to me, Tim. More flexible. I need to be open to possibilities. I'll need even more capital to take the enormous leap I'm considering."

Elliot flipped to the last page of the contract, took out his favorite pen, signed the thing, and dated it, September 23, 2002. He put the pen away and handed the contract to his attorney.

"There. Done. Let me know when the proceeds are in the Cayman accounts. Oh, and tell Mark he's fired. He really pissed off Chairman

Mao." Mark Firelock was the flamboyant CEO of the company. One stunt too many for Chairman Mao, and now he was gone. Elliot hoped Mark would learn a lesson from this, then smiled. No, Mark was immune to lessons.

"Will do, Elliot. Anything else?"

"What else could there be, Tim?" asked Elliot. "Oh. Yes. You're now the Chief Financial Officer for Perry Capital. Can you handle that, Tim?"

"Of course, Elliot." Tim Shorter smiled with a pleasant set of medium teeth. "Thank you for your confidence in me."

"A win-win. Now go move some money around and make me a few more billions."

Tim Shorter smiled his medium smile, put the contract in his portfolio case, and left. Elliot looked out his window. The nanny had vanished along with her stroller. Time for lunch.

"Liberty or death."

"Excuse me?" asked Tim Shorter.

"That's what Tom Paine said, 'Give me liberty or give me death.'"

"I knew that, Elliot."

"Why is America choosing death, Tim?"

Elliot Perry glared at the big-screen TV with the huge celebration of the 2008 election results in Chicago's Grant Park. Elliot's boyfriend, Oscar White, had gone out for the evening, being unable to stand watching it all. But you had to see it to believe it. McCain lost 365 to 173 in the electoral college. A joke. The man was a joke. Both men were jokes, just one wasn't funny.

"America is in its death spiral, Tim. The Republicans couldn't win an election if they tried. They've lost the Senate and the House. And McCain single-handedly put a Black man in the White House." He grimaced. "Something has to be done. And I'm the guy who's going to do it."

"Bit what?"

"Bitcoin, Elliot. It's...I don't know what the hell it is, but you're gonna love it."

Tim Shorter handed his copy of the June 16th 2011 *Economist* newspaper to Elliot. He stabbed a stubby finger at the Babbage column.

Elliot read the article in a gulp, processing the basic facts. "A decentralized currency. Jesus Christ, Tim. No central monetary authority? They'll never let it happen."

"It's happening, Elliot."

Elliot felt the old entrepreneurial excitement growing in his chest. This bitcoin stuff might be It. The answer. Decentralized currency, no government involvement, and bam—people could get on with their lives without government harassing them and stealing all their money in taxes and fees and regulation. This really might be It. He had to learn more.

"Who in the stable knows about this stuff, Tim?"

Tim Shorter, now promoted to Senior Partner in Perry Capital, said, "I figured you'd be interested, so I asked around this morning. It's all about the blockchain."

"The who, now?" Perry scanned the article in the *Economist*. "Nothing in here about 'blockchain.'"

Tim walked over to his desk and tapped a little on his computer. "The website has a more complete article. Oh—here's a paragraph full of 'blocks.'"

Perry joined his partner and read that paragraph and the next one and the one after that about ten times. He understood why the editors omitted this part from the printed version. Too much technical detail. Way too much. "OK, Tim. Offer a raise to whoever can explain this and assign them to the company apartment for two weeks."

"There's no one like that on our team. But I've found the ideal man, Elliot. A guy named Jeff Morrow. Graduated from MIT in CompSci in May. Rumor is he's quite the hacker. And a talented hacker is what you need to engage with the bitcoin ecosystem. I've looked into this stuff. It's like a river full of piranha and crocs, and you need an expert to survive."

"Well, then." Elliot Perry smiled.

* * *

Elliot knocked on the door of the corporate apartment in the condo complex on Cowper Street, right across University from the company's offices in Palo Alto. It was where they accommodated people who had business with company headquarters for short periods rather than paying the outrageous Palo Alto hotel rates.

The door opened. Elliot smiled. Yep, looks like a hacker. No suit or tie, six-three and 250 pounds, and long hair under a Houston Astros baseball cap. Let's see if the brain supports the look.

"Mr. Morrow? Elliot Perry. Glad to know you." Perry stuck out a hand and vigorously shook the paw offered.

"Call me Jeff, sir."

Elliot started with academic achievement. Jeff had breezed through MIT's computer science curriculum but spent most of his time developing hacks into secure sites all over the world. When he wasn't hacking, he was exploring the latest programming technologies and software frameworks.

"Where's your family, Jeff?"

"Don't have any, sir." The man smiled. "Born in Texas. Orphaned a few years ago, auto accident. And my grandma in Houston just died and left me some money, so I set myself up in Frisco to get me a job. Take my time to figure things out."

"Sorry for your loss, Jeff. And call me Elliot, please."

"OK, Elliot." Jeff grinned. "Still getting adjusted to the Bay Area. It's wild here, ain't it?"

"Yes, it can be. So you set yourself up in the City?"

"You mean Frisco? Yeah. Thought it would be best, I'm used to Boston and Houston, big cities."

"You'll find the tech boom is peaking up there. Consider moving down here for a while. And I can give you a job."

"So Tim said. Sounds interesting, but he was kinda coy about it all." Jeff grinned. Elliot figured he was on the fence, interested, but he didn't like barriers.

"Well, get used to that. Everything's secret around here, to keep the tech safe until we can monetize it."

"OK, that explains the ten-pager nondisclosure, right?"

"Right. Standard stuff."

"Like a drink, Elliot?" The big man twisted and looked at the wet bar next to the fireplace. "Got all kinds of hooch. I drink Corona, but ain't none of it here. I've survived on Margarita Mix and that high-end tequila. Excellent stuff."

"A little early for me." It was ten in the morning. "But I'll see about getting you a case of Corona. You use lime?"

"Nah, don't like vegetation with my brews. And I kinda lost my sense of day-and-night at the Toot."

"The...."

"Sorry, MIT. What we call it."

"So, Jeff. How familiar are you with blockchain software?"

"Which one?"

"Any."

"Great tech. They still haven't figured out who that guy Satoshi Nakamoto is, but he's a fucking genius."

"Satoshi Nakamoto, he invented the technology." Elliot, having read an article about bitcoin, knew that much, but not a lot more.

"Wrote most of the original blockchain code." Jeff raised his eyebrows. "You getting into that? It's open source, not much money in it for venture capitalists, I'd have thought. Your coin exchanges that cream off coin, or coin mining, that's where the money is now. Or tools. Not much scope for hacking, either. It's more of a social engineering deal with those guys. Kinda like pick-pocketing but scaled. Not my thing."

"You've lost me, Jeff. What are coin exchanges, and what do you mean by mining?"

"Huh." Jeff grinned. "So, coin exchanges translate digital coin into fiat money, like dollars. For a fee, of course. And every block that goes into the bitcoin chain gets there by mining, solving computer puzzles with a lot of CPU time to earn coin. Do I need to explain social engineering?" He looked as though he'd rather not.

Elliot smiled. "Yes, conning people into giving you their passwords or personal information."

"Right. Then you use the information to hack in and steal whatever you can. Hacking the blockchain itself isn't a recipe for minting money. Hard to do. It's more of a professional challenge, something you do for fun. Now, hacking an exchange, that's fun work and lucrative, too. You can take millions if you do it right."

"Money isn't everything, Jeff. And I'm not a venture capitalist. I'm private equity. Very private."

"OK, now you got *me* confused." Jeff smiled and gestured around him. "All this ain't peanuts, Elliot. What do you want if not money?"

"Liberty."

Jeff rolled his lips around the word. "Lib-er-ty, huh?"

"You're a Texan. You must know a lot about that."

"Remember the Alamo? Sure." A gleam started in Jeff's eye. "You got somethin' specific in mind, Elliot? Or are you just blowin' smoke?"

"I want to explore the possibilities, Jeff. And blockchain and bitcoin have real possibilities."

"Yes, sir, they do. Ain't no question. All kinds of 'em." Jeff grinned. "OK, tell you what. Whyn't you set me up in a little office down here somewhere, give me a bunch a green, let me hire a couple of friends, and we'll explore for you. Get you some lib-er-ty."

"Who might these friends be?"

"Just folks from the Toot. A guy from New York, hella smart. And a girl from Pakistan I've been mentoring. Now, she's *really* smart. She's a way better hacker than me. But she'd want—"

"I don't want to involve anyone but American citizens, Jeff. Sorry."

"OK, but you're missing a true opportunity. You can get her an H1-B or even a green card, easy. And she's drop-dead gorgeous."

Elliot smiled. "That is not relevant for me, Jeff. I hope you don't mind."

"No, sir, not at all. Well, I got a backup idea, guy from Boston, a townie, not a tool."

"A tool?"

"Tech tools, MIT undergrads. This guy is at Bunker Hill Community College, but he hangs with us. Just can't afford the Toot."

"We'll try it, Jeff. Welcome to the team." Elliot stood and shook the big man's hand.

CHAPTER FOUR
1WeakLink

ALEC SMILED AS THE ELEVATOR climbed to the fourteenth floor of the downtown office building on Harrison Street in San Francisco. The majority of VCs he had met with in the past four years were in Palo Alto or Mountain View in one- or two-story buildings. But in 2016, the action moved to the skyscraper-filled South of Market district of the City. The recruiter gushed about deep-pocket investors, venture capital, and futuristic technology development at a stealth startup. Hints of large stock option grants and a lucrative salary added to his interest. Pumping the recruiter proved futile, as she wouldn't tell him anything specific.

The receptionist led him down a quiet hallway. The conference room had a large redwood table and a stunning view of Yerba Buena Island through a wall-to-ceiling glass window. He set down his backpack on the floor. He hadn't known what to expect in the interview, so he'd brought his laptop and keyboard along with a stack of papers he'd published on secure blockchain protocols. The recruiter suggested that because that's what interested the San Francisco VCs. They didn't care about his four years of startup experience in the Valley or his academic credentials, and they didn't need references. They had all the information they needed. Alec sat in one of the padded leather chairs and stared out at the bright January day, the entire bay spread before him.

"Alec Chenais? Glad to know you," said a youngish man upon entering. He gently closed the door to the conference room and shook Alec's hand. "Sorry for the delay. I needed to verify some things before talking to you."

Crispin Bannon had a goatee and a slight British accent, the kind you'd find in long-term transplants in Toronto or British Columbia. He also had a hungry look. Not for lunch, for money. Alec had seen it a lot in boardrooms over four years in Silicon Valley. VCs wore it when they thought they'd landed the big one. They were usually wrong.

But Bannon didn't have the appearance of a venture capitalist. His eyes were too sharp, and his clothes were a notch downscale. His demeanor suggested techie, but his tan hinted at beach time. Marketing? Product marketing? Three-letter level?

Alec sank back into his chair as Bannon swung another chair around and sat next to him at the table. "Could you explain the details of the position? The recruiter wasn't very forthcoming, Mr. Bannon," Alec said. "But she made it sound like an opportunity I shouldn't pass up."

Bannon laughed. "Yes, it is. And call me Crispin. But before we get started, please sign this NDA."

Alec skimmed the fifteen-page document and signed it. Then they talked about blockchain. Crispin had read Alec's papers, and many others as well, including the Satoshi white paper. He turned Alec inside out. Alec opened his laptop and showed Crispin some tools he'd developed, and Crispin brought up some blockchain-related websites, talking all the while about the prospects for the technology. After about half an hour, Alec realized Bannon wasn't testing his knowledge so much as his interest in blockchain, along with his interest in entrepreneurship. Instead, he pressed Alec on how far he would go to build a software system in the blockchain ecology?

Alec tried to pin Crispin down. "Are you offering me a lead software position on a real project, Crispin? I have a lot of unvested options in my current position, so—"

"I'm offering you founder status and the CTO role at full salary in a new stealth startup, Alec. Initial stock grant and options. Very secret, very well funded. Blockchain software. You get to build your own team. But our sponsor requires a security clearance. Will that be a problem?"

"I have dual citizenship. Canadian and American. Two passports. I was born in Boston, but my dad is Canadian."

Crispin grinned and replied, "That's fine. Last time I checked, Canada was on our side."

Alec thought the Quebecois would disagree with Crispin's claim. But Alec and his family were solid citizens. Too solid. Surely a security clearance wouldn't be a problem. And it sounded like he'd hit pay dirt—ground floor in a minting-money startup with fascinating tech that would yield all the cash he needed. Then he'd have the potential to make a difference in the world.

"Let's talk details, Crispin."

And he'd have to do his due diligence on Crispin Bannon and his henchmen. He had to make sure Crispin wasn't scamming him or leading him down the primrose path. That this was all real. Alec didn't want to waste time on bullshit. He'd done enough of that at home with his father.

The due diligence on both sides of the 1WeakLink equation satisfied all parties. Crispin proved his bona fides with a flush bank account at Silicon Valley Bank and references from three major venture capitalists. Alec made several phone calls to people he knew in Silicon Valley, all of whom gave Crispin the thumbs up. The security clearance for Alec came through in record time, according to Crispin. Something to do with Crispin's advice to the corporate sponsors, according to 1WeakLink's CFO, Yuriko Nakamura. Crispin took on the role of CEO, while Alec filled out the executive suite as CTO. Yuriko found a suitable three-story building in SOMA that Crispin and Alec both approved. The third floor was all theirs. It had three large rooms and a smaller conference room that overlooked the I-80 freeway approach to the Bay Bridge.

Crispin, after some shuffling around, confessed to Alec that their corporate sponsor and first client was the National Security Agency. The NSA wanted a system to hack blockchains. Alec, despite being a super-programmer, had some blind spots. Specifically, hacking. He knew how to stop hackers, but the hacking itself was foreign territory.

Alec got busy with his network from CMU and soon hired several world-class blockchain developers. Crispin then scheduled a company meeting to coalesce the diverse and remote team. Alec had struck gold with Peter Reynolds in New York City who was not a CMU alumnus but the cousin of one. He was a staff developer working on a poorly managed coin exchange project. The abuse irked Peter enough that he was ready to leave. Peter had then led Alec to two other developers, Marcus Creasy in London and Maksym Shevchenko in Ukraine. And Maks brought along his wife, Olyena, the best among them. She excelled as a developer and had a kind heart. The team needed that, since the rest of the developers were asocial introverts. The one missing skill: hacking.

Crispin scheduled the WebEx meeting for 7 a.m. on Monday, April 18, 2016, to cover business hours in all the time zones involved. Crispin, Alec, and Yuriko gathered around the new conference table. Yuriko yawned, unused to the early hours. Crispin had requested a 5 a.m. start for the meeting because he always got up at 4, but Alec talked him out of this absurdity.

Alec started the meeting off. With cheer in his voice, he said, "Hi, everyone. All together for the first time! In a minute, Crispin will explain his vision and our mission. First, congratulations on joining a blockchain company that's going to change the world. You won't regret it. Just one thing: we need someone with hacking experience. We'll pay a $10,000 bonus to the person who finds a great hire with that background. Time is short to bring this hire on board because we have a super-tight timeline from our sponsors."

Crispin's lips were thin. Yuriko rolled her eyes. Alec disregarded the inevitable lecture from Crispin. Getting this done required a strong motivator, and money moved people more than anything. But the team members, unfortunately, looked blank. No suggestions, just silence.

"Think about it, talk to your friends, and find us this hire," Alec urged. But as he watched the WebEx images of silence, he realized he'd have to lead the search himself. He was emotionally torn between his excitement at the chance to expand his knowledge beyond technology to people and his need to dive deep into software systems. Being a CTO entailed more than just showing off programming skills. A great CTO hired exceptional individuals, even if it meant traveling the world.

Traveling to the June 2016 VivaTech conference in Paris was Alec's first foray into heavy-duty tech recruiting. Crispin had given him carte blanche to hire anyone he thought could get product out. He'd handed Alec a corporate credit card and told him to spare no expense but to come back with a hacker. Rumors were already circulating that this new European conference would attract thousands of people from all corners of the web, including the dark ones.

"Crispin, one problem. Most of these people won't be American citizens. If they need a security clearance—"

"We can keep their status between us, don't you think? And the NSA isn't that picky with talent they absolutely, positively must have. We've already got a Brit and two Ukrainians, for Christ's sake. I'll convince them."

In keeping with his theory of sparing no expense, Alec booked a room at *l'hôtel* Le Meurice, a top five-star hotel on the *rue de Rivoli*. This would impress the people he'd interview there. But he wasted no time luxuriating in the well-appointed rooms of his suite; today, he was hunting.

But fate intervened. Opening his door to leave, he discovered a woman about to knock. Alec froze in the doorway, overwhelmed all at once.

"*Vous êtes Alec Chenais, n'est-ce pas?*" the woman said in a deep, silky voice. Her sleek, night-dark hair, parted down the middle, fell over her shoulders and behind one ear. Her face was faintly Asian, with beautiful cheekbones and eyes that hinted at a smile under elegant black brows as they looked directly into his. Heart-shaped lips curved in a slight smile, and she wore no makeup and didn't need any. She dressed expensively, all in black, with a butter-soft leather jacket opened to show an exquisite body in a black silk blouse. Her French was perfect Parisian, sounding elegant and rich to Alec's vulgar Quebecois ear.

"I'm sorry. I assumed you spoke French, Alec," the woman said in flawless American English.

"*Je…le fais, quand je peux parler du tout,*" Alec stammered in his nasal Quebec accent, regaining his senses.

The woman smiled broadly, making her even more exquisite, and offered a hand raised at the slight angle that indicated a handshake. Alec lifted a suddenly heavy arm and gave the short French shake. The woman said, "I am Ludivine Moureaux. I imagine you've never heard of me."

"I would certainly remember, Mme. Moureaux. You have the advantage of me." Alec was careful to use the formal *vous*, so unlike his informal Quebecois, so as not to offend.

Ludivine Moureaux smiled again. "What a good place to start our relationship, Alec. And please, call me Ludivine. All my friends do."

The dots connected in Alec's stretched mind, and he said, "Are you looking for a job, Ludivine? Is that why you're here?"

"Oh my, no, Alec." She took his arm and gently pulled him toward the lift. The door closed quietly behind him. She continued in Parisian French, "I'm here to show you the real Paris, the Paris you need to comprehend for the long-term success of your company. We will meet people of use to you and see things you must see. Then, lunch. And talk." Despite her mention of business, Ludivine used the *tu* form. Three times in one sentence. She did not offend.

Alec, electrified by her touch, had no objections to this revised plan for his day.

Ludivine smiled as she said, "I am sure you will find today's events far more interesting than anything at this conference. But we must go to parts of Paris that are rather…off the beaten track. My car and driver await us downstairs."

* * *

The quiet, powerful Mercedes Maybach twisted and turned through the streets of Paris. The driver, introduced by Ludivine as Octave, had the physique of a professional fighter but wore a subdued but very expensive dark suit and a black silk tie over a white shirt. Ludivine's bodyguard? Alec, in the back seat with Ludivine, had lost his bearings after Octave's first few turns. He'd spent time in Paris in his university days, but Paris was much more complex than the familiar Rive Gauche. The streets, arrondissements, and banlieues passed in a blur. The two of them spoke French; it seemed the right thing to do. Octave spoke not at all.

"And where will you take me, Ludivine?" Alec asked.

"Some small places with big people," Ludivine replied. "Left there, Octave. And stop before the bollard."

In that small apartment, as well as the subsequent basements and Internet cafés they visited, Alec encountered individuals who were difficult to categorize but clearly understood both the intricacies of the Web and the darker aspects of software development. Ludivine greeted them all as friends with *la bise*. The majority were young men, with a handful of older guys and young women mixed in.

Ludivine introduced Alec as her American entrepreneur friend who was curious about "what we do in the night." He categorized them by which circle of hell they occupied. His attraction to Ludivine grew as his rational mind pigeonholed her as a dark Virgil rather than a lustrous Beatrice.

By noon, this diverse array of hacking expertise had overwhelmed Alec. Ludivine said, "And now, lunch. Let us go to a small bistro in the 11th, Alec. I know the *propriétaire*. We can sit and talk for as long as we wish. And, my friend, please do not try to pay for anything."

They talked until 3 p.m. over glasses of excellent wine. Ludivine turned Alec inside out, a pleasant experience that left him warm and inspired. This mysterious woman captivated him. She clearly had many connections and a penchant for profit. Alec sensed that there might be darker impulses lurking within her, and the mystery stimulated him to reveal more about himself than he usually did.

At length, Ludivine glanced at her watch and frowned. "But I have kept you away from your work all day, Alec. I am so glad I had the chance to show you our world here."

Alec, his mind alive with what he'd seen and with Ludivine's presence, said, "Perhaps we can explore more of your Paris while I am here, Ludivine?" He understood she might be the key to his search for the right people. But she might offer even more.

Ludivine let out a throaty laugh. "I will drive you back to your hotel, my friend." She handed him a card. "And here is Octave's phone. If you need transportation during the rest of your stay, or should you need to consult with me about my services, please call him."

They drove back to Le Meurice, which wasn't far.

Alec, fueled by wine and curiosity, asked, "Would a digestif interest you, Ludivine? A short while will not exhaust our conversation."

Ludivine smiled and reached for his hand. Holding it in both of hers, eyes locked on his, she brought him down to earth in her low, smooth voice. She said, "Alec, my friend, I must tell you I never sleep with a man with whom I will do business. And we will surely do business eventually. Then, we will see. But for now, *au revoir.*" She released his hand with a reassuring pat.

Octave, anticipating this conclusion to the day, had Alec's door open. He mumbled his own "*Au revoir*" and scrambled out of the car, embarrassed. Octave smiled, eyes sympathetic. Alec walked with as much dignity as he could muster into Le Meurice as the Maybach silently pulled away from the hotel. Waiting for the elevator, Alec breathed deeply. The air in Paris had led him astray, but he was willing to breathe more of it.

CHAPTER FIVE
A New Hire

The first of July, 2016, was a glorious Friday in Paris. AJ had come for the VivaTech conference, but her interest in tech presentations had dwindled after the silly posturing in several panel discussions. Ludivine rescued her by suggesting that they might enjoy a drink at a cafe. But Ludivine never did anything without a motive. And since her schemes usually involved large sums of money, AJ was more than willing to forgo the afternoon's breathless tech updates for an excellent glass of wine.

It was a break in tradition, as she'd grown up believing alcohol was the devil's drink. But now that she worked for the devil herself, it seemed the thing to do. And it was marvelous wine, always, with Ludivine.

The two women sat at a table on the sidewalk overlooking the Troca, enjoying the sun and the people and reminiscing about other days in other countries. AJ owed Ludivine a lot. Like, maybe, 300,000 euros. Not literally, of course. The difference between what she was making in Cambridge fooling around with the boys in the back room of a large consulting firm and what she was making with Ludivine. Adventures—one could not seriously call them "jobs"—that Ludivine had arranged for her over the past twelve months. And now, Paris. Ludivine had sent her the registration for the conference and had asked her to attend. That meant only one thing: another adventure.

Ludivine came to the point. "AJ, you are a software virtuoso. Perhaps the best in the world. Except for me, of course. You can choose your work and charge whatever you want. I helped you realize your talent, did I not?"

"Yes. And what enterprise do you propose?"

"Do you remember a friend of yours from MIT named Jeff Morrow?"

Jeff, Big Jeff. How could she forget him? She'd told him to go fuck himself when he made a pass at her. He was the only such person AJ remembered taking no offense and continuing to teach her what he knew.

AJ smiled. "My first mentor. Before you." Then she frowned. "You're not suggesting I work for him, are you? Because—he's good, I'm not saying he's not good. He taught me a lot. But he's, well, not the brightest business bulb in the room."

"No, but he teamed up with one."

"Who?"

"A man named Elliot Perry."

"Isn't that the Silicon Valley billionaire who's getting Trump elected?"

"That is one facet of the gentleman. Another facet is his interest in blockchain technology."

"You want me to work with him on blockchain?"

Ludivine smiled, her cheekbones showing as her eyes crinkled. "No, my love. I want you to work *against* him. Perry wants to control blockchain technology and, through it, the dark web. He is a threat to my business interests. He is also a threat to the political and financial systems of the world, but I have no interest in protecting those."

"So I would work directly with you?"

"Ah, no. There is a startup in San Francisco, secret and very well funded. I want you to take a job with them. The CTO is here at this conference looking for people."

"Why not write this software yourself?"

"Why bother, when someone else will do it for me? With your help. The opportunity cost of having my team work on such software would be too great."

AJ's interest grew. Blockchain fascinated her, especially the challenge of getting inside the so-called impossible-to-hack systems. She had explored the technology thoroughly but had no opportunity to dive deeply into the challenge of hacking it. Ideas about that rapidly formed and swirled in her brain, then changed to speculation about the rewards. Ludivine's adventures usually yielded good money, but this one had the smell of a killing, a breakthrough project that would propel her to financial independence.

Knowing Ludivine as well as she did, AJ had to ask the next question. "And what must I do for you there?"

"Write the best software you can, my love. Create a great product. Make sure it does what their clients want."

"And then?"

"And then, give it to me."

AJ smiled. "You will have to compensate me well for outright plunder. You may find it cheaper to become a client of the company."

"I am not the client the company desires, AJ. Not at all. That is why I need you inside. I also need that software to be the best it can be, because I'm going to use it against Perry and his hackers. And that also requires you on the inside. As for compensation, I am sure we can negotiate a satisfactory amount, much less than it would cost to develop the software myself with my team."

AJ had learned Ludivine's story in bits and pieces over the year she had worked with her. Penniless, she moved to Singapore after the 2008 meltdown. She played a role in the 1MDB scam, stealing millions by helping Jho Lo steal billions. Curious, she bought 200 bitcoins at the price of $233, then sold them at the price of $65,000. She then moved back to Paris, went into business for herself, and amassed a coterie of hackers and brilliant software developers whom she rented out on the open market. The *dark* open market. Ludivine was financially independent and getting more so every day. Now she could help AJ make that leap as well.

"Tell me everything," AJ commanded.

Alec answered the knock at the door of his hotel room. Last interview of the day, thank God. Spending a Saturday cooped up in a hotel room talking to idiots was an insane waste of time. It was the last day of the conference, and he had lost hope.

"Hi, I'm Aamna Jaffrey."

"Hello, Aamna. Have a seat," Alec said, waving at the couch. "Your resume? Call me Alec."

Aamna took a sheet of paper out of her backpack and handed it to him. It had her name, her education and two lines summarizing the fact that she was a well-paid consultant.

"This is it?" Alec waved the paper in despair. He had met with fifteen software developers during his day of interviews. He was tired, exhausted from endless conversations, and drained from probing people's unfounded self-assessments of their programming skills. He hadn't found anyone to rival even the youngest of Ludivine's connections, but he wasn't yet ready to risk selling his soul to help his company.

Aamna Jaffrey smiled. The smile did what her resume had failed to do. It made him pay attention to her. The more attention he paid, the more alert he became. This was a truly beautiful woman. Full of life, *joie de vivre*. He looked at the resume again. A Bachelor's and a Master's from MIT, the latter from the Center for Computational Science and Engineering. He'd heard great things about that graduate program, and an MIT undergraduate degree itself was hard to ignore. Big consulting firm, then out on her own. But as beautiful as she might be, he could do his job and put his attraction aside. He'd interview her on the merits.

Aamna said, "I understand, Alec, that you want a software developer for a startup in the blockchain space. Super top secret." Her British accent and her smile distracted him enough to slow his understanding of what she'd said. He caught up: super top secret.

It was. She wasn't supposed know anything about the company. But she did.

"So, Alec, there's no need to bother with coding exercises and language tests. I'm deep into blockchain tech at every level. *Every* level, including the ones I am sure you know nothing about. I have a green card. I want to leverage my blockchain skills to their greatest. Your startup will allow me to do that."

This was top secret. Had Crispin been talking?

"Ms. Jaffrey." He kept his voice stern. "Who told you about us? Who suggested you come here?"

"The grapevine, Alec. I have a lot of good friends in the industry, especially in Silicon Valley. I was here at the conference and saw your signup sheet. So I asked around, heard some fascinating details, and here I am. And call me AJ, please."

Interest in the technology, check. Interest in and knowledge of the company, check. "Why should I consider hiring you, AJ?"

"I can hack out any code you need. I can do that in far less time than anyone else you'll hire. And with much higher quality. And I know everything there is to know about the dark web."

Confidence, check. If you believe her. Somehow, he did. Maybe a less formal setting would allow him to understand this woman better. He smiled. Paris certainly lived up to expectations, its secrets relentlessly thrust upon him. But AJ was much more straightforward than Ludivine. He knew they were similar, he just needed to unearth the details. And, somehow, AJ seemed much safer than Ludivine and her demimonde.

"Look, AJ. I'm done for the day, here. This hotel room is elegant and comfortable and I hate the carpets after dancing around on them so long. How about dinner? There is an excellent restaurant here in the hotel, Alain Ducasse. On me, of course."

"All right, but I won't sleep with you after one dinner. If ever." Totally self possessed. And prickly.

Alec grinned. The earlier contretemps with Ludivine had hardened him even to the air of Paris, though perhaps his attraction to AJ was too obvious. He reassured her, "Just to test your bona fides, AJ. If you can talk blockchain tech and the dark web over a good Parisian dinner and maintain the illusion you've created, I'll hire you. If your references check out, of course."

AJ smiled. "Promise?"

"Promise."

The early morning light filtered through the shimmering satin curtains of Le Meurice, filling the room with a soft champagne hue. Alec looked at AJ's face beside him in bed. Stunningly attractive, even with her beautiful black eyes closed in sleep, her black hair tousled from sex, and the rest of her body covered in sheets. Her elegant nose, her firm mouth, her golden skin. OK, maybe the chin was too big for classic beauty. But when she laughed and spoke passionately, her face faded into the background. And when that body made love, you forgot everything but the passion. He longed for that warmth in his life. Ludivine had awakened something in him. But Ludivine was unreachable, out of his league. Love had nothing to do with Ludivine, only passion. But AJ made him feel fully alive.

At dinner, he had understood the depth of her mind and her abilities. He'd finally met someone far smarter than he was. He'd worked out from her degree history that she was twenty-seven years old, his age. Years at MIT and consulting on innovative projects had only enhanced her natural software genius. She had a charm that fascinated him. By the dinner's end, he was more than halfway in love with her.

And the miracle happened. She shared his love. You could see the hesitation and the prickles disappearing as the evening wore on. His own inhibitions loosened as they talked. Toward the end of dinner, he'd asked where she was staying, and she said with friends. So he asked if he could walk her there to continue their conversation. Ludivine's gentle refusal of the day before pushed its way into his head. He didn't want a similar repulse from AJ, and he knew he wanted to hire her. Propositioning her would lead their relationship away from that, and his company needed her. He decided not to say anything that would jeopardize the job offer.

That resolution lasted until she counter-offered to walk him back to his hotel. She tipped the last of the Chambertin from her glass, set it down, and said, "I take it back."

"Take what back, AJ?"

"The bit about not sleeping with you after one dinner." Her eyes smiled as they locked with his.

Alec smiled back warily. "Um. I don't think, from the HR perspective…." Alec's stomach clenched a little, realizing that he didn't care if it was a bad idea at all. His voice trailed off.

AJ smiled. "Fuck the HR perspective."

Alec knew he was lost. "Right. I'll call for *l'addition*. Oh. You're hired. Whether or not you sleep with me. I'm sure your references will be fine."

"Of course I'm hired. Would I sleep with someone stupid enough not to hire me?" She grinned and took his hand.

As the first rays of sunlight entered the room over the trees outside in the Tuileries, Alec gently woke AJ with kisses. He explored her body as she awoke and responded, and they made love again. They had all the time in the world.

AJ considered herself a seasoned world traveler as she ventured onto the streets of San Francisco in search of a place to call home. The August weather in the City was unlike most of the places she'd lived. Cambridge and Somerville were humid and hot, Paris was empty and hot, Islamabad was dry and hot. San Francisco was downright cold and foggy. In August.

Alec offered to put her up in his condo on Mission Street. As much as AJ considered herself modern, this was too modern for her. She loved Alec. She loved the touch of his body and the ecstasy of making love to him. But her intuition told her that living with Alec would not help their relationship. Not because of incompatibilities or lifestyle differences, but because of her strong wish for independence. And living with an unmarried man would be shameful; that feeling bubbled up from her distant past. She had no wish to be ashamed of her relationship with Alec.

Years away from her family in Islamabad had hardened her to many things. Searching for an apartment prompted her to reflect on those things. Independence was fine, but so many deeper feelings lingered, little threads that pulled tight in the wee hours of the morning. Especially when she slept next to Alec. Whom she would betray by stealing his software for Ludivine. For money. And independence. AJ postponed the thought, not yet ready to think about the betrayal. The money from the outrageous salary at 1WeakLink and Ludivine's even greater rewards would eventually snip those threads. But when? Not yet. First, her own home.

Yuriko, sensitive and helpful, told her to try the Haight. She told AJ that rents had soared all over the City, but with her salary and personal references she shouldn't have any problem finding a nice one-bedroom apartment.

After two weeks of fruitless competition with others in her position, she finally heard about a nice little second-floor flat up the hill on Waller Street near Buena Vista Park. She got there before other seekers swarmed it. Sunny and quiet, it suited her needs, and the friendly Lebanese landlady who lived in the downstairs flat proved ready to rent to her. And the landlady assured her that there was a fiber gigabit Internet connection. The previous tenant had it installed, then later fled to Texas for some inexplicable reason.

Alec offered to help her move her things in. Since she had no things, she declined with a smile. She ordered the basics from an Internet furnishings company and had them delivered and installed by several friendly men, who perhaps lingered a little too long. Her landlady explained they were not creepy lechers, just waiting for their tips. And she bought a bicycle to commute down the hill to 1WeakLink. Now that she had a home and an Internet connection, there remained the work for Alec—and for Ludivine. That work would complete the process that renting the flat had begun.

Work—she remembered Yuriko's warning about sleeping with her boss, too. She had to be careful. Independence also meant being free of the contempt that others in the company might have for her as Alec's lover. She would keep the flat to herself and sleep with Alec only in his condo. That way, as she strove for independence, she could uphold a facade of decency. For herself and the world.

CHAPTER SIX

A Shameless Lust for Power

"I SHOULD HAVE RUN, GOD damn it!" Elliot Perry exclaimed, his face etched with frustration. Oscar White, his husband, looked across at him with a grin. "Oscar, remind me why I didn't run."

The 2018 election results rolled by, with Newsom crushing his Republican opponent, Cox, 62 percent to 38 percent.

"You didn't run, Elliot, because you wouldn't have won. You endorsed Trump. Then you gave that interview about California seceding from the Union. To cap it all off, you proposed to me. I don't think Republicans would have turned out in droves for you, Elliot. None even showed up for the wedding."

Elliot Perry smiled. "It was private, Oscar. And so am I."

"You'd make a great governor. But 80% of Californians would hate your fucking guts. They'd hang you from a lamppost the first chance they got. Metaphorically speaking, of course. But look at that dude, Elliot. He can't even find a good barber. And who gets the name 'Gavin,' for Christ's sake? Ten-to-one they'll recall him within two years."

The handsome governor's beaming face on the huge hi-def TV only made Elliot madder. He called Tim Shorter.

"Are you watching this debacle, Tim?"

"Sure am, Elliot."

"How much money did we put into that bastard's campaign, Tim?"

"You don't want to know, Elliot."

"Did we not do enough?"

Tim's voice sounded resigned. "No, Elliot. Californians simply won't elect a Republican to a major office in the state of California."

"Did we realize that when we gave him the money?" Because Elliot hadn't really understood. He figured that with enough money, he could elect a bonobo to state office. He grimaced at the TV, watching resentfully as the Democrats easily accomplished what he could not.

"Yes, Elliot. I explained it all to you. Your response, if I remember correctly, was, 'This money is what we make in an hour, Tim. Let's take a flyer.' So, we were the largest donor to Cox's campaign, $5 million."

"Well, that wasn't a flyer, Tim. That was a Hindenburg."

"Lesson learned, Elliot?"

"Fuck you, Tim," Elliot snapped and hung up.

"You should be nicer to Tim, Elliot," said Oscar, laughing. "He's all that stands between you and Leavenworth."

Elliot cheered up a little at his husband's laughter. Oscar always lightened up awful situations. It was a major reason Elliot married him. But Elliot had gotten the message. The truth had sunk in with its full weight. Elliot wanted power. Elliot wanted to end government interference in business affairs. He wanted to end the endless grabbing of other people's money through unnecessary taxes. Most people, the right people, would be better off for it. They didn't seem to realize that enough to vote for it. So, politics was not the answer. Compromise was not the answer. Kissing the ass of The People was not the answer.

He needed to move faster to the tools he knew *were* the answer. Elliot felt a vein throbbing in his forehead as his anger returned. Rather than running for office, he needed to change the world with his own two hands.

Elliot Perry walked briskly into the Den at 9 a.m., the morning of November 7th, 2018.

The "Den" was shorthand for the offices of TANSTAAFL Software, a startup privately funded by Perry Capital. It was his secret weapon for world domination. Occupied by Jeff Morrow and his six hacker friends, TANSTAAFL's Den was the one place Elliot felt he was not in control. This was no illusion; no one could control these people.

The Den occupied the second floor of a three-story office building on Hamilton Street, easy walking distance from the Perry Capital offices. The Denizens had claimed the space as their own. Elliot tried to stay away from it, as it offended his sensibilities. The developers preferred working with the shades down during the day. "Too much glare," Jeff had told him. "And we're used to basements, not sunny rooms." Elliot fantasized they might be vampires. But vampires were exactly what he required at the moment. Werewolves, too.

"Hey, Jeff," Elliot said, picking out the big man sitting alone at a monitor in the dark room. "Where the hell is everybody?"

"Most guys come in later. Night owls. I been here all night, Elliot. Whaddya need?"

"Action."

Jeff pushed his chair back and shifted his bulk to get comfortable. "Have a seat, Elliot."

"No, I think better walking around."

"Suit yourself, man." Jeff leaned over and grabbed his Corona from his desk. "Beer's in the fridge."

Elliot kept walking, back and forth, until Jeff got nervous. "OK, Elliot. What's this all about?"

"I want to change the plan, Jeff."

"Whaddya got in mind?"

"Let's speed it up. I want to take it international. I want to *be* international."

"What happened to Lady Liberty?"

"She got fucked one too many times, Jeff. She's done. Used up. I want to speed up the blockchain plans. Server infrastructure all over the world. Out of government control."

"What's wrong with the cloud? We've done fine. Servers means sysadmins and network guys and God knows what else. And power bills." Jeff grinned. "Make global warming worse."

Elliot grimaced with annoyance. "Fuck. Go solar. Liberty means independence, Jeff. I want to avoid being at the mercy of Amazon, Google, or, God forbid, Microsoft. Or PG&E. They're all tools of the government now." Elliot's brain expanded. "We're going to need our own network. Satellites. Connected to the regular Internet, but completely under our control. So no one can interfere with us."

Jeff grinned. "Paranoid this morning, ain't we?"

Elliot stopped pacing and confronted his employee. "Did you watch the election results?" he demanded.

"Christ, no."

Elliot threw up his hands. "If anybody gave a shit about the government, this couldn't happen."

"What couldn't happen?"

"Elections like yesterday."

"Who was running exactly?"

Elliot sighed, disarmed by Jeff's naiveté. "It's why I love you guys, Jeff. You really don't care, do you?"

"Why should I? I mean, as long as you're paying me. Us."

Elliot wanted to scream at the man. He breathed, then toned it down to a fierce but softly spoken tirade. "OK, Jeff. I'm paying you. So listen up. Within two years, I want to be completely independent. I want a secure blockchain with my own unregulated currency. In four years, I want the power to render any currency worthless globally. In five years, I want complete control of all major blockchains and digital currencies. And elections. You can already see that blockchain will be the future of elections. The future of democracy lies in governments recording votes in a secure blockchain, or so they're thinking. In six years, I want to control every election anywhere that uses blockchain. Can you do that, Jeff?"

"Jesus Christ, Elliot. What brought this on?" Jeff tossed his empty bottle in a wastebasket and got another one from a mini-fridge next to his desk.

"Can you do it, Jeff?" Elliot paused. "You're not telling me you're afraid of breaking the law?"

"Elliot, the last time I paid any attention to laws was a speeding ticket in Barstow. But lookit. What you want is heavy stuff. Satellites? Needs a lot more green. Especially for servers and networks. And people."

"I've got a lot of green, Jeff. I know parties who have more green. And we all want to spend it."

"I can do that for ya." Jeff Morrow smiled happily, his eyes crinkled with pleasure. "Gonna be fun."

"I'll bring in some people for management, CEO, CFO, that kind of thing."

"Naw. We can handle it."

"Huh. How about your Pakistani wonder girl? We need good people, and I don't care about Americans anymore."

"Shoot, Elliot. I just gave her a reference a few months ago. She works for some dude up in the City. Company called 1WeakLink. Too bad."

Elliot paused, mouth ajar. "Really. 1WeakLink."

"Yeah. She won't tell me a damn thing about it. Says she's sittin' pretty and won't even talk to me about coming down here."

"Keep talking to her, Jeff. Take her to lunch. Hook and gaff her if you can. And get me all the information you can about the company. I've heard of them, they're heavy into blockchain tech. Anything you can discover has value, right? Your priority is to recruit more people like her."

"What about satellites, Elliot? I cain't just pull those out of my ass."

Elliot smiled. "Starburst."

"What?"

"This guy I fired from my company, the one I sold for billions? He started a spaceship company, Starburst, and did pretty well. You know—the one that littered all the beaches in South Texas with rocket fuel and blast debris."

"Oh, those guys." Jeff grinned. "Ya fired him? How does that help us?"

"I'll explain it was the Chinese buyer who fired him. That will get his attention. I'll give him a billion dollars to put up our satellites." Mark Firelock loved liberty even more than Elliot did. And he loved power. He'd be on board, no question. A moon shot! Elliot grinned. Mark's actual goal was Mars. He was just making money on satellites while he designed bigger things. Elliot would persuade him to stay closer to Earth for a while, making money and accumulating power. But Elliot knew he'd address Mark and his megalomania eventually. Once Elliot had the tools to take all the power he needed. He could just send Mark off to Mars and keep Earth for himself.

"Fuck me." Jeff seemed to accept the vastness of Elliot's vision for the future, Corona forgotten in his hand.

"And we'll set up a headquarters on my yacht, so we can move to international waters."

"I ain't never been on a boat, Elliot." Jeff showed the first sign of any concern about Elliot's plans. He put the Corona bottle on his desk and scratched his beard nervously.

"Ship. Don't worry about it. Just *move*."

Jeff grabbed his beer, swigged and swallowed, and raised the bottle toward Elliot for a cowboy salute. "Aye aye, sir."

Ludivine Moureaux scrutinized the email she'd just received, looking for hidden clues. Someone was hiring, big time, and had one of her public-facing emails on their spam list. Nothing in the text revealed the source. The sender email was fake, a non-existent domain. She used a tool to dump the content from the link in the text, a simple contact form on a server with no WHOIS record other than the service provider in Kiribati. She'd worked with the Kiribati admins before. No chance she would learn anything from them.

She examined the email header and saw what she expected, a long list of sender servers with domain names from all over the world. A world traveler, this email—but no Kiribati. The sender was spreading the wealth. The top of the list was a server with a fake domain that resolved to an IP address she recognized. It was part of a block of IP addresses linked to servers in a Russian botnet on one of the darker corners of the Internet. Sasha. Someone had hired Sasha for this email campaign. She occasionally used Sasha's botnet herself because it was secure from prying eyes. But Sasha had a weakness, and she could exploit it.

Ludivine clicked on a contact on her cell phone and waited. The man who answered spoke in Russian-accented French.

"Ludivine the Magnificent! *Privyet!* Do you finally desire a date with me? Are you in Saint Petersburg?" The Russian's excitement had the usual false ring to it. Ludivine began the back-and-forth Sasha seemed to need.

"Not a chance, Sasha. I don't date suppliers."

"Is that all I am to you, my ravishing love? A supplier?"

"No. You're also a snitch and a cheat, Sasha. That's why I love you."

"You don't love me if you won't go out with me."

Enough. Sasha could do this forever. *Une petite domination* was required. She demanded sharply, "Can we cut the crap? I need some information. About one of your servers."

"Ask me anything, Ludivine. Anything at all." Sasha's voice made an overheated attempt to present the image of himself lying at her feet. Sasha was 150 centimeters tall with a straggly, graying beard, a bald head, and a squint. This image might have sent a more emotional woman into uncontrollable laughter, but Ludivine was not an emotional woman. She coolly recited the IP address along with her email address. "Who uses this one for emails, Sasha? Sent 8 November 2018 at 09:33:30 UCT."

"Is some piece of shit stalking you, Ludivine? I can have them killed for you. I don't want anybody stalking you but me."

"No, it's a mass email scam, a phishing expedition, and it's interfering with my business. I dislike that. Besides, your prices are too high for assassinations." Not that she had ever paid for an assassination. But there was little point in encouraging Sasha's enormities.

"I'm crushed, Ludivine. Hang on while I check the SMTP logs. It's a proxy IP, so it may take a few minutes to find out which server. My God, the things I do for love." The silence of the universe filled her phone as she waited. "Ludivine? You're in luck. The logs tell me a domain called luna.taanstaafl.net sent that email. *Gospodin* Morrow, I suspect. His VPN choice is unimpressive. A minnow, not a phisher, at least so far in his career. Do you know him?"

"Not personally, only by reputation. *Merci*, Sasha. That's all I need."

"Where do I send the bill?"

Switching to Russian, a much better language for emphatic declaration, Ludivine crushed this ridiculous attempt at profit. "Stuff it up your ass, Sasha. You owe me. For the last time."

Sasha groaned. "How am I supposed to make money with people like you, Ludivine? And you won't even go out with me."

"Goodbye, Sasha."

Jeff Morrow. Perry. Their plan was in motion.

Ludivine clicked on another contact.

"Hello, AJ. We need to talk."

AJ sat in the window seat of her Waller Street apartment and looked out over the City. The fog had lifted, revealing rows upon rows of Victorians stretching out toward the Bay. So different from her home in Islamabad.

Ludivine's call had shaken her, and she sat at the window, thinking seriously. Her mentor pressed her on the 1WeakLink system, saying that AJ must send the code to her as soon as possible. Ludivine remained amiable in her cool way, of course, but she was insistent.

AJ explained the status and schedule. Her part of the codebase lacked a breakthrough technology for manipulating the encryption in blockchains. Solving the problems wouldn't be easy. The blockchain manipulation tools were only half complete because the other developers coded much more slowly than her. Except for Alec, of course. The system was not workable in its current state. Ludivine's prolonged silence before accepting this disappointment added to the pressure on AJ. But there was more to consider.

Over the past few weeks, AJ had settled into a blissful routine with Alec: code, sex, code, and more code. To her, sex and code had become indistinguishable. But she had repressed her secret agenda: stealing the 1WeakLink system for Ludivine. She'd also repressed the guilt she felt toward her incipient betrayal. She clasped her hands together, the anxiety and shame of what she intended to do overwhelming her. To betray Alec. What sort of person was she, that she could do this to him? But she could.

She rented this apartment to hide her shame, not avoid it. She realized now that this was a psychological trick she'd played on herself. So much shame in her behavior. The guilt of the sex, of *enjoying* that sex, and the shame in her heart over enjoying it. The shame of loving a man her parents would certainly not consider marriage material. They still insisted she consider marrying now that she had a master's degree from MIT. And now the guilt of betraying love for money. And yet, it was an enormous amount of money. Enough money to allow her to play the psychological trick forever. And so she would do it. But the shame still lurked underneath, waiting for her like a djinn hidden in a cave.

Still, the 1WeakLink software was far from done. Yes. It might be better to wait for the event to process the shame. Allah does not burden a soul more than it can bear. And her soul could bear this. For now. *Ma sha'a Allah.* The saying came easily to her lips from the many repetitions of it during childhood. She was not religious, but sometimes Allah proved useful.

AJ took one last look at San Francisco, shook her head, and went to her workstation to bury her shame in coding.

CHAPTER SEVEN
The Server Hack

AJ SAT NEXT TO ALEC at the long worktable in the 1WeakLink developer's room. Long, small-paned windows overlooked the busy freeway approach to the Bay Bridge, with a view of the never-ending stream of cars. Alec had told her the landlord's history of the building. A hundred seamstresses working away at sewing machines had occupied the semi-industrial building's third floor for many years in the main room. The business stored the finished product in the smaller room in which they sat. The new owners had sanded and refinished the old, splintered, and worn wooden floors to a gleaming sheen. Metal beams crisscrossed the rooms to reinforce the brick walls, reducing the risk of collapse in one of those nasty San Francisco earthquakes.

AJ had lost herself in the programming flow. She was using her improved version of an open source big data processing system to efficiently trace blockchain links across nodes. Not algorithmically challenging, but countless details consumed her mind.

A small window popped up on her monitor, flashing a red exclamation mark. Her flow broke in an instant.

"Alec," she said, fingers raised above her keyboard.

"Yah, one minute—"

"No, Alec. Now. Someone's hacked into our secure server. My tripwire went off."

"Shit!" Alec slid his wheeled office chair across the polished floor. "Shit! Where are they?"

AJ's fingers flew across the keyboard as she relentlessly tracked the server breach. Alec stood up and hovered intently over her shoulder, watching her progress. She felt the warmth of his body as she chased the intruder, the hunt transforming the flow into the increasing heat of arousal. He put his hand on her shoulder to encourage her, and the warmth grew.

She followed the thread of the hacker's commands and smiled with satisfaction. "They found the honeypot, Alec." His hand squeezed her shoulder.

"Hi, guys," Yuriko said as she came in from the front office. "What honeypot?" She stopped short as she took in the tableaux. "Oh. Please." She covered her eyes with one hand.

AJ sat bolt upright with her heart pounding as Alec's hand hastily withdrew. She said, covering her embarrassment, "Sorry, I'm just dealing with a nasty hacker attack on our server. The honeypot is a decoy system we created to detect and divert attackers. It lures them in. It's like the real system but with fake data. So I'm tracking them now without their knowing it. And Alec is helping." This last statement wasn't really true, but it explained what Yuriko saw, or at least AJ hoped it did.

Yuriko uncovered her eyes and tilted her head with a sardonic smile. "So I see. Well, I'm so glad we have such fine technical minds working for us. Be glad it's not Crispin, you idiots. And, oh, he wants a meeting. To explain our client's latest concerns. He'll be here in five minutes. Will you be done with, uh, the 'honeypot' by then?"

AJ glanced at her monitor. "Russian. Only to be expected. The…wait a bit. The tracer is moving on…the origin…Yangzhou. China. They used the Russian server to hide their identity."

Alec's jaw clenched. Then he said, "We have the topic for our meeting. The People's Republic of China is interested in our products." He reached to pat her on the shoulder but withdrew his hand and accompanied Yuriko to find Crispin. She stared after them in dismay.

* * *

Crispin's "office" was the sweatshop supervisor's office, from which he ensured the seamstresses' diligence. Alec smiled as he looked at Yuriko's cubicle, the only one now occupied in the room.

He joked, "It must be nice having Crispin watching you all the time, Yuriko."

Yuriko looked at Crispin's observation window and snorted, "Like hell." She smiled. "Exactly like hell."

When Alec and Yuriko entered the small room, Crispin's hands were folded in front of him, and he glared at his management team with tight lips.

Yuriko sat in the only extra chair, and Alec leaned against the door after closing it. He asked, "What's up, Crispin?"

Crispin got right to the point. "I've had a disturbing phone call with our NSA board member. They're furious."

Alec raised his eyebrows. "About what?"

"Elliot Perry."

The private equity billionaire? "What's Perry got to do with anything?"

"I took a call from him yesterday. He offered to buy the company. And the NSA was listening in."

"What do you mean, listening in?"

"They monitor all our communications, apparently." Crispin's eyes challenged Alec with this bombshell.

Alec clenched his jaw and stood silent, thinking about how to express his outrage. The NSA had no right to monitor their communications in secret. This NSA action violated their privacy rights. Before the complaint reached his lips, the main point hit home. Perry. Casting aside human rights for the moment, he said, "But we've just started the company! I hope you told Perry no?"

"Surely. But the NSA had heard enough to confirm Perry's knowledge of our work. They want to learn who told him."

"It wasn't us—the dev team. Yuriko?" He looked at the CFO.

Yuriko shook her head silently, her lips tight.

Alec said, "It could even be the NSA, Crispin. They have a history of leaks themselves."

Yuriko said, "Tell him, Alec."

"Tell me what?" demanded Crispin, his hands pressed on his desk, frowning.

"AJ just caught a hacker breaking into our honeypot server." Alec took a deep breath and added, "Chinese. PRC."

"Bloody hell, Alec!" Crispin thrust his head forward. "And the NSA will have monitored that. They'll be frantic. The PRC? That's a mission-critical breach."

Alec considered what might make the PRC mission critical. 1Weak-Link's mission was to build a blockchain hacking tool for the NSA. Blockchains and China. Where might China see itself as vulnerable because of blockchain technology? He put it together. Belt and Road. It was crucial for China's commercial dominance, and the NSA wanted to hack it.

He said, "One Belt and One Road. The NSA wants our tool so they can hack the Belt and Road blockchains around the world."

Crispin lost his patience. He folded his hands again and leaned forward, looking directly at Alec. "Brilliant, Alec. Got it in one. Imagine the NSA's reaction to their hacking us." Crispin rose, contemplating the Bay Bridge through the window, hands in pockets. He turned back to Alec. "Remember Snowdon?"

Everyone in the tech world had followed the Snowden NSA leak adventure and the government's dramatic response to it. Alec said, "Are you saying they're going to arrest us or something?"

Crispin grinned and shook his head. "Might have done in the past. They're quite a bit more hands-on now, Alec. If they decide you're a leaker, they could make you disappear. Or any member of your team. They will do whatever it takes to remove the threat to the project."

Alec said, "I'm sure we didn't leak, either to Perry or to China. Why would we? I'm betting the Chinese just hacked in randomly as part of their industrial espionage tactics, not because they've detected a threat to the BRI. Perry, the Chinese, the NSA—we're in a great place, Crispin. Everyone wants a piece of our work." Alec grinned, then sobered. "I'll meet with the team and stress security, OK? And it might help to give people more stock options to give them even more reason to help us succeed. Can I do that? Yuriko?"

She replied, "If the board approves it. And the NSA is on the board."

Crispin sat back down in his chair. "I'll call our contact and reassure him, then propose the increase. But Alec. You must make it absolutely clear to them that any leak will have dire consequences. For the company and for them, personally. Remind them of their nondisclosure agreements, but let them know that being sued in an American court will be the least of their problems if they cock up. Right?"

"Right," Alec sighed. His dream of funding his altruistic human rights ideas had become more pragmatic. And AJ would hate this new reality. But at least he could trust her. What about the rest of the team?

AJ listened in growing horror as Alec laid out the frightening new reality of 1WeakLink.

"Disappear?" she asked. "What does that mean, Alec?" Her mind filled with the images Reema had sent her of the horrific conditions for women in Pakistani prisons. This was Reema's work now. She had started an NGO to help these women, and their plight was terrible. Injustice and oppression had destroyed their lives. In Pakistan, the legal process differed from those of western countries. Or so she had understood. Now Alec was shattering her illusions by telling her that the American authorities might ignore the legal system altogether. This was not good news.

Alec admitted uneasily, "I don't know what the NSA might do, AJ. In the States, you have habeas corpus. That means your lawyer can challenge your imprisonment in court. Even the prisoners at Guantánamo Bay. But—"

A chill crept up AJ's spine. "Guantánamo? You mean the NSA can just take us and imprison us forever without trial? Torture us? Or worse?"

Alec, appearing dismayed by her reaction to his news, took her hands in his. He said, "Look, we both know that won't happen. We won't reveal anything about 1WeakLink to outsiders. So there's nothing to concern yourself about."

Was there not? The image of a smiling Ludivine pushed the images of the poor Pakistani prisoners out of her mind. Ludivine's image was anything but reassuring; it was terrifying.

Alec released her hands and drew back. "AJ, I have to ask. How did you discover the purpose of the company? Back at your job interview, remember?"

Her heart froze. Ludivine. Ludivine. Ludivine. She replied, "I don't remember, Alec. I must have heard it in a conversation somewhere during the conference." She shook her head and looked him in the eye. "I just don't remember."

Alec didn't pursue the point. Instead, he asked, "AJ, I don't want to lose you. Will you stick with us? With me?" He looked her in the eyes.

AJ forced a smile. "Of course, Alec. There's nothing. Nothing at all." She hugged him, her chin on his shoulder, her eyes closed, as her mind began its desperate search for a solution.

"So that's the situation, folks," Alec said, staring at the green dot next to his laptop camera. AJ sat next to him at the conference table. The anxious and indignant expressions on Alec's WebEx audience's faces begged for reassurance. It was 7 a.m. on a Wednesday morning in San Francisco, late in the day in Europe.

"I'm a U.S. citizen!" exclaimed Peter from New York. "What the hell." He glared at Alec through the monitor, the effect ruined because he was looking sideways at his monitor instead of at his camera.

"I know. So am I," Alec said. "Makes no difference. Don't mess with the NSA, and they won't mess with you. The upside is you all get extra options. 300,000 options vesting over three years. You'll all be very wealthy."

"Or immured for life on some Caribbean desert island," Marcus grumbled sarcastically from London. "With no beach privileges."

"What is 'immured,' plis?" asked Olyena from Lviv.

"Oh, take a guess, woman," Marcus replied, his irritation seeping through.

"It means locked up, Olyena," said AJ. Olyena blew her a virtual kiss, and Alec smiled.

"Do we still get the stock options if we're locked up?" asked her husband, the practical Maks. His wife slapped him on the shoulder in exasperation.

"Yes, we'll lock those in as soon as you agree to the terms." Alec grinned. "Pun intended."

"Do we sign something?" asked Olyena.

"A smart contract on the NSA private blockchain," Alec replied. "As long as you all keep everything top secret, the contract will vest your options on schedule. If the NSA detects a problem, the smart contract will cancel your options. What else the NSA will do to you? I don't know, but please don't find out."

The team members expressed varying levels of anxiety at this vague threat and anger at the NSA's spying on them, but in the end, they all agreed to move forward. Alec, relieved that he could now trust his team, held AJ's hand under the table out of sight of the camera. She gripped his hand with extra pressure.

Later, AJ asked to stay at his place for the night, and Alec readily agreed, aware that the NSA's threat still bothered her a lot. All evening, she stayed close to him, and later, in bed, their loving was more passionate than ever. As they relaxed afterwards, she wrapped her arms around him and murmured, "Everything will be all right, won't it? Alec?"

He pulled her closer, kissed her, and said, "Of course."

CHAPTER EIGHT
A Hacker's Progress

JEFF MORROW CALLED JOEY OVER to his workstation. He had learned that Joey had majored in political science at MIT. Jeff, who rarely left the Stata Center, hadn't been aware that MIT *had* a political science department. Joey had scoffed. Now, his breadth of knowledge might prove handy. Jeff asked him for advice on elections that would be suitable candidates for hacking. Joey took a piece of paper from Jeff's desk and wrote furiously on the back. Low tech, Jeff grinned to himself.

"OK, Jeff," Joey said, handing the paper to Jeff. "Here's a list of fifteen 2019 elections around the world."

"Fifteen! I need one, dude." He looked at the list and scratched his beard.

"Shoulda said so. Well, it's obvious. Astana."

"Where the hell is that?"

"Kazakhstan."

"I'm none the wiser, dude."

"Just take my word for it, Jeff. It's a snap election for the Majlis, the country's legislature."

"What makes it snap, dude?" asked Jeff, the image of a Kazakh gator flashing through his mind.

Joey grinned. "Jeff, you really are clueless. A snap election is a special election. Called suddenly and not on the regular date."

"Why that one?" asked Jeff, annoyed.

"Four reasons. First, it's tomorrow, the last day of February. Second, you have a baseline 'cause they know the results before the election. Third, the election won't affect any legislation, because the government always wins. Fourth, nobody gives a shit about Astana politics. Or Kazakh politics, for that matter. So, this is an ethical hack. Sorta." His lips twisted. "It's always possible the hack will set off riots. Kazakhs can be unstable."

"Great place. Sounds like Texas."

"Right. Very similar." Joey was from New York and thought Texas was a foreign country.

Jeff grinned. He needed to show Elliot something positive before the Den moved to his yacht. Hacking the Astana voter rolls wasn't rocket science, but the tools would scale once Elliot decided which elections to experiment with. It wasn't blockchain hacking either, but they'd get there soon. Sooner, if he could convince AJ to join them.

"Let's get started," Jeff said.

"What do I do?" Joey asked eagerly.

"Set yourself down in that there chair, dude, and watch a master hacker at work."

Jeff wanted to avoid giving Joey the idea that he was more knowledgeable than Jeff. Valley management 1A. This election is really going to snap.

Jeff hacked into the Astana elections department server with a zero-day, then deployed the trojan-based tool. He ran the programs he'd written to mix up the names and addresses in the database, recording everything as he went. One minute and thirty-nine seconds later, Jeff turned off the recorder and exited the server, leaving Astana to its own devices. He was glad he'd recorded everything, because he was 100% sure the Astana Majlis election would not make the *New York Times*.

Elliot turned to the international news section of his copy of the March 19 *New York Times*. The office was quiet. Some employees had left for the yacht while others had been laid off. Elliot read the daily *New York Times* along with the *Wall Street Journal*. He liked the quality of real newsprint under his fingers. Web news didn't cut it. Though he kept it to himself, he hated computers. Of course, they would make him extraordinarily powerful and rich. And power and money defined life.

Speaking of power, Elliot scanned the paper, and there it was: Nursultan Nazarbayev had stepped down as president of Kazakhstan. Tim heard about the crisis through a friend invested there. He also mentioned that the protests that led to the resignation resulted from Jeff's manipulation of the Astana voter rolls. The extensive and growing corruption frustrated people, and the hack sparked rumors that intensified their anger.

Before this, Elliot had little interest in Kazakhstan, either financial or intellectual. There were plenty of opportunities for financial gain elsewhere in the world. No reason to expose himself to that level of corruption and greed. But the hack was a brilliant choice for a dummy run of the tools. Jeff had done a great job. He changed his mind about Kazakhstan. Why not?

Elliot picked up his cell phone and called Jeff in the Den to congratulate him. "And Jeff, a new assignment. The paper says Nazarbayev is going to make his ridiculous daughter president. Let's explore our options, shall we? Investigate the supposed suicide of her ex-husband in Vienna in February and go from there. Let's see if we can make the regime change permanent."

"OK, boss, sounds like fun!"

Elliot rose and walked to the office window, peering out at the Palo Alto park. He changed the subject. "How's your Pakistani girlfriend? Ready to join us yet?"

"Girlfriend, hah. AJ's too focused on her hacking to have a boyfriend."

"Anything about the company?"

"Naw, zipped lips. And I been kinda busy, Elliot."

"Now you're busier. Charm her into getting you into their systems. Social engineering, right? Wrap up your mainland affairs and tell your team to get ready to shift operations to the yacht. Tim will arrange transportation. Talk to him about tickets and baggage shipping and such. No pets on board. We sail from Miami on April 3rd."

Ludivine followed Jeff Morrow's efforts to dash Dariga Nazarbayeva's hopes and dreams from a cafe on the rue St. Michel. It was a cool day, and she was wearing an ankle-length hunter green quilted coat open over a black sweater, black leather pants, and black boots.

She had just met with potential clients. It had not gone well. Ludivine had decided, early in her business adventures, to avoid people she would not invite to her table. One look at these prospects convinced her they were not the right fit for her services. She left and spent the afternoon at the cafe, sipping excellent wine, people watching, and following up on various projects.

She once again persuaded Sasha to share his knowledge and learned about Jeff Morrow's hack of the Astana database. Sasha's interests in Kazakhstan involved botnet servers and bitcoin mining. He didn't care about the president, just the people he'd paid off further down the corruption tree.

From other sources, she'd learned that, shortly after the Astana hack, Jeff switched from his Palo Alto Internet connection to a secure satellite system, Mark Firelock's Starburst. Her team could not access that network. Not yet. They'd have to speed things up. For the moment, she could track Morrow's efforts on Sasha's servers. The change suggested that Morrow had moved to a new location, somewhere off the main Internet networks. She made a note to investigate the move and Perry's whereabouts.

Ludivine sipped her Chablis as she assessed Jeff's progress through her notepad. This series of small regime-change hacks wasn't important. And there were no blockchains involved. Jeff had not yet achieved any significant results there. But soon she would have to intervene when Elliot Perry's quest for world domination threatened her international interests and her powerful status in the dark world of the web. Unlike Sasha, she took no direct interest in Kazakhstan's internal politics. But she knew

Perry would not stop at a minor regime change in an irrelevant nation-state. Her last phone call to AJ told her that Jeff had tried unsuccessfully to recruit her into Perry's organization, and that he had tried to break into 1WeakLink. Ludivine liked to be three steps ahead. And that started now.

She picked up her phone and texted Raoul, her deputy, to activate the surveillance plan they'd worked out for Perry's operations. She advised Raoul to take care to avoid the surveillance-aware measures and counter-measures that Perry's henchmen would surely have in place.

Ludivine put away her phone and notepad and smiled at the well-dressed, handsome gentleman at the next table, who had been eyeing her for half an hour. She shook her head slightly, dashing his hopes and dreams, and headed for the Pont Neuf. Jeff Morrow's hack meant she had work to do.

Jeff Morrow was on a roll. The Kazakh operation went so well that Elliot gave him a $25,000 bonus and said he should share it with any outstanding members of the team. Jeff thought about it and decided the guys were competent, not outstanding. So he kept the bonus. The hack that ruined Dariga Nazarbayeva's reputation was a classic disinformation operation. The key was to make 'em believable. Since Nazarbayeva's past was an open book to his team, it was not only believable, it was true. A non-disinformation operation. Unusual for this type of attack. But Elliot paid for results, and he got them when Kassim-Jomart Tokayev took over the government.

But Elliot's second assignment proved harder, much harder: hacking into 1WeakLink in Frisco. And the move to the yacht compounded his problems. Hacking needed concentration and a lot of beer, and moving to a boat across the country disturbed both. But now he'd settled into his cabin and set up his hacking consoles in the converted nightclub lounge. A crew member stocked the wine coolers with Corona, and he was back on track. The TANSTAAFL crew dribbled aboard one by one. Now they had sailed into the Atlantic, destination unknown. He'd made no progress on Elliot's task. And he was seasick. Very seasick.

AJ, as stubborn as ever, had only given him two lunches. He'd probed her system, but she'd locked it down tight in all the obvious ways. He'd taught her well. And now he was sailing the seven seas. But his Starburst satellite Internet connection was excellent, so he continued to probe AJ's secrets, which so far had remained secret.

Alec met AJ for breakfast at the Jackalope cafe, a block from the office. Since she only stayed over on Fridays, they had breakfast on Tuesdays at the Jackalope to catch up.

Today, her preoccupation told him she had something on her mind. She stared out the cafe window at the passing commute traffic on Howard Street, her eggs cooling on their plate.

"What's up, AJ?" asked Alec.

She smiled disarmingly, her eyes coming back to meet his. "Well, I didn't want to make you jealous, but I've been keeping in touch with a friend of mine from MIT, Jeff Morrow. Two lunches. He's been recruiting me to work at his company down in Palo Alto. I keep telling him no. I thought I'd better tell you because now he's trying to hack into my computer at work."

Alec frowned. "Stalking you? Is that why you're—"

"No, no, Jeff's fine. I've known him for years. Since MIT. He's a mentor. But he's a hacker first. Like someone else you know." She smiled and reached out for Alec's hand. He took it and gripped it. "He's just having fun."

Alec was doubtful. Extremely doubtful. "His fun isn't funny. If he hacks in—"

"No, of course not." She was indignant. "I set up our security, didn't I? No one gets in, ever."

Except the Chinese. But she caught them red-handed. Another pun. "Who is he working for? The Chinese?"

"Oh, no, not Jeff. He works for a private equity billionaire, Elliot Perry. USA all the way. He's a Texan."

Alec suspected Jeff wasn't just having fun, despite his patriotism. Perry had tried to buy the company. Now that had failed, he was trying to steal the software. If the NSA discovered this hacking, they'd go ballistic.

"I'm not jealous," he lied with a smile. "But could you please take a break from Jeff?"

AJ grinned and nodded in agreement. "He's going on a long trip, anyway. A cruise, he said."

"Good." Hope the ship sinks. Alec grinned at his inner vision of the Titanic heading down. AJ smiled sunnily back.

They finished their breakfast in harmony.

CHAPTER NINE
Working from Home

"Aamna, Aamna, when are you coming home?"

Her mother's voice came through perfectly from halfway around the world. The phone call told AJ nothing new. Her mother always said the same thing. Home, home, home.

"San Francisco is home, Mama. I live here now."

"Oh, Aamna, no! Pakistan is home. Your family, your friends are here, and they miss you. It has been years since we have seen you. Please, come home."

These pleas worked on her emotions. She'd left so much behind in her pursuit of knowledge and wealth. She had to remind herself why: to achieve all she could with her computer skills, the financial rewards, the sheer joy of hacking the impossible. Not to mention avoiding marriage. Farazman had married while she was at MIT and was no longer an issue. But the longer she stayed away, the more family and home pulled at her. AJ missed her father and mother. She missed Reema and her other friends. She even thought fondly of her brothers.

Throughout her freshman year at MIT and all the years that followed, her family called her regularly, urging her to return to Pakistan. By the summer of 2019, their pleas had turned to desperation as she remained steadfast. Her father was alternately proud and appalled by her salary at 1WeakLink. Proud because it exceeded that of all the men in his company combined; appalled because it rendered useless the greatest influence he could wield over her: money. Through it all, Papa remained kind and supportive but deeply disappointed in her absence from Pakistan.

Alec was unconditionally supportive. "I understand, AJ, I do. I see why your parents are acting the way they are. Do what you have to." And AJ loved Alec for his idealistic belief in human rights. He reminded her of Reema, who was always doing something for some abused refugee or prisoner of conscience. She knew her own concerns were different, but she appreciated their good intentions.

Ludivine's calls added to the pressure at work, already great from the insane project schedules she had been meeting by sleeping much less and cutting back on social activities. As she spent more time with Alec, her guilt now joined with a serious loss of productivity. She limited her sleeping with Alec to once every two weeks. He accepted this reduction with resignation and a comment about his own workload that sympathized with her.

As the project progressed, doubts about her actions in San Francisco plagued AJ more and more. Alec was great, of course. That was the problem. She wasn't. She was playing both sides, a covert agent for a criminal mastermind. The idea of betraying Alec was getting harder for her to accept, despite the future riches. She sent bits and pieces of the software to Ludivine as she finished them, each transmission renewing her guilt. Then Jeff started calling, recruiting her. And trying to hack into her system. Telling Alec about Jeff had been a mistake. He got jealous.

She loved the pleasure and the intimacy of making love to Alec. At first, she ignored the guilt. Then the doubts grew, and the guilt swelled, and the jealousy surfaced, and the sex changed. For both of them. The guilt of breaking the rules she'd grown up with surfaced and joined with her betrayals. For her, the sex rarely matched the first ecstasies of their relationship. Did Alec feel the same way? Was it the jealousy?

And then there was Thanksgiving.

* * *

Early in their relationship, Alec had told AJ about his own parents, who fortunately did not call often. Really, never. He called *them*. His mother, Dr. Mary Bethune Chenais, a computer science professor at McGill University in Montreal, was emotionally cold and uninvolved with her son, even though they both loved computers. His mother had a deep understanding of the field of quantum computing and its biomedical applications but had little interest in her son's work. Their conversations were brief; life updates, never important things. Alec's conversations with his father only made him angry.

"He's so full of shit, AJ," Alec would complain. "Every time I talk to him, he interrupts to talk about his latest ad campaign. It makes me sore because he could help, but he's all about the fundraising, not the people."

Attending the Chenais family's October 2018 ritual called "Thanksgiving," which seemed to have nothing to do with thanks or giving, exposed her to the full range of Chenais emotions.

Alec's mother made fun of certain people they both knew in the computer science community, making AJ laugh and wonder just how naïve she had been in school. But Mary was sharp, critical, and often disrespectful. AJ was certain that Mary would criticize her after she left the room. She criticized Alec when he was *in* the room.

AJ did not like Paul Chenais, Alec's father. There was something sinister about the man. Paul loved to hear himself talk, especially about his human rights work. At Thanksgiving, Paul held forth about all the moral ills of Pakistan, her old home. She told him about Reema and her organization, but he laughed it off as too little, too late. He launched into a diatribe about the politically motivated assassination of Prime Minister Bhutto—the daughter, not the father. More disrespect.

The sole benefit from that 2018 family gathering was her discovery of "cranberry sauce." Paul claimed Canadians made better cranberry sauce than Americans. AJ replied that they certainly made better cranberry sauce than Pakistanis, and everyone laughed. But as she traveled home on the plane from Canada, she compared the warmth and kindness of her own family to the coldness and bitterness of Alec's. Her longing for her own family grew.

On a cold Wednesday night in early October 2019, AJ and Alec were in bed in Alec's condo. AJ knew that depression and guilt would soon overtake her. Now she lay comfortably in Alec's arms, warm and drowsy after making love.

"We need to schedule in Thanksgiving with my parents, October 13," Alec murmured in her ear.

Images from the previous year flooded her mind. All the pressure and guilt flooded back. Cranberry sauce was not enough.

"Is this your idea of love talk, Alec?" She sat up in bed, the warmth fleeing. "Or are you just thoughtless? Because I'm not going."

"Be reasonable, AJ. They're my parents. Liking them is unnecessary, but we have to—"

"*We* don't have to anything, Alec. We don't. *You* go. I won't."

"You're being childish. And stop interrupting me."

"What?" She turned to him, now wide awake. "Childish? Interrupting you?" AJ clenched her teeth so that she wouldn't bite her tongue off to control the words flooding out of her brain. She got up and dressed. It was all too much. The guilt, pressure, and disrespect fueled a sudden and unusual anger in her. She had to leave.

"What are you doing, AJ? Please, calm down." Alec got out of bed, naked, his face alarmed. He reached for her, but she shook him off and continued to dress.

"I'm going home. I don't have to lie here and listen to your bollocks."

"AJ, I'm trying—"

She walked out, slamming the front door to his condo, and walked through the cool October air to Market Street. She cried a little at one point. The Muni took her home to the Haight, and she spent the rest of the night lost in her code and ignoring texts and emails from Alec. She slept most of the morning and skipped work.

The next day, Alec called. "AJ, I want to apologize. I love you. I don't want to hurt you or to impose anything on you. Thanksgiving is out, I'll go by myself. All right? Can we make up?"

AJ's anger had cooled, but she had to do something. She loved Alec, but there were so many pressures: her family and the sex and his parents. And Ludivine. She needed space but couldn't end things with Alec. The thought of Ludivine's reaction was unbearable. Her guilt over betraying Alec to Ludivine wasn't enough to risk walking away from her future riches and the independence they represented.

"Alec, we need a break. I love you too, but I need some time for myself. There's too much going on. I can't handle it all." She imagined walking into the office and seeing him there every day. "May I temporarily work from home? You don't need me in the office. Only for a month or two, OK? Then we'll sit down and figure things out."

"All right, AJ, all right. Whatever makes you comfortable. We'll make it work. Do you have everything you need at home? I mean, for work. Is it all secure?"

"Yes, Alec. Trust me on security, you know me. I even have food here and everything." She smiled.

"AJ, I need to ask. Are you going to leave the company?"

"No, Alec, no way. I love the work, I love what we're doing. And I love you, I just need…time. To figure things out for myself."

"You got it." He swore undying love and hung up. She carefully placed her phone on her kitchen table, opened her laptop, and lost herself in coding.

At the beginning of February 2020, AJ was still working at home. She spoke to Yuriko in her HR capacity about the situation with Alec. She wanted to assure the company of her commitment and to reassure them about her and Alec. Yuriko said she was fine with that. Alec said he was, but how could he be if he really loved her? And he did. Things would work out. They would.

Then Yuriko called and asked, "Have you heard about this Chinese COVID virus?"

"Oh, yes. Terrible."

"Well, it's getting worse. I have good information that the authorities are going to restrict international travel soon."

"What do you mean?"

"It may not be possible to travel anywhere outside of the United States while they get a handle on the transmission of the virus."

"When and for how long?"

"A month or two, or even a few weeks? Some people predict the lockdown will be over by the end of the summer, others think it could be a year or two."

AJ's stomach lurched. No travel at all? For years?

After Yuriko hung up, AJ walked into her living room. Why did this hit her so hard? She'd worked for years to be independent from her family. Their old-fashioned idea to marry her off had made her run away. And she'd worked hard on her career. She'd agreed to Ludivine's plan precisely because it would make her financially secure, secure enough to tell her parents to go to hell.

But deep down, AJ knew she didn't want to do that. Marriage was out of the question, of course, but she loved her family. She loved Islamabad, where she'd grown up. She loved her friends there. There were ways to avoid an arranged marriage.

If she had her family to fall back on, she could deal with Alec's. If she had her family's acceptance of him as a husband, she'd rely on their warmth and kindness to counter the trials and tribulations of her American life. And having her own family with Alec in America would create a new, stable base for her.

But what about Ludivine? If she were careful, Alec would never find out about her treachery. He hadn't suspected anything so far, even though she'd given Ludivine several pieces of the system. What if he found out and left her in disgust? What would be her fallback?

Not her career or her money or even Ludivine. Her family.

Not to see them for years?

She had to think this through.

By February 7th, AJ had postponed her visit to her family in Pakistan. She needed to make up with Alec and find her footing in America. The logic was simple, but her feelings still drew her to Islamabad. She suppressed them.

The following Tuesday, she called her parents to tell them.

"But, Aamna," her mother wailed. "I am sure the government will bring you home. Yes, COVID fills the newspapers, but we need you here."

Her father said, "Asya, we have no insight into what the government will do. But, Aamna, there are still flights. Could you come home for a visit? Even a short one?"

"But I might not get back, Papa. To America."

"Is that so terrible?" her mother asked.

Aamna realized she could as easily work from home in Islamabad or the Haight. A quick visit home? Possible. But the risk—not possible. She told them so.

"Oh, Aamna. I did not want to tell you, but I am sick," her mother said.

"COVID? Is it the virus?" AJ asked in alarm.

"No, the doctors tell me nothing," her mother said.

"But, Asya—" her father said.

"Now you be quiet, Mahmood, and let me talk to my daughter. Off the phone, please."

Her father said, "I hope you know what you're doing, Asya."

"I do. Please."

"Goodbye, Aamna. Take care."

"You too, Papa." He hung up. "Now, Mama, what's this about being ill?"

"I've had these pains for some time, Aamna. But I didn't want to worry you."

"For how long?"

"Long enough. But I do not want to talk about my problems. It is just that not seeing you for years—I do not know if...." Her mother trailed off, leaving the future to AJ's imagination. "Will you at least consider a visit home? Before something makes it impossible?"

"Oh, Mama."

"Yes, my darling, yes."

AJ was on a United flight to Heathrow late the next night, with a PIA connection to Dubai and Islamabad. She called Ludivine while waiting to board at SFO. Her mentor expressed no surprise at her travel. But she had never seen Ludivine express surprise about anything in their time together.

"How does this affect our deal, *ma chérie?*" Ludivine asked.

"I will work from Pakistan, just as I do from home. But...it's not secure. I won't be able to send you code updates from my parents' home. We'll have to work something out, later."

"Of course. And your relationship with Alec Chenais?"

"We—I have stopped seeing him for a time, Ludivine. But I am sure we will reconcile. I need to be with my parents, and he accepts that."

Ludivine said in her smoothest French, "Very well, *ma chérie*. I am sure it will be fine. But, please take care not to burn any bridges. Much depends on your success. Do not jeopardize this project with a virus, a lover's quarrel, or even your mother's health. This is important to me."

"Yes, Ludivine. I do see the importance. I will call Alec. There is no problem. Everything will happen as we have planned."

"Good. Stay focused on the code. We will arrange for secure access soon. And stay healthy, *ma chérie*."

CHAPTER TEN
Crisis

The background noise on AJ's call was loud, making it hard to hear her. Alec pressed the phone to his ear.

"Hello, Alec. I…to tell you.…"

"Can you speak up, AJ? Too much noise. Where are you?"

"Heathrow."

"Uh, what?"

Her voice grew louder. "I'm at Heathrow. London. I'm flying to Pakistan. Islamabad."

"But—"

"No, Alec, just listen for a moment. I have to go home. The pandemic is coming. And my mother…Alec, she is ill, very sick. I want to go to them, to my family."

"When will you be back?" Alec asked, shaken.

"I don't know. But Alec, I will work from Islamabad. Is there any problem with that?"

"If you have a fast Internet connection, no problem. This shouldn't change anything."

AJ's voice became urgent. "Alec, my flight is boarding. I must go."

"Call me. Call me when you get to Islamabad. I need—"

"Yes, yes—I must go. My plane is boarding."

The phone went silent. Alec put it down on the counter and stared at his coffee, now cold. AJ, working from Pakistan. This changed everything.

A half hour after AJ's phone call, Alec sat in front of his breakfast, uneaten, still processing AJ's departure. His phone rang. An unknown number. He pushed away his unproductive questions and answered it.

"Ah, Alec, I am so glad. Can you talk?" The voice was deep and familiar.

"Ludivine? Moureaux?"

"Yes, *mon ami*. I am calling you from Paris."

"I haven't heard from you since...."

"A marvelous day four years ago, yes. A lovely memory. But I call because I must warn you."

"Warn. About what?"

"Elliot Perry." Ludivine switched to French. "Alec, you know that my business interests are very broad. People tell me things. Since I am your friend, I listen attentively when I come across things of interest to you. A rumor, Alec, about your company, has reached my ears."

"If you mean Perry's interest in the company, I'm aware." But Ludivine's shared awareness shattered the NSA's crucial need for secrecy. It was a mirage.

Ludivine said, "Then you must also know Perry is a major danger to your company. He is more dangerous that you can know, Alec. You may need my help soon."

"What kind of help?"

"The kind only I can give. I need not explain. You've met my colleagues."

Alec grimaced. Too much for him to take in. Perry, AJ, Pakistan, the NSA. And now Ludivine, from Paris. His problems were piling up out of control. Did he want Ludivine's help? She might cause more problems than she solved if the NSA found out. He'd have to be careful.

"Ludivine. Thanks for the warning. I will take it seriously. Unless you can suggest something for the present?"

"Not just yet, *mon ami*. We must await the crisis that provides an opportunity. I will be in touch. *Au revoir, mon ami.*"

And she was gone.

AJ plopped her carryon down by a seat in the arrivals lounge at the Islamabad airport. Her limited sleep on the flight from Heathrow left her feeling irrational. She had promised to call Alec during the chaos and rush of boarding. So many conflicts swirled in her mind. But she'd promised. And during the flight, she'd had time to think.

She pressed the contact call button and held the phone to her ear. Alec answered on the first ring. They exchanged greetings, and AJ told him she needed to go through customs, passport control, and find transportation.

Alec was silent for a moment, then said, "I have to ask you, AJ. You wanted to take a break. It's been months. Is…are you…"

His hesitation and concern gave her clarity. She loved Alec, but the relationship had changed. How had she ended up here? Working for Ludivine to steal the software didn't bother her in itself, but betraying Alec was unbearable, even with their separation. She had to choose. So many things weighed against her love for this man. It wasn't worth everything she would give up by staying with him. How could she convince him to let her go?

She said as firmly as possible, "It's best, Alec, that we end our relationship."

"AJ, we can work this out. When you return to the States—"

"It may be some time before I return, Alec." She paused, hardening her resolve. "Alec, I need to tell you something. My family…they are very traditional."

"That's OK, AJ. I can adapt once I get to know them. I can fly—"

"No, no, you don't understand, Alec." She pressed her lips together. It wasn't really a lie, just an exaggeration. But it would solve her problem. She said, "I am to marry. My parents have arranged a marriage for me. It is our tradition."

"But you love *me,*" he cried.

She refused to lie about that. She remained silent.

"Do you love this man?" asked Alec in a choked tone.

"I don't know him. It is an arranged marriage."

Alec groaned. "This is…you can't, you mustn't do this, AJ. They can't do this to you. To us."

AJ's heart went out to her now ex-lover, but she would stand firm. The situation was painful. She would end it now. "I must, Alec. Please understand. This is Pakistan, not America. Now I must go."

"But, AJ—"

"Goodbye, Alec. I will email you when I am ready to work again."

AJ ended the call and lowered the phone to her lap. She looked out at the giant plane that had brought her home. She sighed, stood up, and headed for customs and her family.

Sleepless and fixated on AJ, Alec had to act. He hadn't spoken to his father since the Thanksgiving visit. The one AJ didn't want to attend. Because of his father. But Paul Chenais had the information Alec needed. He checked the time: 10:30 a.m. in Montreal. He clicked on his father's contact to call him.

"Good to hear from you," said his father. "Did you see our latest campaign on the Rohingya?" The implication being, why else would you call?

"No, but I'm sure it's—"

"We got a large grant from a Singaporean donor who wanted to think differently, so we're blanketing the region with TV and social media drops. We're breaking into the region, so this is big, Alec, huge."

"I'm sure. Listen, Dad, I need some advice."

"OK, like what?"

"Pakistan, Dad. You remember AJ is Pakistani? She's in Islamabad with her family now. Update me about things in Pakistan. What's happening there that I should worry about?"

"Oh, Christ. What isn't happening? Corruption, torture, arbitrary executions, kidnappings, murders of journalists, murders for blasphemy, forced marriages, gender-based violence, terrorist attacks, honor killings. I can't remember it all without looking it up on our flyer. Why would she go to Pakistan?"

"She's *from* there, Dad. Her family is in Islamabad."

"Still. My advice is to get her out."

"She won't come." Alec hesitated. Then his father finished his words of wise advice.

"Forget about her. Find yourself a nice Quebecoise. Or a Swede. They're very nice."

"It's not funny, Dad," Alec said, his voice hushed with controlled indignation.

"Sure it is, you just don't have a sense of humor. *She* sure didn't when we met her. What's her name again?"

Alec's finger hovered over the End Call icon. The urge to hang up on his father gripped him. But he had gotten nothing useful. Would he ever?

Fortunately, his father remained oblivious to his son's emotional state. Alec took a breath to control his anger, then asked, "Dad, how would you go about stopping an arranged marriage? Where the family forces the woman to marry someone she's never met?"

"Huh," his father snorted. "Now I see. Did you get her pregnant? Did she go there to have the baby? And her family's marrying her off to save face?"

"No, that's not—"

"But she's being forced?"

"Yes, she has—"

"How do you know? Did she call you for help?"

"No, she called me to tell me about it. She's going along with it for her family. I have to—"

"So she's doing this voluntarily."

"But she doesn't want to. She loves me. I'm sure she does. I have to go —"

"Nothing you can do, Alec. It's not against international law if it's not forced. And you'd have a hard time unless it was your child she was covering up for. No standing to sue."

"But if I flew there, found a lawyer—"

"Barrister, for human rights cases. But they're all crooks. My opinion, of course. Waste of time and effort, anyway. It's voluntary. If they're not forcing her, she doesn't love you enough to stand up for herself. Forget her, Alec. Hey, I've got to go, staff meeting about the Rohingya campaign. Bye."

And the call was over.

Crispin showed up at the office around 4 p.m. After a few minutes, he entered the development room and walked over to Alec's worktable.

"Alec. What's all this shite about AJ?"

"Did Yuriko tell you—"

"Why don't you tell me, thanks. Horse's mouth and all that."

"AJ flew to Pakistan to be with her family. Her mother's sick. She'll be working from there."

"That's it?"

"What are you insinuating?" Would Crispin confront him about his relationship with a subordinate? He had said nothing before. Why now?

"Insinuating. A big word, that. No, I'm asking. I'm asking because the NSA is going to ask me. And our key hacker is now based in Pakistan, well known for its unreliability."

So, not the relationship. The spooks. And Crispin was peeved.

Alec justified himself. "I can't help it, Crispin. She just did it, and she's Pakistani, and her family needs her. And she can work from there. Otherwise, we lose her and her skills. We can't afford to lose her, Crispin."

"You should have made her think twice," Crispin said.

"She surprised me completely with this. But I can't order her to turn around. She'll quit."

Crispin took out his cell phone and made a call. He summed up events to the person he was talking to. "Here," he said. "The NSA wants a word."

Alec took the phone. "Hello? This is Alec."

"Alec," said a smooth voice. "Good to talk to you. Listen, this Pakistan thing is very serious. Drastic consequences. Do you understand that?"

"I do."

"Well, good. Pakistan is not a friendly place. Things may happen if secrets get out. Very nasty things. Everyone involved may suffer consequences." The voice continued smoothly, no violence in the inflection. "Everyone involved. Oh, and how is the blockchain software coming?"

"We'll have something useful in a month, sir. If you—"

"No, no, doesn't matter. Whenever. No rush. You should concentrate on your work. And…take care." The phone went silent.

Alec handed the phone back to Crispin, who put it in his pocket.

"Are we good?" he asked.

"Yeah. Just fine," Alec replied. Crispin left for his office, leaving Alec to his worries.

CHAPTER ELEVEN
Return to Pakistan

The 28-hour flight from San Francisco to Islamabad via Heathrow and Dubai was now only a memory. In the customs line, everyone examined each other with nerves on edge, wondering if others had the virus. Anyone with a slight cough cleared the surrounding area in an instant. Those few wearing masks avoided eye contact with the unmasked.

AJ daydreamed she was safe in the warm embrace of her family, in her old house, in her old room. Then the man behind her pushed her forward, as the line had moved on. She gave him a dirty look, and he told her to wear her *dupatta*. The headscarf was in her backpack, but she'd forgotten about it during the long flight. She was once more in her old world.

That old world had traveled there to welcome her. Even her two brothers were there. As her father approached her with a smile and a hug, she noticed her brothers smirking behind him.

Her father inspected her and said, "Ah, my daughter, you are even more beautiful than when you left."

"It's good to be home," she told him. He hugged her.

"Can we go now?" asked Babur, the older of her two siblings. Sohail, a year younger at 17, smirked again and punched his brother in the shoulder, and they scuffled. Their mother admonished them.

AJ looked her mother up and down. She presented no visible signs of illness. Mama appeared unchanged since AJ's last seeing her.

"Mama, are you feeling well? You should not have come. Did your doctors discover what is amiss?"

"We can talk about all that later, my dear," her mother said as she hugged her. Her brothers smirked again with no empathy, but they were family, and AJ hugged them too.

"It's good to be home, mama," AJ said. Her mother reached to adjust AJ's *dupatta*.

"Can we go now?" Sohail asked. "We're late for cricket, papa. You know this."

"Cricket can wait, my son. It is not every day that we welcome our dear Aamna home," their father said.

"Aamna is rich, now," Babur said. "While we rot here, she can freely travel the world. But you will not even let us go to India with our football teams."

"Do not argue, Babur," her father said. He hugged her again and repeated, "Welcome home, my daughter." She returned his hug with the warmth she truly felt for him, preparing herself to reintegrate into the family. Despite the pandemic and family conflicts, she would manage.

Their driver picked up her suitcase. They fought their way through the airport crowds and exited through the shiny glass front of the building to the parking area. They led her to a new black SUV and put her in the front passenger seat. Her mother gushed over her from the back seat the whole way home.

Two days later, AJ walked down to the lake along the promenade in Lake View Park, and there stood Reema. AJ rushed forward and embraced her old friend. The two had a heartfelt moment filled with memories and emotions.

"It is so good to be with you again, Aamna!" Reema said, holding her friend's shoulders. "My, you've grown so beautiful since I last saw you.

And a new name. AJ." Reema struggled to form the American English sounds. "I like it too, but it's so strange! You're American now."

"Not really. But, Reema, I was so sorry to hear that your parents have died. We belong to Allah, and to Him we shall return."

"Yes, it was a heavy loss," Reema said, casting down her eyes. "I am alone in the world, AJ. Oh, it is so good to see you!"

"Yes." AJ pointed to a table. The small picnic area in Lake View Park was filling up. "Shall we sit? And share?"

Reema lifted the bag. "I brought daal chawal and roti and kebab masala for us," she said. "Is that enough?"

"Oh my goodness," AJ said. "Let us sit down and eat! I have so missed proper food!"

The friends shared out the food onto small plates and ate while they talked.

Reema said, "Your emails did not contain many details about your work in San Francisco."

"Yes, it is confidential. Silicon Valley startups make you sign all kinds of documents promising dire consequences if you say anything about your work. But the work is exciting. And how are your prisoners?"

Reema waggled her head. "I am not sure the Mehrasa Foundation does any real good, Aam—AJ. Oh, I find it so hard to remember your new name."

"Call me Aamna, my dear one," AJ replied. "Aamna is my name, after all. Here, anyway."

"And everyone in America has such strange names?"

"No, but America has such different people. Names take on a life of their own. For example, my boss is Quebecois and has a French name. He is a nice man."

"There must be nice men somewhere, Aamna," Reema said.

AJ grinned again. "Please do not try to convince my parents. They think America has ruined me for life in Pakistan. I dare not tell them about Alec."

"Alec." Reema sat up straight. "Is that his name?"

"Alec Chenais."

"And he is your boss?"

"Yes. It's...complicated, Reema. Very complicated." AJ looked at her friend, hoping that she would understand, that she would not disapprove. That she would still be a friend.

Reema then showed that she was no fool. "If your parents find out, it *will* be very complicated, Aamna. Very complicated indeed."

AJ discovered that, after two weeks at home, she had mostly reverted to the patterns of her youth. But instead of studying for school, she was now working remotely on the 1WeakLink infrastructure. She could work without thinking of Alec. But his presence loomed at the end of the chain of source code uploads, halfway around the world. Reema was her lifeline.

AJ's parents considered too much of her life in America as forbidden territory. They at once rejected her nickname. Fortunately, they did not ask for details. They didn't want to know.

As for her brothers, they were not people to talk to except for coaching instructions or disciplinary warnings, neither of which was AJ's business. And their only contributions to conversations with her were jibes about American life. And marriage.

That, of course, was her mother's primary goal in life: to get her married. Aamna tried to get her mother to talk about her illness, but her mother deflected her concerns, focusing instead on marriage. And so, in the fourth week at home, her parents sat her down and told her that Begum Rabia Safdar had approached them about another candidate.

"How did that old biddy hear of my return, Papa?"

Her mother interjected. "I informed her, Aamna, dear one. It is necessary for Begum Rabia to make the match. Her connections with prominent Islamabad families are very strong."

"But Mama, I do not wish to marry some stranger."

Her mother stroked her face. "Oh, Aamna, what we wish for and what happens are two different things. Believe me when I say the dearest wish of my sick heart is to see you married before I die." Her mother clasped her hands over her heart and raised her eyes to the sky.

"You will not die, mama. I won't let you." She hugged the older woman, seeking to lessen her anxiety by deflecting any discussion of marriage. She again pressed her mother on the details of her sickness, but her mother claimed to be too tired to discuss such matters. Only marriage.

AJ herself had other ideas. Yes, no doubt her experiences in America and Europe shaped those ideas. Certainly her occasional trysts and her relationship with Alec informed them. She already regretted her breaking up with him. Did she want to marry him? Oh, so many conflicting ideas. Why could not her mind be silent? Had she come back home for nothing? No—she needed to be with her family. She needed to be with her mother in her time of trial. Why would her mother not tell her what was wrong?

She asked her father, but he just shook his head as her mother pursed her lips. "She doesn't want us to talk about it, Aamna. Please leave it alone. Things will work out. Just be here for her. And please consider Begum Rabia's offer."

"Papa, the world is a big place. I have worked with companies all over it. There may be someone with more advantages as a potential husband. An American, say, or a Canadian."

Her mother jumped in. "Aamna! What is important is our home. The family relationships, the benefits of coming together, keeping our traditions. Raising your Pakistani children in those traditions. The infidel Americans and Canadians only care about money, not family, my dear one. Here, you are safe and privileged; there, you are alone, divorced when you are no longer young and beautiful." Her mother talked about this for some time, while her father nodded. Her mother must have gotten all this from watching bad American television.

Seeing that she could not shake her mother's determination, she worked on her father. "I need some time, Papa. The pandemic won't help anything. Let's see what happens in the summer or fall. Is that all right?"

"Yes, my dear one." Her father sounded pleased at her acceptance of the inevitable. "You are here with us at last. That is enough to make us happy."

CHAPTER TWELVE
Mergers and Acquisitions

Elliot Perry gripped his satellite phone tightly.

"Mark, that's not what I wanted to hear."

"Sorry, Elliot, it's physics. Physics doesn't care what you want to hear."

Elliot gritted his teeth. "Explain the physics again, Mark."

"Well, OK. It's politics and physics. I can only launch a few rockets a year. My landing pads won't tolerate any more. And the Texas statehouse won't tolerate even as many as I could launch. And I can't get other states to let me build more pads. Not after what happened in Galveston."

Elliot, isolated on his yacht, the *Mugwump,* did not know what had happened in Galveston, but he didn't care.

"Mark, you promised me the satellites and the bandwidth to do what I want. For 2023. I paid you a lot of money for that."

"You'll get them, Elliot. In 2024. December."

Two years and nine months from now. That wouldn't do. "Damn it, Mark, pay attention. 2023."

"Elliot. Physics. You need more satellites to get area coverage and to send data faster. Close together over a fixed-size globe. Plus, there's only so much undeveloped coastline in Texas. The launch pads are on the coast. If something happens, the rockets crash in the Gulf. Mostly. That's the way it all works, Elliot."

Going out on deck for some fresh air, Elliot watched the Norwegian fjords slowly pass by. Goddamn politics. It's always politics. On top of physics, he had to navigate American politics, as if it weren't already challenging enough. Hell, *Texas* politics. They bound liberty with political chains, and he had to break them.

He'd use the less secure ground-based Internet connections until 2024 with higher security at the endpoints. Jeff's team can handle that. But Elliot needed things to happen now, to move forward with his—what? Country? No, no government. Organization? No, too structured. Pirate crew? Too low class and questionable. Captain Nemo, that's what he was. With a yacht, not a submarine.

But Jeff couldn't keep up with Elliot's need for speed. A little management intervention might help. Elliot smiled. In the past, keelhauling ensured progress. He ought to discuss possibilities with the *Mugwump's* captain. Later. First, the Seacave.

The Seacave was the converted nightclub lounge on the yacht that replaced the Den in Palo Alto. Elliot thought the huge, dimly lit space was perfect for Jeff and his team. And they had converted the refrigerated wine racks to hold a variety of bottled and canned beverages to sustain them in their daily work. The captain had put a stop to acquiring Aeron chairs. He pointed out that wheeled chairs don't work well on moving decks. Instead, the team got upholstered leather benches along with workstations bolted to the deck. It wasn't exactly Silicon Valley or SOMA.

"The problem I got, Elliot, is I can't get enough people." He looked across the dimly lighted salon to the three people staring at their monitors. "Best one so far is that Manchester girl Susie, got real lucky with her when we docked in the UK. The other guys are good, but we need more, and I can't get 'em."

"Why, Jeff?" asked Elliot. More delays. Keelhauling appeared more and more appealing as a solution. But Jeff had his reasons.

"Well, shit. 'Yeah, we got our startup offices on this boat. Cruising the seven seas, or however the hell many of them there might be.' I've fucking lost count, Elliot. Guess how many people don't want to work on the high seas." He looked across again. "Susie loves it, she thinks it's a cruise adventure. But nobody else wants to work on the cruise, Elliot. Even I'm not hot about it."

Elliot looked down at Jeff's workstation. No bucket. Jeff's chief complaint about his life aboard ship had been the difficulty of adapting. After a few weeks on the *Mugwump,* he'd ditched the bucket next to his workstation, but clearly his stomach still wasn't happy about being at sea. Maybe Jeff wasn't the right leader for this venture. Wait and see.

Elliot sighed. "Jeff, make do. Use the pandemic as bait. *Mugwump* is the safest place on Earth with the virus spreading on land."

"Yeah, no shit." Jeff Morrow coughed nervously. "The other problem is we're inventing all this crap from scratch. We need hackers and hacking tools."

"It's your job, Jeff. Find them. Shanghai them if you have to. I'll see what I can do about tools." Elliot paused, then added, "What happened to that Pakistani friend of yours?"

"I been busy since Kazakhstan getting blockchain together. On this boat."

"Ship. Well, ask her if she's up for a salary of $1 million a year."

"Yikes. Even I don't get that much."

"You will, if you get results, and you'll get a bonus if you hire her. I'll let Tim know." Pakistan. Now, what did that remind him of? Ah. Varoozh. It might be possible to use Varoozh Paracha's expertise to move forward.

The old radio cabin on the *Mugwump* had given way to a new layout in one of the medium-sized staterooms as Elliot's communications needs expanded. A digital time zone display showed capitals around the world, and monitors lined the walls. The ports had closed curtains to reduce glare. Thick carpeting minimized noise. Steve, the primary comms crewman, looked up when Elliot entered.

"Hey, Steve. Great job you're doing down here," he said.

"Thanks, Elliot." Steve smiled a lopsided smile, but Elliot guessed he knew full well that the yacht's owner did not wander the ship giving people warm encouragement. "What can I do for you?"

Elliot grinned, appreciating the directness. "Steve, I need to set up a call to Pakistan, then a conference call between the Pakistani and a company in San Francisco. I want to listen in on that call without the participants knowing I'm doing it. Is that possible?"

"Sure thing, Elliot. Just give me the numbers."

Elliot gave Steve the private number of his friend Varoozh Paracha in Karachi and the number of 1WeakLink in San Francisco. Steve said, "You can take the call to Mr. Paracha over there, Elliot." He gestured to a workstation sitting empty at the side of the stateroom. "Do you need privacy?"

"Only if I can't trust you, Steve," Elliot said. "Of course, if that were the case, I'd have to throw you overboard."

Steve grinned at this joke, though his smile contained some uncertainty. "OK, Elliot." He turned to his console and fiddled with it for a while. "I've got Mr. Paracha on the line, Elliot. Transferring the video and audio to the workstation."

Elliot put on the headphone set at the workstation.

"Elliot, good to see you," Varoozh said. He was a middle-aged man with graying hair, a smiling Pakistani businessman's face with a goatee, and lively, light brown eyes. After meeting the man at a Ron Paul Institute conference in Karachi, Elliot had run a background check. Varoozh's unsavory connections and checkered past, plus his success in accomplishing difficult mergers by any means necessary, were exactly what Elliot needed for the 1WeakLink acquisition.

Elliot would normally use Tim and his team for acquisitions, but this one had some aspects that might need a unique set of M&A skills. Varoozh's skills. Elliot had already made one foray to acquire 1WeakLink.

That company's software was critical for his plans. Mark and Jeff had let him down. He intended to acquire the 1WeakLink software without revealing himself. Let's see what Varoozh can do.

Elliot cut right to the chase. "Varoozh, I need your deal-making expertise. Right now."

Varoozh's smile widened. "Anything you like, Elliot. First thing tomorrow?" It was 9:30 p.m. Pakistan time. But it was 9 a.m. in San Francisco.

"In half an hour, Varoozh—San Francisco time. I want to acquire a company, 1WeakLink, headed by a man named Crispin Bannon. Any amount for the offer. Persuade them."

"It would be my honor to take this on, Elliot," Varoozh said. Delicately, he added, "And me?"

"I can offer you fifteen percent of the stock in the company, a five percent commission, and a bonus of $100,000 at deal close. In whatever currency you prefer, even crypto."

"I would never touch that stuff, Elliot. Dollars would be fine. But I'd need a ten percent commission and $100,000 if the company won't sell."

"Seven and fifty."

"Eight?"

"Seven, Varoozh. That's my limit. Unless you go crypto, then I'll make it nine and seventy-five." Elliot didn't care about the percentage, but the negotiation was everything. He wanted Varoozh to contemplate the future. Which was crypto.

"I'll take the seven percent, Elliot. Deal."

Elliot hunched over the small table in the comms center. He activated the headset's noise cancelation to muffle the sound of the yacht's engines rumbling up from below as the *Mugwump* moved toward the Atlantic.

"1WeakLink Corporation. How may I direct your call? Please speak clearly the name of the person or department you are calling." The state-of-the-art voice recognition used a pleasant woman's voice.

Varoozh said, "Crispin Bannon." Varoozh pronounced the name with an excellent English accent.

"One moment, please, while I connect you."

No fuzzy music during the wait. That impressed Elliot. Someone at 1WeakLink had taste.

"Hello. This is Crispin Bannon."

"Morning, Mr. Bannon. My name is Varoozh Paracha. I am the CEO of a company in Pakistan, Paracha Information Systems Limited. Perhaps you know of us?"

"I'm afraid not, Mr. Paracha."

"Varoozh, please. We have similar businesses, but I don't sell my software in the US. That's why I'm calling."

"We're not at a point where we can consider international OEM agreements. Perhaps—"

"No, no, you misunderstand. I and my principals wish to expand our operations to the United States. The easiest way to do that, Mr. Bannon, is to acquire companies with reasonably similar products. Your company would be an excellent acquisition candidate for us."

"Oh, I see." A moment of silence. "Mr., uh, Varoozh. Thank you for the offer, but we can't entertain such a deal. Other commitments."

"What would change your mind? Make me an offer, Mr. Bannon."

"Varoozh, we just can't make a deal in our current situation."

Come on, Varoozh, impress the man. Make a genuine offer.

"Mr. Bannon, to show my sincerity, I'm offering you $100,000,000 for the company. Your capital and revenue projections must tell you that's an attractive offer. The potential for worldwide sales is quite large and worth our while, and our international connections with governments and industries are solid. We would be happy to provide any information for your due diligence on the transaction."

"A hundred..." Crispin paused, then asked sharply, "Who are your backers, Paracha?"

"Mr. Bannon, they would prefer to remain anonymous for now."

"Not good enough." Crispin's voice smoothed out and turned persuasive. "Varoozh, you must know I would need my board's permission to even consider your offer. They'll want names. Who are your principals?"

The Blockchain Killing

Varoozh again deflected. "It's a genuine offer, Mr. Bannon. Cash, no questions asked. And a bonus for you if you close within a week."

"Are you fronting for the PRC?" asked Crispin. "Or a hacker group? Elliot Perry? He's already tried this."

Elliot signaled to Steve, who ended the call. Elliot sat back and removed the headset. Varoozh had done his best, but clearly Bannon was more than reluctant. He was suspicious. Bannon's questions and the size of the offer and bonus suggested to Elliot that he was more interested in the attempt than in making money. In his Silicon Valley experience, no startup CEO behaved that way. Unless…unless they were working for somebody else. The NSA?

He'd have to go deeper into the company. To its people. To the Pakistani woman or her teammates. Varoozh could handle that, no problem.

Crispin stared out his window at the Bay Bridge. The NSA would dislike this development. A Pakistani fronting for someone else? No, they wouldn't like it. And they already had it on their surveillance record.

"Crispin, what was that about?" He turned and noticed the open door. Yuriko must have heard the whole thing.

"Some bloody idiot pretending to offer us $100 million for the company. I questioned—"

"How much?" interrupted Yuriko, startled.

"It was utter nonsense, Yuriko. Nothing to concern you," he said to calm her.

"But Crispin, you should have at least kept him dangling until we investigated. That's real money. With that much money, we could become wealthy without delivering the software. Crispin, you—"

"The NSA would do something drastic, Yuriko. I've told you before, we can't afford to upset them."

"Yes, but $100 mill—"

"Yuriko. I'm the CEO. To keep your position as CFO, go back to your desk and complete your tasks. This conversation is over." He stared her down. "Close the door on your way out."

Yuriko, mouth tight with offense, shook her head and complied.

Mr. A would not like this. Referring to him by that name seemed silly when Crispin knew exactly who the Admiral was. But that's how the NSA worked. No names, no pack drill. Just a lot of flaming, bloody hell when things went sideways. As they were now doing. He had to consult. He picked up his phone.

Jeff heard the Seacave hatch open. He looked up from his code to see a grinning Elliot Perry. That was rare these days. The grin, not seeing the man. He had been in every day demanding action.

"What's up, boss?" he said.

"The Jaffrey woman, Jeff. Do you know the purpose of her iWeakLink software?"

"Who knows? She's never told me. But it's gotta be hacking, because everything AJ touches is hacking. She's good."

"Yes. She is. According to my sources."

"What the hell, you're checking references?"

"No, Jeff, I'm investigating. How did I make so much money?"

"Pure luck. Sure wasn't by being cheap."

"No. It wasn't. Luck or cheap. It was having excellent sources of information. About people. People, Jeff, make you money."

"Haw. Maybe I should get out more."

"I talk to people so you don't have to, Jeff. And the people I've talked to about your friend Aamna Jaffrey are well-connected. iWeakLink. What do you make of the name?"

Jeff hadn't thought about it. No reason to. He wanted AJ, not her software. "Gotta be the chain, right? Weak link. So, government plus hacking plus chain equals—oh." He smiled. "Ah."

"Yes. They're building a toolset for hacking blockchains. For the government. The NSA is their first customer."

"Well, shit. That's gotta be something we should worry about. We should put protections in place."

"Think bigger, Jeff. And hire the damn woman. Then get her to bring along their codebase. Once we have that, and her, we can protect ourselves from the government, sure. But we can also use that toolkit to dominate anything that gets in our way. She can add lots of good things as we go. But, Jeff. If you can't hire her, I'll have to explore other options to get her on board. You hire her, you get your million. If you don't, I'll use the money to pay the consultant I'll hire to get the software another way. All right?"

Jeff grinned. "Got it. OK, I'll see what I can do."

"You do that, Jeff. You do that." Elliot smiled with all his teeth.

"Hey, gorgeous. Been a while," Jeff said, using his best cowboy-optimism phone manner.

"Jeff? Is that you?" AJ exclaimed.

"How you doing, AJ?"

"I'm—not so good, Jeff. The COVID pandemic."

"Don't tell me you got the damn virus," he said.

"No, but I had to come home. To Pakistan. Islamabad, where I grew up."

"You never talked much about home. What's wrong?"

"Family. I guess the truth is you can't go home again."

"Hey, now you're done with those City bozos, why don't you come work for me?"

"Oh, Jeff. Thanks, but I'm still working for 1WeakLink. Remotely. And my mother is sick here."

"Damn. Well, what'll it take? To get you into the right operation. Mine."

"Jeff, I need to be here with my parents. My mother. And my brothers."

"Would a million bucks a year help?"

"Sure, Jeff. Of course it would. Why not? What rubbish," AJ laughed.

"Am I kidding you, gorgeous? I am not. Genu-wine offer. Right here, right now."

After a long silence, AJ said, "You and I go way back, Jeff. In what we do. It's dark web, no? For millions."

"Naw. Well, kinda. But not really. Outside the web. You remember I work for Perry, right? He's got his own setup. We need smart people to join us. Hacking, sure, but you're already doing that."

"I didn't tell you anything about what I'm doing, Jeff."

"No, but I know you. What makes your eyes light up and your heart go pit-a-pat. AJ, you're a born and bred hacker. It's your meat and potatoes."

"1WeakLink is a successful company, Jeff. Nice, smart people. I can't just walk away. I've got stock options that will be worth millions. And I have other commitments."

"The damn government, right? You don't want to tie your future to the suits, or worse, the spooks, gorgeous. And options are optional, AJ. Risky. Our money will be in your hands tomorrow. A giant bird without a bush in sight."

"The government, sure, but other things too. I'm not a pirate like you. I have ties."

"Holding you down, gorgeous. Cut 'em. I'll even sweeten it with a signing bonus. Another million."

"Bloody hell, Jeff. You're completely, bloody insane."

"You bet I am. And the only cure is you, hacker princess."

"Let me think about it, Jeff. I will, I promise."

"OK. Don't rush, but things are moving fast. Look, I'm hard to reach, but call this number and I'll get back to you, OK?"

Jeff gave his secure voicemail number to AJ, who repeated it.

"Bye, Jeff. It was good to hear your voice. Oh, I'm so alone here."

Jeff listened to the pain in her voice. Yeah, he could use that. Let her stew for a week, adjust the heat, and boom. Done.

CHAPTER THIRTEEN
A Heart Attack

Alec never used the elevator in the 1WeakLink building. Too slow, and the stairs provided some exercise in his sedentary existence. Today, he was breathless by the first landing. By the third landing, he had to grab the handrail to stay upright. He paused, panting, before exiting the stairwell and walking to the 1WeakLink office door.

He placed his finger on the biometric entry lock, which clicked open. Still panting, he walked through the reception area and into the development room. He braced himself and looked out at the freeway through the small-paned windows. His legs gave way, and he fell to the floor, pain coursing through his chest and arm.

He must have fainted, because now Yuriko was kneeling beside him and shaking him.

"Alec, Alec, what's wrong? Are you OK?"

"Yuriko...," he started, but he couldn't finish the thought. The pain closed in.

"Oh my God," Yuriko said, getting to her feet. She took out her cell phone and dialed.

"Yes, one of our employees is having a heart attack. Can you send someone?" She gave the address and suite number and other information. Alec tried to roll over and failed. Yuriko kneeled down and rested a hand on his shoulder.

"Relax, Alec," she said. "The ambulance is on its way."

In no time at all, two paramedics were kneeling beside him, taking his pulse and blood pressure and assessing his breathing, which was heavy and labored. Alec wanted to tell them nothing was wrong. That was so obviously not true that he just concentrated on getting enough air. The paramedics attached monitoring electrodes to his chest and studied the results, explaining what they were doing to him and Yuriko.

"Arrhythmia," a paramedic said. "Heart's beating, but irregularly. Let's get you to the hospital." They unfolded a stretcher and maneuvered Alec onto it, then lifted him and carried him out. Yuriko walked by his side.

"Will he be all right?" she asked.

"He has an irregular heartbeat and breathing problems, ma'am, so we're taking him to the hospital for specialized treatment. I can't give you any more details—privacy, you know? But we're doing everything we can for him."

Alec tried again. "Yuriko. AJ…." But again, he couldn't finish. What the hell was happening to him? His thoughts went to Russian nerve agents and Chinese spies, and he tried to sit up.

"Lie still, buddy," a paramedic said, patting him on the shoulder. "We got you."

Alec concentrated on breathing as they rode down in the elevator. The ambulance ride to the hospital was short and loud. At least he was alive to hear it.

The emergency room nurse assured Alec that the doctor would be with him soon with the test results.

"You said that half an hour ago," Alec complained. "I'm having a heart attack, damn it."

The chest pains hurt, though not as severely as in the office. He was still short of breath, too, but the oxygen mask helped.

The nurse smiled, looked at the monitors, and shook her head. "You're stable now. I'm sure the doctor will explain—"

Alec stopped listening. The air was cool on his bare chest, festooned with suction cups and wires leading off to beeping machines. He sat in a curtained-off area of the emergency room. This was a science fiction set, not reality. He was sure he was going to die, despite the nurses' reassurances.

"Good news, Mr. Chenais," the emergency physician said, pushing aside the hanging curtain. "It's not a heart attack."

"Then what is it?"

"From everything you've told me, it's Broken Heart Syndrome."

Alec shook his head in awe of modern medicine. "That's a thing?"

"Yes indeed," smiled the doctor. "I suspected it after you told me about the breakup. Takotsubo cardiomyopathy. The EKG was wrong for a heart attack. The angiogram shows no blockages in the arteries, and the blood test shows enzyme levels inconsistent with a cardiac emergency. We'll do an echocardiogram later to confirm the ventricle movement abnormality, but I'm sure that's the problem."

"I've got a lot going on. Besides the breakup, that is."

"Makes it all the worse." The doctor frowned. "Are you constantly thinking about her?"

"Of course."

"OK. Thought boundaries. Obsessive thoughts make depression worse. Here's something to try. Make time daily for thoughts of her. Thirty minutes. Only think of her during that time."

Alec, mouth open, obsessed about AJ. He said, "I can't. She's just there. All the time. And I work with her. I'm her *manager*."

The doctor sighed. "Try. Here, I'm going to set you up for some cognitive therapy sessions with our psychiatric department. That should help."

"Fine. Just fine." He'd fit it in between coding sessions, the only therapy he'd tried that worked.

The doctor typed in the referral into a workstation. He turned back to Alec and asked, "Are you having suicidal thoughts?"

"Not until you mentioned it."

"If you can joke, you're not clinically depressed. At least not yet. We'll monitor you. Let's check in after a week of CBT. We're going to admit you to the hospital until the chest pain goes away and you're breathing better, OK? A day or two, no guarantees. We'll do the echocardiogram in Cardiology later today. And try not to think about your girlfriend while you rest. Thought boundaries." The doctor tapped his forehead with a finger. "Find a happy place and go there."

"If I'm OK, I have a lot of work to do, Doctor."

"No. You don't." The doctor smiled again. "Don't make me call an orderly, Mr. Chenais. You need rest, time to recuperate. In the hospital, so we can monitor your heart. I'll have a beautiful psychiatrist come and keep you company for a while. How's that?"

Alec groaned and said, "If you can joke, I'm not at death's door. You're sure?"

"That you need rest? Yeah. Real sure."

The doctor left, and the nurse drew the curtain around and began removing the suction cups, one by one, while another nurse wrapped a hospital band around his wrist.

"That son of a bitch needs sensitivity training," Alec complained.

The nurse smiled and gave the last suction cup an extra hard tug.

CHAPTER FOURTEEN
Blockchain Strategy

JEFF FOUND THAT RESTING ON his laurels, or, really, resting on his ass, wasn't going to cut it on the *Mugwump*. Two things. First, Elliot was ever more impatient about getting results. He defined results as successful hacks that showed progress toward the kind of software mastery that would fulfill his ambition for world domination. OK, maybe that was paranoid, but Jeff felt the heat.

Second, he hadn't fully grasped the difference between sitting in an office somewhere useful in the United States and sitting on a bench on a yacht a thousand miles from anywhere. Quitting was not an option when the exit was jumping into the Norwegian Sea. And a ship owner had more say in one's life than, say, a dopey CEO. Elliot had proven himself a master of the carrot-and-stick school of management. All the beer you could drink, enough money to retire on if you ever got to shore, and all the hackers you could use. But you had to deliver. Astana wasn't enough, you had to keep going and find new ways to disrupt the world to keep proving yourself.

So Jeff streamed a recorded presentation from a conference on COVID response. A physician and researcher from the CDC in Atlanta passionately discussed his new blockchain software, already in use at the CDC, and its potential to combat the pandemic.

"This technology addresses the challenges of data access, privacy, and storage," the doctor explained. "Blockchain's decentralization enables efficient data collection through smart contracts, ensuring HIPAA compliance. Its immutability prevents data corruption, while its transparency links the data to a known source. It also supports contact tracing and effectively manages medical supply chains."

Jeff listened to the rest of the twenty-minute presentation. Most of it bragged about the deep learning methods the scientist had applied to the blockchain data to detect COVID symptom patterns. None of these methods had yielded anything useful. Jeff was familiar with both the software and the failure-brag syndrome. He'd seen it endlessly at MIT. But the point was the existence of the deployed blockchain, not the failed analytics. He carefully took a screenshot of the website references at the end and the PubMed ID for the accompanying detailed article, which he downloaded and skimmed. Lots of nice, juicy details about the software. Immutable? In your dreams, sucker. Should he tell Elliot? Nah, let it be a pleasant surprise. This hack could make the *New York Times*.

The ward nurse led Crispin and Yuriko to Alec's bed, which was one of six beds in the small hospital ward reserved for patients under observation. No doctor had come by for two days, so "observation" was misleading. His nurse replied that she had updated his records every two hours. The doctors didn't need to check on him because nothing had changed.

The nurse took away his lunch tray, half-eaten and left for any passing vultures to consume. Yuriko carried a small bouquet. Crispin glowered as Yuriko placed the flowers in a glass and asked, "How are you feeling, Alec?"

"I'm fine. Just a little chest pain. Nothing to worry about, the doctor says."

"Why are you still here?" Crispin asked bluntly.

"Got me," Alec replied. "The nurse says I'm still under observation."

Crispin rolled his eyes, then snapped at Yuriko, "Give me a minute with him, please."

Yuriko pursed her lips and her eyes narrowed at the rudeness, but she drifted to a chair away from the bed.

"What?" asked Alec, who was beyond polite exchanges.

"The NSA wants you to help with a problem," Crispin said.

"I can't do anything until I'm released, Crispin."

"I can see that." He shuffled closer to Alec and leaned forward. Keeping his voice low, he said, "The NSA reports that someone tried to hack a blockchain system at the CDC. The IT people freaked out because they couldn't stop the hackers from getting into their servers. The NSA says we know more about blockchain hacking than anyone at the agency. So far, the blockchain system is unaffected. But the CDC raised it with the NSA, and the NSA raised it with me, and I'm—"

"Raising it with me, the end of the chain," Alec sighed. "Can't do it, Crispin. But I know who can."

Alec reached for his phone and called AJ.

AJ rolled over in bed and grabbed her phone from her nightstand. Alec. Alec?

She answered the call and said, "Alec. Do you know what time it is? Two in the morning."

"Sorry, AJ. Emergency. We need your unique skills." The voice was calm and collected.

"Alec, you can handle any emergency yourself. You don't need me," she said sharply.

"I'm in the hospital."

"You're—" She stopped, eyes wide, unable to speak.

"Yeah, long story, no concerns. Anyway, Crispin has a problem that I can't do anything about here in the hospital, and you can. Are you willing to talk to him?"

"I guess. But Alec, why—"

"Too long a story to tell you now. Here's Crispin."

AJ called the number Crispin gave her and talked to the CDC security guy. He was short on details, but the VPN connection he gave her got her into the CDC's network without a problem. He told her what they'd found, and she navigated to the target server and immediately guessed what was happening. Some kind of zero-day, a bug that no one had found yet, got them in and let them log into the server as root. Then they would have installed some kind of hacking trojan to attack the blockchain server.

She typed a few Linux commands and found the hack extension to one of the Linux tools. She dumped the system error log and found the thousands of rejected attempts to get access to the blockchain server in Atlanta. How long before they used the same zero-day access to hit the other blockchain node servers scattered across the United States?

She downloaded the hack code to her workstation and ran a reverse compiler on it to see what the hacker had done. She recognized the hack as one she'd tried a few weeks ago and rejected because it was based on a bug the Ethereum folks had patched. Whoever this was, they were behind the curve on the latest blockchain software.

She verified the version of the blockchain software and told the IT guy, "This hack is harmless because the software they're attacking has fixed the bug they want to exploit. Let's see how they hacked in."

After an hour of log tracing and examining Linux source code, she discovered the entry path: not a bug, bad configuration. The hackers gained entry through a firewall backdoor, a connect-back that allowed download of a zero-day malware hack to the target server. This was eerily familiar; it was a path she had taken many times herself, learned at MIT. Only the zero-day was new. She walked the IT security guy through the firewall reconfiguration that would fix the backdoor.

She suggested installing a network threat detection system as soon as possible, one that covered all the blockchain nodes. The CDC guy claimed ignorance. She believed him. She stored the CDC VPN security credentials in her encrypted information store, just in case she had some use for them later. Trick of the trade. Of course, if the CDC people had any intelligence, they'd change everything. But she knew from experience intelligence was thin on the ground in such places. Having her own backdoor into the CDC systems wouldn't hurt a thing.

She texted Alec a quick message telling him she'd blocked the hacker, then went back to bed. She lay awake wondering why Alec was in hospital. Nothing serious, he'd said. She wanted details, but she'd burned a bridge by telling him she was to marry. Still, she cared too much to just abandon him. Maybe a short note of concern would make him tell her everything. She'd have to phrase it carefully. In the morning.

Jeff, frustrated beyond belief, knew that he had to tell Elliot about his failure to hack into the CDC. He debated his options. He could fall on his sword, or pretend it never happened, or swim for the Norwegian coast. Or Iceland, or wherever the hell they were now.

He grinned. No, he'd just avoid the whole mess and let someone else tell Elliot. His gaze swept over his minions in the Seacave. Which one would he sacrifice?

He never got to choose. Elliot made the choice for him. A crewman entered through the aft hatch and made a beeline for him. The crewman, Jeff didn't know his name, was apologetic but insistent. Elliot wanted to see him in his stateroom right away. Jeff sighed. Sword it was, then.

"I have my own sources, Jeff," Elliot said, after Jeff's account of the bright idea followed by the failed hack of the CDC. "I don't like surprises. So I make sure I'm aware of what's going on. Now, I've been putting a lot of pressure on you for results." Elliot grinned. It was not a pleasant grin. "The key word is results, not pressure. I like results. My business thrives on results. Do you know what we do with our companies that don't show results, Jeff?"

"No, sir."

"We close them down, Jeff. Closing down the Seacave would be bad for your career, Jeff. Think about it. Next time, make damn sure it works and leaves no trace. We can't afford to have spooks or competitors find out what we're doing. We can't afford to fail. Get it solid, then get it done. Got me?"

"Yes, sir. Uh. Aye-aye, sir." Never could remember the lingo.

"And what about your girl in Pakistan?"

Can you fall on two swords? Nah. Get it done. He related his calls to AJ and his failure so far to convince her to join the Seacave crew.

"All right, Jeff. Don't worry about it. I'll see what Varoozh can do. After all, he's Johnny-on-the-spot. I'll call him." Elliot waved him away in dismissal.

Jeff found his way down the gangways and ladders abaft to the stern boat launch platform. He hung over the rail and emptied his lunch into the midnight-dark Norwegian Sea. When they returned to American shores, he'd look up the son-of-a-bitch who'd blocked him and make sure he got paid well for his work.

By Friday, four days into his hospital stay, Alec was reduced to reading blockchain papers on his phone. And the hospital Wi-Fi stank. By 10 a.m., he had reached his limit in navigating the intricacies of Web3 dapp programming on the Ethereum blockchain. Even brilliant programmers need to take a break, he reasoned.

Five minutes into the break, thoughts about AJ coalesced into the need to contact her. Alec rejected several questions he could ask her, finally settling on a solid VPN for effective hacking. He sent off his question. She replied with a business-like efficiency, pointing him to a VPN that connected to the Tor network, telling him he'd be secure in whatever scheme he was up to. A kind wish for his recovery and hope for a swift return to health followed.

Should he reply and tell her everything? He lay back in bed and realized he was too embarrassed to reveal his broken heart syndrome. She'd think he was making her feel bad about her marriage and about ending her relationship with him. He loved her too much to risk the possible blowback. He sent a reply thanking her for the VPN advice and telling her he'd be out of the hospital soon.

Alec installed VPN software on his phone, all the while pondering how to fix their relationship. There had to be a way. Talk with her about the 1WeakLink tools she was developing? Ask innocuous questions about her family? Were there any such questions, given her impending forced marriage? And that led Alec down a rathole of despair that reminded him of his doctor's advice. Thought boundaries or a broken heart.

By early afternoon, Alec had immersed himself in the stories of Edward Snowden and Reality Winner, lunch uneaten. The NSA's extensive surveillance and its inability to protect its own assets astonished him. He marveled at Snowden's audacity at leaking millions of classified documents.

During his research on Winner's leaks, Alec came across a mention of blockchain technology. This led him to a 2019 paper describing an NSA project to store classified documents on a private blockchain. Smart contracts and encryption keys ensured document accessibility while maintaining confidentiality.

Sitting up in his hospital bed, Alec realized the private NSA blockchain was more important than he had understood. The NSA's fascination with blockchain hacking had become crystal clear. They had funded 1WeakLink to build tools to hack China's blockchains. But the tools would also show how adversaries and turncoats could compromise their own blockchain. They didn't want that technology in enemy hands until they figured out ways to stop the hacks.

He pressed the button to summon the nurse, aware that she would not appreciate his initiative. Tough. It was time to go to work.

CHAPTER FIFTEEN
Family Trouble

"Sohail! Stop that noise! I am working." Her brother and two friends were abusing electric guitar, bass, and drums. Six feet away from her door. Loudly. She stood, arms akimbo, looking out at them.

"Fuck you, Aamna. We're practicing. We have a gig."

"Sohail. I earn more in an hour than you do in a decade. But I can't work in peace! Do I have to involve Papa? Go out to the garage. Or the backyard."

"It's too cold out there."

"It is June in Islamabad, Sohail. June! Sohail, if you don't stop making that noise, I swear I will smash your fancy bass and throw it in the garbage."

"You will not." The boy marched up to her, the bass hanging around his manly belly. As manly as he could be at seventeen. Sohail considered himself a rock star and wore clothes to match, an open shirt with gold and silver chains, and tight black pants. "You think you are in America? You think you can tell men what to do just because you are older than us? Not in our house."

"Tell her, man," the drummer said, grinning—no, leering. "And why is she not wearing her *dupatta*? Showing off for us?" A cymbal crash punctuated his critique.

"You see, sister? You are shaming me in front of my friends. Please return to your room, work, and earn us money for better amplifiers instead of screaming. And wear your *dupatta* when my friends are here."

"You...little beast. You are beastly!" AJ's rage welled out of her eyes. She slammed her door. Her tears shamed her to herself. Cry over that little prick? She'd get him back. Sohail had no respect for her work and education. He had no respect for age, for women. For *her*. This was not how families should work. But for now, *she* had to work. Her noise-canceling headphones drowned out most of the noise. You could not call it music, the noise they were making. The song was unrecognizable to her. But Sohail's bass thumped in her stomach all the same. Jeff's offers lingered through her attempts to get into the code, but the flow finally came as she delved into the encryption hacking algorithm.

Lights flashing. Red lights. Something was wrong. AJ checked her bedside clock—3 a.m. Noises outside and inside the house. AJ got out of bed, pulled on her robe, and opened her door.

Two men in masks and hazmat suits carefully carried a stretcher down the stairs. On it lay her father, his face covered by an oxygen mask. He was panting, wheezing, coughing. Her mother, right behind them, was screaming something unintelligible. They carried her father out to the front courtyard, ignoring her mother. AJ rushed to the door behind her mother and saw an ambulance, back doors open, waiting for her father.

"What is happening, Mama?" She swung around and grabbed her distraught mother's arms and shook her. "Please, Mama, you are sick! You must not do this. Mama, tell me what is happening!"

She led the weeping woman to a couch inside the house. But her mother would not sit down. AJ's brothers came out of their rooms shouting nonsense.

Her mother screamed, "We have to go with your father, Aamna! He is dying! He cannot breathe!"

Her mother ran out the door. Her brothers followed. AJ ran after them.

"No, madam, you cannot come. Please, get down from there!" Her mother had climbed into the ambulance. An attendant got her out.

"But I have to go with him! I must be with him!" her mother cried. Her brothers stood by helplessly with their mouths agape. AJ, increasingly worried about her mother's illness, grabbed her arm.

The attendant shook his masked head. "You cannot. The government will not allow it. Not with COVID. Please, madam, go back to your house and stay there. You must quarantine. You and your whole family. To prevent the spread of the disease. Call the hospital later to get more information about your husband. You need to get a virus test, everyone in your house. We have to go now."

The evil word was there. Her father had the virus. He could not breathe. He would soon die, and what would happen then? The ambulance attendant's words came back to her. Quarantine. The virus had trapped them in their own home. They would all die. She closed her eyes. This could not be happening.

The ambulance rolled out the front gate and turned on its siren, splitting the night with its wail of death.

AJ's mother met with the family and servants after a long night of phone calling. She waved the June 17th *Daily Times* at them.

"The government has shut down Swat and Abbottabad and Allah only knows where else," she shouted. "They are shutting down sectors in Islamabad! They will soon shut down the entire country!" The family, including AJ, stared at her in shock. The servants whispered to each other in the back of the room.

"I have called the minister about the situation," her mother continued, not specifying which minister. "He cannot help me see your father. It is out of his hands. Useless. He himself has tested positive. This newspaper reports it. He insists on our quarantining for a week. That means you, too," she said, waving the paper at the anxious servants. "You all must stay here. We will accommodate you all."

"We have cricket practice, Mama," Babur objected.

"You will not be wasting your time with cricket for a week, Babur," his mother replied with a stern look. Babur sat down, his tight mouth and glaring eyes a telltale sign of his disappointment and potential rebellion. It would serve him right if he went out and engaged in virus-laden activities.

AJ asked, "When will we know, Mama?" No one asked what she meant.

"A week, they say. Of course, they know nothing. They say your father is critical, and he may die soon. We will all die or live. *Inshallah*."

One of the younger female servants wailed. Her father, the gardener, held her and comforted her. AJ's brothers whispered to each other. Her mother frowned at them. "You two. Stop whispering. You *will not* go out. I will lock you in your rooms. And you, daughter, you will stay in your room. The servants will bring you food. We do not want you to catch the virus. You are our only source of income, Aamna, now that your father is gone."

AJ said nothing, worried anew about her mother. This illness of hers, she must be using all her strength to command the family in this emergency. It could not last. AJ did not want to be an orphan. She swallowed as tears fell. Her mother sighed. "Daughter, daughter. You must be strong. Dry your tears."

"I can work, Mama," Babur said.

"My band will—" Sohail started.

Her mother reacted sharply. "Be quiet, both of you. You cannot work, Babur, because the authorities have quarantined us. You cannot leave this house. Do you not understand? And the same goes for you, Sohail. And your band makes no money."

AJ turned her mind to practical matters. "Mama, how are we going to get food? If we cannot go out?"

"I have called Mr. Kharal at the grocery. He knows the situation and will deliver food when we need it. And Mr. Roy at the restaurant down the street will deliver cooked meals if we want them."

"What can I do to help, Mama? What about your illness? You cannot do it all by yourself."

"*You* must stay healthy. Do not worry about me. If you are to marry and save our family, you *must* stay healthy and beautiful. If you die, we will be destitute."

"Destitute? But Papa's business, surely—"

Her mother shook her head. "The business is not profitable. There have been problems for some time. All the more reason for your marriage to a strong, successful businessman who can help us."

AJ processed this statement of her mother's logic. She had not meant that AJ's computer work was their only source of income. After all, unlike her brothers, she worked at home. That work meant nothing to her mother. The marriage would ensure the family's survival if her father died. AJ was their only asset outside of the family business. Her father's illness threatened that business. Her marriage would secure their future by allying the family with some other wealthy family who would take over the business and secure the family's income. This could not stand.

"Mama—" she began.

"I do *not* want to hear it. Please go to your room. Close the door and pray to Allah that you do not catch this evil plague that has fallen upon us."

CHAPTER SIXTEEN
AJ's Plight

AJ SAT AT HER DESK, unable to code or even think, staring at the monitor. There were too many troubles, and they paralyzed her brain. Her contract with Ludivine and the pressure to betray Alec. The pandemic. The illness her mother tried so hard to hide. Breaking up with Alec and rejecting him as her soulmate. Her brothers' disdain and disrespectful behavior. Her father's getting COVID. The quarantine. Her mother's insistence that she stay in her room.

AJ picked up her phone and called her lifeline.

"Hello, Aamna. How are you?" asked Reema warmly.

"I am quarantined in my house, Reema. My father—" AJ stopped and swallowed, tears falling. "My poor papa is in the hospital with COVID."

"Oh, Aamna, I am so sorry."

"And that is not all. My mother has brought back the marriage broker, Begum Rabia."

"Oh, Aamna! I know this pains you. But arranged marriage is the way in our country, is it not? Surely this marriage will bring you into a new family with honor and dignity? Perhaps you should accept the reality of it, if you cannot escape it."

"But…" AJ hesitated. Reema was pragmatic, but she was also the more traditional of the two women. How would she react? But she had no choice. She sighed and said, "Reema, I had an affair in San Francisco."

Reema gasped and said, "I suspected something when you told me about your boss. The way you said it, the tone in your voice…but, oh, Aamna. An affair. You slept with the man?"

"Yes, Reema. As shameful as that may be. I slept with him, and I enjoyed it." AJ's eyes closed in guilt. "But I left him. And now, with this quarantine, I can no longer control my life. With Papa gone, Mama is insisting on this marriage. What can I do? Reema, can you help me? You help women in prisons, do you not?"

"I cannot fly you out of Pakistan like a djinn, Aamna." Reema was always the practical one. "I work with women in prison, yes. They go in, they are desperate, and there they stay, growing ever more desperate. I can help them with legal aid, and I can help them with the assurance that someone cares about their plight. But I can never relieve their despair, and most times I cannot get them out of prison. I give them what hope I can. I can give you hope, Aamna, but it will not be enough."

AJ heard her friend's voice tremble. Her own throat closed, and she did not answer.

Reema broke the silence and whispered to Aamna, "You can easily end this marriage idea." Her voice hesitated. "Tell the Begum about your lover. That would at least remove the burden of marriage from your life."

AJ pressed the phone to her ear. "I…am not ready, Reema. For the accusations and anger such a revelation would bring from my family."

Reema replied, "You cannot hide from it forever, Aamna. And you cannot change the past. Truth escapes the prison of silence. Is it not better to embrace the truth and live it?"

AJ replied, "Reema, you are giving me excellent advice, but I am not ready to accept it. I must find another solution."

"I would help you in any way I can, my dear one. Just let me know."

AJ had worked through the night on a crucial feature for BoltCutter. At nine in the morning, she stretched and thought about breakfast. The doorbell rang. What now? AJ's mother's voice came. "You must go away. Quarantine! What ever you wish to sell us, we do not want it!"

AJ went out to the living room. The tinny voice on the intercom replied, "Madam, you must listen. I must speak to Aamna Jaffrey. It is vital, a matter of great financial importance and urgency. You must listen, madam."

"Who are you? What do you want?" her mother asked sharply into the intercom, rolling her eyes.

"My name is Varoozh Paracha, madam. To whom am I speaking?"

"You are speaking to Asya Jaffrey. What do you want?"

"I need to speak to your daughter, Mrs. Jaffrey. At once."

"She is in quarantine. We are all in quarantine. Why not call on the phone?"

"I *have* called on the phone, madam. No one picks up."

AJ remembered the series of calls on Wednesday and Thursday from an unknown number that she ignored, along with all the other spam calls. No voicemails.

"My daughter needs to stay in quarantine."

AJ could tolerate no more of this officious control of her life. "Mama, let me talk to Mr. Paracha."

"You cannot, Aamna. It isn't proper. You are to marry soon."

"Oh, Mama, just let me speak with the man." AJ searched for a rationale that would convince her mother. "He says money is involved."

Her mother paused, caught between the twin imperatives of propriety and greed. AJ approached the intercom and took her mother's place.

"Mr. Paracha, this is Aamna Jaffrey. Who are you? What do you want with me?"

"Ah, Ms. Jaffrey. *Alhamdulillah!* I am offering you a job."

"I have a job."

"I have a better one for you. I work directly with Mr. Perry and Jeff Morrow."

"Oh. But I have told Jeff I wasn't interested in his offer. I am happy with my current job, and I cannot leave my house because of the virus." But now this man was here, physically here, offering her an escape from her troubles. Should she...?

Paracha responded firmly, "Yes, I understand. This will pass soon. Ms. Jaffrey, my company in Karachi works with Mr. Perry. He has instructed me to hire you as a special contractor. The terms—frankly, Ms. Jaffrey, we need to discuss the terms privately. Can we do that?"

"Can you wait for a few minutes? I must call and check with Jeff about this. If you don't mind?"

Paracha's voice expressed exasperation, but he agreed. "Yes, yes. I will wait. But this is urgent."

AJ called Jeff's number and left a message, and within a few minutes, he called back and verified that Paracha was who he said he was. After talking to Jeff and contemplating her difficulties, she decided to listen to the man. She said, "Mama, Mr. Paracha needs to talk with me privately."

"I heard the man, Aamna." Her mother's lips tightened. "Perry. Is that —"

"Yes, the billionaire American capitalist. He's interested in my work."

"Aamna. Who is this person Jeff?" Her mother's eyes were half closed in suspicion.

"Jeff Morrow, Mama. A man I met at MIT. He works for Mr. Perry."

"And you've spoken to this man? Without telling me?"

"I knew you wouldn't like it, Mama. But Jeff is an old friend."

"What did this American say to you? Is he seducing you?"

"In a way, Mama." Her mother's angry reaction made AJ reconsider her sense of humor. "No, no, Mama. He's offering me money. For a job."

"How much money?"

"$3 million."

Asya gasped. "Three…Aamna, what nonsense is this?"

"Software is a lucrative industry, Mama. If you would just listen to me —"

"Spouting nonsense! Money comes from selling machines or clothes or food, not from playing games on computers."

"I do not play…oh, Mama. You do not know what I do."

"And what does this Mr. Paracha offer?"

"He needs to meet with me to tell me. He is waiting, Mama."

The doorbell started in again. Mr. Paracha was impatient. In AJ's opinion, not a good quality for a manager. Still. She pressed the talk button. "Mr. Paracha, we can talk outside, in the garden."

"I am fine with that, Ms. Jaffrey. But this is urgent."

"Yes, all right. I will be out directly."

"Aamna, you cannot—" Alarm filled her mother's face.

"Yes, Mama. I can." AJ went to get her *dupatta*. And her mask. At this rate, she might as well wear the hijab and have done.

"Well, Mr. Paracha?" AJ sat at one end of the ornate stone bench positioned to take advantage of the May blooms in the garden. Birds sang and bees buzzed around the flowers. Her mother had positioned herself behind the parlor window as a chaperone. This simultaneously reassured AJ while talking to this stranger but also oppressed her with the weight of all her family problems. But Mr. Paracha claimed to be there to solve those problems.

This Varoozh Paracha was a nice-looking fifty, with graying hair and clever eyes under heavy black brows. AJ spotted a salt-and-pepper beard under his mask, and his voice was deep and pleasant as he introduced himself and again referred to Jeff and Perry.

"Mr. Perry is offering a fixed-price contract for two years of your time and effort. My company will be the contracting party and will pay all taxes and fees in Pakistan over and above the contract fee. No American taxes, unless you deposit the money in an American bank."

"Hmm. And the fee?"

"$20 million."

AJ was silent. Her mask kept the astonishment she felt hidden while her thoughts crashed around in her mind. She remembered her startup hiring negotiation training. Wetting her lips, she said, "I want $40 million. I have stock options in my current company that will—"

"No problem, $40 million. And more to come, I am sure. Mr. Perry is a generous man when he needs something."

"Ah, oh. Yes, I see." I should have asked for $100 million. *The thought pulsed wildly through her shattered mind.*

"We will, of course, deposit the money in the currency of your choice wherever you like. I would recommend dollars; other currencies may be riskier."

AJ knew this was so and agreed. Then an idea burst into her mind. "Certainly. But Mr. Paracha, I must ask for one more thing."

His eyebrows raised, Paracha asked, "And what is that, Ms. Jaffrey?"

"I want to get out of Pakistan. After the quarantine period. I will work for your company, but it has to be somewhere else. Somewhere that will accept a Pakistani passport." Somewhere her mother, her parents, could not force her into an unbearable marriage. "And my mother is sick. I must see to her care."

"I can arrange all that. But I too have another need."

"And that is?"

"You must bring along the 1WeakLink codebase."

AJ gasped. Another thief! Stealing the code and betraying Alec to Ludivine was already bad enough. Now she would betray *both* Ludivine and Alec. She'd broken her ties with Alec, but she still loved him. However, Ludivine presented a unique situation. Was $40 million enough to evade the consequences of betraying Ludivine in their illegal dealings?

Paracha misinterpreted her reaction as an aversion to illegality. "For $40 million, Ms. Jaffrey, we can dispense with irrelevancies. Mr. Perry can make sure you incur no penalty for this action. Only we will know. We insist on absolute secrecy. Mr. Perry does not intend to sell the software; he intends to use it. And to expand it." He smiled. "With your help, of course. And having that amount of money and Mr. Perry's goodwill provides a great deal of security." He meant, of course, regarding the NSA. But his words reassured AJ about Ludivine's response as well.

"There are special circumstances, Mr. Paracha."

"We are aware of them. Irrelevancies." Paracha smiled, his hand flung up in a gesture of dismissal.

"How soon can I fly out? Our quarantine ends next Wednesday."

"Well, you can't *fly* out. Too many restrictions right now. Go by ship. Mr. Perry's yacht. He has moved all his operations onto it. This allows for certain liberties. On the high seas, you understand. For example: your passport. No longer a problem."

"Erm…" Visions of sex trafficking filled AJ's mind. "I am afraid—"

"We will, of course, deposit the money in an account of your choice before you board the ship, Ms. Jaffrey. The ship has all the amenities. You will have no expenses on board. I can assure you, this is a legitimate offer. I refer you again to Mr. Morrow, who is aboard the ship."

Not legitimate. But she trusted Jeff. He had called her from a ship? At sea? No wonder she could not reach him directly. A ship? That would….

"When can I go aboard this ship?" she asked hurriedly.

"Mr. Perry tells me he can dock in Karachi in two weeks, possibly sooner if weather and the sea routes permit. I can offer safe transportation to Karachi whenever you like. Is that satisfactory?"

Two weeks. To escape marriage, to leave her bedroom, to have the money to help her family, to avoid the plague. To secure her future. Two weeks. She had no choice.

"Yes," AJ said. "That is satisfactory."

"But, Aamna. No, really? You must be joking."

Reema's voice on the phone was incredulous at the news AJ had given her. But she had not told Reema everything, only about the $40 million job offer.

"It came out of nowhere, Reema. All my troubles, gone."

"But your…" Reema seemed unable to get a word out. But she did. "Lover. Your lover in San Francisco, Aamna. What about him?"

"He is in the past, now, Reema. Despite my love, I am still angry at his behavior."

"It is hard, Aamna. We are the both of us romantics," her friend said. "So many problems! I am so sorry. And so much money, Aamna! The temptations you must feel."

"That's another reason I wanted to talk to you. I want you to have some of this money for your organization."

"Oh, no, Aamna, I could not—"

"Please, Reema. I must donate some of this money to a good cause to keep my self-respect. Your cause. $5 million."

"No, Aamna!" gasped Reema. "I thought you meant a few hundred. $5 million is far too much."

"I want this very much, Reema. Please do not refuse me."

After a brief silence, Reema asked, "Aamna. Is this money…is it legitimate?"

"Yes, Reema. It comes from a rich American who wants my help." And wants me to steal my company's software. Legitimate? Once in the bank, of course it is legitimate. A fee for a service. Reema doesn't need the details.

"And you leave in two weeks?"

"Yes. On Mr. Perry's yacht."

"This is a fairy tale from the *Thousand Nights,* Aamna."

"Ah, Reema. Many of those tales end badly. I can only hope mine turn out well."

"Yes. Will we meet again? Before you leave?"

"Tomorrow, or the next day. After my quarantine ends. You can come to our house. In the meantime, text me your bank information for a wire transfer. As soon as I receive my money, I will send my donation to you."

"Oh, Aamna. I do not know whether to cry for sadness or joy! I shall just cry."

"And now you see exactly how I feel, Reema."

"The Jaffrey woman accepted Varoozh's offer of $40 million. That extra digit got her." Elliot grinned. "Cheaper than buying the company, too."

"Well, hot diggity damn!" Jeff Morrow raised his hand. Elliot peered at it a moment, then realized it was a high five. He responded with what he hoped was the right slap.

"Boss, you can't believe how slick this news is! AJ on board. Oh my God, you got no idea. And all their software, too."

"I'll take your word that she's worth it. The software certainly is." Elliot gave Jeff a hard look. Was the man's joy solely because of having his friend as a co-worker, or were there other factors involved? Jeff had been showing worrying signs of attraction to his co-worker Susan. To each his own. But with Aamna Jaffrey added to the mix, the emotional complications could undermine his organization. Island fever was one thing, but he had no desire to get himself into a Below Decks or Love Island mess. Such things were fine as entertainment, but he had a business to run. Jeff ignored the look, still overwhelmed with the joy he felt.

"Oh, boy, are you in for a treat sweeter than peach cobbler." Jeff rubbed his hands together and grinned. "Brings back memories of the basement in the Stata Center all those years ago. When we hacked—"

Elliot held up a hand, then lowered it as he realized Jeff might slap it. "I don't want to know, Jeff. Let's just leave it at the cobbler. And get back to work."

"When's she coming?" Jeff paused. "She's in Paki land. How's she gonna get to us?"

"The mountain is moving to Mohammed, Jeff. We've already set course for the Cape of Good Hope."

CHAPTER SEVENTEEN
A Mourning Family

AJ awoke in the early morning to screams. She grabbed her robe and ran into the living room. Her mother was standing by the phone, screaming. The handset lay on the floor.

AJ ran to her mother and led her to a sofa. "Mama, Mama, what is it? What is wrong?"

Sohail and Babur ran into the living room wearing only underwear and T-shirts. They stared at the women on the sofa.

"He is dead!" screamed their mother. "Dead, and we are lost!"

Sohail lifted the phone and spoke into it. He blanched. He looked at the others. "It is…Papa. He has died. From COVID. It is the hospital."

AJ fell back against the sofa, hands pressed against her mouth, almost as affected as her mother.

Babur approached the sofa and touched his mother's head. "Mama, Mama, please. Compose yourself. Decisions and actions await us."

But their mother was inconsolable, unable to frame a thought other than that her husband was gone forever.

AJ, chest heaving, came to her senses and spoke. "We need to get her to bed, Babur. Can you…."

"Sohail. Help me." Babur grabbed his mother's arm. Sohail came and grabbed her other arm, pushing AJ aside. "Come along, Mama," Babur said. The two boys lifted their mother to her feet and led her to her bedroom. AJ followed and watched as they dumped their mother onto her bed. She went in and helped her mother into the sheets, still crying inconsolably.

"Mama, don't worry, we will see to everything," said AJ.

"*I'll* handle things, Aamna," Babur said sharply. "I am in charge now, and everyone must follow my instructions. Stay with her, Aamna, until she calms down. One day of quarantine remains. It will be hard. But we will do what is necessary."

"Mr. Paracha, I have to leave sooner than I expected. When can you wire my money?" AJ moved the phone to her other ear as she picked up a biro.

"Ms. Jaffrey, we have already wired the money to the offshore account you provided. It should be available to you within the hour. May I ask why you are now in such a hurry? Is there trouble with the Americans?"

"No, nothing like that. It is…personal. I…my family…my father has died."

Paracha smoothly expressed his sorrow and empathized with her loss, then articulated his chief concern. "Then your father's sad death creates a problem for you?"

"My brothers are now leading the family, but our relationship is strained. I fear they will prevent me from leaving if I do not act soon. Oh, this evil plague! It is destroying everything I hold dear."

"Well. Perhaps…yes, I can transport you to Karachi and lodge you in a safe house. On Mr. Perry's instructions, I have wired the funds to you, and you must deliver the code as contracted. Will that be a problem?"

"No, not at all."

"Can you send it to me today?"

AJ considered this and saw all the security flaws involved. "No, we must meet in person, Mr. Paracha, and I can give you temporary access to upload the code then. It will only take a few minutes. The quarantine is over, so we can meet secretly. Tomorrow my father is to be interred at the H-8 graveyard, near the park." AJ swallowed and suppressed a sob and steeled herself to finish her plan. "Can you meet me at the Pakistan monument in the park nearby? The funeral will end at around 1:30. Can we meet at the monument at 2?"

"I can do that, Ms. Jaffrey. I will bring my laptop with a satellite connection."

"Very well, I will see you tomorrow," AJ replied.

"Goodbye, Ms. Jaffrey. I am exceedingly sorry for your loss," Paracha said.

AJ sat on her bed, holding her phone in her lap. A tear ran down her cheek. It was done. Except for one thing. She accessed her money transfer account and sent Pakistani rupees to Reema's account. One promise kept. How many broken?

"Aamna! Where do you think you are going?" Her mother glared at AJ from where she stood at her father's gravesite. Her mother, overcome by her husband's death, had recovered when confronted with the need to organize the funeral and mourning reception.

AJ pleaded, "I need some time alone, Mama. I feel sad, and I need to walk for a while."

"No, my girl. You'll stay right where you are. Begum Rabia will meet us at home right after the funeral, before our mourning visitors arrive."

"But, Mama—"

Asya grabbed AJ's arm and shook. "No, no, no. Stay right where you are. Babur, make sure your sister gets in the car with you."

"Yes, Mama. Sister, you hear? I will watch you."

AJ looked at the sky for help, but Allah was not listening. How was she to deliver the goods? Mr. Paracha would wait and wonder. Allah alone knew his thoughts and reactions. Mr. Perry might take back his offer. She considered calling Paracha, but the intimidating presence of her brother forestalled her. The terror rose in her throat.

Reema, who had come to the funeral to support her, edged up to her.

"Aamna, what is it? What is wrong?"

AJ pulled her friend away from the family and whispered, "Reema, you heard? My family says I have to stay here. I am to meet the matchmaker.

They insist I must marry. I cannot. Oh, I am so angry! But I must...I have...something I must do." Aamna stared at Reema's kind eyes above the mask. "Reema, I must ask a large favor." Babur took a step toward them, and AJ smiled at him in fake reassurance.

"Anything, dear friend," whispered Reema.

AJ typed a note on her phone, then pushed it at Reema. She whispered, "Take this. My passcode is 7567. Can you remember it? 7567."

"Yes, but—"

"I want you to meet someone at the memorial." She pointed across the river. "It's just a short drive. There will be a man, Mr. Paracha. He will have a computer. He will log into my account on GitHub. Here, open the Authenticator app." She showed Reema the codes for authentication. "This one, here, is for GitHub." She switched to the note she'd typed. "Here is the GitHub login and password. Meet him at 2 p.m., all right? Now go while I deal with my rotten brother. Bring me back my phone tonight or tomorrow."

"But, Aamna, what—"

AJ glanced nervously at Babur, who was showing signs of impatience. "Please, no questions, Reema. Please? Go."

Begum Rabia had arrived shortly after the family had returned from the funeral, a cheerful, smiling presence among cheerless people. AJ now had this grinning old woman on top of everything else.

Begum Rabia's phone rang, and she stepped outside to answer it. AJ didn't care what the old biddy was doing. Her mind was on Reema and Paracha. The torturous ride home sitting next to her brother Babur had given her a headache. Mama lamented the loss of Papa and their fortune. She would have to tell her mother about the money soon, but not here with her mother crying and her brothers listening. She would get a private moment with her mother after the mourning ended and the visitors left.

Begum Rabia came back through the open front door, no longer smiling.

Asya Jaffrey asked, "Is there a problem, Begum Rabia?"

The old woman's lips curled into a sneer at AJ. "You. And your shameful family."

"What?" her mother asked. "What are you talking about?"

"This woman. This unspeakable slut of a girl. She has fornicated. In America. She has lived with a man. She has fornicated with many men."

"No! This is not true. She is a good girl, my Aamna!"

"She is not. I have learned the *truth,* girl!" The matchmaker's eyes blazed with lost revenue.

Her mother looked at AJ with shock. "Is this true, Aamna? Tell me it is not true."

"I…I love him, Mama. Alec Chenais. Yes, I have slept with him. I—"

Her mother screamed, beating her breast. Throwing her hands up, Begum Rabia walked out, leaving the door open. Babur and Sohail burst in from the kitchen, chewing on the guests' food.

"What is it, Mama?" asked Sohail.

"What is wrong with her, Aamna?" asked Babur. "Why is the door wide open?"

AJ just shook her head.

"She," her mother hissed. "She has shamed us all! Aamna has slept with many men while in America! America was her ruin! We are destitute from your father's debts. We will all starve on the streets of Islamabad."

The two boys stood like statues, their mouths agape. AJ sighed. This moved Babur to grab her by the arms.

"Is this true, sister? Is it?" He shook her.

"Let me go, you beast," she said, pulling away from him. "Yes. No. I have not slept with many men. Alec is my lover and we will marry." But would they? Only Allah knew what the future held.

Babur became very red in the face.

AJ turned to her mother, worried about her health. "Mama, because of your illness, it is unwise—"

"We cannot worry about that now, Aamna. Your shame, our shame, is everything now!"

"She is not even sick, you stupid *kothi*," Babur shouted.

"What?"

"Babur, be quiet!" their mother sputtered.

"She said it to bring you here to marry. And now look what has happened." Babur practically spat in her face. "*Fahisha!*"

This insult was too much for AJ. Donkey-woman maybe, believing her mother's lies, but she wasn't indecent. She said to her mother, "Mama—"

Her mother hissed, "Go. Go to your room. We will deal with this somehow. Go!"

AJ closed the door of her room. She sat on her bed to think. Her secret was a secret no longer. She was finally free from any arranged marriage, but how did that old biddy discover her affair? And her mother had lied. The whole family had lied. To get her here. She would forgive Alec and make it work. Go back to San Francisco. Now she saw what she had done. The folly of accepting Perry's offer. She would return the money. She would—the code!

AJ rushed to her computer. GitHub was still open in her web browser. She'd been working on some code changes earlier. She committed the changes to GitHub, then navigated to her account settings and changed her password. It was unfortunate about Reema and Mr. Paracha, but the damage would be too great to overcome if Alec understood her betrayal. Or if Ludivine found out. She would make it up to Reema. Oh. $5 million. Could she get that back from Reema? Reema was pragmatic. She would understand.

AJ looked at the time on her computer screen: 1:55. She had changed the password in time. When she got her phone back, she would call Alec and tell him…that she loved him. Forgive him his insensitivity. It was the truth! Just not all of it.

AJ would weather the storm in her family, wait out the pandemic, then return to San Francisco and decide whether to marry Alec. She'd appease Ludivine somehow. All would be well.

All would be well.

CHAPTER EIGHTEEN
The Dark Web

A crewman summoned Elliot to the comms cabin to take the call from Varoozh. He expected great news.

But Varoozh reported failure. "She reneged! Changed the password on me. She did not come to meet me as promised. Instead, she sent a friend. With her phone. And with her GitHub password. But it failed!"

"What do you mean, it failed?" Elliot felt the burn of frustrated anticipation.

"She changed the password. Before I tried to download the code. I slapped her friend around to get the story. But it was too public to take proper measures."

"Call her. The Jaffrey woman."

"I can't. The friend has her phone."

"Pay her a visit. Right now." Elliot rubbed his eyes. "No, wait. She planned this. To steal my money and disappear without delivering. The girl was part of the Moureaux group before she went to San Francisco. Moureaux! That witch could be behind this!"

"What do you want me to do? I want to do something. People do not trick me without consequences."

"Your ego is not my problem, Varoozh. The 1WeakLink code and Jaffrey are. And Moureaux. Hmm. Give me some options, Varoozh."

"If I go to her house openly, her family might interfere. The mother would make trouble. But their house is not secure. I will break in while they sleep and force her to give me the code. Or take her where I can deal with her effectively. And her friend, too. And get that code."

"That all sounds complicated, Varoozh. I don't like complications. But I want that code. And I do *not* want anyone to know we have it. Silence the two women. I'll leave it to you. Just finish it."

"What about Moureaux?"

Elliot set his jaw, then loosened it to say, "I've got a little list, Varoozh. She's on it. Let me worry about Moureaux. Just...finish it."

"I'll finish it. Tonight."

"Jesus Christ, Elliot, what the hell is that?" asked Oscar.

Elliot, waking from a deep sleep, grunted. The sound came again. A faint tapping.

"God damn it." Elliot rolled out of bed, found his robe, and walked through the several rooms of his stateroom to the hatch and opened it. Jeff. Jeff Morrow, looking agitated. Better than queasy, but—

"What the hell time is it, Jeff?" he asked sharply.

Jeff checked his watch. "Uh, 4 a.m. South African time, boss."

Elliot looked up, then down, teeth clenched. "Why are you banging on my hatch at 4 a.m., Jeff?"

"Boss, you gotta come and check it out, OK?"

"What's going on, Elliot?" asked Oscar, emerging naked from the bedroom.

"I'd tell you if I knew," Elliot grumbled. He glared at Jeff, who was staring hard out the window, obviously embarrassed. But still excited.

"The code, boss. The code. It's here," Jeff blurted.

The grogginess disappeared. "When?"

"Five minutes ago. Come on!" Jeff turned and headed toward the ladder down to the lower decks.

"Fuck," said Elliot, who turned to find his deck shoes. Oscar was holding them out, dangling from one hand, with a mischievous expression on his face. Elliot smiled and said, "Work never stops, Oscar, even on board."

"Is it really…?"

"We'll see." Elliot followed Jeff down three decks to the Seacave. It had only been fourteen hours since Varoozh had made his dramatic promise. Now he'd delivered. Warmth radiated throughout Elliot's body as he clambered down the ladders to the lower deck and followed Jeff into the Seacave.

Jeff jabbed a thick finger at a small notification. "I got this ping from the cutout server, boss! Someone uploaded a file. Checked it out, and guess what: a ZIP file from GitHub. All the 1WeakLink code!"

"Get it secured, Jeff."

"Already moved it to the secure code server, boss." The TANSTAAFL crew used a server in Transnistria accessible only with a private PKI key as their front door to the dark web. Their working code lived on a very private repository accessible only by key, and only Jeff had the key. Their dark web code wasn't on GitHub or any other public site, too risky.

"What's next, Jeff?"

"Spend a few days understanding and integrating the code. Then pow! We do something big. Enormous." Jeff rocked back in his chair with glee.

Elliot slowly smiled a broad smile. He said, "About time."

Elliot roused Steve, the comms tech, from his bunk at 5 a.m. to set up Elliot's call.

"Yes?" answered Varoozh.

"Varoozh, Elliot here. Where are you?"

"On the M-5, in my car."

"We have the code. Why didn't you call us?"

"No time. I planned to call as soon as I got back to Karachi. Besides, no one would man your comms that early."

"How did you access the code?" Elliot's curiosity overcame his rational decision to stay ignorant.

"I went to her house at one in the morning, while everyone slept. I picked the lock and got into her room. She wasn't there, but her workstation displayed a browser with GitHub open. I downloaded the code and transferred it to your server, and left. Took five minutes."

"But what happened to the woman? Is that all?" Elliot was sure Varoozh hadn't told him everything. Did it matter?

"That's all I want to talk about. Sleeping dogs, Elliot. Sleeping dogs. Check the news; the Jaffrey woman's dead. Send me the fee when you can." Varoozh hung up.

Elliot had the code. Perhaps he should stay ignorant after all.

CHAPTER NINETEEN
The News

Alec Chenais settled in for the night's work around 8:30, getting into the coding flow. The pandemic lockdown made night and day irrelevant. At 9:12, a text message popped up on his phone. The header said it was AJ. Her usual mode of communication with him now was through the project management system, so this was novel. Alec's heart tightened as he imagined what else she might have to say. The small message bubble appeared as the phone recognized his face. "Sorry alec to inform you of aamna jaffrey's death in a traffic accident so sorry for …" The size of the bubble cut the rest of the message off.

Alec grabbed at his phone, but his sudden movement knocked the thing off the table. He jumped out of his chair and scrabbled furiously on the floor as the device slid along just out of his reach. He finally caught it, like a trapped rat, and swiped and clicked.

"…the loss you must feel she talked about you all the time what a wonderful friend she was to us again so sorry to have to tell you reema"

Alec texted back, asking for more information, but the phone remained silent. Reema? AJ had mentioned a childhood friend with that name once or twice. But why did Reema text on AJ's phone? Scenarios flew through Alec's mind until he forced himself to stop: AJ was dead? He had to know. He couldn't give in to denial. But he only had a single text message from an unknown person with AJ's phone. Unknown? He remembered AJ's childhood friend from that awful Thanksgiving when AJ described her work with Pakistani women prisoners to his dad. Reema. Reema Kathia. The Mehrasa Foundation.

He clicked the call button to return the call. But the phone was now off. Voicemail. AJ's greeting. Oh my God. From beyond the grave.

"Reema Kathia, this is Alec Chenais." His voice trembled with fear. "Please call me. I must know what happened to Aamna. She can't be dead. Please call me at this number. Please."

The phone sat silently on his desk as he waited for it to ring, dread filling his mind.

He called again and left another urgent voicemail. Then he started searching for the news, finally finding it on the *Express Tribune* website and others, some in Urdu, some in English. All the same, they no doubt quoted from a single police statement. The machine-translated Urdu, garbled as it was, said nothing more than the English. The story was on the *Tribune's* Islamabad page, not important enough to make the front page. Dated May 16th, 2020, the article reported the police had found the body of a young woman from a good family, Aamna Jaffrey, on a side street, the victim of a hit-and-run accident. An investigation was underway, and the family was distraught.

AJ was dead. Alec's future was gone.

Alec grabbed his peacoat and took the elevator ten stories down to Mission Street. The pandemic closures had emptied the usually busy street during the day. At night, it was a ghost town. Alec walked down toward the Bay, hands in the pockets of his peacoat for warmth. Far from a Montreal winter night, but Alec was too upset to care about temperatures.

Yerba Buena and Moscone Center loomed off to his right. If only AJ had listened to him, heard his apology and how much he loved her. But she wouldn't listen, she wouldn't. If she'd just listened, she'd be alive, living in San Francisco, and loving him. But she hadn't. She flew to Pakistan. She'd used the pandemic as an excuse to run away.

Alec walked down to the Embarcadero and out to the edge of the Bay Trail and the long walkway of Pier 14. He stopped at the viewing platform at the end.

He stood there for an eternity, growing colder by the minute, gazing at the coruscating light show on the Bay Bridge. With fewer people coming downtown, the usual stream of headlights on the bridge was gone, leaving only the shimmering art lights and the dark silhouette of Yerba Buena Island. Staring down at the water. It would be so easy. So easy.

If only he hadn't called her childish and interrupted her and made her angry enough to leave him. If he'd only found the words to apologize, to make her listen, to make her understand how much he loved her. He'd given her space and time. Had that been the right decision? If he'd been more forceful, she wouldn't have left. But he didn't believe that, really. She knew what she wanted and what she was doing. He knew deep down that he couldn't change her mind until she was ready to change it, and that never happened. Never had a chance to happen.

Was it the arranged marriage? Did that pull her away from him, even though she loved him? Did she have to go along with the family's plans for her? Was there a darker motive behind this? Perhaps psychological or financial pressure that coerced her into the marriage? Alex laughed bitterly to himself. Human rights didn't matter when the woman you loved was just gone. Forever. What about her rights? And his own?

Small waves slapped at the pilings as he leaned over the waist-high metal railing. The slaps assaulted his ears with a percussive guilt, and the lapping water pulled his mind deeper into the blackness. He held himself still, afraid to even think about his feelings.

As the eastern sky brightened into a pink and orange sunrise, he sighed and turned to retrace his steps, taking the elevator up to his condo.

Alec sat at his condo workstation, preparing his mind for the emergency company meeting. He turned on the ring light behind the giant monitor and closed his main window curtains to block out the rising sun in the east. He made himself a *café au lait* and stared at his monitor, waiting.

When he started the Zoom session, he saw everyone was already waiting. Maksym and Olyena from Ukraine appeared together, and Pete from New York, and Marcus from the UK, and Crispin and Yuriko from their San Francisco homes. They traded the usual greetings and jokes, but everyone seemed a little nervous. Crispin's what-the-hell frown did nothing to help the situation.

Alec said, "Hi everyone. I called this meeting—"

"Alec," Olyena said, "AJ isn't here yet. Don't you want to wait for her?"

Alec took a deep breath. He said, "She's not coming. She's dead."

The conference erupted in chaos as the team members broke into each other's exclamations.

"Guys, guys, quiet," Crispin said. "Let Alec talk."

"I found out late last night," Alec said. "From a friend of hers in Islamabad. Police discovered her body on a side street and are currently investigating. I can't get any more information."

"Oh, Alec," Yuriko said, stricken.

Alec scanned the other Zoom frames. Surprised expressions, but only Olyena showed any genuine emotion. Crispin's lips were tight. He was probably thinking about schedules and trying not to say it.

"Alec, wait, was she murdered? Assaulted?" Marcus's question was sharp and urgent, as if his wife had been the victim. Olyena groaned and grabbed her husband's arm.

"I don't know, Marcus. I only know what I just said. No idea when it happened or any other details."

Maks said, "She dropped some code on GitHub on Tuesday, Alec."

Pete said, "Yeah, I got a notification about it." He consulted his phone. "About 5 a.m. Tuesday morning. I was asleep, didn't get it until later that day."

"So, 2 p.m. her time. Tuesday afternoon." Alec filed this into his memory, one of the many facts he'd collect.

Pete said, "Yeah, I guess. Hey, Alec. I've been integrating those API changes in my modules, but there are so many bugs, it's—"

Yuriko had recovered enough to intervene, steering the meeting back to AJ's death. "Alec, we need to focus on supporting the team and AJ's family. Does she have family here?"

Alec shook his head. He struggled to express "Just me," but couldn't, the pain getting in the way. "No, Yuriko. They're all in Islamabad." But his brain processed another fact: AJ's last code integration was of poor quality. But her code always worked the first time. Always. What—

Olyena was crying by this time. "I loved her," she sobbed. "She was strong and good, a real woman." Maks hugged her and wiped away her tears. Looking into the camera, he said, "Ukrainians are emotional. Sorry guys." But Alec noticed his dry eyes and even tone.

"I want to thank Alec for arranging this meeting to give us the news," Crispin said, firmly taking over. "He and I will meet later to figure out the implications of poor AJ's death on the company. I'll schedule another Zoom session when we have something for all of you. Until then, keep doing what you were doing. If you need anything, text Yuriko."

As Crispin spoke, Alec saw a line from him appear in the private chat window. "Alec, meet me at the Jackalope at 9, OK? In-person talk." Alec just nodded to let Crispin know he'd be there. He ended the session in silence, as there was nothing more to say. He turned off his ring light and sat in the semi-dark room, staring at nothing.

The Jackalope Cafe on Howard Street, Alec's favorite, was one of the few downtown cafes to survive the pandemic lockdowns. Its customers were the work-at-home crowd who lived in SOMA. These folks liked fresh air, strong coffee, and reliable 1000Mb Internet, but they lived in sucky apartments in rundown buildings with no such amenities. The cafe now only did takeout from a table in the doorway. For outdoor dining, they'd built a platform with plywood walls on three sides and a fiberglass panel for a roof in the street parking spaces in front of the cafe. They called it a parklet. It had murals of jackalopes drinking coffee and typing on laptops.

Crispin, always five minutes early, sat at a table in the middle of the parklet nursing a latte. Alec disdained such foreign concoctions and got a *café au lait* from the takeout table. The barista recognized him and ensured the correct roast, cup, saucer, French press, and preferred brand of whole milk. He took his coffee and sat down across from his co-founder. Alec felt a little awkward because he didn't have his laptop in front of him. He glanced over at the cafe window where he and AJ had always eaten breakfast, then prepared himself for his CEO.

"Hi, Crispin," he said.

Crispin's thin, light brown beard twisted with his most sardonic smile. "Alec, let's cut the social crap and get to it. Without AJ, we're fucked."

"That's..." Alec's throat closed with the pain and anger.

"That's *true*. We are fucked." The CEO took a sip of his latte. "AJ had it all in her head. Besides you, she was the sole developer who could rip out the code. Now she's dead and we're fucked."

"I can take over, Crispin. She was...the best I've ever known. But I can produce."

"Alec, you're a super-programmer. You're brilliant. You grok the different blockchains, no question. As CTO, you're perfect. But you're not a hacker like her. She has explored the holes, the tunnels, the fucking secret passageways into the dark dungeons, Alec. You haven't."

"I...have sources. Crispin, I can learn. Or I can find someone."

"Yeah. How the hell can you find someone when everyone is locked up?"

"It's called the Internet, Crispin. It doesn't matter where people are anymore."

"Alec, the days of dogs playing on the Internet are over. The people we need dislike the light. And they don't post resumes. I repeat—how are you going to find someone?"

"I can do it myself, Crispin."

"Alec, with Aamna dead, you're having trouble forming complete sentences."

"I'll be fine, Crispin." AJ had been his future, but the future was now the product. He could lose himself in his original goals, the ones that had driven him even before he met AJ in Paris, the ones that led him to create 1WeakLink.

"The NSA wants a demo in two weeks, Alec. Can the team produce something that won't embarrass me?"

Alec noted the pronoun and drew a Venn diagram in his head, with two completely separate circles: one for Crispin, and one for "the team." No overlap between the sets. Crispin had NSA contacts, one thing he brought to the table as a founder. No, the only thing, aside from enough capital to pay the cloud service bills for a year for a development product that ate CPU hours like candy. Other than that, he was a useless *espèce de merde*.

Alec opened his mouth to express this rational conclusion, then closed it as his brain finally kicked in to stop the downward spiral of blame. He cleared his throat of the bile. He would complete the product, using the resulting fortune to combat forced marriages worldwide, something AJ would appreciate. That would get him over his hill of grief.

"I will do it, whatever it takes. Or die trying. I will. I owe it to her."

"OK, Alec, brilliant. You do that. You have one week to show me something, then one week to clean it up enough to demo. Got it?"

"Yeah." Alec finished his *au lait,* carefully set the cup down on its saucer, bused it to the cafe table, and walked away.

CHAPTER TWENTY
Dealing with the Devil

Alec curled up in a ball on his couch with headphones playing the Goldberg Variations on a loop. He wasn't into gaming, so this was the best he could do to avoid working on or even thinking about the alpha release. Or about AJ. But he needed to buckle down soon or Crispin wouldn't get his demo.

Unsure if it was the third or fourth time through the music, he sighed, uncurled, and went to his three large monitors. He stood debating whether to make another au lait or work.

Alec jerked his mind to the software. Distracting himself with music or coffee technology or by reading French existentialist philosophy: useless. The point: endless distractions don't produce code.

Finishing AJ's code was the moral equivalent of chiseling hieroglyphs on her sarcophagus.

She'd been working on the heart of the BoltCutter tool, the cryptography subsystem that was key to the 1WeakLink toolset. Alec knew the basics of the math involved, but he didn't have AJ's intuitive feel for the twists and turns of the numerical algorithms required.

Alec examined AJ's final GitHub Python code upload. Final. On the last day of her life.

Last day of her life.

10:30 at night on Monday, and he had to deliver by Friday. Focus on the code. Pete said it had bugs. Focus on the interfaces. Wow! That couldn't be right. That meant....

An hour later, Alec leaned back. Progress, but...coding was distracting. Could you be distracted from being distracted? AJ must not have been herself when she checked in this code. Her code never failed. Until now. Then she died. He'd deal with the implications later. If there was a later.

He'd hit a wall. He simply didn't have the intuition he needed to solve the numerical problem presented by one part of the block decryption algorithm. AJ had missed or ignored this problem. Her code failed even basic functional tests.

Just like in the real world. If you ram your nose against a brick wall to the point of blood, change direction. He saw three options.

Hire a new tech staff member. Difficult. Particularly considering the scarcity of the required skill set and the tight deadline for solid code.

Or hire a consultant from the ocean of self-employed software developers. Easier, but that ocean had a lot of poor quality fish, and there was no time to sort through the catch.

Or call Ludivine. He'd seen what her demons could do, and they offered exactly the software help he needed. But if the NSA was already holding its nose with his existing employees, hiring Ludivine would make them want to wear gas masks. So he'd have to keep it under wraps, even from Crispin. And he'd pay for it himself.

Alec's time in Paris with Ludivine had been excellent marketing on her part. But he'd clearly understood the underground nature of her operation. AJ's ability to work her way into any software system never raised his moral anxiety the way Ludivine and her demons had. They had few ethical concerns and fewer inhibitions about their work. Yet he'd called her earlier in desperation because of the pressure from the NSA over the CDC hack. Alec considered that emergency a walk in the park compared to his current situation. Ludivine was right. That hadn't been a crisis worth involving her. But now his need to complete the alpha release far outweighed his moral concerns, and the crisis was real.

It was 2:30 in the morning, 11:30 Paris time. Alec retrieved Octave's card and made the call, then waited for Ludivine's callback, which came within five minutes.

"*Bonjour,* Alec. How nice to hear from you." She spoke in French, and Alec replied in the same language.

"The last time we spoke, Ludivine, you expressed reluctance to consult for my company, if you recall."

"Yes, Alec. The opportunity was not right for me. But it was right for AJ. I am very sorry for your loss, Alec."

"You…know about AJ?"

"Of course. I follow events closely. But how can I help you, Alec? With your business?" Ludivine, having exhausted her empathy for his loss, wanted to move on.

"Yes, all right. AJ was our expert in cryptography and…security." He couldn't bring himself to say "hacking." He continued, "She was good, Ludivine. As good as your friends."

"Yes, Alec, I agree. I spent some time with her, back in 2016. A wonderful person, and a demon with software."

Was AJ one of Ludivine's demons? Ludivine being Ludivine, she could very well have set him up for AJ. Groomed him. Not relevant to today's problem.

Committing himself, he said, "She—her death interrupted the work she was doing for us. We must deliver an alpha release in a few days, and I've hit a brick wall. I can't figure out what's wrong with her algorithm. And learning the required math would take too long."

"What sort of math?"

"Probabilistic graph theory and combinatorics, primarily. With a little advanced number theory. I need someone trustworthy, Ludivine. This is… government work."

"How exciting, Alec! Everyone I recommend you can trust. Yes, I can help you with this."

Alec laughed. "How much, Ludivine? To ensure trustworthiness? To help?" Alec was certain that Ludivine's concept of trust would not be credible to the U.S. government.

"15,000 euros, Alec. The equivalent in ether at today's exchange rate. I will send you the QR code for the Ethereum wallet. Once I have transferred the fee, I will put you in touch with my friend, who will be happy to help you. It would be best, Alec, if you only revealed the part of your code relevant to the problem. Do you comprehend?"

"Yes, of course, Ludivine." She meant that the code he revealed might end up on the dark web. He paused, moved by his grief and need, then said, "I appreciate your help. I'd like to see you again, Ludivine. When all this is done."

"You will, Alec. Someday soon." She switched to English. "But we'll always have Paris." The phone went dead.

"It's good. Absolutely fantastic!" Crispin was ecstatic. "You've worked miracles."

"*We've* worked them, Crispin."

"I didn't do much, but thank you."

"No, Crispin. I mean, the development team did."

"Of course, Alec." The CEO's voice bubbled with enthusiasm despite the implied criticism of his interpretation of pronouns. Alec was sure Crispin didn't get the point. He rarely did. He possessed the shell of a tortoise.

It was just the two of them in the Zoom session. Alec figured his team didn't need the thrill of watching Crispin rave about the working version of the 1WeakLink tool suite. Making them stay awake all night to witness Crispin's response wouldn't be a reward. But the demo had gone well. Ludivine's consultant found a hack to bypass a mathematical singularity in AJ's code. The consultant admired AJ's originality but noted her failure to analyze the math deeply enough to understand the singularity. He'd reworked two functions to use some routines buried deep in the numerical library to approximate a solution, and now the subsystem worked fine.

Alec made the code transfers completely sub rosa rather than working in the normal way through GitHub. When he uploaded the finished work, it looked like it was all his. His and AJ's. He had smiled as he uploaded the code. He felt guilty over his pretense that he had solved the problem, but Ludivine would keep that secret.

Alec sat still, unable to get out of his chair. What did it matter now that AJ was dead? Could he return to his original goal of taking an obscene amount of money from the government and using it to solve the world's problems? The prospect was all too foggy now. Especially after involving Ludivine. AJ had brightened his life and filled his thoughts with the future, and that was gone. None of it made sense anymore.

"How much polishing is left, Alec?" asked Crispin, interrupting Alec's downward spiral.

Alec returned his mind to the project. "Peter and Marcus can get everything done in a couple of days. Then we'll run a security audit. That will find the vulnerabilities that are the first thing the NSA techies will look for. But it shouldn't be a problem for next week. Once everything is ready, we can do the rest of the production checks."

"All right, I'll set up the demo meeting with the NSA brass for Friday. Does that work for you?"

"Sure, Crispin." Alec heard the lack of enthusiasm in his own voice.

Crispin recognized it too. "The company's future *depends* on this demo, Alec. Your share of the company depends on it. Make sure it goes well."

Alec nodded. AJ's death burdened him, but he knew he had to move forward. For AJ. For the future. Get the release done, get the demo done. No matter the cost. He had to.

CHAPTER TWENTY-ONE
Cape Town

Elliot Perry stood outside the Seacave, debating with himself whether to goose the crew inside. "Herding" these cats was not a useful management technique. They moved at their own pace. And they communicated little, if at all. He'd attended CEO discussions about remote work years ago. Frankly, he thought remote work might be a solution, not a problem. Sure as hell, office work on a yacht would not yield huge productivity gains. Not in the Seacave.

He wanted to apply the software where it benefitted him the most. Today, the coin exchanges. Tomorrow, the world.

The hatch opened. Jeff Morrow stood there, a queasy grin on his face. Clearly, Jeff was no sailor.

"Hi, Elliot. Say, boss: look up." Jeff jabbed a thick forefinger upwards.

Perry smiled and tilted his head up. Oh shit, those fucking bastards. They'd installed a tiny camera looking down the passage. They saw him standing there like an idiot.

He forced out an embarrassed laugh. "OK, Jeff, you caught me. I've got a serious itch that needs scratching. Can you help?"

"Betcha I can. Come on in."

The Seacave had beer bottles and cans, pizza, and other snacks from the galley scattered about, lit only by the glow of thirty monitors. Some were in dark mode, others had bright white screens glaring out in the darkness. TANSTAAFL Software at work.

Jeff staggered slightly as he walked over to one of the darker monitors. He plopped down on the fur lined bench he'd ordered from Germany through the steward while they were cruising the Baltic Sea.

The ship gave a small shudder as the Atlantic surge crested. The sea anchor held them in place, but the waves off the Cape of Good Hope thrashed the ship unmercifully.

"Jesus Christ, boss, how much longer are we gonna sit here in this mess? I'm sick." Jeff gripped the edge of the bench and swallowed.

"I'll let the captain know it's time to sail around the cape. Might as well. We'll head for Singapore on the way to San Francisco. Interesting things going on with the money markets there. I'll meet with some principals in person. And we need to refuel, maybe in Mauritius." Elliot smiled. Jeff wouldn't appreciate that course too much; the Indian Ocean was shaping up to a heavy typhoon season.

"Fine, just get me the hell off this roller coaster. Anyway. We've integrated most of the 1WeakLink toolset into our codebase now." Jeff shook his head. "Damn shame about AJ, boss. The code had some serious problems. AJ would have worked them out real quick. It took us a week to get our heads around her code and fix it. That guy Chenais ain't no slouch, either. He wrote some damn fine code in this thing."

Jeff waved a fleshy hand at his screen, which showed an unintelligible display of several windows containing code gibberish.

"I'm sorry, Jeff. There was nothing I could do," Elliot lied. "Varoozh said nothing about what happened when he downloaded the code from her computer." Elliot didn't care, but he wouldn't tell Jeff that. All he cared about was her silence, and that was now guaranteed.

"Killing her was unnecessary, boss. I could have talked her around."

Elliot shrugged it off. "Water under the bridge, Jeff." He sat down next to the big man on the bench. Fur lined. Very nice. Have to consider that for my stateroom. "Show me what you've got."

***

The captain of the *Mugwump* decided he preferred Cape Town as a pit stop. Elliot guessed the captain was the kind to look for gas stations with the tank at three-quarters empty. Elliot arranged with the port authority for the yacht to dock at the cruise terminal. When he applied for shore leave for the 200 crew and employees, the port authority laughed hysterically. They informed Elliot they'd locked down the entire city because it was the COVID hotspot of South Africa. Diesel fuel was fine, tourism was right out.

Elliot dealt with Jeff's disappointment by pointing out that at least the ship had anchored in a quiet harbor. Then Elliot put him to work.

Two days later, Elliot ordered a copy of the morning *Cape Times*. The paper reported a mysterious hacking of an Ethereum coin exchange. 15.5 million Tether tokens from one of the exchange's largest accounts disappeared overnight. The theft had baffled security investigators. The affected blockchains didn't show any wallet movement or missing tokens.

Elliot wrote a note to himself in his diary to have Tim give Jeff a $1 million bonus from the new funds. Then he read an article pleading for funds to help a baby baboon blinded by a paintball shot. He scratched out the $1 million, wrote in $100,000 for Jeff, and wrote in another $250,000 for the baby baboon. Why not? Plenty more where that had come from. Still, he'd have to work on reining in his altruism.

CHAPTER TWENTY-TWO
Selling the NSA

"How many slides here, Alec?"

Crispin Bannon scrolled through the PowerPoint presentation that Alec had sent him. Crispin had scheduled this Thursday-afternoon Zoom session for a complete walkthrough before Friday's presentation to the NSA.

Alec checked the slide counter. "126, Crispin."

"For a one-hour presentation. Alec. We're looking at ten slides. No more."

Alec's jaw dropped. "But, Crispin, they won't understand—"

"The NSA techies don't need to 'understand,' Alec. They need proof. Convincing. Confidence. What they don't need is a forty-five minute nap while you drone on and scroll through your 126 slides."

"We could can the presentation. The demo will be enough."

"Huh. Maybe a baby in the bathwater problem, but I'll bite. What are you going to demo for them?"

"We've developed four demos for different blockchains. I don't know which one to choose." It was a challenge to decide while the emptiness of missing AJ weighed on him. Getting this demo done would clear the decks. It would let him focus on the business. Instead of her absence from his life.

"You need to narrow it down to *one* and commit to it, Alec."

"Let's go through them, and you can choose. The CIA has a blockchain to manage field assets and intelligence transactions. Anonymous assets transact and get paid in digital currency."

"Um. Does the CIA know…that we know?"

"No, they don't, Crispin."

Crispin pursed his lips as he thought about it. "The NSA might like it. But no, better not. No need to risk getting the CIA mad at us. They're a potential client. What else?"

"We hacked a Chinese supply chain app for fentanyl ingredients. Importers use invoices to trigger anonymous blockchain shipments in digital renminbi. We can reroute these through our shipping clients and send the ingredients to the DEA."

Crispin's face didn't move, only his eyes. Then he smiled. "No way. The Chinese won't let that go. We don't need them mad at us. And getting the DEA on board might be unwise. The NSA likes to work alone. Next?"

Alec smiled in return. "A major European newspaper uses a blockchain to manage sensitive international news items from worldwide correspondents and anonymous sources. The blockchain guarantees traceability and allows editors to audit the reporting chain."

"Can you change the news?"

"No, we haven't managed that. We can insert fake ones, but we can't change anything. They use proof of work, which makes it very difficult."

"Proof of work?"

"It's a consensus protocol where nodes solve hash puzzles to process transactions, requiring significant compute time. Altering a transaction forces regeneration of all hashes across the entire chain, making it far too costly."

Crispin again thought it through. "The NSA might love just having access to the stories and sources. Huh." He grimaced, then shook his head. "Too boring. You said four? What's the last one?"

"An auditing app for a financial firm lets auditors in London access blockchain transactions remotely, the trust making personal inspection unnecessary. Because it's proof of stake, we can alter values if we hack nodes undetected." AJ's code made that possible. AJ. Alec's attention wandered to the empty void in his life.

"Any downside? What's proof of stake?"

Alec explained, "Another protocol that lets nodes post digital coins to compete for block creation, with a round-robin algorithm choosing the winner. We can hack the process to pose as the winner, but large changes risk auditor detection. A big hack would steal colossal sums in an instant and get out. But we can demo the potential."

"OK. Do you have any voting or election blockchains to hack? The NSA mentioned an interest in it."

"Election blockchains are scarce at the moment. A few professional nonprofits use them in internal officer elections, not anything important. When they appear, we'll be able to expand to them, but they're just not there yet."

"Let's go with the trade application. That's not too controversial." Crispin smiled. "Great job, Alec!"

At 9:50 a.m. on Friday, May 29, 2020, Alec logged into the NSA teleconference site. The date must be important, Alec judged, because the site told it to him seven different times during the login process. It involved a 24-character password, a 256-bit private key from a thumb drive, a text sent to his cell phone, his Social Security number, and a question about his mortgage. Alec felt very secure.

Alec waited. At 9:55, Crispin came on, and then a nondescript man wearing a white shirt with a solid red tie and a pocket protector with pens appeared with the screen name "Mr. B." He was followed by "Ms. C," a college-age woman with stringy blonde hair, a plaid men's shirt, and thick glasses that hid her eyes. Crispin acknowledged them, then lapsed into silence.

At 10:03, another man, this one in a naval uniform, came on. Crispin greeted him deferentially, and his screen name was Mr. A. Clearly the big boss.

"Are we all here?" asked Mr. A.

A chorus of "Yes" greeted this tautology.

Crispin introduced Alec as his CTO, then said, "All right, Alec, explain what you're going to show them, then we can start the demo."

Alec smiled an insincere smile and launched into a brief explanation of the trading audit blockchain.

Mr. B asked, "What's the point of it all?"

"This company has offices all over the world. Their auditors had to fly to every office to check paper files or separate databases on site. The travel expenses cost them a mint. Now they just sit in London and query blocks from the chain, because they can trust that the block can't be changed. That's what they think, anyway." Alec smiled.

Ms. C. had a high, squeaky voice that grated on Alec's ears, and she used it a lot to ask highly detailed technical questions about the application. Mr. B looked bored, and Mr. A had a poker face.

When Alec mentioned hashing, Mr. B perked up and asked some probing questions about how the blockchain used the hash codes. As Alec got deeper and deeper into the weeds, he realized Mr. B was baiting him with questions he already knew the answers to. A skeptic.

Crispin heard the skepticism and stepped in the get the demo back on track. He appealed to Mr. A. "Alec can show you how effective the product is. We're proud of what we've accomplished so far."

Mr. A said, "That's why we're here—to see the product. Please go ahead, Alec."

"Thank you," Alec said, sharing the auditor's application to their screens. "See the trade labeled '7CUR8745'? It's a small yen adjustment for an exchange rate update. I've highlighted it."

Ms. C said, "Add 3 cents to the dollar side."

"Okay," Alec replied. "Using the 1WeakLink Gaslighter tool, I'll paste the network ID, block hash, and trade hash. See the trade structure appear?" General agreement followed. "Now I set the value, click OK, and here's the updated transaction in the company app—reflecting the 3-cent change."

"Incredible," Mr. B said, leaning into his camera. "How did you do that?"

Alec smiled. "Magicians never reveal their secrets." AJ's code made it happen, though even Alec didn't fully understand how—but it worked.

"Can you delete a transaction?" asked Mr. B, frowning.

Alec pulled up the BoltCutter tool. "Again, copy and paste the information for the transaction, click OK, and it's gone." He pointed out the "Transaction not found." The BoltCutter was also AJ's work, with final input from Ludivine's consultant.

Toward the end, he had Mr. B nodding, his skepticism waning. Alec said, "A lot of these blockchains are private. They're only accessible via VPN connections through firewalls with whatever level of application security their policies require. We can only apply our tools if we can access their applications and blockchain. So it involves some, uh, 'access management.'"

"You mean, we'll have to hack in to use the tools," Ms. C said, grinning. Her glasses flashed reflected light. She squeaked, "No problemo!"

The two men rolled their eyes but said nothing. Quite a team.

"We're out of time, guys," interjected Crispin, who had said nothing else during the demo. Probably holding his breath the whole time. "I'll follow up with you on Monday, Mr. A. All right?"

Mr. A agreed, shared contact information, and ended the session. Alec's cell phone rang. Crispin. Alec had to spend fifteen minutes talking the man down from whatever cloud he was on. He hung up after Crispin had finished complimenting him and sat there deflated, thinking only of AJ and what to do about the void she'd left in his life.

A message pinged on Alec's phone at 6:03 after an all-night coding session. He picked it up and swiped. Reema. Reema? Finally! And not from AJ's phone.

"alec sorry to tell you aamna murdered"

He quickly typed in, "reema please call me need to talk."

His phone rang. "Reema?"

A woman with a strong South Asian accent said, "Yes. Alec Chenais?"

"Yes. Please tell me, what happened to AJ?"

"I am so sorry, Alec. The police came to question me today. They told me she was murdered. Her family thought it was a car or something, a road accident. But the police came and said murder. Someone beat her badly, and she bled to death from internal injuries. That is all we know right now. I am so sorry."

Wiping away his sudden tears with his free hand, Alec spoke into the phone. "I'm sorry too, Reema, it's a shock." Heat coursed through Alec's body as he absorbed this new information. Murdered. "Who did this to AJ? Do the police have any suspects?"

"No, Alec. The police in Pakistan, they do not communicate well or often. They told me it was murder only because they wanted information from me, and that was all."

"Reema, can you give me the phone number of her parents? I'd like to talk to them."

"That is not a good idea, Alec. They...will not wish to talk to you."

Murder cries out for justice. The heat grew inside him. "Should I come over there? To help with the investigation?"

"To Pakistan?" A long pause. "I do not think you can, Alec. Things are so hard right now. The pandemic, the airline restrictions...and the police would not want your help. Let me find out more." Reema paused, then said, "You must understand, Alec. You. And Aamna. Her family. It is so difficult, this situation. You should not come here."

Alec, defeated for the moment, said, "Please, keep me informed. If there's anything I can do to help the police, please let me know."

"Yes, I can do that."

"All right. Thanks for telling me all this, Reema."

"Goodbye, Alec."

Alec ended the call and buried his face in his hands. He got up from his desk, went to his bathroom, and splashed cold water on his face. He stared at his reflection in the mirror. Too much pressure, too much coding, not enough sleep. And now this. Murder. What did that doctor say about his Broken Heart Syndrome? He needed rest. To set boundaries on thinking about AJ. Sure.

In the kitchen, he made himself a *café au lait*, using his meticulous process to steady his nerves. He carried it to his desk to continue his programming work. He would bury himself in the code to avoid fixating on AJ and the life they could no longer share. And on the justice he knew he'd have to pursue.

CHAPTER TWENTY-THREE
The Breakthrough

After his windfall bonus, Jeff kicked back, enjoyed a few brews, and pondered his options for the money. What to do with it when they got to shore. Any shore. He gazed at Cape Town from the upper deck, admiring the magnificent view of Table Mountain. Plenty of bars he could hit with the guys. And Susie. She'd have a great time, loosen up that stiff upper lip.

But no. Damn COVID virus had shut down the entire city of Cape Town. Just when he was ready to get his land legs back and party, they wouldn't let him ashore. At least the boat was stable anchored in the harbor.

He could share the bonus with Susie. After all, she solved AJ's bug with some heavy math. Way out of his league. But he was sure Susie wasn't out of his league in other ways.

She'd come aboard from the U.K., a friend of a friend. Susie hailed from Manchester, a city with a lot of slums and a great football team. Jeff tried to get her interested in the Cowboys, but she set him straight right away. Forcefully.

"It's *football,* you twit, innit. Not that shite you Yanks do, all lined up and big helmets. Football."

Susie sported a glorious mass of tattoos and spiky hair and piercings in the oddest places. He'd asked about other, less obvious ones, and whether she'd like to show them to him. She'd given him hell and a two-finger salute. Then explained what that gesture meant. In detail. A challenge. She didn't speak English very well either, though she claimed it was mint, whatever that meant. She gave him the salute after that question, too.

Money might do it. But Jeff didn't like the idea of paying for it, so to speak. And he liked the idea of giving away money even less. Imagine his surprise when he'd found out that his parents had given away all their millions while he wasn't paying attention at MIT. He'd learned this wonderful fact when the lawyer called him after the accident to tell him he was in for a residual amount of $65,438.23 under the terms of his parents' wills. They'd locked up the rest in some kind of charitable trust for roadrunners or something. That day, he developed a disdain for any type of charity. Technically, Susie wasn't a charity, but still. He'd keep his money in his pocket and try something else.

He'd considered partying on the yacht, but he caught some vibes from Elliot that stifled that idea. Elliot was not the party type. This boat deal looked worse and worse. At least a cruise constituted an end-to-end party. The *Mugwump* was end-to-end work. With brews, but work.

Susie's voice called out to Jeff across the Seacave. Jeff unloaded his legs from the worktable where he'd propped them, set down his brew, and strolled over to Susie's workstation.

"Whatcha got, Susie?"

Susie turned her head to give him a black look. "Don't call me Susie, innit. Susan, ya facking twit. Have a gander at this comment in the 1WeakLink code. It's by that ace hacker lass."

She pointed to her monitor screen, and Jeff leaned over her shoulder to read it. She moved away, huffing, and he grinned. Then he read. His eyes widened.

"Shit. You're kidding."

"Yeah. Figured you'd fancy it."

Jeff, his mind now on code instead of sex, did fancy it. A lot.

He was looking at the access paths and codes for an internal blockchain at the NSA.

Thank you, AJ. Hacking the NSA was the ultimate goal for any certified hacker.

"Let's get to it, Susie," Jeff said, rubbing his hands and seating himself next to her on the upholstered bench. "I'll let you drive."

Elliot sat in a chair next to Jeff's workstation in the Seacave. Jeff had summoned him once more to show off his latest effort. As Jeff explained what he'd done, a frisson passed through Elliot's body. The kind of frisson that meant someone was walking over your grave. The NSA. Jeff had hacked the NSA.

He interrupted the self-congratulatory flow. "Jeff. Stop. Good work, yeah. But...." Elliot thought things through. "Did they catch you? Lock you out?"

"Naw, they never noticed. We were careful not to trip anything, just looking around. It's all encrypted, of course." Jeff pointed to some gibberish on his screen and told Elliot he was looking at encrypted blockchain information.

"Witness the power of 1WeakLink code, Elliot! Every box is a node in the chain pointing to secure documents or code in their servers. They've encrypted the content with double PKI encryption, and we can't crack that yet, but AJ's code makes a start on it by decrypting the blockchain. She was using this as a hard case to test her hacking code, I bet."

"And you can crack this?"

Jeff's smile twisted as he hesitated, then told the truth. "Not me, but Susie can. Ace, that's what she calls it. Ace hacking. She's good, boss."

Elliot looked away. How dangerous was this? NSA? Worldwide top-secret information. Big, but dangerous. Useful, but dicey. Extremely dicey.

"Hold off on doing anything about this, Jeff. Let Susan work on the encryption. Having all this in our back pocket is great. But no blowback from the spooks, please. It's too early, and I'm not ready. Mark's still working on getting his satellites in place, so we're still dependent on land-based servers and networks, and the NSA can easily disrupt those. They won't do that if they don't consider us a threat."

Susan, leaning against a beer fridge, walked over. Elliot raised his gaze to her, seeing her obvious wish to say something. Jeff appeared nervous and shook his head, while Susan's face showed determination.

"Mr. Perry."

"Elliot, Susan," he replied with a smile. "Everyone's casual on the ship."

"Soz, still gettin' me 'ead round that. We're dead posh in the UK, like, Elliot. Ta, Jeff, for the nice one." Jeff looked relieved.

"Do you have any suggestions, Susan?" Elliot asked.

"Well aye, I do. This hack came from that ace hacker lass, Jaffrey. If you want to stop them Yank spook wankers being brassed off and handing us a load of burning rubbish, there's a way. Insurance, like." She smiled a wolf's smile. Elliot, after some interpretative work on this foreign language, nodded. Susan continued, "We can drop some proper dodgy spoofs that make it look like this bloke Chenais is the one dogfooding, like. Then whatever we do won't gen up a lot of dead mither, innit? At least, nowt for us. Done and dusted, like. We could do it easy peasy for the lass, but she's croaked, like, and the spooks wouldn't believe it. See?"

"I do see," Elliot replied, smiling at the assault on the English language. Jaffrey, dead, was not a suitable scapegoat, but Chenais would do quite well. "Fine. You do that. Keep up the good work, Susan. And Jeff: just make sure no one finds out it's us."

"Got it, boss," Jeff responded, gazing at Susan with sheep's eyes. To each his own.

CHAPTER TWENTY-FOUR
Men in Black

The week after the NSA demo, Crispin emailed Alec to say they needed to get together to talk about the next steps. Needing some fresh air after several days of coding at his condo, Alec suggested they meet at the Jackalope late Thursday morning. Crispin said he had phone calls that wouldn't allow him to set a specific time, but he'd drop by before noon. So Alec sat in the Jackalope parklet with his laptop, sipping a *café au lait* and reviewing some code changes from the Ukrainians. They'd cracked one piece of the Ethereum puzzle, if he could believe their ecstatic emails.

A verbal argument caught his attention. A man and woman nearby quarreled. Something about Jerry and sleeping around. Alec smiled. Life on Howard Street. Looking at his phone, the man at the next table stood up to leave.

Alec's phone rang. Crispin. He answered.

The man at the next table grabbed the phone from his hand. A thief! He rose from his chair, turning. The couple stopped arguing and came over to help. But they didn't. They grabbed his laptop. Thieves.

Alec's mouth opened to shout for help. From behind, someone pulled a hood over his head. Strong hands twisted his arms behind him and bound his wrists with plastic ties. Gloved hands dragged him, stumbling. Street sounds. Hands pushing him into a van. His head hit metal, stunning him. Doors slammed, and rough hands tied his feet together as the roar of the engine assaulted his ears. Nothing was visible through the hood. He struggled to sit up and shouted, "What's going on?"

"Shut up," a gravelly voice said.

"Who are you? What are you doing?"

"Shut. Up." Alec felt a pin-prick in his arm. His muscles gave up and went slack, he slumped to the floor of the van, and blackness overtook him.

Two voices, both men, traded jokes. The voices reached Alec dimly as his confused brain processed data again. No more van, a mattress. Face up, arms tied. Legs tied. Muscles so weak he could barely move. The voices were harsh, the laughs loud and hard. He recognized one voice; he'd heard it earlier, in the van. A door opened and a third voice spoke.

"What did you give him?"

"The usual."

"Why is he still out?"

"'Cause he's an asshole."

"Idiots. Undo the restraints and lose the hood. Let's have a look at him."

"Ma'am. Take my word, he's OK."

"I can't interrogate him like this."

There was a note of impatience in the rough voice. "No, you can't. So? What do you want us to do about it?"

"You're working for me, damn it."

"Yes, ma'am. Sure. But he's out, and he's gonna stay out for a while."

"Jesus Christ."

A door slammed.

"Stupid bitch. Desk jockess."

"Yeah."

The third voice. The questioning one. Somehow familiar. The tone resolved itself. A female voice. Not soft, squeaky. His brain gave up the fight, and he went back to sleep.

* * *

"Is he awake?" the voice squeaked.

"Let's find out."

Powerful hands grabbed Alec's arms and lifted him, sitting him none too gently on a hard wooden chair. The hood came off, and he blinked into the harsh light. His vision readjusted. He occupied a windowless room. Its walls were white, its door solid and equipped with a lever handle. The room contained him, two men in black body armor, and Ms. C from the NSA.

"Whrg," he croaked. "What," he asked, "am I doing here?"

Ms. C smiled. "Talking. To us."

Alec licked his dry lips. "I…water. I need a drink."

"Fuck," said one man in black. The nasty one. "I need a drink, too. I get one first, asshole." A short black beard framed his broad face, eyes fierce under his black watch cap. He cracked his big knuckles and smiled. Not a pleasant smile.

Ms. C's glasses glinted as she looked at Mr. Nasty under the bright ceiling light. "Get him some water."

"Get it yourself. Ma'am."

Sighing, Ms. C left the room, closing the door behind her. A minute or two later, she returned, holding a paper cup.

"Free his arms," said Ms. C.

"You sure?"

The woman glared at the armored man. "Yes, I'm sure. Do it."

Mr. Nasty pulled a large, evil-looking knife from a belt sheath and walked behind Alec.

"Don't move a muscle, asshole." He felt the tie separate, his arms free again. Mr. Nasty stayed behind him.

Ms. C handed the cup to Alec. She said, "Here. Sip, or you'll…"

Alec had already drunk the entire cup.

"Asshole," Mr. Nasty reaffirmed.

"So, Alec," Ms. C said.

"What's going on?" Alec asked. His brain cleared as time passed.

The squeaky voice asked Alec to share his thoughts. Ms. C smiled. The pain coursing through his head told him not to trust that smile.

"Give me a clue. What do I call you? Ms. C?"

"Good as anything, Alec. But let's cut to the chase. You hacked us. And we want the person who took the 1WeakLink codebase, Alec. In Pakistan."

Alec blinked, uncomprehending. Shaking his head, he voiced his mystification. "What?"

Ms. C took this simple question as a challenge. "I ask the questions, Alec. Not you." The squeak was really irritating. And the woman, seen live and up close, was on the short side with stringy blond hair, thick glasses, and acne. Alec had seen a lot of thrillers on TV and the big screen, and none of those big-time government interrogators looked like Ms. C. He thus made a mistake.

"Fuck off," he said. "I want a lawyer."

Ms. C nodded at Mr. Nasty.

A large hand rested gently on Alec's shoulder. He turned his head to see Mr. Nasty grinning. He still held the knife. He weighed it thoughtfully, as though judging where best to use it.

"Now, Alec." Ms. C smiled. "I'm sure you didn't mean what you said. It's way too soon for lawyers, anyway. We're working on a security breach. Lawyers come when we discuss your criminal liabilities. Right now, we're working on intelligence." She smiled her dubious smile. "Your intelligence. Now, you didn't mean it, did you?" She glanced up at Mr. Nasty.

Mr. Nasty's fingers tightened on his shoulder.

Alec adjusted his attitude. "No no no I did not! Please...."

"Fucking weak, that's what he is," said Mr. Nasty. "Kid, this won't hurt a bit. Until later."

"Hold off a bit, Chief," said Ms. C. "Let's take it one limb at a time. OK, Alec. The hack. You hacked us, Alec. Our blockchain. My boss didn't like that. It wasn't friendly. It wasn't loyal." She shook her head. "It was stupid, Alec. What were you thinking?" She nodded. Mr. Nasty again gently squeezed Alec's shoulder, this time resting the knife on his other shoulder. Alec could see the sharpness of the edge in his peripheral vision.

"Hacked you? I didn't hack you. What are you talking about? I haven't—"

"Alec, Alec. Evidence shows you did it. You hacked us. We didn't hire you or your company to open our kimono for a major security breach. Why did you hack us?"

Alec shook his head, then stopped as the headache returned in force. Two possibilities: either Ms. C was making it up, or somebody had made it appear as though he had hacked into the NSA's systems. He explained this to Ms. C.

"We don't make things up, Alec. The right explanation is the simplest one. Why involve strangers when you're clearly the culprit?"

"I didn't do it. What evidence is there?"

"I'd like you to concentrate on answering our questions, Alec. Not asking your own." The knife moved a little toward his neck and pressed against his shoulder. Alec flinched.

"Why would I do this? I'm on your side," he said.

"You're a security risk, Alec. The stolen codebase told us that."

"What?"

Ms. C sighed, and Mr. Nasty's fingers tightened. He stropped the knife back and forth on Alec's shoulder.

"About that codebase. We track all the data that interests us in the world, Alec. That's our job. And your Ms. Jaffrey rode off the ranch. Pakistan. We're very interested in Pakistan these days. We intercepted her phone calls, Alec. $40 million from an unidentified man in Pakistan. Two days before she died. Why did you conspire with her to upload the code? And to whom?"

"I didn't. She…we broke up. She left." The accusation percolated into his brain. "Upload? What do you mean, she uploaded the code?"

"Come on, Alec. You helped her, you're the code guru at 1WeakLink. You were aware of her behavior."

"I didn't help her," said Alec. "She broke up with me. I loved her, but —"

"Aww," sympathized Ms. C. "So, you were close. Very close. You slept with her, Alec. What's your share of her loot? Who gave it to you, and where is it? Are you working for somebody in Pakistan? The talibs? The ISI? Why maintain an offshore account? And then came the mysterious Ethereum hack a week later—but she was already dead. Was that your hack too?"

"What are you talking about?" asked Alec, frustrated and very aware of the large knife right next to his neck. "What code? Where—"

"More questions, no answers. Need a reminder, Alec?" She glanced at the man behind him, who patted his shoulder and raised the knife in front of Alec's eyes so he could inspect the edge. It was very large and extremely sharp. It had a serrated, curved tip for doing serious damage to anything ranging from a tree trunk to an elephant.

"No! Tell me what happened. Please." A thought struck him. "The murder. Did AJ die because of the code upload?"

"Don't you mean, what code upload? Alec, her body turned up the next day. Did you give her the money? Did you snaffle up the rest of the stolen Tethers? Where are those stablecoins?"

"No!"

The black glove pressed down on his shoulder.

"Ahh, no! No money! I was here, working! The code wasn't working fully. Bugs. AJ merged and pushed changes in a hurry without checking them. She finished her night with that. But she hadn't finished testing."

"But *you* could finish it, Alec, and test it. You finished it in a few days. You just demo'd it to us. We got your laptop and your cell phone. Both were open, and we examined everything on them. You've accessed the code every day for weeks. So, who's tweaking it now? Who do we go after? Who are you working for in Pakistan?"

"I'm working for 1WeakLink. I'm…*Mon Dieu*."

"What?" Ms. C perked up.

"I hired a…consultant. A woman I met. To help fix the bug. But she's not Pakistani."

"Another woman. How romantic, Alec. What woman?"

Alec hesitated. The gloved hand pressed down harder.

"Ludivine, Ludivine Moureaux! Please. Stop."

Ms. C shook her head with a smile. "Ah. Her. But Ms. Moureaux did not upload the code, Alec. It went to a satellite and then somewhere else. The NSA tracks Moureaux. We see everything she does. Ms. Jaffrey has been feeding her code all along, up to when she left for Pakistan. We just hadn't sprung the trap. And you gave Moureaux money from your personal account. For what, Alec? Tell us who Jaffrey was working with in Pakistan. Who you were working with. Who killed her? Tell us where your share of the money is."

"She was with her family. They're not—they're just regular business-people. Not technical. She didn't work with anybody. There. Just us. The company. I got no money, none. I don't know who—"

Alec's pain-induced logorrhea suddenly stopped. Reema. Was Reema involved? She wouldn't be the hacker. She didn't have those skills. But maybe she saw something. He didn't want to give her name to the NSA. Ludivine could look after herself, but Reema was a bystander. He desperately wanted to ask her about AJ before anyone else. Reema wouldn't talk to him if the NSA got there first. But he had to extricate himself. He remained silent.

Ms. C stared at Alec through her thick glasses. She didn't smile anymore. "Something came back to you, Alec? What? And, Alec. Jaffrey's phone is missing. Its last known location was a park in Islamabad, then it disappeared from the cell network. Her family knows nothing about it, and it wasn't on her body when the police searched it. Who has her phone, Alec?"

"I don't know." Reema had it, he was sure. But he wanted to find out himself. Find out what was going on with her and AJ. "I only called her once, back in April, about a hack at the CDC."

"On this phone." She pulled a smartphone out of her pocket and waved it. Alec recognized it as his own. "We know all about that hack, Alec. But you got a message the day after she was killed, Alec. From her phone. After she was dead. Who was it?"

"Somebody called me to tell me AJ was dead."

"A text message from 'reema,' Alec. From that phone. And later a phone call from Reema Kathia, from her own phone. In Pakistan, Alec. Is Ms. Kathia your control?"

"Reema is just a friend of AJ's. She runs an NGO in Pakistan."

"We've checked her out, Alec. She doesn't have the code. And her profile doesn't show she's in the game. But her nonprofit's bank account received $5 million from Jaffrey on the day of the code download. Jaffrey got the $40 million. Where is it? Stop dancing around. Tell us who got the codebase. Tell us where the money is."

"For Christ's sake...."

Ms. C pursed her lips and shook her head. "Let's start from the beginning, Alec. You hacked us."

The man in black tapped the knife on his shoulder. Alec flinched.

CHAPTER TWENTY-FIVE
Wrongful Dismissal

After two more interrogation sessions, Ms. C accepted that Alec knew nothing. She then gave him a choice: detention in a secure government facility and access to legal advice, or going home after signing a release. He signed. Why make waves? He'd find out what was going on soon enough through Crispin's contacts. Mr. Nasty seemed disappointed to see him go, sheathing his knife in disgust. He didn't seem to like Ms. C very much, either.

The van dropped him off at 3rd and Mission. They removed the ties and hood and shoved him out of the back. They didn't even wave as they drove off.

He let himself into his condo. It was chaos. Drawers pulled out, contents scattered. Mattress slashed open with foam spilling out the sides. Pillow feathers everywhere. Leather couch a set piece from a slasher movie. Several holes in the walls, smashed with a sledge or something like it. Coffee beans strewn across the kitchen floor, along with sugar, flour, and baking soda. Counters ripped off. And of course, no computer. In his office, the monitor lay upside down on the floor with a cracked screen. He pushed around the litter; no burner phone. They'd taken that, too.

Alec's muscles ached from the tension of the interrogation and from whatever drug they'd given him. He was exhausted and in no mood to clean up the mess. A long, hot shower might help. But the bathroom was just more disaster. Toothpaste on the mirrors. Towels on the floor. Toilet paper off the roll. You could hide government secrets in a roll of toilet paper. That was what they were worth. Toilet unbolted and on its side; at least they'd shut the water off first. Alec ran the shower. No water. Upon inspection, he found the hot water heater in its closet was empty, topless, and had its pipes shut off.

Alec righted a chair in the living room and considered his life. Human rights, for instance. He was an entitled white male making hundreds of thousands of dollars a year with millions to come in stock from his vibrant startup. In San Francisco, that most progressive of cities. Yet here he was, taking a rest after a government agency tried to dismantle him just as they'd dismantled his living space. AJ had betrayed him and the company. $40 million? Did that justify what she'd done? Did she hate him that much? And who gave her that amount of money? The Russians? The Chinese? Daesh? The Taliban? The Pakistani ISI? Did she plan this from the beginning? The hacker queen from Pakistan taking her share from the decadent Western world? Stealing from the decadent and foolish man who loved her?

No. AJ loved him. He loved her. Sure, she had no real moral sense in the cyberworld. But neither did he. Not anymore. Not after the NSA had revealed its true nature. Right and wrong now were indistinguishable.

And what about Ludivine? She had even less moral sense than AJ. And she'd set them up. To meet Ludivine one day and AJ the next? A hard-to-believe coincidence. Could Ludivine have given her the money? But the NSA said Ludivine had not received the 1WeakLink code. So she was not AJ's Mephistopheles.

The chaos and uncertainty signaled a life-altering change that demanded action. Alec's thoughts coalesced around 1WeakLink. He had to talk to Crispin, who already thought Alec's marketing efforts lacked polish. And the NSA. Crispin's best client treating Alec like a criminal would push Crispin over the edge.

* * *

Since the NSA had taken his phone, Alec had to go to 1WeakLink's offices to check in. Friday at 2 p.m., at least Yuriko would be in the office. He would explain what had happened, get Crispin involved, and somehow salvage the situation with the NSA.

When he pressed his finger to the biometric door lock, nothing happened. He knocked, then knocked again.

Yuriko opened the door and stared at him. Her eyes narrowed. Her lips made a thin line.

She said, "You can't come in, Alec. You're fired."

"What?"

"The NSA informed us they've revoked your security clearance. You can't work on our products without one, Alec, or even come onto the premises. The paperwork is in the mail to you, along with a severance check for $50,000, as per your contract. It includes copies of your nondisclosure and noncompete agreements. The board has canceled your unvested stock shares and options and set the value of your shares to nothing. Crispin says—"

"What?" Alec couldn't take it all in. Fired?

"Is she talking too fast for you?" Yuriko gave Crispin a black look when she heard his voice from behind her.

"Shut up, Crispin. He's in pain."

"So am I."

Yuriko looked back at Alec and tilted her head. Alec liked Yuriko and gave her the benefit of the doubt.

"Sorry, Alec. The best of luck in your future endeavors." Then she winked and shut the door.

CHAPTER TWENTY-SIX
The Untouchable Suspect

STANDING OUTSIDE THE IWEAKLINK BUILDING, Alec took a moment to process his latest disaster. Then, realizing he was now free to deliver justice for AJ's murder, he bought a $35 smart phone and a new Linux computer at a nearby electronics mart. He carried them home to his trashed condo, then searched the floor and found Octave's card among the contents dumped from the drawers. Octave took his call and promised to pass the word to Ludivine, who called within ten minutes.

"Ludivine, I'm calling to warn you. The government has your name. They forced it out of me a day ago. I apologize for the late call; I was incapable of thought."

"The NSA is an old friend, *mon ami*. We act like long-separated lovers with a lingering fascination."

"They professed to know all about you."

"Whereas I know very little about them. Except that they know everything about me."

"Yeah. Somehow, I doubt that." Ludivine laughed, confirming his guess. "But, Ludivine, there might be a snitch somewhere in your group of hackers."

"Of course there is. How else would I keep the NSA informed of my operations the way I want them to be informed?" A brief pause and she got down to business. "So how can I help you, Alec?"

"AJ."

"What about her?"

"The NSA said she had uploaded the code to a third party. That I'd helped her. I hadn't. If it's true, and if we can find out who got the code, we've identified her killer. Can you trace her download? The NSA claimed not to know the final destination of the code download. And I —"

"You no longer have access. Oh, *mon ami*. It will cost you."

"I can't pay you now. This is important to me, Ludivine. I'm asking you for a favor." He hesitated, then doubled down. "And you set us up, Ludivine. You brought her in to steal the code. You owe me."

"It is a good thing we now have no secrets, *mon ami*."

Alec smiled, not believing her for a second. "I want to help the Pakistani police find the killer."

"Alec, the police in Pakistan are not likely to be of help."

"If they won't help, I'll find somebody who will. Listen. She committed changes to the codebase on GitHub the day before they found her body. The NSA said she uploaded the code that night. And, Ludivine, the code AJ checked in was buggy, unusable. That suggests a lot of stress."

"And what about later? The murder?"

"The news reports only mention finding her body. My information is that the police are investigating it as a homicide."

"And who told you that?"

Alec hesitated. Reema was his only lead. Compromising her was unwise. And he had not yet paid Ludivine. "I can't tell you that, Ludivine. Sorry."

"Secrets between friends, *mon ami*, are never wise."

Ignoring this dictum, Alex asked, "Can you find out who uploaded the code, Ludivine? If the NSA can't?"

"Certainly, *mon ami*. With time, and with effort. As a favor. I will begin now."

* * *

Ludivine didn't trace data flows or IP addresses from AJ's home in Islamabad; she already knew the 1WeakLink code had gone to Perry. After AJ revealed Jeff Morrow's attempt to recruit her into Perry's group, Ludivine tracked Perry's dark web activity, which her team found increasingly clear. But Alec needed a name—a Pakistani name.

Alec's anger over AJ's death was palpable. While he claimed to seek justice, Ludivine sensed revenge driving him. To her, death marked the end of an adventure, not something demanding justice or retribution. Yet Alec needed action, and she needed him to move past AJ's death so she could use him to get the completed code and even to add to it. She would support his revenge disguised as justice, as long as it didn't interfere with business.

She considered scenarios: a local might have kidnapped AJ, forced her to download the code, and then killed her; perhaps they coerced her into revealing her GitHub credentials or exploited weak security. Alternatively, AJ might have uploaded the code herself before dying, or someone accessed it from her computer without her knowledge. Too many possibilities.

Ludivine turned to the large window in her apartment overlooking Paris and the illuminated Arc de Triomphe. The city lights sparked her imagination as she prepared for a sleepless night of web investigations. Perry and Jeff Morrow—what were their ties to Pakistan?

While waiting for Ludivine's call, Alec spent two days setting up his new computer. He reset his router to factory settings to ensure the NSA hadn't installed a trojan, reconfigured his firewall, updated passwords, and installed the VPN software AJ recommended. He added the Tor browser for anonymous connections.

The cleanup process was frustrating. His insurance company, sympathetic to the burglary, required a police report. The police filed a brief report and left, never to return. With his scanner shattered on the office floor, Alec went to a copy store to scan the report and emailed it to the insurance company. They politely asked him to contact them again when he had bills to submit.

George Hasselblad, the homeowner's association manager, blanched at the wreckage. "How did they get in?" he asked, scanning the broken furniture.

"No idea, but they bypassed all the security," Alec replied.

"Christ. Alec—let's keep this quiet. We don't want to alarm other owners. I'll have the security firm investigate. If this is due to a failure on our end..." George trailed off, clearly uneasy. Alec doubted they'd find anything; the NSA wouldn't leave evidence behind.

George rubbed his mouth. "We have a list of preferred contractors. Would you—"

"Yeah, send it over. It'll take time to fix everything, but I need the toilet replaced and the water heater repaired immediately. And I'll keep this quiet."

"Thanks, Alec. You're a prince."

George sent the list, and Alec called a plumber. Later, sitting on his slashed couch, feet propped on the coffee table, he stared blankly into space until his burner phone rang: Ludivine.

"Alec, I have news—whether it's good is for you to decide. This information is too sensitive for the net. I do not advertise these services, and no one, especially the NSA, needs an understanding of my abilities. Are you using a secure prepaid phone?"

"Yes."

"Varoozh Paracha."

"Spell it?" She did, transliterating from Arabic.

"Who is Varoozh Paracha?" Alec asked.

"A Pakistani criminal posing as an IT entrepreneur."

"And his involvement?"

"He's Elliot Perry's dark web contact in Pakistan."

"Perry again? How is Perry involved?"

Ludivine laughed softly. "*Mon ami*, that's a secret I must keep. But Perry has your code."

"Where can I find Paracha?"

"He lives in Karachi but recently visited Islamabad." She gave Alec an address in Karachi. "Alec, I wouldn't pursue this. Rumors link Paracha to assassinations and dark web dealings."

"Rumors?"

"Never charged or convicted, but my sources are wary of him."

"So he's the killer? Was he in Islamabad—"

"At the time of AJ's murder? His phone data places him there but was on the move."

"The police—"

"They won't investigate Paracha for murder, Alec. Too much financial interest at stake across their hierarchy."

"Corrupt?"

"That word doesn't capture it fully, *mon ami*. If Varoozh Paracha killed AJ, it was because Perry wanted your code badly enough to pay him for it. That rock you cannot turn over—you haven't the strength."

CHAPTER TWENTY-SEVEN
Advice from Dad

ALEC SLEPT ON LUDIVINE'S INFORMATION to let it sink in. His eyes snapped open at 4 a.m., his mind racing over the ways he could use the information. Most of them involved going to Pakistan, getting an automatic weapon, and shooting Varoozh Paracha once he'd found him.

Rational thought set in at 4:05 a.m. He took a long shower and made his usual *café au lait*, having stocked up the day before. One does not live by computer alone. Breakfast was another problem—no edible food. Or any bowls to put food in. He'd head out to his favorite cafe on Jessie Street later.

But first, advice. He needed, for once, to talk to his father.

Paul Chenais was the executive director of a human rights NGO based in Montreal. Its mission was to help prisoners of conscience wherever in the world they were imprisoned. He'd raised Alec on a diet of human suffering unparalleled in the history of the world. He said so, often. Alec had absorbed the logic of human rights from his father, but he despised the man. His father was overbearing, narcissistic, and clueless about his effect on other people. Especially on Alec.

And yet, Paul had earned his self-confidence. He literally understood where the bodies were buried. Paul impressed Alec with his knowledge of relevant people and places around the world. It was what he did with his knowledge that made Alec furious. Paul's central ability was getting money for his NGO. By any means necessary, short of armed robbery. To talk to Paul was to donate.

But, surely, his father would help in this little murder. Knowing the victim, he would be willing. Wouldn't he? And his attitude towards the NSA would help.

His father cheerily answered the phone. "Hi, Alec. Good to hear from you. How's your project going?" Alec's father always started their conversations on a cheerful note. It wouldn't last.

"They fired me, Dad."

"That's too bad. What did you do?"

"I offended the NSA."

"Uh, what?"

"See, the product I was working on.... I can't talk about it much without making them even angrier. Let's just say the NSA believed the software tool would help their mission."

"Fuck me. The NSA. My son. What were you thinking?"

"Have you ever come across effective altruism, Dad?"

A snort. "Sure. I get those guys to pony up twice as much as anyone else. They have no idea what effective means."

"Yeah, well, I do. I figured with the money I got from the NSA, I'd finally be able to do something about human rights."

"Meaning I'm not?"

"Let's move on, Dad. I need help."

"We had this discussion when you went to Carnegie-Mellon instead of McGill. Your mom—"

"Dad, I'm not talking about money. I'm talking about human rights."

"Human rights? I'm lost."

"AJ, Dad."

"What about her? Nice girl."

"She's dead, Dad. Murdered. In Pakistan."

"Wow. Your life is going great, Alec."

"Dad, can you please shut up and listen? I need help, not contempt." Paul's concern and empathy for AJ's death was nonexistent. But Alex understood his father well and had expected none.

"I don't disrespect you, son, but murdered? Jesus."

Alec summarized the situation with AJ and Paracha, mentioning Perry and only obliquely Ludivine.

"I'm at a loss for words, Alec. Christ."

"I'm asking you to give me suggestions on how to get justice for AJ."

"What kind of justice?"

"Putting Paracha in jail."

"In Pakistan?"

"That's where he is, and that's where he killed AJ."

"I didn't mean somewhere else. I meant justice is not possible in Pakistan."

"Why?"

"I'll send you the reports from Transparency International, Human Rights Watch, and our own summary of the catastrophic level of corruption there. The police in Pakistan are one of its worst institutions, and that's saying something for Pakistan."

"You said all that to AJ at Thanksgiving, Dad."

"And she ignored me and traveled there? Well, I hate—"

"Don't go there, Dad. I loved her."

"OK, OK. You loved her, and she's dead, and Pakistan is Pakistan. Let me think."

The line fell silent. Finally, his father spoke. "Alec, you need to start a PR campaign to shame the Pakistani government into doing something. It will take a lot of money. How much do you have?"

"I have $50,000 in severance from my company plus $20,000 in savings and $45,000 in a 401k."

"These things are expensive. Ads in the world's major newspapers, the *New York Times, WSJ, USA Today, Washington Post, Guardian, Independent, Times of India, China Daily, Bilt,* and all the Pakistani newspapers. We recently completed a campaign to free prisoners in Nicaragua. It cost about $2 million Canadian."

"I don't have that much money. I hoped you would do something through your organization. Do you know anyone in the Pakistani government?"

"We're over-committed as it is, Alec. And fundraising is down this year. And everyone in the Pakistani government hates our guts and wants us dead. Sorry. Crowdfunding. That's the answer."

"Um."

"Start a crowdfunding campaign. We've found that it helps to give away gifts like a T-shirt. Put AJ's picture on the front and your message on the back. Wearing them at worldwide protests would put pressure on the Pakistanis to act. It would also fund the PR campaign."

His father was off and running on his favorite approach to ensuring the world's respect for human rights. Alec had subscribed to the NGO's newsletter after leaving home. He'd followed the campaigns in the news reports on the Web. The Nicaragua campaign had been one of his favorites. He gave his father a chance to own his failure. "Was the Nicaragua campaign successful? How many prisoners did the government free?"

"That's not important, Alec. We generated a huge response, both in terms of pressure on the Nicaraguan government and in terms of donations."

"I read that the government jailed another 123 opposition members because of the protests your campaign sponsored."

"Irrelevant, Alec. I just said—"

"Yeah. And you said it's not possible to get justice in Pakistan, but you advise me to start a crowdfunding campaign. Gee. Maybe I'll try a different approach. I might need your help in getting out of jail, though. Afterwards."

"Alec...."

"Bye, Dad. Love to Mom."

CHAPTER TWENTY-EIGHT
Islamabad

Islamabad's airport was more modern than Alec had expected. Somehow, he had imagined a small building filled with destitute beggars. Instead, it rivaled SFO's new international terminal in elegance and convenience. Wealthy business people and families with masses of luggage surrounded him.

The pandemic disrupted the airline's schedule, forcing him to travel from Heathrow to Manchester for the flight. He had plenty of time to reflect. Unproductively. His father's approach to human rights would get him nowhere. Diplomatic channels were useless because AJ was Pakistani, not Canadian or American. Her green card meant nothing. A local affair. And he knew no useful local contacts. He'd have to make some.

But now he was in Islamabad, he could seek justice for AJ through direct action. He'd talk to the Jaffrey family to learn about the murder investigation. To get the police on Paracha's trail, he'd need local help. After the Jaffreys, he'd call Reema Kathia. She'd help him, of course she would. Another human-rights NGO leader, but probably more effective than his father. And she had been AJ's best friend.

First, he found a taxi. Second, he got a recommendation for a hotel from the taxi driver. Third, the concierge at the hotel was eager to help. She found the Jaffreys' address and phone number. She offered her desk phone for the call, but Alec smiled and said he'd call later. Should he call beforehand or simply arrive? The family could easily refuse to talk to him on the phone, especially if the murder got a lot of media attention. He would introduce himself as AJ's manager. They wouldn't refuse him if he showed up unexpectedly and expressed concern about AJ's murder.

Alec told the taxi driver to wait and gave him a handful of rupees. Despite his lack of English, the driver understood Alec's hand gestures.

Alec looked through the ornate gate set into the high wall surrounding the house. The house was modern in style and luxuriously appointed. A courtyard led to the garage, and Alec noticed a garden next to it. A black Mercedes SUV sat elegantly in the courtyard, ready to take Mr. Jaffrey and his family to any destination they desired. From the size of the house, Alec imagined they had a coterie of servants, including a chauffeur, but no one was visible.

He rang the doorbell under the intercom and waited, but no one answered. He rang it again.

Finally, a male voice came, peremptory, in a language Alec did not understand. Urdu? He should have brought an interpreter. Maybe the taxi driver? No, no English. Or perhaps Jaffrey spoke English?

"Mr. Jaffrey? Do you speak English?"

"Yes. Who is this?" the voice responded in English.

"Hello, my name is Alec Chenais. I've come to Islamabad to find out what happened to AJ."

"What? Find out what?"

Alec realized that AJ's father would not know her by that name.

"Aamna, your daughter."

"Aamna is dead and is not my daughter, you fool. What did you say your name was?"

"Alec, Alec Chenais." Had Aamna's father disowned her?

"You." And nothing more.

Two young men rushed out the front door. Both looked furious. They marched up to the gate and glared at Alec. Their eyes burned with hatred, or so it appeared to Alec. They were definitely not happy to see him.

The younger boy carried a cricket bat and shouted something in Urdu. The older boy confronted the younger one, poking a finger in his face, causing him to back away. Then the older boy addressed Alec, anger dripping from his voice. "You. You are the one. From San Francisco. Are you not?" The boy's voice dripped with hostility.

"That's where I'm from, yes. I was Aamna's manager at the company she worked for. I came—"

"You are the one that ruined our sister, seduced her to become a whore! You—"

Alec responded heatedly. "She was not a whore! We were lovers!"

"Scum! Infidel! You are—" Words failed the boy.

Alec forced himself to calm down. "I want to talk to your father. Please."

"Our father is dead! Our sister is dead! You have ruined our family, shamed by her. And you are the cause!"

"Babur!" exclaimed the younger boy. Then something in Urdu, shouting and waving the cricket bat. The older boy reached for the gate to open it.

A woman, older, emerged and trotted over, shouting in Urdu. The boys argued with her. The woman shouted them down. Several people gathered in the doorway to the house. They looked like servants.

Babur, the older boy, passionately spoke to the woman. She must be his mother.

Alec said, "Mrs. Jaffrey? I need—"

Babur turned and shouted, "Shut up, you bastard! You are the cause!"

Mrs. Jaffrey shoved her son aside. Her eyes held more ferocity than her sons'. She grabbed the bars of the gate and rattled it in her anger.

"You ruined my daughter! You! How can you live with your shamelessness?"

The younger boy grabbed his mother's arm and spoke. She turned and shouted at him.

"Mrs. Jaffrey, someone murdered Aamna," Alec said.

She faced him, pounding her fists on the gate like a drum. "Go back to America. Leave, or I will allow my sons to beat you to death. I would kill you myself if I could!" She grabbed her younger son's cricket bat and hit the gate with it. The two boys grabbed her arms, and two male servants left the doorway and trotted toward the group.

Alec needed little intuition to tell him he would not get any useful information from the Jaffrey family. They unmistakably knew about him and AJ, all the details. He'd have to find another way.

The small group inside the gate grew louder, turning into a mob. Before they could open the gate and attack him, Alec walked away, back to his taxi, striding rapidly. The taxi driver, alarmed by the commotion, started up his car. Alec jumped in and the driver roared away. Alec glanced back to see the Jaffreys emerging from their gate, shaking their fists at the retreating car. A rock bounced off the back, and the taxi driver moaned and sped up.

Shaken by his reception at the Jaffrey house, Alec settled into his room at the Marriott and reconsidered his approach.

Alec needed an interpreter. He wouldn't make much progress with Canadian English. He knew precisely one person in Pakistan, and that person spoke English. Reema Kathia. He punched her number into his burner phone from memory and waited. Voicemail.

"Hello, Reema, this is Alec Chenais. I'm in Islamabad, at the Marriott Hotel, and I'd like to meet and talk with you. Could you please call me back at this number?" He recited his phone's number and hung up.

Five minutes later, his phone rang. Reema.

"Alec Chenais?"

"Yes. Reema, thanks for returning my call so promptly."

"You're here? In Islamabad? Really?"

"Yes, I flew in this morning. I visited the Jaffrey family, but—"

"You didn't! They know, Alec, about you and Aamna. They will be angry."

"I discovered that, Reema, when one of her brothers came at me with a cricket bat. Then the mother did the same."

"Oh! Are you all right?"

"Yes. Luckily, they were on the other side of a metal gate. I left before they could get out."

"Oh." Reema drew a shaky breath. "I'm speechless, Alec."

"So am I." Alec smiled to himself. What do you say to people who want to kill you?

"But Alec, why are you here?"

"I want to learn more about AJ's death. Aamna. I want to help find her killer working with the police."

"Oh," Reema sighed. "The police."

"Did the police catch anyone? Did they offer further information about the crime? Find a motive?"

"I do not know, Alec." Reema cleared her throat. "I spoke to the family. They are reluctant to say anything. And the police…Alec, I must go."

"No, wait, please. There are things, complications, to the murder."

"Complications? What does—I'm not sure I understand the word."

"Things are not what they seem, Reema. There are governments involved, in dark ways."

"Dark. Dark?"

"I can't really explain on the phone. Can we meet up? How about a drink at the bar in my hotel?"

"I…cannot. It is not possible for me to be seen drinking in a hotel. With a man. It is our way here."

"I see. How about meeting at a cafe tomorrow?"

"I think…it would be best if we did not meet. Alec, there are things you don't know. Too many things. About Pakistan, about Aamna. I must go."

Alec took a breath. Reema was his last hope, the only person he knew in Pakistan. Without her help, he was reduced to knocking on doors and joining the lines of people pleading with the police.

"Reema, you're my last hope," he said. "I desperately want to find out who killed AJ, and I need your help. I'm begging you, Reema. Please talk to me. I need to understand what to do. Please, Reema."

"Aamna was my best friend." Another shaky breath. "I owe it to her, even if…All right. But we have to meet outside. You are at the Marriott?"

"That's right. Near the center."

"Yes. There is a park with a lake. Lake View Park. If you take a taxi, they can drop you off at the parking area. Walk straight down to the lake. To the left, by the pavilion, there is an overlook with a viewpoint. We can meet there. At 2 p.m. Is that all right?"

"Yes. How will I recognize you?"

"I'll be the person who comes up to you and calls you Alec." Meaning, of course, that he'd stick out like a sore thumb. "But I'll be wearing a simple, white *dupatta*—that's a scarf that covers the head. And I'll be carrying a shopping bag. And, please, wear a mask."

Alec followed instructions and walked down the promenade to the lake. Breathtaking views and many people enjoying a stroll on a sunny day. Reema had predicted it: he stuck out like a sore thumb. He attracted more than one stare as he turned towards the large pavilion.

And there was Reema with her white *dupatta* and shopping bag. She arose from a bench and approached him.

"Alec."

"Reema. It's wonderful to put a face to the voice." Though the mask and dupatta hid most of the face.

Reema eyed him warily. "Yes. We can sit on the bench to talk, or we can walk."

"Let's walk. Wonderful views here."

"Alec, I don't want to prolong this. I feel very uncomfortable talking to you about Aamna. Your relationship…goes against our traditions."

"And you're traditional?"

"I try to be. I'm not like Aamna, looking for freedom and new ways of doing things. But what can I tell you?"

"Anything to uncover more about the murder. Can you go along with me to the police station to interpret for me?"

Reema looked down and shook her head. "No, I cannot do that. I am far too busy with my organization. Things that need my attention are going begging while we walk here."

"Then what would you suggest I do? Hire an interpreter?"

Reema's eyes crinkled as she smiled under the mask. "I can do better than that. I have a friend who might help you. He's not working right now, he's between jobs."

"What sort of work does he do?"

"He is a programmer. He works in IT departments as a consultant. I hired him for a time two years ago to build our international website."

"And he speaks English?"

"Pretty well. He attended college in the city of Boston."

"Can you arrange for him to meet with me today?"

Reema took out her phone and made a call, speaking in Urdu. When she disconnected, she said, "Abdul will meet you in the lobby of the Marriott at 3 p.m. today. Is that all right?"

"Yes, fine. What's his full name?"

"Abdul Ali Jalali. He is a very nice young man. He will help you."

"And you, Reema? What else can you tell me?" Alec looked directly at the eyes above the mask. How truthful would this unknown woman be?

Reema averted her eyes as she contemplated her response. "I have poor Aamna's phone, Alec."

"Did she give it to you?"

"Yes." Reema told Alec a story about AJ's father's funeral, the last time she had seen her friend. She paused, and told Alec in a trembling voice about AJ's request to her.

"I went to the Pakistan Memorial, in a big park over there," she said, pointing west. "I found the man Aamna wanted me to meet, a Mr.

Paracha. He was surprised when I spoke to him, but when I explained, he opened his computer and we tried to access the website Aamna had talked about. I held up the phone with the Authenticator running, but suddenly the man swore an oath and closed the computer. He tried to grab the phone, and I backed away. He slapped me and demanded the password, but I had no idea what he was talking about. After another slap, I turned and ran."

Alec was stunned into silence. This all sounded like AJ had intended to allow Paracha to download the 1WeakLink code to his computer. But that meant—no, she couldn't have done that. Could she? But he should be sure of the details.

"Did Paracha tell you his full name?"

"No."

"Can you describe him?"

"He was a good-looking, middle-aged man, about fifty, with graying hair, medium-sized ears, and large black eyebrows. The man wore a mask, so I don't know what his face looked like, but he had a short beard. He was of average height, strongly built, blue suit, white shirt, no tie."

Alec entered this description in a note on his phone. Not much to go on, but this man might be Varoozh Paracha. He asked, "Have you told any of this to the police?"

"No, I saw a policeman only once, to answer questions about Aamna." She hesitated. "They are not aware that I have Aamna's phone. I deactivated it so that they could not trace it. Alec, in my position, I cannot just go to the police. My organization helps women in prison, and the police do not support my work. I am not sure if Aamna was doing something illegal, but I cannot take the risk. And the police, well, they are rarely helpful."

"You mean they are corrupt?"

"It is best not to talk about such things."

"But, Reema. How can the police find the murderer if they don't know about this? This man could be the killer."

Reema stepped away from him and looked at him with frightened eyes. "I cannot, I cannot." Alec was losing her, his only witness.

"All right. But think about it, please. I'll talk to them and see what they've found out. Did you talk with AJ after the man attacked you?"

"No. She had no phone, you see. I went to her house. Her mother would not let me in. She said Aamna had shamed them and was not available. She was furious. I rushed away, terrified. I should have given her Aamna's phone, but I just wanted to leave. And then…the next day. The news came." Reema blinked away a tear.

"I'm sorry. It must have been terrible." Alec had seen Mrs. Jaffrey's anger, and he had little trouble imagining Reema's terror. AJ's mother's anger was palpable, and he knew why. "So they had learned about our relationship by then. Is there anything else you can tell me?"

"Just that there was a lot of money involved." Reema's eyes looked away again.

Alec asked, "Was there anything about the money that you didn't tell me?"

"No. Yes."

"Tell me, Reema, please. I'll keep it to myself."

"Aamna, Aamna," Reema said, tears in her eyes. She wiped them away. "Aamna was such a wonderful friend. She donated to my organization. She sent it on the day of her father's funeral. Aamna told me it was the least she could do, that it was only a small part of the money she had received."

"She gave you the money before she gave you the phone?"

"Yes. Oh, how I loved her!"

Alec whispered, "I loved her, too." He pushed away the things he didn't want to think about. Not yet. When he was ready. When they'd found the killer and done something about it.

But stolen software, money, and a violent man? He was on the right track, and eventually Reema would have to tell what she knew to someone who could do something about it.

CHAPTER TWENTY-NINE
The Police

Elliot went to the comms cabin for a video call with Varoozh. When a consultant called days after a job was done, it meant money. Consultants never called just to say hello. He'd already wired Varoozh's fee to his Cayman account as requested, so it meant more money than Varoozh had negotiated.

"Varoozh. How nice to hear from you," he lied. "How are things in Karachi?"

"What? Oh. It's a charnel house, people dying everywhere from the virus. Why?"

Small talk wasn't working, it seemed. "Varoozh. Why did you call? What do you want? Is there a problem with your fees?" Cayman banks were averse to causing problems for people like Elliot, but he had to ask.

"Fees? No, no." A pause. Elliot's sixth sense about the connection between people and money kicked in.

"What's happened, Varoozh? How much do you need?"

"Allah be merciful, Elliot. Do you read minds?"

"No, I read people." He left unsaid that the primary connection between Varoozh and himself had to do with currency exchange, and reading those kinds of relationships posed no challenge to Elliot.

"Listen, Elliot, here's the thing… I need to pay off some police."

"Why?"

"I accidentally left a fingerprint on the woman's computer." He breathed. "I was in a hurry, Elliot."

Elliot closed his eyes.

"They came to me in Karachi and asked me politely what I was doing in the woman's room touching her computer."

A long pause followed this revelation. Elliot scratched his chin and said, "And what did you tell them, Varoozh?" Please, please, pretty please say you did not tell them my name. And please don't think you can blackmail me for millions.

"I asked for their bank account number, and they were kind enough to give it to me."

"I see. And you propose to forward this critical information to me, is that it?" Half blackmail, half business expense.

"Yes, Elliot. I need a favor, just this one time. After all, I delivered the code, and there is no connection to you. It is only 15 million."

"Dollars?" Elliot choked out.

"Rupees."

"Well, thank God. Only $50,000, then. Sure, Varoozh. This favor will only enhance our long-standing relationship." By which Elliot meant Varoozh had better damn well respond within minutes to anything Elliot needed from him for the rest of his life. And Varoozh knew it.

"I...understand. Thank you, Elliot," Varoozh said. "You won't regret it. Here's the account information."

Elliot noted the numbers and said, "Stay in touch, Varoozh. And take care. More care. Much more." He hung up. He stepped out of the comms cabin and looked up at Table Mountain. The *Mugwump* would have to leave Cape Town soon. Jeff's efforts might attract too much of the wrong kind of attention if the yacht stayed in one place. Indian Ocean or South America? He tossed a two-rand coin and failed to catch it. The coin hit the gunnel and bounced into the harbor. An omen. Wait a week or two, just to make sure. It would give him time to decide whether to leave Jeff here.

* * *

Alec got up from his seat in the Marriott lobby as a young Pakistani entered and looked around.

"Abdul Jalali?"

"Yes. Mr. Chenais?"

"Alec, please."

"And I am Abdul." He held out a hand, then stopped and raised an elbow. Alec smiled and elbow-bumped him. They both wore masks.

"I'm still not used to all this," said Abdul, shaking the mass of tight curls trimmed close to his head covered with a Boston Red Sox baseball cap.

"No one is. Are you a Red Sox fan?"

"This?" Abdul tapped his cap. "No, never seen them play, even when I lived in Boston. A friend gave it to me years ago, and it's stuck to my head. Cricket, that's my game."

"You speak American English." Despite his slight accent, the man would blend in effortlessly at any bar in the City.

"Yeah, I spent four years at college in Boston, Boston University. Weird place. Loved the summers, hated the winters." He shook his head. "My family's poor, couldn't afford the English universities. I got a scholarship and a job and worked my way to a degree."

"Reema says you're a programmer."

"Yeah, comp sci major. I can program my way around a website. You?"

"I'm CTO of a blockchain startup in San Francisco."

"Wow, the real thing!" exclaimed Abdul, bouncing up and down. Abdul seemed to have trouble staying in his chair, exuding kinetic energy.

"Has Reema explained what I need?"

"She just said you're a friend and you need someone to translate for you."

"Well, it's more than that. You should hear the complete story before you decide to help."

"OK, lay it on me."

"My Pakistani girlfriend came back here to be with her family, and someone murdered her."

Abdul's frenetic energy stilled. "Murdered?"

"They found her body in an alley. And Reema told me the police decided it was murder. Beaten to death."

"That's terrible. I'm sorry for your loss."

"Yes, thank you. I'm here to investigate what happened. I need to talk to people, specifically the police. I need an interpreter for that."

"So the police haven't caught the killer."

"Not to my knowledge." Alec wondered how much he should confide in Abdul. He seemed friendly enough. "I can't get any information from the family. You see, they found out about our relationship in San Francisco and weren't happy about it."

"Girlfriend. You mean you were lovers?"

"Yes, that's the rest of it. Can you get past that?"

"Sure thing. I'm not all caught up in the traditional shit. I learned a lot in America." His mask moved with his cheeks, and Alec deduced a knowing grin.

"Tell me what you think I need to learn about you," Alec suggested.

"Nothing outrageous. I don't have a criminal record, I have a Bachelor's degree, I know Javascript, I don't like dogs, and I'm not married. My parents and two sisters love me in their own unique ways."

"How do you know Reema?"

"I worked for her."

Abdul's curt voice and brief answer hinted at withheld information.

"And?" Alec probed.

"And…I'm in love with her. She's shy. But what a powerhouse! The way she runs the organization and deals with the prison idiots." Abdul grinned under his mask. "And I'm going to get her to marry me, eventually."

"Does she know that?"

"Yes, but she doesn't like the idea. She wants to devote her life to the unfortunate. I've tried, but she doesn't think I'm unfortunate enough. So I'm toughing it out on crumbs until she thinks I'm unfortunate enough to marry."

"Did she tell you about her friend Aamna?"

"The girl who went to America? Mentioned her a few times. Why?"

"She was my girlfriend. Aamna Jaffrey. AJ. The murder victim."

"Oh, shit." Abdul's eyes opened wide over his mask. "Reema can be tight-lipped about emotional things like losing a best friend. This must be excruciating for her."

"So, are you on for this?" Alec extended his elbow.

Abdul's mask moved into a grin, and he elbow-bumped. He said, "You bet. Wouldn't miss it."

"OK, Abdul, your turn," Alec said, waving the other man forward.

Abdul approached the police station counter and spoke to the woman officer behind it. Her eyes narrowed as he spoke, and she looked at Alec with a frown. He had tested English on her but received a blank look. They had visited three police stations near where AJ's body had been found, but so far they had no luck finding anyone to talk to.

After some discussion, the desk officer dialed a number and spoke.

"She's asking for an inspector. Maybe the right one, who knows?" Abdul whispered.

The officer ended the call and spoke to Abdul, who gestured for Alec to sit against the wall. "We'll have to wait until the Inspector is free. She wouldn't say how long."

"OK. Ask her if they have wireless. I can handle some things on my phone."

"You're joking. This, my friend, is a *police* station, not a fucking Marriott."

Alec sighed.

An hour later, a striking officer in full uniform emerged from a side door in the reception area. He spoke. Abdul brightened up and said, "This is the inspector. He wants to know what this is about."

"The murder of Aamna Jaffrey," Alec said.

The inspector's eyes narrowed at the name. After Abdul translated, he spoke in a stern voice. Abdul translated, "He wants to know if you have any new information on the case."

"Ask him if we can talk in private, or at least somewhere not public."

The inspector nodded, his eyes still sharply focused on Alec, then moved toward the door. Alec and Abdul followed him down a hallway to an open office with several desks. The inspector spoke to another officer, who gathered three chairs near a desk. Abdul said, "He wants us to sit here. The inspector's name is Qureshi, and this is Sub-Inspector Arshad. The inspector says he is in charge of the Jaffrey murder case. He wants to see your passport."

"Do they speak English?" From the lack of response, Alec guessed not. Abdul confirmed as much. "OK. Translate as we go, Abdul." Alex took out his passport and handed it to the inspector.

Alec summarized who he was, leaving out the lover part. Then he summarized what he knew: AJ's work in San Francisco, her hasty departure for Pakistan, her buggy code. He said nothing about Reema's revelations about AJ's last day or the phone adventure with Varoozh Paracha. He was certain the police would dismiss everything as hearsay, possibly implicating Reema. Abdul translated. The inspector asked several clarifying questions but expressed skepticism about Alec's claim that a code bug meant AJ was deeply upset. Then he looked at Alec's passport again and his tone sharpened into an abrupt question.

Abdul snorted and said, "He asks why you didn't mention that you seduced and ruined Ms. Jaffrey."

"I guess he's been talking to the family."

"Bet on it."

"We're screwed."

"I'd take that bet too."

"Explain that things are different in America, and that I'm very concerned about justice for Ms. Jaffrey."

"May I call you an infidel?"

"No."

Abdul sighed and spoke. The inspector replied sharply. Abdul said, "The Inspector says you have no standing here. Standing—is that the right word, Alec?"

"Yeah."

"And that you should go home and stay away from Pakistani women."

"Ask him if he's made any progress in solving the murder."

"He says that's his business, not yours, and that inquiries are proceeding."

"Anything else?"

The inspector and the sub-inspector stood up. The inspector handed Alec his passport, and the sub-inspector took Alec's arm and pulled him toward the door. Abdul followed. He said, "They say this interview is over and you must leave. He says next time he will keep the passport and will have you deported. Alec, I think they don't like you."

"Yeah. I got that too."

CHAPTER THIRTY
Islamabad Encounters

ALEC AND ABDUL WENT BACK to the Marriott and sat in the cafe, drinking more tea. The stuff made Alec realize that he hadn't drunk anything like a decent *café au lait* since he'd left his condo in San Francisco. That he hadn't noticed this said a lot about how distracted he was after the NSA interrogation. Not to mention the joyful greeting from the Jaffrey family and his failure to get anything from the police. He stirred sugar into his tea with a scowl.

Abdul grinned and said, "Time for a private detective?"

"I'll consider it," Alec said. "But can we find one that will take on the cops?"

"Sure we can," replied the optimistic Abdul. "I have an uncle who knows everyone in Islamabad. He will know the right detective agency to work with on this."

Alec was lukewarm to the idea of hiring a detective. Given the situation with the police, he might need to do that. Yet, something continued to bother him.

He needed to talk to Reema again to get more details about her encounter with Paracha. That's what he would say to Abdul. Abdul wouldn't approve of what he would really do: question Reema more deeply about AJ. What she was doing, how the problems with her family had developed, and what else she could tell him about the 1WeakLink software scam that Paracha had run, or tried to run. There must be something there he could use to get justice. Even if it meant confronting AJ's betrayal of 1WeakLink and himself.

Betrayal. Was he just rationalizing his inner need to know how AJ had betrayed him? His anger at her? He sipped his sugary tea as he considered his own motives for trying to find out more. The search for justice would reveal truths that he knew would hurt. It didn't matter. The pain would let him grieve and accept AJ's death.

Truths. Reema certainly hadn't told him everything about what AJ had asked her to do. He would also try to persuade her again to go to the police with her information. That would point the police in the right direction. He considered leaving Abdul out of it but finally decided that excluding him might create more problems than it solved. But he'd have to be sure not to upset Reema. Abdul, his best source of help in Pakistan, would not react well to that.

He said, "Let's go see Reema, Abdul. Maybe she can suggest something. Can you call a taxi for us?"

"You'll go broke taking taxis all over the place. Why not just take my motorbike? There's enough room for two." They walked outside the huge hotel complex and down the street to where Abdul had parked his pride and joy.

The motorbike was worth no less than the Kohinoor diamond to Abdul. He told Alec that he had saved up for it for ten years, ever since he turned twelve. A Honda CD 70, it cost about $500. Alec assured Abdul that he would pay him that much again for his services. Then he asked about a helmet and got a scoff. Alec pointed at two helmets hanging on the bike, and Abdul explained.

"These things are required by the government. Nobody wears them. They're dangerous. Two years ago, a study confirmed our worst fears: these substandard helmets can actually kill you in an accident."

"I've never ridden a motorcycle without one, Abdul, and I won't start now."

"OK, OK, my friend. Here, take the blue one. But I take no responsibility for you if we crash."

Alec strapped the helmet on. If we crash? Or when. Alec hefted the helmet. Lightweight, but better than nothing. Abdul's idea of responsibility was entertaining.

Abdul called Reema to let her know they were coming. He got on the bike and fired it up. Alec climbed up behind him, and off they went, destination Reema's apartment. Her office was closed because of the pandemic, and she was working from home.

Abdul weaved in and out of the busy traffic, confident in his ability to navigate the madness of Pakistani drivers. The engine, deafening, throbbed between Alec's legs. He hadn't ridden a motorcycle for years, and the thrill came rushing back to him, pushing his darker emotions back into their cave.

Reema lived in an apartment building in the G-5 sector near Lake View Park and the national government offices. A few minutes of artful dodging on the motorbike got them there. Abdul parked the bike on the sidewalk and led Alec to Reema's building.

Her apartment was medium-sized and well-designed, with one room she'd converted to a home office. She explained that she'd grown up in the apartment and had taken it over when her parents died. The pandemic had closed her small office in central Islamabad, leaving her in this small space to coordinate her NGO's teams across Pakistan. She wore the same mask and *dupatta* she'd worn to meet with Alec at the park. The pandemic restrictions mirrored those in San Francisco. Except for the *dupatta*.

The two men occupied a small couch while Reema swung her dilapidated office chair around and sat down.

"How is your investigation going, Alec?" she asked. "Is Abdul helpful to you?"

"Enormously helpful." Alec smiled at Abdul. "He's one in a million."

Abdul said nothing but grinned, his eyes thanking Alec for the plug.

"I suppose so," Reema said, her eyebrows signaling her agreement.

"But my investigation stopped dead the moment we entered the police station. The police threatened to deport me."

Reema's mask moved in what Alec took for sympathy. "I feared that would be the case."

"I'd like to ask a few more questions about AJ—Aamna. Is that OK?"

"Yes," Reema sighed, obviously reluctant but committed.

"Did AJ mention anything about her agreement with Paracha?"

"No, not really. She just gave me access information, but she never told me what was behind it all."

"What exactly did she tell you?"

"She asked a favor, in great distress. She had to meet Mr. Paracha at the Pakistan memorial at 2 p.m., and her family would not let her go. Aamna handed me her phone and gave me the passcode, then showed me how to bring up the Authenticator. She gave me a username and password. I was to give them to Mr. Paracha."

"To access GitHub?" Jesus, she'd really done it. Betrayed Alec and the company. Alec's stomach hurt. He refused to believe it could happen. But it had.

"Yes, that was what she said."

"What did she say about Paracha's download from GitHub?"

"Nothing. She said he'd use his computer, but nothing about what he would do."

"Was she very upset?"

"Extremely upset, at least with her family. She felt they were holding her back. And they wanted her to marry."

Her eyes above the mask glanced at Alec, then looked away. This emotional description of AJ reminded Alec of the poorly tested code, confirming that AJ was not herself that day. And it also meant....

"So her family was not aware of her relationship with me. And she didn't want the arranged marriage."

"No, I am sure they were not. They would not have behaved…Aamna would not have been there at the funeral." Reema's fingers twisted around each other in anguish.

"And she'd agreed to marry someone?" he insisted. She'd told him so.

"No, she did everything she could to avoid that," replied Reema. "She hated the thought of it."

This information shook Alec. AJ had lied to him about the arranged marriage. She had lied to get him to accept the breakup. His stomach hurt even more.

Reema sympathized without understanding the full extent of his pain. "I am sorry, Alec. I can see you still feel the pain of her loss." But he'd lost more than AJ herself. He'd lost faith in her. How much of their love had been a lie?

Alec changed the subject, unwilling to wallow in that pain. "Did Paracha say anything about their deal? Or who he was working for?"

"No. Nothing."

"And then he tried to access GitHub, and the password didn't work? What did Paracha do then?" Alec wondered if AJ had deliberately given Reema the wrong password, or if she'd made a mistake in her desperation. Did Paracha just type it wrong? Easy to do given the circumstances. But Reema's answer put those thoughts out of his head.

"He grabbed my arm, slapped me, and kept asking for the password. He was furious. I gave him the password again, and it failed again. Then he slapped me a second time, and I broke free and ran away."

"He slapped you?" asked Abdul. He stood up from the couch. "You were aware and kept this from me?" he demanded of Alec, eyes on fire.

Reema held out a hand to Abdul. "It is in the past, Abdul," she said. "Do not worry yourself about it."

"But—"

"No, please, Abdul," Alec said. "Let's focus on what is important. Reema's story gives Paracha a powerful motive, and his angry reaction shows he's a violent man. See?"

Abdul muttered, "I guess so."

"And, Reema, please report all this to the police. To Inspector Qureshi. The police have no clues to the murder, and they won't make any progress unless they know this. And you need to give them the phone."

"Alec, I have explained why that would not be good for me," Reema replied earnestly.

"But Paracha is here somewhere, and it's vital the police get to him and question him. Don't you understand, Reema? AJ will never get justice if you don't tell them. Come with us to talk to Inspector Qureshi."

Reema got up and walked into her small kitchen and shuffled pots around. She shook her head from time to time as she considered Alec's request. The mask she wore hid her feelings, but her body language signaled distress and indecision.

Abdul spoke up. "She doesn't have to do this."

"Yes, she does. She has to. It's her moral duty."

"No. She will put herself in danger. From the police."

"We'll be there to help."

"Be quiet, both of you," said Reema from the kitchen. "I need to think."

Reema and Abdul took the motorbike, leaving Alec to explain to an anxious taxi driver that he wanted to go to the police station. Abdul explained everything to the driver twice before leaving with Reema, but he kept muttering and shaking his head. Finally, Alec begged the man to go, waving a folded wad of bank notes at him. That at least convinced him that he wouldn't lose money on the trip.

Abdul and Reema waited at the station door for the taxi's arrival. Abdul came over when Alec got out.

"Do you want the taxi to wait, Alec?" he asked.

"No, that's OK. We're close by the Marriott."

Abdul turned to the taxi, but the driver had already driven off, not wanting to take risks with crazy Americans seeking the police.

They walked into the police station, where Abdul again harangued the officer at the desk, this time asking for Inspector Qureshi by name.

Qureshi came to the door, very tall and immaculate in his police uniform. Reema recoiled a little, and Abdul took her hand to reassure her. He then clarified the situation to Qureshi. The officer raised his eyebrows and looked at Reema, assessing her. He turned and told Abdul something.

"We're to follow him," Abdul said. Reema didn't move until Abdul pulled gently on her hand and ducked his head.

The three followed Qureshi to a small conference room. The officer sat them down, then left and returned with his sub-inspector.

Reema told her story and placed AJ's phone on the conference table, along with the SIM card she'd taken from it. As the story unfolded, the inspector's eyes grew stern over his mask. At the slapping incident, he started tapping his finger on the table, his eyebrows furrowed.

When Reema placed the phone on the table, the inspector picked it up, inserted the SIM card, and turned the phone on. At the passcode prompt, he looked at Reema, who gave him the passcode. He glanced at the phone, then pocketed it and glared at Reema. Abdul translated quietly to Alec as the inspector spoke.

"So, Miss Kathia, you kept this information from the police. And now, you come and lie to us."

Reema gasped, her eyes wide. "Lied? No, sir. I did not lie. Everything—"

"You have lied. Mr. Paracha is an upstanding businessman, well known in Pakistani business circles. He would never be involved in something like this. He has told us as much."

"How did you know—"

"We are not as incompetent as you seem to think, Miss Kathia. You yourself are not unknown to us. You have never come to our attention in any criminal matter. It was unwise of you, I must say, to bring attention to yourself with lies."

Paracha, and through him Perry, had already gotten to the police. Inspector Qureshi would not listen to Reema's evidence or do anything about AJ's death. Alec deliberated on what he might say to the inspector, but events moved too fast for him.

Abdul could no longer contain himself. His voice had grown increasingly raspy as he listened to Qureshi accuse Reema. Now, he was shouting at the inspector in Urdu and pounding on the table. Reema tried to restrain him, but he was beyond restraint.

Qureshi didn't move, but his expression hardened. He waved a hand at the sub-inspector, who stood and grabbed Abdul, pulling him out of his chair. He threw Abdul against the wall of the room, twisted his hands behind his back, and handcuffed him.

Reema stood and wailed out words in Urdu, and the inspector said something sharp to her. She sat down, clasping her hands in front of her as if in prayer.

"What is it, Reema?" asked Alec.

"He's arrested Abdul. For insulting a police officer and obstructing justice." She reverted to Urdu, pleading with the inspector. He sat stone-faced, ignoring her. He spoke to his sub-inspector, who led Abdul out of the room.

Alec stood up, not sure what to do. The inspector spoke sharply in Urdu again.

Reema said, "We must leave, Alec. The inspector orders it."

"But I have to—"

"Alec! This is Pakistan, not America or Canada. The inspector will arrest you, too." She closed her eyes, then opened them. "Or worse. He has told me I was lucky not to be arrested. We have to leave now. Please, Alec. I will find a lawyer for Abdul. But we have to go before anything else happens. You see that they have suborned the inspector." She looked at the officer with wide eyes.

"I understand, but—"

The inspector spoke again, looking directly at Alec, who had remained standing.

"Alec, he is threatening you with arrest and deportation if you do not leave at once. Please, let us go, Alec!" Reema arose from her chair and walked to the door. She looked at Alec with pleading eyes.

"Very well," Alec said. He had no other helpful words to offer. Expecting help from the Pakistani police was a pipe dream. They would never find the killer, because he had paid them off.

Reema seized his hand and pulled him out of the room. He looked back to see the inspector sitting stiffly upright in his uniform, his eyes unflinching, his hands folded in front of him on the table.

Reema's lawyer got Abdul released from the police station two days after his arrest. The lawyer said the police would overlook Abdul's actions if he did nothing more to aggravate them, or polite words to that effect. The lawyer bumped elbows with Abdul and Alec, who had accompanied the lawyer to the police station. Abdul and Alec stood in the alley behind the station and took stock.

"What do you think, Alec?" asked Abdul. "Does this mean Reema cares about me? Should I ask her to marry me?"

Alec looked at the sky and decided on the truth. "I wouldn't. Reema feels responsible. She's a very conscientious person, Abdul. She's helping you out of obligation, not love. At least, that's how it seems to me. She doesn't show her feelings easily."

"I must thank her. Why did she not come with you?"

"I don't think she likes the police station."

"I can't imagine why!"

"She's at her apartment. We'll thank her properly, then you can judge for yourself if she'll marry you."

"They gave me back the keys to my motorbike. Let's go find it. Unless a thief has stolen it!"

They walked down the alley and onto the main street where Abdul parked his motorbike two days before. Miraculously, it was still there. Abdul grinned his thanks and mounted the bike. "Hop on." He started the engine.

Alec grabbed the blue helmet, strapped it on, and got on the back. Abdul pulled out onto the street and made a roaring U turn across three lanes of traffic. An approaching car slowed. Alec expected to hear a horn, but the driver forgave the transgression.

Alec saw that the car was a black Mercedes. As the car approached them to pass, he saw over Abdul's shoulder that the driver had a gun. The driver's side window was open. Alec yelled, "Go go go, Abdul! He's got—"

But it was far too late. Alec heard several "phut" sounds as the gun with its suppressor fired. The motorbike spun around. Alec felt a sharp blow to the back of his head. Abdul flew to the side, knocking Alec backwards as he tumbled. Alec landed on his back, skidding along the street and knocking the wind out of him.

Groaning, Alec rolled over onto his stomach and pushed himself to his knees. Several cars stopped, and people came to help the accident victims. Alec got to his feet and looked for the Mercedes. Nothing. The shooter had fled the scene. The motorbike lay on its side, motor roaring. Someone reached and turned off the engine.

Several men gathered around Abdul while a couple came over to Alec and steadied him, asking him questions in Urdu.

"Does anyone speak English?" cried Alec.

A man on his knees beside Abdul looked up and said, "Yes. Your friend is badly hurt. I have asked someone to call the police and ambulance." He looked down. "But it is too late. He is dead."

Alec pushed through the crowd and kneeled down. Abdul had a bloody mess on one side of his head. There was more blood on his shirt. A hole in the shirt confirmed that some of the shooter's bullets had found their mark. And Abdul, poor Abdul, was not breathing. He had no pulse. Alec threw himself into the CPR techniques he'd learned in school and kept at it until the police and paramedics came and deemed it useless.

The Pakistani paramedics looked at Alec and determined that he was uninjured. They showed him his helmet, which was cracked and scarred. He held it, turning it over. That mark. A bullet had scored the outside, just missing him. Abdul's Red Sox hat lay next to his unmoving head. Alec picked it up and turned it over and over in his hands.

A policeman speaking broken English asked Alec to wait on the sidewalk for his superiors. Alec stood there and watched the policeman working on the crime scene and the men loading his friend's body into the ambulance. He recalled the moment of the shooting. The man in the car matched Reema's description of Varoozh Paracha. Who else would shoot at him?

A hand gripped his arm. Inspector Qureshi. Alec asked for an interpreter, but Qureshi and his sub-inspector pulled him away and handcuffed him, then frog-marched him to the police station, which was just down the street. The officers said nothing. They didn't take him to the interrogation room. They took him to a jail cell, removed the handcuffs, and locked the door.

The cell contained Alec and a bucket. Alec sat down against the wall and wrapped his arms around his knees. He noticed he had blood on his sleeves and hands. Abdul's blood. He put his head on his knees and cried for his friend.

CHAPTER THIRTY-ONE
Pakistani Justice

THE PAKISTANI POLICE DID NOT bother with hoods or sophisticated interrogation techniques. They had no need for questioning because they had no need to know anything. Instead, they wanted Alec to learn certain things.

The chief interrogator was a small man with higher rank insignia than Inspector Qureshi's uniform showed. Alec never learned his rank or his name, but he did learn every line of the man's face. The man wore no mask, and neither did Alec after the police tore it off his face so they could slap him more effectively. They never asked any questions, not to Alec's knowledge, because they said everything in Urdu.

The man showed Alec his motorcycle helmet, which one of Paracha's bullets had struck. It had glanced off the helmet instead of going through Alec's head. The point, as Alec gathered from gestures, was that this luck on his part had inconvenienced the police by forcing them to arrest him instead of just burying his body.

From time to time, Alec demanded to see the Canadian consul. This request usually resulted in another beating. Alec suspected a flaw in his response to behavioral stimuli, as the beatings increased his likelihood of asking again.

The cell they kept him in was nine square meters. It was more than big enough to swing a cat, since no one else occupied it. Other cells echoed with nonstop screaming in various languages. Silence came when the lights went out. By the third night, Alec was used to sleeping on the concrete floor. He ate whatever they brought him, though he was unable to name anything except the rice. At least none of it moved.

On the fourth day, the chief interrogator brought in a police officer who thought he could speak English. He was mostly wrong about that, but Alec gleaned enough to understand that he was being held on suspicion of espionage, sabotage, and murder. The police explanations of these charges were incomprehensible but seemed to suggest that he needed to stop asking questions and leave the country. He attempted to explain what had happened on the motorbike, but the police officer just waggled his head and ignored him. So he made his ask for the Canadian consul again, and the police officer relayed this to the chief interrogator, who rolled his eyes and responded in Urdu.

The translator said, "Canada consul knows. She can allowed see you at future. For now, shut up."

Alec seized the chance to inquire about the Jaffrey investigation, as this response was more than anything that had come before. He suggested that the police could do more about it. Three slaps and no dinner.

The Canadian consul general was a tall woman in her early sixties with graying hair and a deceptively maternal face. On his fifth day in jail, a guard led Alec into an interrogation room where she awaited him. Wearing a mask. She rummaged in her purse, brought out a blue surgical mask, and handed it to Alec, who put it on.

"Alec Chenais? Margaret Girard, consul general at the Canadian Embassy."

"Ms. Girard. I am so happy to see you. Finally."

"Yeah. Not my fault. They wouldn't let me in until today. What the hell did you do? This is extreme, even for the Pakistanis."

"Nothing. I've done nothing."

"That's...unlikely."

"Can we sit down? I don't have a chair in my cell, and I'd like to maximize my comfort time."

"Yeah, sure. Sorry." Ms. Girard sat, as did Alec. They looked at each other.

Alec finally said, "I need to get out of this place."

"I daresay," the consul general replied. "But I need some more information before I charge ahead, eh?"

Alec clarified his purpose in Pakistan, recounted his experiences, and provided specifics about the motorbike incident. He fully described Varoozh Paracha and stated his conclusion that Paracha had bribed the police to ignore AJ's murder. He made sure the consul general understood that Paracha was responsible for Abdul's murder but didn't mention the NSA, blockchains, hacking, or Elliot Perry.

Ms. Girard scratched her chin under her mask and considered his story.

"I'm not saying I don't believe you, Alec," she said. "It's pretty far out there, though. We don't get many Canadians targeted for assassination in Islamabad, eh? It's usually someone who's lost their wallet or something."

"Can you find out the charges against me and why I'm being held?"

"I'll ask."

"And could you let my father know about me?"

"Sure, I can do that." Ms. Girard rummaged in her purse and pulled out a notepad and pen.

"Paul Chenais in Montreal." Alec gave her his father's number.

"Why does that name sound familiar?"

"He's the head of the human rights NGO Human Support International, based in Montreal."

"Oh. Him."

"Yeah. You know their work?"

"Eh." Ms. Girard was noncommittal. "I've heard of him."

"Anyway, please let him know my situation, OK? I have no one else."

"All right, Alec. I'll see what I can do."

CHAPTER THIRTY-TWO
Alec's Visitors

A GUARD ESCORTED ALEC TO the familiar interview room. Reema wore the same *dupatta* and mask but had dark shadows under her eyes, and she sat stiffly in her chair.

He said, "Hello, Reema. It's good to see you."

"Alec. I have come only because I must. They finally allowed me to see you. I have had no peace since…the accident."

"Reema, it was no accident. It was—"

She cut him off. "I know, Alec. Please let me finish, then I will leave." Reema's eyes stared unblinkingly into his. Her voice trembled and was harsher than usual. "I have come to share my feelings with you. I cannot keep them bottled up inside me."

"Reema, I'm very sorry—"

" I cannot sleep. I cannot live with this."

"Abdul was—"

"Do not say his name! Do not pollute his memory with your lies and excuses. You are responsible for his death. There; I have said it." She sat back in her chair, eyes glaring at Alec.

Alec understood. Reema was in pain. She had lost someone she loved, and she blamed him. She blamed herself for connecting Abdul with Alec despite the danger. But he needed Reema. She had to grasp their shared concerns.

He said, "I came here to find justice for AJ, for Aamna. You tried to help. Abdul tried to help. But things just snowballed." He swallowed. "Abdul loved you, Reema. Take comfort in that. I'm sorry."

"Do not say his name!" Reema glared at him. "And do not say her name either. You are responsible for her death as well. So many deaths, all from America. From you." She rose from her chair. "I am finished here. With you. My words are spoken. I cannot be in the same room with you anymore."

She walked to the door and knocked. The guard let her out, then took Alec back to his cell.

"Well, Alec, here we are," Paul Chenais said. "You weren't kidding, were you? When you said I'd have to help you get out of jail."

Behind the mask, his father's face was inscrutable, but his voice dripped with condemnation. It was the voice his father always used when the shit hit the fan in the Chenais household. Every word bore its own inflection of contempt.

Responding to the contempt would only make it worse. His father thrived on argument and the ad hominem attack, which usually served him well in the human rights world of fundraising. It served him less well in handling his family. Alec's mother, long accustomed to the style in her academic context, dealt with this gracefully—she ignored him. Alec had learned that technique the hard way.

"Have you seen the consul, Dad?"

"Silly woman. Totally useless. Nobody at the embassy gives a single shit about human rights."

"What about me, Dad? Do they have any thoughts about me?"

Paul glared at his son. "This is an opportunity, Alec, a goddamn big one. Don't you see? Their putting you in jail for nothing gives us a chance to blow the Pakistani police out of the water."

"Dad. I just want them to stop slapping me."

"Damn! It's details like that. We can mount a major campaign over this, Alec. Pictures." His father reached out and hooked a finger over Alec's mask and pulled. "I don't see any bruises or red marks."

Alec recoiled and adjusted the mask back into place. "No, they've eased up recently."

"Well, damn, boy, get 'em to slap you some more. We need pictures, eh?"

"Dad, I'm sleeping on a concrete floor with a bucket and ten thousand bugs to keep me company. I don't need more slaps. I need out."

"Yeah, yeah. Toughen up. Two weeks. Yeah. I need another two weeks. That gives us time to build pressure and flood channels with pledge requests. It will only—"

"No."

"What?"

"I refuse to stay here for another two weeks just for your fundraising."

He couldn't love, respect, or tolerate this man. He couldn't tolerate that way of life anymore. Then his father confirmed that judgment.

"It's not me, Alec, it's the organization, it's the movement. This is so—"

"Fuck you, Dad."

"Look, Alec, you don't really have a choice, do you? They're going to keep you in any event. So why not use it? Do some good for once?"

"Is there any water here?"

"Alec. Concentrate."

"No, really. I need some water so I can work up some spit."

Paul Chenais wrinkled his nose. Alec saw it despite the mask. "That's uncalled for," his father said.

"Really? I don't think so. Can we wind it up here? My pets need me in my cell." Alec stood and banged on the door. "Guard! Hey, guard! Yoo-hoo." When a startled officer opened the door, Alec made hand signals to take him back to his cell.

Alec was now all too familiar with the small interrogation room. He had been sure his father would generate publicity by staging a sit-in. But he was gone. He'd lost Reema and rejected his father. Who was left to visit him?

The door opened to reveal a tall, mustachioed police officer in an immaculate uniform, no mask. His epaulets showed more doodads than the inspector's, so Alec suspected this was a senior officer. He stood up. Why not show some respect? It might stave off more slaps.

"Alec Chenais. I am Deputy Inspector General of Police Khudiadadzai. Please. Sit down." The DIG waved his hand at Alec's chair, then sat stiffly in the other chair.

"You speak English?" asked Alec.

"Of course. Now, let us get down to business. This affair has consumed too much of our time."

"What affair would that be, sir?"

"This nonsense."

"You mean my father's effort to—"

"Father? No. I mean *your* nonsense. Enough is enough. The charges against you do not justify putting up with any of this. We have so informed your consul." Meaning that the money Paracha had paid wasn't enough. And that he wouldn't pay to keep Alec in jail.

"So, you're letting me go?"

Amorphous plans formed in Alec's mind: reconnect with Reema, find another interpreter, locate Paracha....

"No, we're deporting you. To Canada. Let them worry about you." The DGI smiled a cold smile. "And they are paying for it."

The DIG stood up, clearly ending the meeting. Alec scrambled up and said, "But the murder, two murders. I have to—"

The DIG smiled as he cut Alec off. "Enjoy your trip to Canada, Mr. Chenais. Don't come back."

Ms. Girard, seeing the airline personnel opening the gate door, stood up. "Well, Alec, I guess this is goodbye, eh?"

Alec, sitting handcuffed to a morose Pakistani police constable, smiled. Inside, he was a mass of despair. His trip to Pakistan had been a complete failure, and he had gotten someone killed. Now he was flying to Vancouver, a nice place, no doubt, but not where he wanted to be.

The constable looked up and smiled. That was a first. Alec interpreted the smile. The constable's duty escorting Alec out of Pakistan was almost done, and he saw the end in sight. He would escort Alec onto the 10 a.m. plane, remove the handcuffs, and deliver him to Canada. Abandon all hope, ye who enter here.

"I'm curious, Ms. Girard," Alec said. "Have they ever charged me? Has there been any resolution of Abdul Ali Jalali's murder?"

"No, and I don't know. I don't follow the crime news."

"Can you find out and tell me?"

"No."

"God, you're so helpful."

"I try."

"Not very hard."

The consul smiled and offered her hand. Alec shook it as the constable tugged at the handcuffs. The airline was boarding families with children and people with special needs. That was Alec, no question. He considered lying down and refusing to board, but something in the consul's expression suggested that this would cause immediate action in the constable, backed up by airport security. The constable tugged again. Alec, numb with despair, felt nothing but the pull on his wrist.

Ms. Girard smiled and said, "Goodbye, Alec. Enjoy your trip to Canada. Don't come back."

CHAPTER THIRTY-THREE
Vancouver

Alec found a bar table at Tap House in Vancouver airport and settled in for some reflection. After ordering fish and chips and a *café au lait,* he waited for inspiration.

He had nowhere to go.

His home in San Francisco was a wreck.

He had no job.

His only way to return to Pakistan involved human smuggling and more money than he had in his bank account.

He had lost AJ forever.

The coffee arrived, and he gingerly sipped with a grimace. The drink didn't meet his standards, but it would have to do. He considered ordering a craft brew instead but had discipline enough to vow to wait until evening for that. Whenever evening was; his biological clock had stopped. By his phone, it was noon on the same day he'd left Islamabad at 8 a.m. Time travel wears you out.

On the arrival of the fish and chips, the day got better as he realized he hadn't had decent food in what felt like forever. Not poutine, but at least the chips gave him hope for the future.

Alec pushed back the empty plate and pulled out his cell phone. He topped up the prepaid account, which was running low. He checked the clock on the phone to see the time in Paris: 10 p.m. He sighed. A long wait until business hours.

He headed for the exit to find a room at an airport hotel.

Alec's phone alarm woke him from a restless sleep at 1 a.m.. Time to call Paris. He dialed Octave's number from memory and reached him. Alec requested a call from Ludivine as soon as possible.

At 2:17 a.m., his phone rang.

"Alec? This is Ludivine. Where are you?"

"Vancouver. British Columbia."

"Oh. What happened in Pakistan? I haven't heard from you."

"Deported. The police didn't want me to investigate the murder."

"Hardly a surprise, *mon ami*. No?"

"I guess not. But I want to finish this." He debated whether to tell Ludivine about the attempt to kill him, but she steered the conversation in another direction.

She asked, "Are you aware of the latest blockchain news?"

"No. I assume that's relevant?"

"Very. Do you have access to the Web?"

"Yes." Alec opened his laptop and brought up a browser. Ludivine gave him a URL that took him to a news article describing a serious Ethereum Tether hack. He looked at the dateline: two days ago.

"It certainly looks like my blockchain code," he said.

"My sources tell me it is untraceable and the best hack they've ever seen on a coin exchange."

"Must be my code, then. Perry's team? They must have hacked the NSA too. That explains why the NSA kidnapped and interrogated me. Perry's integrated everything AJ and I created. He couldn't have done it without our code."

"Ah, so modest. But the conclusion is fair."

Alec blew out a breath. He needed to fill her in on the murder. "You said Elliot Perry was behind Varoozh Paracha. Paracha tried to assassinate me in Islamabad. He killed a good man right beside me. Was Perry behind that? And behind AJ's killing as well?"

"I honestly do not know, *mon ami*," she replied coolly. Ludivine had no reason to care about these murders. Maybe he could give her a reason.

"Ludivine, what would it take to galvanize your interest in these murders?"

"More credit that I can allow you, *mon ami*. Much more."

"I have no way of paying the debt I already owe you."

"Not true, Alec."

Alec stretched his tired mind to fill in the blanks. He failed, so he asked, "Why is it not true, Ludivine?"

In a warm and persuasive tone, Ludivine said, "Come to Paris, *mon chér*. We will dine and discuss the matter. Tomorrow evening. And perhaps we can discuss other matters of interest to us both. Agreed?"

Alec hesitated, uncertain about diving into this black well of doubt and iniquity. Did he want this future? But he had little choice. And after his time in a Pakistani jail, he believed he could put up with anything as long as it didn't involve bugs. A vacation in the City of Light. Dinner with a beautiful woman. Why not?

"Agreed. Where?"

Ludivine gave him the name of a restaurant, an address in the 17th arrondissement, and a time: nine o'clock.

CHAPTER THIRTY-FOUR
Ludivine's Covenant

The restaurant was just north of the Arc de Triomphe. Alec had booked into a nearby hotel and walked, enjoying the beautiful weather and the lively streets of the 17th arrondissement. The restaurant was a brasserie, modern in appearance, with white tablecloths and a well-appointed set of outdoor tables. Since the loosening of the lockdown with its restaurant closures, indoor dining was available. Alec wore a black silk mask he'd purchased earlier in the day from a shop near the hotel.

He entered the brasserie and greeted the hostess in French.

"I am meeting Mme. Moureaux, if you please."

"Ah, yes, monsieur Chenais, isn't it? Please, follow me."

She led him past busy waiters in the restaurant to a side door. She opened it and said, "*Bon appétit,* monsieur."

Alec entered the private dining room to find Ludivine in an elegant but casual shirt and pants. She arose to greet him with *la bise*. Alec's hand lingered on her arm a moment longer than strictly necessary. She gently disengaged and sat.

She said, "I have taken the liberty of ordering a few special dishes from the chef, prix fixe. I am sure you will enjoy the cuisine."

"I share your certainty, Ludivine. How are you?" He took a risk with *tutoyer*.

Ludivine smiled, not offended by the familiarity. The smile lit up her beautiful Asian eyes and cheeks. "I am well, *mon ami*. I trust you are too?"

A server appeared and poured Alex a glass of an elegant Montrachet. He then served them an artistic dish of crab in a truffled creamed haricot sauce and a plate of ice holding a dozen oysters in shells covered with mignonette and a diced fruit called poha berries, slightly underripe. So much for poutine. But Alec's mood had shifted from the prosaic to the sublime, at least as represented by Ludivine and the excellent cuisine.

Alec answered Ludivine's question indirectly. "Pakistani food did not agree with me," he said, savoring the flavors. "Especially the last few days there." He slurped an oyster from its shell.

"Prison food is seldom pleasant, I suppose. I wouldn't know. Regardless, I thought this would set a more favorable context for our negotiations."

"Good so far. What kind of agreement do you have in mind?"

"First, I would like to express my deepest sympathy for the loss of AJ. She was a dear friend of mine, and a wonderful woman."

"Yes, she was. I loved her very much." Alec hesitated, then took the bull by the horns. "Did you set us up, Ludivine?"

"Ah, now, *mon ami,* you are on the verge of business. I only admit that I saw an excellent fit for her in your organization. I did not expect romance. But I welcomed it."

Alec dipped a bite of crabmeat into the creamy sauce. "AJ was the best coder we had, even better than I."

"Modest indeed. And yet, your company dispensed with your services."

"They could no longer trust me. The NSA…intervened." He told the story of his kidnapping and interrogation.

"And that was when you called me for help."

"Yes. I couldn't tell you the complete story. Too strange. Too embarrassing."

"In your world, perhaps. In my business, one must always learn the dangerous undercurrents in the surrounding sea of trouble. To avoid situations such as you experienced, you understand?"

"Yes. I am not used to such things."

"That will change when you start your new career."

"With you?"

"If we can come to an arrangement." She passed her napkin lightly over her lips and touched the button for service. The main course came, a pork loin glazed with honey and soy sauce seasoned with Basque red pepper and a wonderful Xérès sherry vinegar. The server poured a glass of Chambolle-Musigny after getting Ludivine's approval of the wine. He placed the bottle on the table and withdrew, closing the door.

Ludivine's tone became businesslike. "Alec, business awaits. I need to ensure that your motivation suffices for the work. It must be to enter my world. What is it that you want? Is it money? Revenge? Power? Or are you lost and searching for redemption from your sins?"

"I was lost on the plane to Canada. I really was. And my sins are many. But when I called you, I had found my purpose, Ludivine."

"Revenge?"

"In part. For my friend Abdul and for AJ and myself. Yes. But much more than revenge. What do you know about my family?"

"*Rien, mon ami.*" Ludivine's gaze was quizzical as she sipped wine and pondered this irrelevancy.

But Alec was skeptical that she knew nothing about his family. This woman seemed to know everything. But he plunged ahead, describing his father and mother in terse but informative statements as he carefully carved bites of pork loin from the rib bones. He described his father's reactions to his desire to investigate AJ's death and his imprisonment. He wasn't sure what to expect from Ludivine. In the event, she grinned with amusement as he described his dismissal of his father.

"So what does this mean, Alec?" she asked, sipping her burgundy. "More revenge?"

"No, please don't misunderstand. I love my parents. I value human rights and have always wanted to do something about the human condition. Just—not like my father. Not at all like my father."

"So? Revenge or human rights?" Ludivine, her face like a mask, ate a bite of her pork.

Alec smiled. "Why not both?"

Alec finished his wine as Ludivine considered his motives in silence. Her lips rose slightly at the corners. "Both?" she asked.

"Revenge and human rights. Wrapped in a single package: Elliot Perry."

"Ah." Ludivine ate the last of her pork. When she saw that Alec had finished as well, she pressed the button for service. After clearing the table and brushing up the few crumbs, the server looked at Ludivine, who nodded. "The mousseline, Charles." He nodded.

When the door closed, Ludivine folded her hands, elbows on the table, and regarded Alec. "And what do you have in mind for our friend Perry?"

"Shutting him down. But I need your help. Your botnet. Your sources. I don't know where he is or how to get to him and his operation."

"Those are precious things, Alec. Beyond the budget of...someone in your situation."

"You mean an indigent, unemployed refugee."

"Perhaps not quite so bad, but...as you say."

"I can contribute in kind to your operation, Ludivine. I will work for as long as it takes to pay my debts."

"Hm. Allow me to consider the proposal while we eat." The door had opened to admit the waiter, carrying two plates. Each contained three small profiteroles, cut in half and filled with a lemony pastry cream. Each profiterole was dusted with powdered sugar and small green specks of rosemary. A few raspberries on the plate set off the pastry. Alec bit into the puff, and lemon and rosemary filled his senses.

"These are incredible. Incredible."

"I am here for these, Alec. The rest of the meal just keeps one alive to get to this point." Her lips closed around a bite of profiterole. She swallowed and said, "I think we can work together, *mon ami*. But I do not need an indentured servant."

"I have only a few thousand dollars in assets, Ludivine. I cannot—"

"It is not what you have, *mon ami;* it is what you can get."

As Alec swallowed his second profiterole, he saw clearly for the first time the whole of Ludivine's plan. AJ, the setup, the seduction, the glimpse of a new way of life. The prolonged grooming during this dinner.

"You've planned this all along, haven't you?" Alec smiled, taking the accusation out of the words. "You're a master of deception and seduction, Ludivine." He ate his last profiterole. The last meal for the condemned. "You want the code. My code. AJ's code. And me, to make it all work."

"I do. All of that." She again wiped her lips with her napkin. "I had hoped to accomplish this without all this fuss, but your affair with AJ and her murder changed the terms of engagement. As have the efforts of Elliot Perry and his team. It's war."

"War? And if I don't agree?"

"You have had an excellent dinner in a beautiful city." Ludivine regarded him with a calm face and said nothing about war. Alec didn't press her; he wasn't ready.

"With an exquisite woman." The woman of my nightmares? No, not that.

"You are too kind, *mon ami*."

"There is just one problem. I do not *have* the code."

Ludivine smiled. "Yuriko does."

"Yur—" Alec stopped, mouth open. He slowly closed it. "Yuriko. Yuriko?" His understanding of Ludivine's plan expanded. His earlier clarity disappeared, replaced by a sense of being lost in a maze of Ludivine's construction.

"Yuriko is a close friend of mine. She is finance, not coding. Nevertheless…" Ludivine waved a hand.

"She has access."

"She does."

"Why do you not just get her to give you the code?"

"I cannot risk her. She is an agent in place and is more valuable to me than the code. I cannot risk her being uncovered. But she can help you."

"My God. The duplicity." But that wink. As the door to 1WeakLink closed. Yuriko. My God.

"Welcome to my world, *mon ami*. About your motivation...."

"I am more than motivated. Let's do this."

Ludivine reached out a hand and caressed Alec's hand on the table.

"Yes. Let's."

"I thought you said you never slept with a man you're doing business with," Alec said, half afraid he was jinxing the project or the sex.

Ludivine turned lazily and rubbed Alec's back. They lay together on the bed in Ludivine's apartment, a large, elegant one-bedroom on a tree-lined street near to the restaurant where they had made their pact.

"I do not limit myself, even by my own rules. Any fool can make a rule, but only a true fool always follows it." She kissed him. "It is a matter of pleasure and of risk. Tonight, I want to seal a covenant. Are you ready to sign?" She felt him with her hand, found that he was indeed ready, and sat up over him, entwining her legs with his, her long black hair hanging down over him as she moved forward.

Ludivine, content, lay in bed and listened. Alec had started his shower.

She got up quickly and grabbed his phone, making sure she'd noted exactly where it was on the nightstand. She took it to her office and plugged it into her laptop. She launched the pin hacker she'd written several years before, and it quickly opened the phone. She downloaded a small piece of software and integrated it into the clock app via the alarm function, a zero-day she'd found a week ago. She closed the phone and unplugged it, then closed her laptop. Putting the phone back where she found it, she returned to bed.

When Alec came out of the bathroom, she told him she'd make breakfast if he'd pick up some croissants at the boulangerie near the corner. He left with his phone, and she tracked him to the bakery and back again on her own phone as she poured two glasses of orange juice, sliced pieces of baguette, found the jar of special jam and the Norman butter, and made French press coffee.

Satisfactory. A most satisfactory evening and night. And the croissants would be excellent. They always were. Ludivine contentedly sipped her coffee. After breakfast, Alec would leave for San Francisco to access the code, and she would initiate the operation against Perry.

CHAPTER THIRTY-FIVE
Yuriko

Alec's condo remained as trashed as before. He had a toilet and hot water, but the place was unlivable. He was exhausted. He closed the shades in his bedroom against the midday sun, turned the slashed mattress over, put some blankets on it, and slept for ten hours.

A loud explosion from outside awoke Alec. He stumbled to the window and saw nothing. More explosions came. Many of them. Ah. July 4, and the Mission was alive with celebrants. He looked toward the Bay; no fireworks display. The sun was down and the fog was in. He checked his phone: 10:30 p.m. Too late to call Yuriko? Last time, it had been 3 a.m. He dialed.

"Yuriko? It's Alec."

"Alec! Just hold on one minute, Alec. I have to—" A voice mumbled something. "It's a friend. I'll be back. Don't move."

Alec grinned. Oops.

"Now. Where are you?"

"More to the point, where were you?"

"Oh, Alec. None of your business."

"Right. I'm just back from Pakistan. And Paris."

"And?"

"It was a shambles, Yuriko. They put me in jail. But that's not why I called."

"Do you need money?"

"Yes, but that's not why I called either. Ludivine."

Silence. "I'm not sure...what you mean?" The trepidation in Yuriko's voice did not sound uncertain.

"Ludivine explained, Yuriko. It's time."

Alec heard a sharp intake of breath from Yuriko. "I don't think this is wise."

"Maybe not, but it's time. It's independence day."

"Can we meet? I can't talk right now."

"I'll bet. Sure. Jackalope, Monday at nine?"

"I'll be there. Now—if you don't mind? I've got something—"

"Have fun. *Au revoir. À demain.*"

Alec sipped his *café au lait* in the parklet outside the Jackalope. He'd come early to make sure he got exactly the coffee he needed. But the barista remembered him. It felt like years, but it had been only a month since his last coffee here. The worst day of his life, even worse than the Montreal Molotov cocktail.

He spotted Yuriko hurrying along the sidewalk on the opposite side of Howard. He watched as she waited for the light and crossed at the crosswalk. Traffic was moderate, much less than a year ago. The pandemic had solved one problem for the City, at least.

Yuriko looked good. She dressed for the office with loose gray pants, white leather sneakers, a black blouse with puffy sleeves, and a glistening necklace with a gold heart. It was a step up from the clothes she'd worn a month ago. Definitely a change in her life. A lover?

She came up to his table. "Alec. It's so good to see you."

"Get some coffee and join me, Yuriko. It's good to see you too."

"Tea. I'll be right back."

Yuriko's body language as she waited at the cafe doorway table for her tea was angular and constrained. He'd have to allay her concerns first. She wouldn't be happy knowing he'd learned her secret affiliation with Ludivine.

Yuriko returned to the table carrying her cup of tea.

Alec said, "You're looking good, Yuriko. A new locket?" The golden heart had an "M" engraved on it.

"Oh…yes. A gift."

"Boyfriend?"

She smiled. "Girlfriend."

"Congratulations."

"She's love bombing me. We'll see."

"I wanted to express my profound thanks for what you did for me."

"You mean slamming the door in your face?" she grinned.

"You know perfectly well what I mean."

"Are you feeling better? I was worried when you vanished."

"The NSA—"

"Yes. You've had a rough time." Yuriko clearly didn't want to discuss the NSA.

"I'm much better. Now that I have a purpose."

Yuriko hid her eyes as she sipped tea, then looked up at him. "Ludivine?"

"You must have known this might happen. Or you wouldn't have taken her money."

Yuriko grimaced. "No money. Not yet, anyway. Only favors and information. She got me the job. She said she wanted an inside person keeping her informed about…progress."

"Is she in bed with Crispin too?"

Yuriko's face scrunched at the thought. "God no. No no no. She had an underground connection to private equity people that knew Crispin."

"And you told her about me. And the trip to Paris."

"Yes. Was that such a bad thing? You got AJ."

"*Ludivine* got me AJ."

"Oh, Alec. AJ…and Ludivine? She never told me."

"Her world is a tiny place, Yuriko."

"So this was her plan all along?"

Alec shrugged. "I guess so. Let's get on, Yuriko. Ludivine and I are now allies."

"And she wants me to do something?"

Alec responded with a question. "Just how close are you?"

"None of your business, Alec." She didn't smile, but her eyes crinkled. "What did she tell you?"

"Only...that you were friends. And that you'd help me access the code."

"Christ. It's come to this."

"How can I get access? I've tried logging in with my old password, no good. And I tried AJ's password too. She trusted me with it a while back. Nothing."

Yuriko hesitated, then said, "Olyena."

"What? Is she in on this?"

"No, but she's taken, er, a *dislike*—to Crispin."

"How is such a thing possible? Such an inoffensive man. But you think she'd open up to—"

"To me. Not to you. We're friends."

"The NSA will learn it was her. They knew about AJ."

"AJ?"

Alec realized there was much that Yuriko didn't know. Too much. Too much to explain now, certainly.

"Never mind. Just accept that the NSA will be all over her."

"There is always collateral damage in wars."

"And this is war. Ludivine's war."

Yuriko tipped her cup back and finished her tea. "Was that all?"

"For now."

She got up and smiled. "I'll be in touch. Goodbye, Alec. And good luck."

"You said that before." Alec hoped that this time the benediction would take.

CHAPTER THIRTY-SIX
Ms. C

Yuriko sat at her usual table in the tiny restaurant on Sanchez Street in the Castro. She and Mallory had discovered the place and made it their rendezvous, their private happy place. Most restaurants in San Francisco closed on Mondays, but this one stayed open the whole week. She looked at her watch: 6:15. Mallory was late, but only by fifteen minutes.

Yuriko sipped her chardonnay. Thoughts of Mallory and Ludivine consumed her. Last night. Mallory was a great lover, the best she'd had since...well, since Ludivine. Very different people, different styles, different feelings. Ludivine the dark, mysterious seductress; Mallory the blonde, flirty whirlwind. Both knowing exactly what to do for maximum pleasure.

Her phone rang, an unknown number. Oh, Mallory had a new phone, that's right. Better answer.

"Hello?"

"Hello, Ms. Nakamura."

"I'm not interested."

"Let's change that, shall we? I'm from the NSA." A woman's voice, high and squeaky. Oh. Ms. C from Alec's demo.

"Ms. C, right?" What do these idiots want now?

"That name will do, I guess. Well, let's get started."

"I'm meeting someone. Can we do this tomorrow at the office?"

"Mallory's not coming."

Yuriko's throat tightened. "What? How do you know—"

"We know everything, Ms. Nakamura. May I call you Yuriko?"

"Hell, no. What's going on?"

"I'm sorry to have to tell you that Mallory is one of our agents, Ms. Nakamura. An exceptional one, wouldn't you agree?"

"I...."

"We know about Alec, Ludivine Moureaux, Olyena Shevchenko, and the code, Ms. Nakamura."

"But I haven't..." She'd told Mallory. About Ludivine. Oh my God. That *bitch*. How could I have been so *stupid!* But how did they find out about Alec and the code?

Ms. C continued, "Just as a token of good faith, Ms. Nakamura? The locket? It's bugged."

Yuriko's hand grabbed the gold locket on the chain around her neck, the one with "M" signifying Mallory's perfect love for her. She jerked it and the fine gold chain snapped. A passing waitress asked if everything was OK. Yuriko forced a smile and nodded, unable to articulate a word. What would she tell Ludivine?

"So, Ms. Nakamura, it's time to talk."

Yuriko noticed movement across the room at the bar. Ms. C put her phone away, picked up her cocktail, and walked towards her table. Yuriko's feet moved involuntarily to get her up and running, but she suppressed the urge. It wouldn't help. Nothing would help.

"If it's any consolation, Ms. Nakamura, Mallory reports that you are an excellent lover. That's a tremendous compliment. She's particularly experienced in that sort of thing."

Yuriko glanced down at the table, the rage engulfing her but quickly quenched by total humiliation. But Ludivine—she had to toughen up, for Ludivine's sake. She looked up with a fierce stare at the NSA agent.

"What do you want?"

"The code, Ms. Nakamura."

"What will happen to me?"

Ms. C smiled. "Nothing. If you get me the code."

"But you'll get it anyway. You're *paying* for it."

"You're assuming I am asking on behalf of the agency. Never assume, Ms. Nakamura."

"I…what?"

Ms. C shook her head. "For a hardened member of an international crime ring, Ms. Nakamura, you don't seem to roll with the punches very well."

Yuriko could only stare at her. Not for the agency. For *her*. This was worse than anything Yuriko had ever experienced.

She said, "You're blackmailing me. To get the 1WeakLink system for yourself. You…you're a fucking criminal yourself."

"Language, Ms. Nakamura." Ms. C cocked her head. "Insults won't get you anything but jail time. Or worse."

"Are we ready to order?" A smiling server had approached the table unnoticed.

Ms. C smiled and squeaked, "Order whatever you want, Ms. Nakamura. It's on the agency's tab. My treat."

Yuriko took up the menu card stiffly and ordered the sautéed halibut with roasted corn and horseradish crème fraîche, her favorite dish. Might as well go out with a full stomach.

"And two more glasses of chardonnay, thanks," she said.

"I don't drink," said Ms. C. "This is their gin-free and tonic." She sipped from her cocktail glass.

"They're for me," replied Yuriko, handing the card to the server.

CHAPTER THIRTY-SEVEN
Preparing for War

The cheap laptop would not cut it as a hacking workstation. Alec needed a lot more CPU and better architecture for that. He'd have to buy, not build, so he visited a sleek store in Union Square. He'd avoided the place on principle for years, building his own systems. No time to tinker with chips and motherboard backbones. He walked out with the top of the line laptop after waiting a half hour for technical support to configure the memory to the max. The machine ran on a native version of Linux with the latest CPU and graphics chips, very suitable for the tools he'd need for his new career. Such as the 1WeakLink system. The salesperson tried to cross-sell a phone to him, but he'd become attached to his burner and turned him down. His money wouldn't last long at this rate. Maybe he could get Ludivine to reimburse him for the business expense.

He returned to his condo with the laptop. He cleared away the debris around his workstation desk by sweeping it to the floor and set up the new computer. The Internet connection was still up. All he needed was access to his account. He ordered dinner delivered from a restaurant and waited for Yuriko's call.

It was midnight when Alec's phone buzzed. He snapped out of a light sleep and grabbed his phone.

Yuriko said without even waiting for hello, "Crispin told the team to change your password but to keep your account, just in case they needed something later. Maks changed the password, so Olyena had the new one. I fed her all kinds of lies about why I needed it." Yuriko read off the password, a randomized string of sixteen characters. Alec entered it into his password vault and logged into GitHub with it. Success.

"I'm in, Yuriko. I'll download everything and disappear for a while. I hope I'll see you again sometime, but I can't guarantee it."

He listened but heard only silence. "You still there, Yuriko?"

"Yeah, yes, sorry, Alec. Great!" But her voice didn't sound like she meant it.

"What's wrong, Yuriko?"

"Nothing, nothing. I, that is, I have to call Ludivine. But I'm fine. I'll be OK."

"Sure. Give Ludivine my regards when you talk to her," Alec said. Then Yuriko was gone.

What concerned Yuriko and prompted her to call Ludivine? Despite his earlier certainty, Alec spent five minutes rethinking everything. Was he ready for this? He thought about Pakistani jails and people with guns. He thought about the NSA.

None of these thoughts changed his resolve or affected his plan to work with Ludivine. Unless she pulled the plug, he would go ahead. Time to take control of his life.

He started the download of the codebase as a ZIP file and watched the download indicator cycle.

Two minutes later, the download finished. Alec logged out, shut down the laptop, and headed to his bedroom.

Tuesday morning, Alec got out of bed at 9:24 and went out for breakfast to the little breakfast place on Jessie Street near his condo. Lousy *café au lait*, but excellent pastries and eggs. Then he stopped at a corner grocery and bought a bag of decent french roast and a quart of milk. The grinder and French press coffeemaker had survived the NSA.

Back at the condo, Alec drank two cups of his own *café au lait* while installing the 1WeakLink systems on his new laptop. He was almost done when his phone rang. He didn't recognize the number, but he answered anyway.

"Yes?"

"Alec, good to hear you're back in town," squeaked a voice he recognized immediately. The last time he'd heard it, it had hurt so much he remembered everything about it. He refrained from asking how Ms. C had gotten the burner phone number. This was the NSA. Maybe he hadn't fully thought things through the night before. But there was no point in being nice. Not to Ms. C.

"What's it to you, lady?" he asked.

"Tch. It wouldn't hurt to be polite. Especially to someone who can have you killed."

"Yeah, sure. Look, I'm busy—"

"We have a special request for you, Alec. We want you to build a kill switch into the blockchain code."

"You should have thought of that before you got me fired. I can't get to the code anymore, and you know it. Will you have Crispin rehire me?"

"Alec, Alec. Yuriko Nakamura was very forthcoming once we made clear the consequences of her actions. We know you have the code. We monitored the download last night with Crispin Bannon's kind permission to access your account. He says hello."

Alec understood now why Yuriko had seemed distracted. A trap. They'd set him up. But did it change anything? Ms. C wasn't sending men in black this time. She was asking for a favor.

"Why not have Crispin do it? Or the software development team. Or even you or your own software developers?"

"We'd prefer to compartmentalize this change. Only the NSA and you will know. And of course you're the best person to do the work. The NSA likes to use the best."

"What are you planning—"

"No questions, Alec. Oh, and Alec, include the kill switch in your delivery to Ludivine Moureaux. You can understand why, can't you?"

Yuriko had given up Ludivine, too. Damn her.

A kill switch. In the hacker world, a kill switch adds a bit of processing that stops the software from working, usually with a hidden key. If Ludivine tried something they didn't approve of, they could shut her down. He could program a kill switch in just minutes and knew exactly where to hide the code for seamless sharing between tools. AJ had created a shared data mechanism already encrypted for security. He'd just write the code, encrypt it with a new key, and give the key to the NSA. To Ms. C.

If.

"I want a guarantee," he said.

"Like what?"

"Like you leaving me alone to get on with my fucking life. From this point on. Agreed?"

"Oh, sure. No problem. You're of little value to us now, too compromised. Alec, we just need this one last ask. After that? You're history to us."

"Can I have that in writing?"

A chuckle. "You're a comedian, too, huh? Who knew?"

Alec only imperfectly grasped what it meant to be history to the NSA. He was sure that it would not allow him to continue his life unaffected. He resolved to take measures. Once he'd written the kill switch. He, too, would have to call Ludivine. About Yuriko, the code, the kill switch, and the future.

He said reluctantly, "All right. I'll add the kill switch. You can check it out of GitHub—"

"No! This version needs to stay far away from any public code site. We can't take the risk. Look what happened with Ms. Jaffrey's code. No. I'm sending you a Tor SecureDrop site and codename. Use the codename to register, then drop the code after you've tested it, with the key and documentation on how to activate the kill switch. Then you can give the code to Moureaux. How long will it take?"

"A few days. Friday?"

"Wow. You're getting slow in your old age, Alec. Let's say tomorrow, shall we? Wednesday. Or there won't be a happy ending this time." It was hard to sound threatening with a squeak, but Ms. C managed it.

This time? He'd experienced damn few happy endings so far. Alec felt the strands of web closing around him, and Ludivine was his only hope of avoiding the spider.

His email buzzed. He opened it to find a nondescript site URI and codename string from an anonymous sender. Some kind of dead drop that the NSA used to keep secret things secret.

He said, "I got the email. I'll drop the code by midnight tomorrow. Is that all? Because I have to get to work."

"Sure, Alec. Have a nice day." Another chuckle and Ms. C was gone.

CHAPTER THIRTY-EIGHT
AJ's Legacy

Alec spent most of Tuesday morning configuring the software on his new laptop. He installed the basic toolset for coding and testing the 1WeakLink codebase as well as various security tools that he knew he'd need before long. After a break for lunch at a local cafe, he got down to business.

Alec used polymorphic coding to hide the trigger code for the NSA kill switch in the shared code library. This little snippet of code built and executed a function dynamically for each tool access. It ran small pieces of code distributed throughout the system, each of which did part of the job of shutting down the software. This hid the code from reverse engineering tools and made it much harder for someone to find. The generated code accessed a private key hidden through an environment variable. Installing the key and setting the environment variable would be the only requirements for a hacker to trigger the kill switch. Hackers running the code wouldn't see it, and they couldn't reverse engineer the code to trace it.

Much of the shared code library was AJ's, built up over the two years she'd worked on the product. Alec looked through it just to feel her presence through her code. One function caught his eye. It loaded a file from shared data into memory, but some additional code processed the file. He worked through it and smiled slowly.

AJ. She'd already built a kill switch into the code. Without telling him.

He looked in the shared data directory but couldn't find any files that might contain a key. She'd kept the key file secret and out of the code. Where could it be? No way AJ would leave it lying around. And she'd make two copies, just in case. And it wouldn't be online or on her laptop.

Alec put on his jacket and walked back to his condo. He went to the kitchen, where the NSA searchers had pulled out and dumped the contents of all the drawers as they searched for items taped to the bottom, he imagined. He searched for a while among the jumble of silverware and broken dishes and coffee beans. He found the key under the fridge.

The physical key to AJ's place.

She'd left it with him. And she'd given him her account password and her secret password, the one she used to encrypt files. She had told him that trust was everything between them. The breakup might have caused her to change that, but he had to try.

For emergencies, she'd said.

This was an emergency.

With the private key file, Alec could stop any use of the 1WeakLink code, regardless of the user. At least, until some clever hacker realized what was happening and removed the kill switch. But there was no one at like that 1WeakLink. Not anymore. And no one at the NSA, or Ms. C wouldn't have tagged him to add their kill switch.

He'd make his own guarantee.

Alec hiked from the MUNI bus stop up the hill to Waller Street, looking around him for suspicious vehicles and lurking men in black suits. The late afternoon sun illuminated the disparate houses on the street. He looked around carefully before climbing the steps of the old Victorian apartment building. Nothing moved except a flock of crows, loudly cawing their displeasure with the world. He felt completely exposed as he climbed the eighteen concrete steps to the apartment doors. A quick check revealed the name "Jaffrey" on the "B" mailbox. He slipped the key

The Blockchain Killing

into the lock on the "B" door and turned it. The door opened with a squeak, and he quickly stepped inside and closed it. At the bottom of the stairs, he faced a seemingly endless climb to the building's second floor. Every. Single. Step. Creaked.

By the time he reached the top of the stairs, he was sweating. A career in software development was no preparation for international intrigue and espionage. Intuition told him that if the noise had alerted someone to his presence, he'd soon know it. And he had his story ready: he was there at the behest of the Jaffrey family to assess AJ's belongings for disposal.

After a few minutes, his heart stopped pounding and he let out a breath. He was alone.

He briefly explored the one-bedroom apartment. Small, antique kitchen. Living room at the front with a view northwards over the City. 1970s bathroom with shower/tub combo, sink, and toilet. The bedroom had a desk with a monitor and wireless peripherals, no computer. No phone, but a fiber-optic Internet connection in the bedroom with a wireless modem that flashed green. Where to start?

The closet. Top shelf, shake out the blanket and extra pillow. Nothing. Search all the clothes, the few of them she'd left behind, nothing. Look for loose boards or covered up holes, nothing. Look up, nothing on the ceiling. Nothing in the light globe. Nothing in the light switch after removing the plate with the screwdriver he'd brought. On to the bedroom.

In the kitchen, he was sweating again, this time from the effort of searching everywhere possible. It could even be a piece of paper with the key written on it. He mumbled thanks when he opened a cabinet and found nothing. Literally. AJ was not a cook and had nothing beyond basic tools and supplies. A few cans and pots, no flour, no sugar. Rice. He poured the rice into a bowl and stirred it. Nothing. Drawers out, upside down. Cavities in the cabinets. Nothing. Removable base plates, cavities under the cabinets. Nothing. He searched the fridge thoroughly. He melted the frozen dinners and ice trays in the microwave, but all he got were poor excuses for Indian meals: chicken tikka masala, butter chicken curry, and vindaloo chicken curry. Frozen naan in a plastic bag. The smell of cumin filled the kitchen to the gag level.

Then he hit pay dirt in the hood over the stove. He had removed a filter, and there, taped to the metal inside the hood, was a thumb drive. He went back to the living room and took his laptop out of his backpack. Then he sat down on the couch to think.

What would a brilliant hacker do to protect a thumb drive? Use autoload to launch a virus that would wipe the drive and possibly the entire computer. A booby trap. Then a second layer of defense, a key file that was really a virus bomb. Third layer of defense: a lockbox file containing the key. It wouldn't be biometric, it would have a password. And he knew AJ's secure password. Or, better, she could have created a hidden partition for the file. His mind wandered back to a beautiful day a few months ago when AJ had sat him down at her computer and shown him a tool for creating encrypted partitions. That's what she would do.

Alec booted his laptop, made sure the autoload feature was off, and inserted the drive. He entered AJ's normal password when the computer prompted him. The drive contained a single file with a PEM private key extension. Far too good to be true. He listed the file size. Twice the size of a reasonable private key file. The booby trap. Alec felt like he should wear a blast vest and mask.

He pulled up a console and unmounted the thumb drive partition. Then he started the partitioning tool and mounted the thumb drive using AJ's secret password she'd shared with him. A single file sat in the partition: a JPEG image file. He opened it up and found a photograph of AJ, smiling that smile he'd grown to love so much.

Alec leaned back. He stared at the screen. It was like looking at a piece of AJ's soul, this photo. And her possessions and her existence surrounded him in the apartment. The apartment he'd invaded, her things that he'd searched. He could smell her. Well, that was the cumin in the kitchen.

Though he mourned her as the love of his life, he had to move on.

A drop of sweat fell on the laptop keyboard. It might have been a tear. Alec wiped his face with his sleeve. What good was a photo of AJ? She must have created it to hide the real key somehow. Then it hit him: steganography. She'd buried the private key among the dense pixels of the photograph. Invisible. The code in the 1WeakLink library loaded the photo and extracted the key. So the photo file was the key file. He copied it into his secure password lockbox. Then he installed the file in the 1WeakLink data directory. He brought up the 1WeakLink GasLighter tool and searched for a blockchain, but the interface immediately froze. Yep, that was the key. He unmounted the thumb drive again, ejected it from the laptop, and shut everything down.

He looked around at the chaos he'd created of the remnants of AJ's life. A powerful impulse to clean it all up suddenly filled him. He had to make it whole again. Put AJ's life back together. But no. Too late for that.

Time to go.

CHAPTER THIRTY-NINE
Honor Among Thieves

Alec finished testing his NSA kill switch at 3 in the morning on Wednesday. He went out for a walk to stretch his legs, but avoided Pier 14, instead walking down to the ballpark and back. The streets were eerily quiet. The days of all-night speakeasies and parties in San Francisco had vanished many years before Alec was born.

He got back to his condo at 6 and made himself a *café au lait,* then sat down to his laptop. He dropped the code into Ms. C's SecureDrop site and sipped coffee, feeling deflated and abused by the extortion. With AJ's kill switch, he could put a stop to anything serious, but he'd need Ludivine to do the hacking, as it wasn't his specialty. It was four in the afternoon in Paris.

He dialed the number Ludivine had given him. She answered with what passed for warmth with her.

"Alec, *mon cher.* I have been expecting your call."

"Yes, sorry for the delay. I had to adjust some things in the 1WeakLink code before transferring it to you."

"Very well, *mon cher.* You can put the code into my private cloud storage." She gave him the URL. He started the transfer.

"While that's happening, Ludivine, you need to know that Yuriko—"

"Yes, Yuriko called me yesterday with her sad tale. The poor woman was frantic, but I reassured her."

Alec, nonplussed, said, "Ludivine, what's it all about? She told me nothing."

"Ah. Too embarrassed, I suppose. Quite understandable. A woman from the NSA blackmailed her into transferring the code before she called you."

Alec ground his teeth. Ms. C. She already had the code, then she extorted him to put the kill switch into Ludivine's copy. Now he had a decision to make. Tell Ludivine or not?

He said, "The NSA would have the code anyway, from Crispin. I don't understand why they blackmailed Yuriko."

"This woman is from the NSA, but she wants the code for herself. Yuriko said she is playing both sides against the middle, using NSA resources to get *kompromat,* then using it to achieve her own rather criminal goals."

"What do you mean, *kompromat?*"

"Yuriko fell in love with a woman who turned out to be an NSA agent. They overheard your conversation about getting the code through a listening device that was given to her as a gift: a locket of some sort."

"Oh, *mon Dieu.* She must be...." That M, on the golden locket. Poor Yuriko. Alec spared that thought before the dread overwhelmed him: Ms. C was going rogue.

Ludivine, unperturbed, continued, "Yes. I reassured Yuriko that no harm was done, but I am afraid she is now useless to us. Compromised. More complications. This NSA woman is an unwanted knot in our tapestry. I will advise my organization to take extra security measures."

He was in too deep. Ms. C had all the resources of the NSA at her beck and call. She'd made that clear. That she was going rogue didn't change that in the least. Alec knew that if he told Ludivine about the extortion and the kill switch, Ms. C would find out and take revenge. Not on Ludivine, who was impervious to such things. But Alec was a newbie at all this. He would be exposed and defenseless. Ms. C's revenge would involve real-world dangers, not the abstractions of the cyberworld.

"So, what's next, Ludivine?" he asked, making his choice.

"Leave it to me, *mon cher*. I have a plan to make it difficult for M. Perry to proceed, one that will serve as a start on our revenge for AJ. I will be in touch, *mon cher*."

"Ee arr, Jeff. Coom have a butcher's at this."

Suze hadn't spoken to Jeff in days, so this was a good sign. The other thing was that Jeff was ready to look at shit in the bilges if it would give him something he could use to impress Elliot. So he jumped on it.

"Whatcha got, Suze?" He stood over the woman's shoulder. She looked up with a grim expression, but without saying anything pointed at a web browser open on one of her monitors. Jeff leaned over her shoulder to read the *Wall Street Journal* article. Susan shifted over, clearly annoyed, so Jeff sat down next to her on the padded bench, smiling.

His smile grew wider as he read the article. The *Journal* had investigated a nice little coin scam. Well, maybe not so little. $2.3 billion missing from the exchange and counting. The article went on and on. Must be a three-page spread in the paper. The guy had moved people's money like cattle going to Kansas.

Suze said, "Right, so me an' Mahmoud 'ave been graftin' on them wallet connections, and we reckon we've clocked this muppet's stash. Where 'e's bunged the readies. 'E's blown some of it, like, and 'e's proper messed about wi' the dosh, splittin' it into millions o' bits an' bobs, but there's still over two billion quid in them stablecoins toocked away in seventeen wallets on dodgy coin exchanges all over t'gaff."

"Well, damn," Jeff grinned. "We can help them out. Consolidate the money. In our wallets." He looked at his co-worker with hope. "Want to work on this together? I can show you the ropes of the blockchain system we're testing, Suze."

"Don't…" Suze pressed her lips together, scratched her neck, twisted her mouth, and said, "Fook yeah. Let's 'ave it."

"Our competitor is taking a hand, Ludivine." Raoul's tone was neutral and analytic, the observer above the fray. Ludivine held her phone to her ear as she walked down the Champs, busy with pedestrians on this sunny Saturday. Raoul had reported Perry's pirate raid on the stolen stablecoins, a true *coup de main*. Perry's group had perfected their version of Alec's blockchain software and were now making their first attempt at controlling the blockchain ecosystem.

But, alas, their *coup de main* ran into problems. They were little fish, the kind that big fish ate. Ms. C was at least a mid-sized fish, with teeth. Sharp teeth, including a newer version of Alec's software. Raoul detailed some of the clever ways she drained Perry's stablecoin wallets of their ill-gotten gains. Ludivine instructed Raoul to observe the details, as her group could learn as much by observation as by action. Ludivine made a mental note to call Sasha when she got back to her apartment. Ms. C had softened up the enemy for her. It was now Ludivine's turn to show Mr. Perry that he didn't control the world.

She put her phone away and switched her attention to her aspiration for today: to acquire a comfortable pair of J. M. Weston black zipped Chelsea boots. The kind with the Louis XV heel.

One cannot live entirely in the digital world, after all.

"Ludivine the Exquisite! My absolute favorite customer. Tell me, how is Paris? Or have you finally come to St. Petersburg for dinner with me?"

"Paris is wonderful, Sasha. And I would never dine with you, even if it were my last meal."

"Ah, the ingratitude! After all I have done for you." A moment of silence. "My records show you paid us an incredible 40 million rubles in the last six months. Dinner would be on me, and afterward—"

"There is no afterward, Sasha. I use your excellent network often. You helped me earn millions. But now, I have a special request."

"*Bozhe moi*, you have but to ask, my beautiful one. Ask, ask!"

"I want to mount a DDoS attack on a series of servers."

"But distributed denial of service is just normal operations, *dorogushka*."

"This is special, Sasha. I do not want the source of the attack requests revealed. Ever. I will pay for that."

"My, my, my love. Is it government? China? The U. S.?"

"Perry."

"So, it is war?"

"Sasha, tell me you are not providing services to the man."

"It is not in my best interest to reveal my customers to my other customers."

"Is it in your interest to force a customer to crash your net? Should you turn and reveal the source, charging for that information, I would have to act."

"I have a strict no double-dipping policy, Ludivine the Beautiful Skeptic. It's offensive to think I would do that."

"You would kill your mother for money, Sasha."

"I was not aware anyone knew of that crime, Ludivine." A grumbly laugh followed. "My mother is healthy and living well in Krasnoyarsk. Or was the last I'd heard of her. You need not fear. I love you more than her."

Ludivine smiled. A base rate bias if ever there was one.

"Just so you know, Sasha. I have ways of settling scores that make Stalin look like a schoolchild."

"I believe you, Ludivine the Bold. Do not doubt me. I will treat you with respect and tenderness in all things."

"*Khorosho.* Here is what I need."

CHAPTER FORTY
DDoS

"Ey up, Jeff! Summat's 'appening." The voice came from the other side of the beer fridge. Port, the port side. Jeff wasn't good at nautical lingo, but practice makes perfect. The voice was Suze's voice. Her lingo was worse than the boat stuff, even with practice. Jeff hadn't made progress with the woman, but he was confident he would. Sooner or later. He slumped in his chair looking at the empty wallets he'd worked so hard to fill.

"Heya, Suze. Whatcha got?" he called. He stayed in his chair. Elliot's latest verbal flogging over the missing $2 billion in stolen stablecoins still hurt too much. If Susan had found the thief, she'd have said so. But it turned out to be something new.

"Fook-all, Jeff. It's all down. Don't call me Suze, innit!" He got the gist. He'd get more when the woman came around to liking him as much as he liked her.

But Jeff often found the terse communication style of some coders difficult. Susie had gone over the edge. All down? He rose, staggering a little as the boat—the ship—heaved against a wave in the Atlantic Ocean, and walked over to his teammate's table.

Susie sat back against the leather bench, her face a mask of frustration.

"What's all down, Susie?"

"Our sites. All over the world." She turned from the monitor and glared at Jeff, her lovely lips in a tight, worried line. "And don't call me fookin' Susie either, ya Yank twit!"

"Um..." Jeff walked around the edge of the table and looked at her monitor. Three browser windows open, three screens. All the same: "The connection has timed out. The server at whatever.com.ru is taking too long to respond." Oh, yeah. "What's the TTL on these sites?"

Sue said, "All of our dark web sites are 300 second time-to-live. Proper fast."

"How long has this been going on?"

"Ten minutes. I tried to update the Singapore site and poof, nowt." She flung a frustrated hand at the message on her monitor.

"Hang in there, Sue. Let me check the routers."

Glum and worried, Sue turned back to her monitor and left him to it.

Jeff stumbled back to his workstation and tried to shell into one of the Singapore firewalls to investigate. Three timeouts later, he was certain: a TCP flood attack on their routers. He cross-checked some routers in Ukraine and Kiribati, and guess what? All fucked.

The Kiribati firewall had a dedicated network tap in front of the firewall router. They'd used it to verify some hacks that they couldn't test at the firewall level. Yep, still attached. Holy shit: millions of SYN requests from IP addresses all over the place. This was major. This was war. Better get Elliot involved.

Remember the Alamo!

Jeff grinned and staggered out of the Seacave in search of his boss. A gift from heaven. It would take Elliot's mind off losing the $2 billion.

"It's that Russian knobhead," said Sue. "Got 'im."

Jeff looked down at his teammate, a big grin on his face. "Mighty fine work, Sue! How'd ya figure it out?"

She grinned up at him from her bench and crowed, "Big data, innit! I nabbed all them SYN requests we logged in Kiribati an' knocked up a geographic model of where they coom from, then pulled in requests from all them botnets we've been keepin' tabs on. Our Mahmoud chipped in wi' that. He built this dead clever botnet recognition tool from that data usin' machine learning. We shoved the SYN data in—got a proper match wi' two of Sasha's botnets. The dodgy ones, the ones he keeps schtum about. And yer can bet yer arse that gobshite Moureaux is behind the attack. I know 'er, me. I know 'ow she ticks, I know who she gets in t'do 'er dirty work an' that. Her and Sasha are tight as owt, them two. 'and in fookin' glove!" Sue's hand tightened into a fist as she glared at the screen. "An' yer know what? I reckon *she's* the one what's been 'avin' it away wi' them two billion quid an' all."

Jeff patted her on the shoulder. A lot of fire in this one. "Hot damn! Terrific stuff, Sue." Time for a hug?

"Don't fookin' call me *Sue,* ya gobshite! It's *Susan!*" The words came in a low hiss of fury. Her fiery eyes burned right into his. Then she turned back to her workstation and ignored him.

"Sure, Susan."

No hugs today. But what a woman! Put everything she had into her work, for sure. As he went in search of Elliot, Jeff's mind moved from love to more practical thoughts about how he would take down the Frenchwoman. One thing he'd learned, though. Elliot had ways of getting things done that outstripped even the best hacking.

Jeff headed up to Elliot's stateroom, where a crewman directed him to the sundeck. He found Elliot sunbathing with Oscar. It was a fine day at the Cape.

"Hi, boss. Uh, we got a little problem."

Elliot sat up on the edge of his deck chair. "How little?"

"Well, see, it's—"

"Spit it out, Jeff," Elliot said, resigned.

"Most of our servers are offline."

Elliot rubbed his forehead. Oscar grinned behind him, and Jeff grinned back. The wrong move. Elliot got that look in his eye.

Jeff explained the attack and Suzie's discoveries about its source.

"Moureaux again." Elliot got up, stood at the rail, and gazed at Table Mountain. "The money. And now the servers." He turned to glare at Jeff. "I want to move all network operations to the Firelink satellites. I don't care whether it's patchy for now. I'll call Mark and get the ball rolling. We can't expose ourselves like this. And Moureaux. Take her out, Jeff. I don't care how you do it, just take out her servers and shut down her business. And keep it shut down. I'll consider other ways to solve that problem permanently. You just focus on her business. Got it?"

Jeff's concerns ebbed as Elliot's attention shifted to the problem at hand, leaving behind his fixation on motivating the Seacave with innovative but painful methods. And anyway, shutting down a major competitor was all the motivation they needed. Nothing like a massive hackathon to cheer people up. And maybe they could snaffle up some more bitcoin wallets first, just to make Elliot happy.

CHAPTER FORTY-ONE
The Counterattack

LUDIVINE RECEIVED THE CALL ON Tuesday while having lunch with a friend in a small bistro on the Left Bank. She excused herself and stepped out to the sidewalk.

"It is bad, Ludivine," said Raoul, her deputy. "They have locked up 75 percent of our workstations and servers with ransomware."

"Clues?"

"To the hackers? Not yet. Raphaël is investigating. But it is obvious, is it not?"

"Perry."

"Only he possesses a hacker organization capable of launching such a massive attack against us, Ludivine. Apart from the Russians, the Chinese, the North Koreans, the British, and the Americans. But none of them have a motive. Perry has a motive."

Ludivine heard the implicit criticism. Raoul had been against helping Alec from the beginning. She couldn't tell him about the 1WeakLink deal because she'd kept it a secret ever since she'd placed AJ in the organization. She'd warned him of Ms. C's entering the fray but not of her NSA connections. It could be her, but much more likely, it was Perry.

Raoul did not believe the rewards of the DDoS attack outweighed the dangers. And he didn't trust Sasha. Had she made a mistake in trusting the Russian? Had she erred in ignoring Ms. C?

"I shall get to the root of the attacks, Raoul. Have the Romanians start our disaster recovery plan. Let me know if any other remediation is necessary."

"Leave no root unturned, Ludivine. These people are despicable, disrupting our business."

She made her excuses to her lunching friends and returned to her apartment. She called Sasha, but the phone rang and went to voicemail. Sasha was like a spider tending a web; he always answered his phone. His unavailability made Ludivine consider whether he might be behind the attack as a tool of Elliot Perry. She needed more information. So, she applied her digital forensics tools. After a brief root cause analysis, she turned to attribution. She fed the forensic data into her machine learning attribution model, which returned an 87.43% probability of attribution to the NSA.

The NSA had hacked her network. Not Sasha, not Elliot Perry. Jeff Morrow was not yet up to the task of delivering a comprehensive ransomware attack.

Machine-led attribution only takes you so far. Ludivine called a friend who was high in the French Gendarmerie national CyberGend network and felt her way through a forest of dark and slippery trees. There was no question of corruption, as her friend owed Ludivine quite a lot on their mutual balance sheet of information exchange. But asking direct questions was never the French way, nor was answering them. Ludivine inferred from the gendarmerie's vague replies to her questions that the NSA had no interest in her organization.

Ludivine poured a glass of Vouvray and let the subtle bubbles stimulate her thinking. The NSA had no interest, and yet the NSA had shut down her business. That could mean only one thing: Ms. C was undertaking a shaping operation before starting her blockchain campaign. Ms. C didn't want the competition getting in her way. If her major operations were at risk, she wanted the competition diminished, demoralized, or destroyed. Ms. C had already executed the theft of Elliot Perry's ill-gotten billions. And Ludivine's group had unwittingly helped her by its secret DDoS attack on Perry's servers. More shaping operations? How many billions was Ms. C after, and where might she get them?

Early in the evening, Ludivine's phone rang. It was a friend of hers in the National Police. Was there a rapid dissemination of information about the war between the security agencies? Her friend was in the *Sous-direction de la lutte contre la criminalité organisée et la délinquance financière*, the SDLCODF. Their focus was on criminal organizations and financial crime. Ludivine had been quite helpful to them in eliminating some of her more unpredictable competitors.

After a brief conversation, she put her phone down and frowned. Her friend had informed her of a contract on offer for her assassination. This was unacceptable. Hacking her network was one thing, but a hit? Only Elliot Perry would be crude enough to engage assassins. Other players of which she was unaware? But she *was* aware.

Ludivine canceled her dinner engagement, prepared and ate a quick meal, made sure her security system was functional, and went to bed to sleep on the problem.

The next morning, Ludivine called Raoul and informed him of developments, including the murder contract. Predictably, Raoul expressed outrage and a commitment to action. Laudable, but unnecessary.

"Let me handle this, Raoul," she said. "I may drop out of sight for a time, as we agreed. You should continue recovery, but do not retaliate. We cannot risk an escalation of this silly cyberwar. And you should take personal security seriously until I resolve the root problem. I will return when I have dealt with everything. Call Octave if you need to make contact."

She packed a few things into a travel bag along with her laptop. She put on her traveling clothes and her new Chelsea boots. Opening the safe concealed in her mantelpiece, she removed a wad of Euros, another wad of dollars, three prepaid cell phones, and her set of fake passports. She turned off her cell phone, extracted its SIM card, and put both in the safe. She called Octave and gave him the number of one phone, along with instructions to call only for the two people she trusted: Yuriko and Raoul.

Ludivine set up one of the burner phones with her tracking app, then checked it. Alec's location was in San Francisco. And Yuriko was there too.

Time to go. Fight or flight? California or Vietnam?

Ludivine smiled. She was a fighter.

CHAPTER FORTY-TWO
A Flanking Operation

ALEC HOLED UP IN HIS condo for a week, ordering in meals from food delivery apps. He divided his time between monitoring the efforts of Perry's team of hackers and building extensions to the 1WeakLink system.

The 1WeakLink WalletWalker tool came up trumps. Alec identified 346 wallets around the world that he could reliably say were Perry wallets. They'd already wormed their way into seventeen different blockchains. They had created a few wallets before stealing the 1WeakLink codebase. After, they really went to Chicago.

He used the ReverseGear tool to find the hacks the Perry people had done. Peter invented ReverseGear as a debugging tool, but Alec formalized it as a part of the security suite at AJ's urging.

Perry's most recent hacks originated from unknown servers using FireLink satellite anonymizers. He postponed work on those because hacking the FireLink network software would be tough. Firelock's people were serious about security. He wasn't ready for that yet. Ludivine would help there. But many earlier blockchain hacks often originated from botnets linked to Russian networks.

As he worked, Alec had two operations in mind. The first one was to empty a few of the Perry bitcoin and ether wallets into a series of wallets he'd created on obscure exchanges. He'd used the 1WeakLink GhostBuster tool to make those wallets even more obscure. The money would fund his work. He'd use some techniques AJ had taught him to launder the money beyond the reach of Perry and his minions.

The second operation was pure revenge for AJ's murder. He coded a new tool to add to the 1WeakLink suite: the Whistleblower tool. It walked the chains using ReverseGear, then notified all the chain full-nodes about the hack. But exposing the toolset would infuriate Crispin and the NSA. So, he'd wait to deploy it until he and Ludivine had flipped the kill switch on the other copies of the 1WeakLink system. He couldn't do that himself because he didn't have the hacking experience to get into the FireLink servers running the 1WeakLink tools.

By Wednesday, he'd finished testing the tools and felt ready to bring Ludivine in. She would help hack FireLink and the other servers for the kill switch attack. He called her phone, but it was out of service. He then called Octave, but Octave didn't answer.

What was going on?

Elliot Perry, simmering, thrust open the hatch to the Seacave. Number One, he didn't like being summoned by employees. He liked to summon. Number Two, he had been napping. Number Three, he couldn't tolerate the very idea of what Jeff had told him: another theft of their hard-earned bitcoins. Any of which would have made him unhappy, but the combination enraged him.

"Well?" he barked when he came to a stop next to Jeff's workstation.

Jeff, who had followed his progress across the expansive space with a nervous grin, got up.

"Come on, boss, let me show you something." He pulled the unwilling master of the *Mugwump* over to another workstation behind the big wine racks. "Hey, Suze, got a minute?"

"Stop callin' me that, mate! You—" said Susan, who then noticed Elliot in the gloom behind Jeff and stopped in confusion.

"OK, Suze. Just show the boss here whatcha found," said Jeff. "You'll love this,' he told Elliot.

"Well?" said Elliot to Susan, who was frozen, hands above her keyboard. Elliot hadn't spoken much with Susan, but the earlier job she'd done had impressed him.

"Erm…OK, Mr. Perry, erm, Elliot. Sorry." Susan's hands unfroze, and she typed. "Here."

"Sit there, boss, on the seat next to her, so you can see the monitor," Jeff said helpfully.

Elliot usually preferred to stand, looming with his 6-foot-2-inches over the programmers, but he couldn't see the screen properly with this setup. He found he still loomed over the woman next to him. There was a large network graph with thousands of lines and clusters of dots outlined in biggish red circles. "What am I seeing, Susan?"

"Our targeted blockchains, Elliot. Cheers!" Susan jabbed a finger at a pulsing red circle. "That's the bugger—erm, person, who's nicking everything. Them lot ain't the same scallies what nicked the last batch o' bitcoins."

"Ah. So now we have multiple enemies, all stealing from us." Elliot grimaced. "Good work, Susan."

"Me and Mahmoud, we got all this Net data from our vendor in Russia, then chucked it into the machine learning system and—"

"I don't need technical details, Susan," said Elliot calmly. "Who? Who is it?"

"Well, we don't exactly cotton who he is. He's not identifiable from owt we've found, but he's in San Francisco, at a dead massive condo palace. But, Mr. Elliot, erm, Elliot, the knobhead's defo usin' the 1WeakLink package!" Susan smiled in triumph. "No bleedin' doubt about it, mate! Erm, Elliott."

"Well," Elliot said. "Jeff, who do we know in San Francisco that has access to that package and would want to steal our money?"

"Gotta be Chenais," said Jeff, giving the name a Texas pronunciation. "Location, means, motive, and opportunity."

"Chenais," agreed Elliot softly. "He's a dead man."

CHAPTER FORTY-THREE
The Water Tower

Ludivine emerged from the all-nighter from the East Coast into a very gray San Francisco day. She had only the leather messenger bag with her laptop and essentials. Her driver met her outside the security area and escorted her to the waiting limousine. She'd arranged for personal transportation from a JFK VIP lounge.

"Your requested items are on the back seat, Ms. Moureaux," said the driver as he opened the door for her. She changed into her leathers during the fifteen-minute drive up I-280 and packed her traveling clothes in the small backpack she had asked for. She complimented the driver on the fit. A Latino with a poker face, he just nodded.

The driver dropped her off at the Harley-Davidson rental shop on Valencia Street, where an attendant was more than happy to show her the details of the beast she'd rented. She thanked him, put on her black helmet, and roared away from the agency. The day had cleared overhead to a bright blue sky.

She met Yuriko Nakamura at a small, out-of-the-way restaurant that Yuriko knew on the border between the Mission and SOMA. The text exchange had been on the cool side; Ludivine suspected Yuriko was upset that Ludivine had revealed their relationship to Alec. But between the first and second kiss of *la bise*, she diagnosed a much deeper anxiety in her friend.

They ordered a light lunch and talked of Paris and their acquaintances there, avoiding the darkness within. The waiter placed several small plates in front of them, and they ate while the conversation turned to business. Yuriko shared all the details of her dealings with Alec and Ms. C with Ludivine. Ludivine listened as Yuriko told her the story of her heartbreaking betrayal by the woman she had fallen in love with. And the resulting blackmail.

As Yuriko finished her story, Ludivine ate a Kalamata olive, ejected the pit into her fist and deposited it in a bowl. She said cooly, "I expected trouble from the NSA, Yuriko. I put you in place at that little startup precisely to handle that trouble. You have done so. It came at a high price for you. I am sorry, but I am satisfied. I have what I wanted: the iWeak-Link code."

"Yes, all right." Yuriko pushed out a breath, her shoulders tense and a frown forming. "But, Ludivine, don't you realize what this means? This bitch from the NSA, on her own account—she knows everything. She'll use it against Alec, too. And she'll certainly use the tools against you. She's a competitor."

Ludivine smiled and tilted her head. "Yuriko. Really? Do you believe me to be a fool? I anticipated all of this."

Confused, Yuriko asked, "Then why are you here? Talking to me about this?"

"Because, *ma chérie,* M. Elliot Perry has issued a contract for my assassination."

Yuriko gasped, speechless.

Ludivine continued, "And this woman, she is as much a competitor of M. Perry as I am. She has her uses for me and is best left to her exploits. M. Perry will find it difficult to defeat her attacks, as they will use the full force of the NSA. I assure you, our organization can weather this storm without undue damage to our operations. But I am now underground for a time, you understand? I have come to San Francisco to find Alec, to help him with his tasks, and to determine if he has betrayed us. I see you to help you through this contretemps. That is important to me as well."

Yuriko shook her head, still confused.

Ludivine asked, "What do you want to do now, Yuriko? The position at your company is perfectly viable as long as Ms. C does not reveal your perfidy to—what is his name? Your CEO?"

"Crispin. Crispin Bannon."

"Ah, yes. M. Bannon. You must know by now that he, too, is an NSA agent?"

Yuriko stared at Ludivine. "Of course he is. Why not? Ludivine, you make me feel like a child in one of those fairy tales with wolves, poison apples, and witches at every turn."

"These stories reflect the reality of our business, *ma chérie*."

"I'm not sure I signed up for all this. Yes, I'll hang on at 1WeakLink, for now. Ludivine, I have missed you, missed our relationship, but…" Yuriko looked at Ludivine with sad eyes.

"I appreciated it, and you, very much. You know my failings in that regard, *ma chérie*."

"But Ludivine, Alec also said that you, I don't know, tricked him into bringing AJ into the company. Without telling me."

"Not every detail of an operation needs telling, Yuriko."

"Operation. Is that the only—"

"My dear Yuriko." She reached out and took the other woman's hand. "There is no need to be upset. This is just my way. I need you for the deal; I needed AJ for the code. Alec's falling in love with her was unexpected but not unrewarding. Especially now. Unless the man has betrayed me, of course."

Yuriko, shocked, said, "No! No. He was anxious about you, about getting the code to you. He hates the NSA. But, Ludivine. Was AJ—part of your harem?"

Ludivine grinned. "A charming metaphor. But no; AJ felt only friendship for women. I sensed tangles there and left her alone."

Yuriko looked relieved. "Yes, she had issues. With men and marriage. We talked, a little. I'm still sad about her death."

"So am I, *ma chérie*. And I will do something about it, have no fear." Ludivine finished her glass of wine. "I think, now, we must part for a time. I will find Alec and do what is necessary. Do you have his current address?"

Yuriko provided Alec's condo address on Mission Street. The women stood and embraced.

"I love you, Ludivine. But you're far more than I can handle."

"I know, *ma chérie*. I know. *Au revoir.*" A soft kiss, and Yuriko was gone.

The doorbell awoke Alec from a deep, satisfying sleep in his trashed bedroom at 3 p.m. Night and day had merged as he concentrated fully on his coding. He had blocked the sun by lowering his blinds early in the week. As he lay in bed in the dim room, he wondered hazily whether he was slowly becoming a vampire.

The doorbell rang again. The hall bell, not the building buzz. Then came knocking. At the front door.

Worrying about security systems, Alec threw on a shirt and pants and stepped barefoot to the front door, carefully avoiding the obstacles on the floor. He said, "Who's there?"

"Manager," came the door-muffled response.

George? He must have some news about the repairs or the security system. Alec shot the deadbolt and opened the door, saying, "George, what's—"

The two men who rushed in were not George. They wore homemade masks, and they were big and in a hurry. One punched Alec in the head, dropping him like a rock. Three minutes later, Alec stumbled down the hall after seeing his new laptop unceremoniously stuffed into a duffel bag along with his phone, wallet, and passport. The blow was wearing off, but he was dazed. He still wore no shoes. The men gripped his arms as they pulled him along. They took him to the service elevator at the rear of the building.

The NSA had struck back, he thought dully. What am I going to do now?

* * *

Ludivine parked the Harley on the street, locking it to a bike loop. She looked up at the tall condo tower and smiled, anticipating meeting Alec once again. She didn't call or text him; better to leave her appearance here as a surprise. You get more information that way. She navigated the communications panel at the door; no response from Alec's condo. She looked at her phone: 3:15 p.m. Not likely to be at lunch, so perhaps on an errand. This was an opportunity. She fished out a small black box from her bag and opened the building door, then took an elevator to Alec's floor. She knocked lightly on his door, no response. She then put on her black face mask and used the box again to open the combination lock on that door.

She walked into a scene of devastation. Not one thing in the condo was in its proper place. She pulled down her mask and sniffed; no smell of death, though there were touches of decay. She quickly looked through all the rooms. A table in one room was upright and clear with only a wireless keyboard on it. The big monitor lay shattered on the floor nearby.

The situation did not look good. Where was Alec?

Ludivine brought up the tracker app on her phone. Alec's phone was on the move. She watched as the small dot moved onto US-101 South.

Her face grim, Ludivine left the mess behind and pushed the Harley to its limit, cutting across traffic on Mission Street to Fourth and to the freeway south.

This time the transport was a car, a beat-up old Honda Accord. Two people in front, two in back, and Alec between them. No hood this time, and they hadn't tied his hands. The masked men on either side of him had guns out and resting casually on their knees, ready for use. The duffel bag with his laptop was on the floor beneath his feet.

This didn't really look like the NSA. Ratty Hondas weren't their style, and the guns didn't look like military issue. Neither did the tee-shirts and jeans.

The car headed south on US-101, Hospital Curve. The driver stayed under the speed limit, no risk of being stopped. After what seemed like hours but was just minutes, the car took the Paul Avenue exit and headed west across Visitacion Valley. Suddenly, they were among trees. Alec wasn't familiar with this area. A park? A big one. McLaren, yes, that was it. The road twisted around and headed up a hill. The car pulled into a parking lot and parked.

"End of the line, buddy," said the man on his right. He opened the door and got out, then pulled Alec out. The second man emerged from the other side and came around to again grip Alec's arm.

"Where—"

"Shut up," said one man, tapping Alec lightly on the side of the head with his gun.

"Tell me what you want," said Alec.

"I want you to shut up," said the man, tapping harder.

The men pulled Alec across the road to a blocked off asphalt path, then headed up the path into some trees. They emerged into a clearing with a huge, blue water tower. They pulled Alec around to the back of the tower, which looked out northwards over all of the City.

"Nice view," said one man. "Yeah," replied the other. He nudged Alec. "You like the view, dude?"

"Why—"

"'Cause it's the last thing you're gonna see." The man laughed, a hiccuping sound that wasn't completely rational. Not surprising. Not NSA.

The other man said, "Hold him." The first man put his gun in his pocket, then took Alec's wrists and twisted them behind his back. The other man walked around in front of Alec and smiled. "Time to go. Mr. Perry says hello and goodbye." The first man forced Alec to kneel.

Alec heard a roaring in his ears. Is this what everyone hears before they die? Blood rushing around. Until it stopped?

Ludivine caught up with Alec on 101-South. She'd stuck her phone in a holder the rental agency had thoughtfully supplied. She followed the dot until it merged with her location. A blue Honda. The car worked its way over to the right and exited at one of the last exits in the City. Ludivine throttled back and followed at a distance. The car went straight down a city street and entered a big park. She almost lost it in the twists and turns in the trees but saw it turn into a parking lot and stop. She eased the bike to the side of the road, pushed up her helmet visor, and watched.

Two men got out of the car and pulled a third man out. Alec. He had bare feet and no jacket. The men dragged him across the road and up a path.

Ludivine looked around. The scene was not right for an interrogation or a friendly chat. It was lonely and isolated. Alec was clearly in trouble. Without him, all her efforts would be for naught. But—and her lips curled into a smile—this was going to be fun, in any case.

She slipped off the big bike and picked up a fallen branch about three feet long and three inches in diameter. She stripped off some side twigs and hefted it. Just right. She got back on the bike and shut her visor. She kicked the beast into action and roared full-throttle toward where Alec had disappeared. She twisted the bike around the barrier to the path and roared up it. She came around a bend and saw a huge blue water tower—but no sign of Alec. She realized they'd taken him around the back. She accelerated to the right and took the curve at high speed.

Alec was kneeling, and one of the men was bringing a gun to bear. Ludivine gripped the branch and opened the throttle. The man's head jerked toward her, and the gun moved, but far too slowly as she blasted past him holding the branch at head level. The man cartwheeled as the branch nearly took off his head.

Ludivine skidded into a reverse turn and roared back toward Alec. The man holding him had released him and struggled with something in a pocket. A gun, probably. The branch had broken. She discarded it and aimed directly at the man. He looked up, face grimacing, just as the big Harley crashed into him and threw him up against the water tower fence. He fell to the ground.

Ludivine recovered and turned again. Alec had stood up. She came up beside him and raised her visor.

"Get on, you idiot! Behind me."

Alec jumped up behind her, pillion.

"Hold on," she said.

He did, but also said, "Get the bag from the back seat of their car. Laptop."

She snapped down her visor and throttled up the bike. Around the tower and down the path, where she saw two men with guns slowly walking up.

"Hold! On!" She screamed it as loudly as she could and hoped for the best. She took the bike into an uncontrolled slide on the asphalt path, wheels first, at full speed. It wouldn't do Alec any good, but if those men had their chance, the result would be worse. She felt her leg in its leather case scraping along the ground as the big machine slid at high speed wheels first into the two men, knocking them away. She thought she heard a shot, but felt nothing other than the grinding of the asphalt through her leathers. As the bike scraped to a stop, she pushed with one leg and got it upright, using what was left of the momentum. Full throttle again. She pulled the front wheel up and flew over the rocks that blocked the side of the path from the road. She crossed the road and pulled up at the mens' Honda, doors all ajar. Her passenger was still aboard, arms encircling her in a death grip.

She said, "Get the bag!"

The arms let go, and Alec eased off the back of the bike and retrieved the bag from the car. His leg was a mess of tattered cloth and blood. But it carried him. Ludivine dismounted and walked around to the front of the Honda. She took out a small Beretta, provided at the same time as her leathers, and put three bullets through the radiator. She then walked around the car and put a bullet into each tire. She put away the gun and remounted. Alec mounted behind her, the bag between her back and his chest. She throttled up and headed back the way she'd come.

CHAPTER FORTY-FOUR
Recovery

THE HARLEY TOOK ABOUT HALF an hour to cover the hills between McLaren Park and the Presidio. Ludivine had Alec shout directions to her and keep an eye out behind for followers. They detoured into SOMA to buy another motorcycle helmet at Alec's request, and Ludivine checked his leg. Scraped up and oozing blood, but nothing that required a tourniquet, a skin transplant, or immediate amputation. He'd need bandaging and sympathy soon, though.

The bike wound through the heavily forested park and down through the old Army base to the historical Fort Point under the Golden Gate Bridge.

They dismounted, and Alec limped around a little but pronounced himself ready for anything. Ludivine stroked his cheek and turned to look at the view of the Bridge and the Marin hills.

Speaking in French, she said, "I do not wish to seem callous, *mon ami*, but we need to disappear for a few days. I fear that means we cannot check into a luxury hotel and get you medical treatment at a local A&E department."

Alec nodded. "OK. We'll have to camp out. There's a state park over there," he pointed to the Marin shore to the north. "China Camp. Isolated. It needs reservations, but I know of a secluded spot where we can camp for a few days and figure out what to do. Private land that nobody checks. Another option, we could just join one of the tent cities in San Francisco. Either way, we need a tent and sleeping bags. And some new pants for me. And first aid supplies."

Ludivine replied with a smile, "I have never slept rough in Paris, *mon ami*, and have no intention of doing so in this fine city of yours. We will call it camping and make do, no?"

"Yes, we'll make do. Er, Ludivine," said Alec, then stopped.

Ludivine smiled, walked over, and embraced Alec. "No thanks are necessary, my friend. Just the code. I hope you understand this is nothing personal. I am simply protecting my investment from dirty thieves and murderers."

"We must buy two tents, then?" Alec smiled.

"I think not, my friend. All this excitement has stirred my blood. Let us agree that we have two nights away from the world, and we may indulge ourselves. After that, we must end the threat to our continued business enterprise. Then, the future. Whatever presents itself." She embraced Alec and kissed him.

"Say, lady," a voice came in English, "Your friend's bleeding. And he ain't got any shoes. Do you need help?"

"*Merci, monsieur*," she responded to the tourist. "He bleeds quite often now. We must attend to it. And to the shoes." She grinned and mounted the Harley. Alec joined her, and she throttled up the bike into a roar, revved several times, then squealed off up the hill, leaving the tourists to their view.

On their second day at China Camp, Alec and Ludivine strolled hand in hand along the beach, taking in the breathtaking views of the East Bay and San Francisco skylines. Alec couldn't help but smile. His leg scrapes were healing beneath Ludivine's competent bandage, and the sandals acquired from a Tiburon shop at great expense were super comfortable. Two software gurus on vacation. He had been on vacation last in 2015, when his then boss in a Menlo Park startup forced everyone to take their vacation days. "Tax reasons," he said, donning his CEO smile. Alec called a recruiter the next day, from the beach in Cancun. "Tax reasons" usually meant "we've run out of money."

After two nights camping, during which Ludivine asked him about his life, Alec realized he had learned nearly nothing of Ludivine's life other than that her mother raised her in a *banlieue* near Paris. She'd told him she'd learned from her mother how to bandage wounds after gang battles. Her mother had learned by bandaging wounded Viet Cong. He remained unaware of the sources of her wealth or the structure of her organization. But they *had* compared notes on software development. Alec, who had been formally educated and systematically exposed to all kinds of system and network programming, had the edge. Ludivine smiled enigmatically and, after kissing him, said, "I hire what I need, *mon ami*. I learn what I must and leave the boring parts to others."

Alec expressed his concern about boring her. She laughed and made a playful remark about hiring him, leading to a charming and intimate exchange of ideas and other things.

Ludivine's actions spoke louder than her evasive answers. She knew more than she let on. Alec's knowledge had excited AJ, in comparison, and AJ had loved their complementary skill sets. Two software nerds melding into one magic whole. It didn't feel that way with Ludivine, but she had other qualities. One thing was clear: they shared a common poor opinion of power structures that made people's lives hell. And of abductions and assassinations. Particularly their own.

Having reached the beach's end, they turned back. Ludivine gave his hand a gentle squeeze, and warmth spread through him. They faced the sun now, but the warmth came from within. He opened his mouth to comment on it when Ludivine's phone rang. She drew it from her pocket and answered. Alec heard only polite acknowledgments, but as he watched Ludivine's face, he saw her mask descend: it was business.

She put the phone back in her pocket, pursing her lips and studying her feet as they walked.

"Ludivine?" asked Alec in a soft voice.

She brushed her hair back over her shoulder and smiled. "Well, *mon ami*, our idyllic holiday has ended. We must turn our thoughts from pleasure to war."

"And what does that mean?"

"We must travel to a place called Seven Oaks, near a military installation called Fort Meade in your state of Maryland."

"The NSA? Why Seven Oaks?"

"It is the domicile of a lovely woman named Donna Hunt. You may know her better as Ms. C."

"Who was on the phone?" Alec did indeed know Ms. C, and he changed the subject to deflect his anger. As far as he was concerned, Ms. Hunt courted trouble.

"My second in command, Raoul. He fixed our server problems and, as a bonus, uncovered their source—a house in that town. Mme. Hunt pays the property taxes on that house. We shall pay her a visit. Tomorrow."

Ludivine slid on her sunglasses and extended a hand, and Alec took it as they walked back to their camp.

The white-painted door of the red-brick Colonial house in Seven Oaks remained resolutely shut. Alec knocked again and listened. Nothing, not a sound. Nothing stirred in the tree-lined street on a Sunday afternoon.

"You're sure this is the right address?" he asked Ludivine.

She sent him a warm smile and took out a small black box. She applied it to the digital door lock, which clicked. "You first," she said, stepping aside.

Alec shook his head, moved to the other side of the door, and reached out to open it. The latch clicked as the door swung open.

"I've got a gun! I'll shoot!"

Alec recognized the familiar squeaky voice and almost stepped into the line of fire, but Ludivine motioned for him to stand back. She called out, "We just want to talk, Mme. Hunt. You are in no danger that is not of your own making."

"Who are you?" the voice squeaked.

"Who we are is irrelevant, Mme. Hunt. If you want your superiors at Fort Meade to comprehend the full scope of your activities, we would be happy to oblige. But surely you do not want that."

"You're that Moureaux woman!"

"I do have the honor to bear that name, yes."

"And who's with you, some fucking assassin?"

Alec spoke up. "Not the last time I checked myself, Ms. C. Just a peace-loving, out-of-work software developer." Understanding Ludivine's desire for nonviolent negotiation, Alec held back his anger at the NSA agent who had upended his life.

"Alec. Of course. Alec Chenais."

"And there is our driver," Ludivine said. "At the curb, anxiously awaiting our return and ready to call the local police should it prove necessary." She smiled at Alec. "He must be getting more nervous as we stand here talking to an open door. Please, Mme. Hunt, we mean you no harm."

"How did you learn my name?"

"Really, Mme. Hunt. Do you take us for fools?" Ludivine tapped a foot. "We do not have all day. We wish to negotiate terms."

"Terms? What terms?"

"An end to your cyberattacks on my network and an alliance, should you be amenable. I am not greedy, and there is more than enough plunder to go around." Ludivine pushed her hair back over her shoulder and frowned. "May we enter, please?"

Silence. Then a squeak. "OK. But keep your hands where I can see them! Or I'll shoot."

Ludivine smiled and strode into the house. Alec scrambled after her.

"You didn't have to hit me so hard," Ms. C complained.

"Yes. I did." Ludivine looked over the wines in the little wine rack on Ms. C's kitchen counter. She put the Glock she'd taken from Ms. C's numb hand on the counter and moved a few bottles around, examining the labels. "You have terrible taste in wine, Mme. Hunt."

"OK, I get it. I'm shit, you're in charge, and I'm dead meat. What the hell do you want?"

Ludivine sighed, pulled out a bottle of red wine, opened the screw top, and poured a glass. She looked at Alec, who shook his head. He needed that head clear if he was going to figure out what the hell was going on.

Ludivine sipped and grimaced, then set the wine glass down next to the gun. She leaned against the counter, crossed her arms, and said, "We want you to help us stop Elliot Perry."

Ms. C's mouth dropped open. "How?" she asked sharply.

"I am quite certain that your agency has ways of tapping into the Firelink network. I want you to use those tools to get me into their servers so I can set the kill switch on their 1WeakLink software. There; am I going too fast for you?"

Alec smiled as he realized the extent of Ludivine's plans. She was turning one enemy into a double agent against another enemy.

Ms. C, who was sitting on her couch massaging the arm Ludivine had assaulted, shook her head. "I can't do that. They'd put me in jail for life."

"Whereas if you do not, and we explain your actions to them, they will put you in jail for life. Surely you are intelligent enough to use the software without revealing yourself to your employer?"

Ms. C, caught between Ludivine's rock and the NSA's hard place, had a defiant look on her face. "Why should I help you? Short of outright blackmail, that is."

"Why not just leave it at the blackmail? But I will offer you more. I have seen your skills and your value. You would be an excellent addition to my organization. And that means rewards. A lot of money, though little prestige. We do not court prestige. It will not help your career as a low-level NSA agent, but it will make that career irrelevant. I can assure you of excellent income and security." Ludivine's lips curled. "Unless you are overly attached to the idea of becoming a cyber warlord. Like Elliot Perry? That desire for strength is his weakness. Why make it yours?"

"You want me to be a double agent? Betray the U.S., betray the NSA?"

"That's right. I *knew* you were intelligent."

"I took an oath."

Ludivine sighed. "That water has passed far from the bridge and out to sea, Mme. Hunt. I remind you of the blackmail."

Ludivine poured two glasses of wine and handed one to Ms. C and the other to Alec.

"Now, I insist we toast to our partnership. *À votre santé!*" She offered the glass, and Alec clinked his with hers. Ms. C pursed her lips, hesitated, then did the same.

CHAPTER FORTY-FIVE
Retribution

"Where did you find those fools, Tim?" Elliot felt the usual signs of serious anger. His pulse quickened and his body tensed, the heat flushing his face. And a growing desire to punch the bulkhead, which would be futile, since it was solid steel. He turned away from the crewman manning the comms center and lowered his voice. But Steve wouldn't hear much over the noise of the increasing gale force winds blowing from the Indian Ocean at the *Mugwump*.

"Tim, this is important."

"Sure, Elliot. But I have limited contacts in, well, organized crime. Apart from your accountants."

"Leave the jokes at home, Tim. Your stand-up skills are crap. So are your operations skills."

"I'm a finance guy and a lawyer, Elliot. Not a *consigliere*. Now calm down and let's strategize. I never should have tried this. It's stupid. And Elliot: it's 10:30 p.m. here and I've had a terrible day."

"You know what, Tim?" Elliot stopped himself and breathed for a few seconds. "You know what? You're right. This is stupid. Letting people steal from me is even dumber. Why? Because they'll do it again."

"Elliot, have you learned nothing in the last twenty years? The world is full of thieves. Thieves rob banks because that's where the money is. Except that you've got more money than any bank. So, guess what? You're a target. Get used to it. And build better defenses. If Chenais can steal millions from you, imagine what governments could do. And *they have the same software,* Elliot. Maybe even better software."

Tim was right, unfortunately. He usually was, except when it came to hiring idiot hit men. Forgive and forget, take the advice, and move on. Stay ahead of the game. Get the Seacave working on new tech. A moonshot. Well, fuck all that.

"You're fired, Tim. I'll get the lawyers to work out a good severance package. Have a nice night."

Saves a trip to the West Coast, anyway.

He said, "Steve, get me Varoozh Paracha." Varoozh would tie off all the loose ends. He'd attend to both Chenais and the Moureaux woman. Should have gone to him first.

Ludivine luxuriated in the hot stream of water that washed the sand and the heat of love from her body. Was it the right choice to take Alec with her on her journey of revenge? Two days in Marin's wilderness convinced her that his core was changing into something resolute and committed. To a new life, a new purpose. A purpose like hers. And she could use his mind and skills to great advantage. She had found pleasure in his body and the way he used it. As long as he was not boring, he would be useful.

She dried herself and walked naked into the suite's central room. The resort in Tamarindo, Costa Rica, was ideal for the kind of operation she wanted. It had cost a lot to convince the reluctant authorities to let them into the country, given the COVID lockdown, but money goes a long way in Central America. No one would suspect she was here. The choice was hers - business or pleasure. Alec was busy at the suite's dining table with his laptop. The sliding glass door was open, letting in the sounds of the Pacific surf from the crystalline beach outside their building.

She paused at the table with its array of technology. They'd purchased ten more burner phones and three laptops, along with some unique equipment she'd had Raoul send over from Paris.

Raoul. He should have had some results by now.

She picked up one of the new phones and dialed.

"*Bonsoir,* Raoul. Any news?" she asked.

"It just arrived, Ludivine. RT, the Russian news channel. The FSB has detained Alexandr Dmitrovich Krupin, a Moscow oligarch, for unspecified crimes against the state."

"Poor Sasha, I wonder what he has done. It must have been something terrible." She knew what he'd done to her, but she didn't really care what Raoul had led the FSB to believe he'd done to Putin. Disinformation went both ways. "*Très bien,* Raoul. Now we can start the Serbian campaign. Is everything prepared?"

"Yes. When can we expect your return? Everyone is anxious."

"How sweet. But I am enjoying myself, relaxing in the sun, out of touch. I fear I must remain so until I complete my current project. I have faith in you and the others to do what is needed. *Vous comprenez?*"

"*Bien sûr,* Ludivine. *Prends soin de toi.*"

"I always do take care, *mon ami.*" She hung up.

Two arms encircled her, hands on her breasts, and lips kissed her neck. "What's the news, Ludivine? Something about Sasha? Who's he?" Alec asked.

"Not now. We have work to do." To divert Alec's attention, she turned and returned the kiss with interest.

"The *Mugwump* is a state-of-the-art 222-meter mega-yacht built at the Benetti shipyard in Livorno. I've hacked into the Benetti information systems with a phishing attack and found the system architecture documentation." The squeaky voice of Ms. C on the phone sounded triumphant, even though getting system docs wasn't exactly a major coup. Ludivine sat up in bed in the Tamarindo hotel and turned on the reading lamp. Alec stirred beside her and opened his eyes.

"And…?"

"And the ship's fully automated. They need a bridge crew to push the on button and enter the destination, and the ship does everything else."

"What makes you confident you're in the right place?"

"I checked the satellites and correlated its position. The *Mugwump's* in the Indian Ocean, heading for Singapore. I downloaded its current navigational data stream. The system is executing automated evasive maneuvers to avoid Typhoon Bangoyo."

"What about getting into the automation?" she asked.

"We have a backdoor into the Firelink network. I've isolated the IP address translation inside the layers of firewalls to reach the ship's central computer. Their system is not up to date. I can get in with an NSA zero-day."

"I would very much like to shell into the ship through your system, Mme. Hunt."

"No names! I thought I'd made that clear! And I can't let you do that, it's too dangerous for me. Just tell me what you want, and I'll—"

"We've had this conversation, *madame*. Danger is part of your job now, unless you want to take an extended holiday at one of your federal prisons. Besides, you do not want the responsibility of what I have to do on that ship, no? Now, the shell?"

After a long pause, Ms. C cleared her throat and said, "Damn you. I'll send you the relevant access information through the Tor drop."

Ludivine thanked her politely and disconnected. Alec, now awake and listening, looked curious. She leaned over and kissed him. "I must work now, *mon ami*. Not enough sleep, but work always comes before sleep. And sex," she said, pushing Alec back into the bed as he tried to embrace her. "Go back to sleep and leave me be."

Ludivine picked up her phone and made a call. She said, "Susan, this is Ludivine. Please call me as soon as possible at the number we agreed upon. It is the moment to grasp our destinies. I hope to hear from you soon."

"Who's Susan? That was voicemail?" asked Alec, leaning on his elbow.

"A friend. A very helpful one. Now go back to sleep, *mon chér*. I have work to do."

* * *

Billionaire's Yacht Lost in Indian Ocean Typhoon, All Aboard Presumed Dead

San Francisco Chronicle, July 28, 2020

GRAND BAIE, Mauritius (AP) - Billionaire Elliot Perry's 222-meter mega-yacht "Mugwump" was lost in a typhoon in the Indian Ocean early Monday, with all crew and passengers presumed dead.

The yacht sent distress signals as Typhoon Bangoyo hit. Despite rescue efforts, no survivors have been found. Authorities suspended the search Tuesday because of the ongoing storm.

Passengers included Perry, his partner Oscar White, and several employees of Perry Capital, Perry's private equity firm.

The incident has shocked Silicon Valley, where Perry was a well-known private equity investor in several major technology startups. An official not authorized to speak on the record confirmed there is little hope of survival in such a storm and that no distress beacons have been detected.

An investigation into the yacht's voyage has begun, focusing on why it sailed into the storm despite the safety protocols of its automated navigation system. The MarineTraffic website reported that the vessel headed directly into the typhoon, contradicting its onboard safety measures.

The tragedy highlights the dangers of severe weather at sea, even for technologically advanced ships.

Ludivine stretched herself out on her beach towel, face down, to dry in the sun. The swim had been delightful, with clear water, gentle waves, and no storm on the horizon. She slid on her sunglasses and folded her arms under her head, the warmth spreading across her back and legs.

"Ludivine? Ludivine." Alec had joined her. She twisted her neck and looked up at him. He wore his swimsuit and beach sandals. His lips were a thin line, and he stood hovering over her, looking like his world was ending.

"What is it, *mon ami?*" She turned over and elevated herself on one elbow, looking at him quizzically.

"What did you do?"

"I am sorry, Alec. I do not comprehend the question."

"The *Mugwump*, Ludivine. What did you do? I just read a news article in the *Chronicle* that said it's sunk with all hands in a typhoon."

"I hoped for such an event after I locked their automated navigation system, *mon ami*. What is your concern?"

Alec crouched down, squatting on the sand. Swallowing twice, his face paled as he gazed into her eyes. "You were…you…there were over a hundred people on that ship! Ludivine. You didn't, you weren't responsible."

"I was, *mon ami*. And so?"

Sitting on his heels, Alec glanced at the sea and the hotel. Then back at her. "You really feel nothing, do you? About killing a hundred people?"

"It seemed an opportunity too good to ignore, *mon ami*. Mme. Hunt opened a door for me, and I went through it. I have no regrets. And M. Elliot Perry is no longer a problem for us."

"I can't…I won't…" Alec rose to his feet and looked down at her, shaking his head. He froze, mouth open. "Sasha. Who is he?"

"Sasha is a Russian oligarch who provides many services to the dark Web, including my organization. Or did until recently."

"What did you do? What was that phone call about?"

Ludivine decided it was time to be blunt. "We discovered Sasha had betrayed us by working with M. Perry, Alec. My organization denounced him to the Russian FSB with disinformation that made it appear he was disloyal to the Russian president. Russians do not react well to disloyalty, and they detained him. We will not hear from him again."

Another name popped into Alec's head. "Who is Susan?"

Ludivine shook her head with a down-turned mouth. "Now there, *mon ami,* you have me. Susan was an old friend, a lover, and I placed her aboard the *Mugwump* as an agent, as I placed Yuriko in your company. I regret I had to sacrifice Susan. She was an excellent agent and a friend."

Alec breathed and asked shakily, "Why didn't you tell me? About all this?"

"I needed you focused on your work with the blockchain software, *mon ami*. And I did not need your particular software skills for these tasks. You did not need to know."

"I see." Alec's mouth resumed its thin line, his eyes narrowed into a frown. He took a deep breath, hesitating, then said, "Ludivine, this is too much for me. You can't go around the world killing people or handing them over to torturers. You just can't."

"These people, Alec, are mostly no loss. One must be realistic and resolute in one's approach to one's enemies, even at the sacrifice of friends. I would prefer a less drastic way to end a conflict, but one must avail oneself of opportunities such as this. Don't you agree?"

"No, I *don't* agree." Alec stood up, clearly upset. "Look, Ludivine. I'm responsible. I'm an accomplice! We need to talk about this."

"Not just now, *mon ami,* you are much too agitated. Why not go for a swim, work out your feelings with the physical activity, then we can lunch and discuss these matters rationally, no? Please. Go for a swim."

Alec took another deep breath and stomped off toward the water, shedding his sandals on the way. He dove into the surf and swam away.

Ludivine sat up on her beach towel and wrapped her arms around her legs. Was Alec about to become boring? She would remind him of the events that had led them here, and that would calm his agitation. If not… well, wait and see. She lay back down on the towel, face up, and closed her eyes.

Alec stared at the sleeping woman next to him in the kingsize bed in their Tamarindo hotel room. The night was dark, and the cicadas had given up their deafening clatter a little after midnight. Dealing with the

Serbian blockchain project and going swimming the day before had left them very tired. And Ludivine seemed drained after their arguments about her methods of getting revenge. At lunch, she'd stayed cool in the face of Alec's condemnation, to the point where Alec realized she was impervious to arguments involving human rights.

Alec realized that, while his attraction to Ludivine was deep and compelling, he couldn't live with her view of the world. He looked at her, peacefully sleeping, the duvet covering her body. His mind spontaneously visualized that face, that body, and his stomach clenched with desire. The heat of the beach in Costa Rica, and the lovemaking that followed later in the evening. Holding her tight, her body taught and pressed against him, as they roared away from the water tank on her Harley. She'd saved his life. He looked away again and thought about Sasha in his prison colony in Siberia or wherever they'd exiled him. AJ, lying dead in the street in Islamabad. What was fantasy, and what was reality?

Alec had understood a lot about the world as he worked to create the blockchain software. He'd abandoned the blind idealism of effective altruism somewhere during his adventure in Pakistan. It could have been seeing Abdul dead, or Reema's total rejection of him. Or the cockroaches in the Islamabad jail cell. Or kneeling behind the water tower. It could even have been his last argument with his father. But he'd lost the naïve belief in an ideal world. And he had to accept responsibility for Ludivine's actions. He was there, he was involved, and it was his revenge, too.

But Ludivine had shown him the downside of swallowing the black pill. Yes, reality was awful. Sometimes, it might need an enormity to set things right. But she'd gone too far. He cared about that. She didn't.

That said, he needed her. She'd been *so* helpful with the Elliot Perry threat. He snorted softly so as not to wake her. Yeah, but she killed a hundred other people to eliminate it. And there was still Varoozh Paracha. He'd killed AJ and Abdul, and clearly the Pakistanis would do nothing about that. Somebody had to. *He* had to. Justice, or just revenge?

But Ludivine possessed the tools and contacts he needed to get it done. And there were still Perry's assassins out for their blood; Raoul had confirmed that with his Parisian sources. Ludivine was adept at keeping herself and Alec safe. Alec was not. So he had to coexist with her until the job was done. He had to get his own revenge while keeping her from perpetrating some kind of genocidal nightmare. She could help him find Paracha. He'd get her to hack Paracha's business, steal his money, make him hurt—financially, not physically.

All that would involve continuing their physical relationship for a time. The downside of that was that it would feed his addiction to her. He'd have to address it on his terms, when the time was right. When he returned to the real world, wherever that might be.

Ludivine stirred and opened her eyes. She smiled the seductive smile that drew him in. He smiled and took her hand. Warm as it was, it felt cold as ice..

CHAPTER FORTY-SIX
Varoozh

THE MORNING AFTER THEIR FIGHT, Alec and Ludivine had breakfast on the hotel terrace. The silence was a little awkward, and Alec fixated on the iguanas as they padded around looking for handouts.

Ludivine said, "You are subdued this morning, *mon cher*. Is there anything I can do to make you feel better? Perhaps a zip-line adventure or some windsurfing?" She grinned, knowing that these activities were not to Alec's taste.

Alec laughed. "We're not tourists, Ludivine. All right, I'll go easy on you. What's done is done, and, yes, I agree it had to be done. Please consult me before taking any drastic action in the future, okay? I'm sure you'll do as you see fit. But I'd like to know what we're getting into before it happens. Is that acceptable?"

"Of course. I count on you to find reasonable alternatives to my proposals and advice, *mon ami*."

Alec smiled, but it was not sincere. Ludivine would do exactly as she wished, of course, regardless of what he said. But he ached for action against Varoozh. He said, "So, next steps. What can we do about Varoozh Paracha? He's he's our only remaining quarry. He killed AJ and my friend Abdul. We must do something about him."

Ludivine replied, "M. Paracha, according to my research, is a very slippery individual. He is ingenious at hiding his illegal operations. My sources tell me he is deeply involved in financial crimes, but also that one might hire him for much darker operations. His record, as you've laid it out, shows that clearly. He is not afraid to kill as part of his business."

"Any idea of his whereabouts?"

"His home base is in Karachi, Pakistan. Unfortunately, because of the pandemic, my usual sources there are limited in their ability to investigate. According to phone logs, he was in Islamabad at the time of our friends' deaths. But since then, his phone has disappeared. He may have returned to Karachi, or he may be conducting business elsewhere in the world. I have instructed Raoul to monitor his firewalls and servers for activity, but so far, there is nothing."

Alec forked some *gallo pinto* and scrambled eggs into his mouth and swallowed, thinking about the problem. "Now that Perry's gone, Paracha may be in the market for more business. Have you tried just calling his business number?"

Ludivine raised her eyebrows. "So simple. There you go, proving your worth again." She took a burner phone from her pocket, looked up the number, and made the call. She waited, then hung up. "Voicemail. Perhaps, with the help of the voice simulator in the hotel room, we could leave a message that would interest him enough to show himself. I shall see what we can do to get some measure of justice."

Alec smiled and nodded. He was of two minds about Paracha. Formal justice was impossible, given his ability to corrupt the Pakistani police and courts. He'd wait to see what informal retribution Ludivine suggested. He could accept anything other than shooting him dead in the street.

Two days later, Alec woke up to bright sunshine. Beside him, Ludivine stirred, stretched, and then headed to the bathroom. Alec got up and got dressed.

He stood at the window and gazed at the beach. Not much progress so far. Ludivine had crafted a devious plan to get Paracha to reveal where he was. Using her voice simulator, she sent a message offering a generous sum of money for an undisclosed task that would intrigue Paracha. But now it was day three, and Paracha had not responded.

Ludivine had informed him the evening before that, because of the continuing threat from assassins, she had obtained a matched pair of Berettas along with ammunition. She had given Alec a short tutorial on how to use the gun and explained it was for personal safety, not aggression. The gun rested on the nightstand next to the bed, a reminder of his vulnerability. Remembering the Molotov cocktail, he decided never to use the gun. Alec hadn't asked whether the contract on him was still active, even with Perry's death. He didn't want to know.

Smiling, Ludivine had expressed her preference for AR-15s but considered them too conspicuous. "And the Berettas were hard enough to get," she had said.

"Do you do a lot of this, Ludivine?" Alec had asked, fingering the gun.

"I have never shot anyone, if that is what you are asking. My revenges take other paths, *mon chér*."

As it turned out, the precautions failed.

Varoozh Paracha walked into the bedroom holding a pistol fitted with a suppressor. Alec gave a desperate glance at the Beretta across the room; no chance.

"Alec, good to see you again," said Varoozh. "Where is—"

Ludivine came out of the bathroom wearing a white robe. "How nice to meet you at last, *monsieur*."

"It will be a brief acquaintance, Ms. Moureaux. Please join your companion. Over there," he waved the gun. "Ms. Moureaux—Mr. Perry, before his unfortunate demise, asked me to give you his regards before killing you."

Alec moved toward Ludivine and said, "Why did you have to kill her, Paracha? AJ. And Abdul. Why?" Could he get to the gun on the nightstand?

Varoozh laughed. "I did not kill Ms. Jaffrey. She wasn't in her room that night. The computer was on, and I just downloaded the code. Never had such an easy time. And the bullet meant for you hit your friend instead. But that is the past, and we must now rectify the mistake, Mr. Chenais." He raised the gun.

Alec dived toward the nightstand and his gun, and Varoozh shot him. The bullet caught him in the left arm. He spun around and dropped to the floor as a second bullet whizzed past his head and shattered a lamp. He looked up.

The panther leaps, Alec thought as the pain closed in. Ludivine plunged toward Varoozh, pulling the belt from her terrycloth robe. She whipped it around Varoozh's neck and yanked backward, and the man fell against her and down to the floor, where they both lay struggling. Two shots from the gun burped, but Ludivine knocked Paracha's arm aside, the gun skittering away on the tiled floor. Alec watched as Varoozh Paracha, legs kicking, hands scrabbling at his neck, slowly stopped breathing.

Ludivine arose, fastened her robe, and said, "You are bleeding again, *mon cher*. You really must take better care of yourself." She went into the bathroom and returned with a first aid kit. Alec's wound was superficial and required only cleaning and a gauze wrap. He yelped at the burn of the alcohol as Ludivine cleaned the wound. She said, "We will place a do-not-disturb sign on the door until we can dispose of that." She nodded at Paracha's body. "Late tonight. There is a dumpster behind the hotel that should serve. Touch nothing about the body until then, *mon ami*. I will go out to get materials to repair the bullet holes, and we can explain the broken tiles as accidental. She finished wrapping his arm. "There! I am sure you will heal quickly."

Alec sat on the bed, arm burning, but at peace with his quest for vengeance. Varoozh Paracha had paid for his crimes. And yet—who had killed AJ?

CHAPTER FORTY-SEVEN
The NSA

LUDIVINE FINISHED THE PATCH TO the wall and stepped back to inspect it. Yes, the color was perfect, since the wall was white. Once it dried, the bullet hole would be undetectable. She smiled with satisfaction.

The police probe of the dumpster body lasted only two days. The hotel had suppressed everything. Ludivine guessed the police understood tourism was too important to disrupt just because of a body. Particularly a body not that of a tourist. The gloves and the nine-millimeter pistol with a suppressor told them that. No one questioned her or Alec. The sensation among the few hotel guests died down the same day.

She went to the window and gazed at the beach. Alec had gone for a swim after finishing a modification to his blockchain code. With the assassination threat gone along with M. Paracha's body, Ludivine was ready to go home. Beach life was relaxing, of course, but it could not replace the boulevards and bistros she loved. She was a city girl.

One loose end, of course. She looked again and spotted Alec splashing into the surf. A good time for the call.

She sat down at the table and pulled the voice simulator towards her. A few clicks on her laptop brought up the phone number she'd harvested from the surveillance systems Yuriko had installed at 1WeakLink. M. Bannon had once referred to "the admiral," when talking to the man at that number. She fed the number into the voice simulator and waited.

"3016890213." The voice was male and calm.

"Hello, Admiral. You will not recognize my voice." The voice was a deep, rough male voice quite unlike Ludivine's. "I wish to inform you of criminal activity by one of your employees. A woman named Donna Hunt has been using your agency's tools to further her criminal activities in the crypto arena. Specifically, your new blockchain system developed by the 1WeakLink company. As a concerned citizen, I felt it imperative to report this when I discovered it."

"Who is this?"

Ludivine pressed the disconnect button on her machine.

Alec would have to know eventually, of course. But that could wait until she was ready. And now she could go home and resume her work in peace.

"Yuriko! Get your bloody arse in here! Now!"

Yuriko got to her feet at Crispin's scream, her mouth tight. Crispin was always rude, but this crossed a line. She walked into his office as calmly as her anger would allow.

"What," she said flatly, making it clear she wouldn't take any crap.

"You. You and that bloody Moureaux woman. Do you realize what you've done?"

Oh, boy. Not good.

"What's happened?" she asked.

"What's happened is I got a frantic call from my…from the NSA. We're compromised. By you and by Moureaux. They got a tip on a person we've been talking to, and you know damn well who I mean."

"Ms. C."

"That's right, Ms. C. They broke her, Yuriko. They're good at that. And she gave you up. And Alec, too."

"I don't know what you're talking about."

"It's over, Yuriko. They're pulling the plug. They're binning the company."

"What does that mean?"

The Blockchain Killing

"You're redundant, as of now. Leave."

"What about—"

"No severance, no final paycheck. You're done. You're lucky the NSA wants to cover all this up. Otherwise, you'd be wearing a hood on your way to Fort Meade. If you talk about this, I guarantee that's what will happen to you. Now get out and leave me alone." Crispin made a dismissive gesture with his hands, his eyes burning.

Yuriko shook her head in disbelief, but she knew it was over. And Ludivine—she'd have to inform Ludivine. Which would not be pleasant.

Ludivine, lying on her beach towel, reached for her buzzing phone. Octave.

"Yes, Octave?"

"Ah, Ludivine. It is good to hear your voice. I have just received a call from Mme. Nakamoto in San Francisco, who wants you to call. She was... most insistent."

"Yes, I expected that. Thank you, Octave, and I will see you soon."

"*Au revoir,* Ludivine."

Ludivine stood, brushed sand off, collected her things, and headed to the hotel. Alec, a slave to his computer, glanced up when she entered through the sliding glass door.

"You're back too soon. What's happened?"

"I have to return Yuriko's call, and I thought you might want to take part."

"Yeah, all right. What does she want?"

"Let us find out."

Ludivine put the phone on speaker and dialed Yuriko, who answered with panting urgency.

"Ludivine! The NSA has shut down the company! They fired me and everybody else. They've found out, Ludivine. About Ms. C, about everything."

"And so you are back on the job market?"

"Ludivine! Don't you realize—"

"*Chérie, chérie!* Do not worry. Everything ends. We are also wrapping things up here."

"But can't you stop it?"

"It is inevitable, *ma chérie.*"

"I don't know what to do."

"I fear I can be of little help, *ma chérie.* But with the NSA knowing your secrets, I cannot risk further association with you. At least, not for some time. With a few words in the right places, I am confident we can secure you a position in Silicon Valley."

"But, Ludivine—"

Alec leaned toward the phone. "Yuriko, it's Alec. When I get back, I'd be happy to help you, OK?" He glared at Ludivine, who smiled pleasantly.

After Yuriko had gone, Alec said, "What did you do?" His voice was calm, but his face was tense.

"I informed the NSA about Mme. Hunt's activities."

"You turned her in. And she broke and told them everything."

"That is true."

"Why? Why betray her? And Yuriko, too."

"I dislike loose ends, *mon ami.* Oh, by the way, you should hasten to empty the bank accounts of M. Bannon and of your old firm. Why not profit from my perfidy? And it would bring a small measure of justice, no?"

Alec slowly shook his head but appeared to be having a hard time suppressing a smile. But of course he cared little for Ms. C or Mr. Bannon, so the pain of betrayal would be temporary. Alec went to his computer without another word. Ludivine turned her ingenuity to where they could have a decent last meal before leaving the charming country of Costa Rica.

CHAPTER FORTY-EIGHT
The Phone

REEMA KATHIA LOOKED DOWN AT the smartphone on her kitchen table. It was Sunday, and it was Eid al-Adha. Another year passed without going on Hajj. And she was thinking about sacrifice.

Following some obscure bureaucratic rule, the police had returned Aamna's phone to her when they closed their murder investigation. The investigation itself had been a sham. They had labeled the killer as "person or persons unknown" and declared a complete lack of clues or evidence. A phone call from someone claiming to be involved in the investigation had warned her not to pursue her claims about the man Varoozh Paracha. And then a plainclothes police officer had dropped the phone in her lap and told her the police had closed the case.

Reema had nothing to remember her friend, just a small photograph taken at intermediate college so many years ago. Should she keep the phone as a memento? But it also reminded her of Alec. And Abdul. Oh, Abdul. Why did she refuse his marriage proposal? But she had no feelings for him. Again, she put aside the inner truth about her feelings for Aamna and her agony over her friend's death. And she had dedicated her life to the women rotting in jail. They still rotted. And now Aamna and Abdul rotted too. And the police had closed both their files.

Much too morbid.

No, she had to get rid of the phone. Returning it to Aamna's family was the right thing to do. Even if it was otherwise useless, the family could treasure it as a reminder of their lost loved one.

Yes. Give it to the family. Sacrifice it. And move on with her life.

The Jaffrey residence looked neglected, like an old man no longer able to care for himself. The deterioration in just a few months since she last saw the place took her aback. Of course, Mr. Jaffrey had died, of course. But surely there were servants, gardeners, drivers. Weeds poked up in the driveway, and one window was cracked, though not completely broken.

With a determined breath, Reema rang the bell at the gate. She waited. Then she rang again.

The door opened, and one of Aamna's brothers poked his curly black head out.

"Who are you?" he asked rudely in Urdu.

She replied, "Reema Kathia, Aamna's school friend."

"What do you want, *kothi?*"

"I'm sorry, sir. What gives you the right to call me that?"

The boy shook his head. "Why am I talking to this foolish woman-donkey? I have things to do." He closed the door.

Now angry, she rang the doorbell again. Years of dealing with prison authorities had accustomed her to insults and rejection.

The boy appeared again, this time stepping outside. "Stop that damn ringing, woman!" He marched over to her.

"May I ask your name, sir?" asked Reema, staring him down.

"My name is Sohail, if that is any of your business."

"Aamna's younger brother."

"Do not mention that whore's name in this house."

"We are not in a house."

The boy's eyebrows knitted together. "You are the best friend. You are the one who encouraged the whore to go to America."

"She was not a whore."

"That is all you know. She was a whore. Whore, whore, whore. What do you say to that?"

"Let me speak to your mother, Sohail."

"My mother is dead, you fool. Last week. From the virus."

"I am so sorry. I did not know."

"What the hell difference does it make if you knew? What do you want?"

"I must give you Aamna's phone. The police gave it to me." She took the phone out of her pocket and held it up.

"We don't want that whore's phone. We have put all her things in the garbage, where they belong."

"I do not think it is proper or right for you to refer to Aamna with such language."

"You. You are another, are you not? Do you sleep with many men like the whore? Do you pleasure Americans for money like the whore?"

"Really, Sohail. This is too much. And why does your house fare so badly? Do the servants not do their work?"

"Servants?" Sohail laughed bitterly. "We have no servants, we have no money to pay for them. The virus took everything when my mother died. None of this is your business, *fahisha*."

Ignoring this deadly insult, Reema opened her mouth to ask whether they had thrown Aamna's $35 million in the garbage along with her clothes, but she closed it. They did not know. About the money.

She left the gate but then returned. "Has there been any news from the police? About Aamna's murder?"

Sohail grinned. "They do not care. When we told them what she did, the whore that she was, they left us alone with our dishonor. They do not care that we killed her."

"You...what?"

"Oh, yes, you stupid *kothi*. With our cricket bats. No man of honor could tolerate such disgrace to the family. The police know, but they do not care. And you had better watch out, *fahisha*, or your family will come for you too." Sohail grinned again and went into his house and closed the door.

Reema slowly slid down the wall of the compound and sat, losing control of her limbs. The phone slipped out of her numb hand. They had killed Aamna. Because…because…no. No. She had only wanted to do Aamna a favor. By telling Begum Rabia. By calling her that day, using Aamna's phone, to tell her that Aamna had a lover in San Francisco. No. No. No.

CHAPTER FORTY-NINE
The Price of Justice

ALEC CALLED REEMA FROM PARIS, three days after he'd left Costa Rica. *His loose end did not involve killing or betraying anyone. He wanted to give Reema some peace in her life.* After the long flight and relaxing in Ludivine's opulent version of Paris, he'd concluded that Paracha had lied: he had indeed killed AJ, even though he wouldn't admit it. Alec's arm hurt like hell, but it was a flesh wound that would heal after Ludivine's expert attention to the wound and Ludivine's physician's attention to it. The doctor downplayed the gunshot wound, saying he had treated more serious injuries for Ludivine's friends without involving the police.

When Reema answered, Alec said, "Reema? This is Alec Chenais. Don't hang up, I have news."

"I am sorry, Alec. For what I said at the police station. I was angry and hurt, but it was unforgivable."

"I forgive you anyway, Reema. Look, I wanted to tell you that Varoozh Paracha is dead. He's paid for his crime."

"Oh! Thank you for telling me! And, Alec, I read in the Pakistani newspapers that Elliot Perry died in a sailing accident. Is that true?"

"Yes, it's true. The whole affair is over. AJ has found some justice."

"Alec…."

"What is it, Reema? You're fading."

"Alec, they didn't kill Aamna," Reema said, struggling to find the words.

"They...you mean Perry and Paracha?"

"Her brothers killed her, Alec. They beat her to death. With cricket bats. It was an honor killing, because...." Reema hesitated.

"Of me. They found out about me. So I was responsible. If they killed him, the police—"

"The police know. They've closed the case. It is the way of things here."

"But *mon Dieu,* Reema, they *killed*—"

"There is nothing to be done, Alec. Nothing. But listen."

"This can't be right! The police—"

"No! Alec, you have to *listen.*" Reema's voice was nearly screaming.

Shaken by her emotion, Alec sat down on Ludivine's sofa. He said more calmly, "I'm listening, Reema."

"I told Begum Rabia."

"I'm sorry? Who?"

"Begum Rabia, the Jaffrey's matchmaker. They paid her to arrange the marriage. I told her you and Aamna were lovers. I told her. On the phone. The day before Aamna died. Before they killed her."

"Why? Why did you do that?" The question tore out of Alec's heart.

Reema begged for understanding. "I wanted to help her. She was desperate not to marry, you see. And telling the Begum about you and Aamna was sure to stop any marriage. And everything went wrong. But, Alec, there's something—"

"There's more?" he interrupted, overwhelmed.

"They, her brothers—they did not know about her money."

"What money?"

"The money she took to betray you."

"Betray—Perry's money? How much?" Alec felt a numbness start in his toes and rise toward his heart.

"Forty million dollars. She gave me five million for my organization. It has helped us grow. But now—"

"Where is the money?"

"I thought maybe with Aamna's phone, you could find the money. And share it with my organization."

"You have her phone?"

"Yes, Alec, I have it."

Of *course* she had the phone. Of *course* she wanted to split the money. Should he just hang up, a rough form of justice for AJ?

Alec decided that action was in order. He couldn't use his own passport, as Pakistan had banned him. But Ludivine would provide an alternative. "To get to Islamabad, I may need a day, possibly two, Reema. I will find the money."

"Thank you, Alec. And thank you for calling me about Varoozh Paracha."

"You're welcome." Alec could barely get off the phone without screaming. He had to think, reason it all out.

Alec adjourned to a small cafe he'd discovered near Ludivine's apartment. They understood how to make a *café au lait* that was better than his. He sat at an outdoor table, overwhelmed by his emotions, watching Paris pass by and thinking about his life. About AJ, about Reema. Ludivine, betrayal, and death. About money and human rights.

Reema had killed AJ, or she might as well have. But indirectly. Alec knew he would find the money. AJ's thirty pieces of silver. He would put it to good use: independence from Ludivine.

But Reema would see none of that money. Sharing the money with her was a far cry from justice. Nor would the Jaffrey family get any of it. He couldn't revenge himself on them directly, but he could make sure they lived in poverty for the rest of their lives. He would steal their identities and make their lives hell.

And Reema's five million? He could take that too. But too much revenge would do his soul no good, so he'd effectively donate it to her women prisoners' charity by leaving it alone.

Alec smiled. Why not donate a dollar of the money to his father's nonprofit in Montreal? He'd mention honor killings when he donated the money. His father could figure out how to best use it, sure he could. At least Reema understood what a human was.

Then he'd set himself up somewhere and do some real good in the world. Enough good to justify all the terrible things that had happened in the last few years, to him and to the people he loved. He'd lost all his illusions of an ideal world, but he'd be damned if he'd let cynicism take over his life. That would be a veritable hell on earth. He could at least do some good in an imperfect world.

But to do good, he had to find the money. And then he had to tell Ludivine goodbye. For good.

"It is good to see you, *mon ami*," said Ludivine, meeting Alec with *la bise*. "Did you have any trouble with *la douane?* I ask only to assess the quality of the *objet d'art* I gave you. A rush job, you see, that could be flawed."

"No, flawless." The fake passport had indeed allowed Alec to pass through the checkpoints at Islamabad and De Gaulle airports without a hitch. His experiences had convinced Alec that French manufactures were far superior to those of the U.S. and Canada, especially in the darker industries. But as much as he enjoyed Paris and Montreal, it was time to find a new home base.

During the long ride in the Maybach to the Champs-Élysées, Alec recounted his efforts in Islamabad to find AJ's bank account and retrieve the money.

"It took me a while, but I uncovered the money. She had it in a digital wallet in bitcoin. I found an exchange receipt that gave me the wallet ID, and from there it was pretty easy to hack the blockchain and steal the funds. One exchange blocked me, but I worked around it. Word is getting out about the 1WeakLink tools, so be careful, Ludivine."

"I am always careful, *mon ami*," Ludivine said, touching his arm.

"I laundered the bitcoins into my anonymous wallets using the tools we developed." He skipped the outraged phone call with Reema from the airport on his way out of the country. He'd explained that he felt it would be unethical to share the money with her. After all, it was tainted with illegality. She'd found words he hadn't known to express her disappointment in him. Alec could live with that.

"You learned well from our adventures, Alec." But Ludivine was pensive.

"Is something troubling you, Ludivine?" He noticed Octave turn his head slightly and smile. Was that a good sign or a bad one? A new adventure or a shallow grave?

"I fear we must part, Alec, *mon cher*. Like your friend Yuriko, you are in too much trouble with the NSA."

"I'm too hot to associate with, is what you're saying." Alec smiled, since Ludivine had spared him from telling her the same thing, albeit for different reasons. "It's for the best, Ludivine. I don't want to fall in love with you. And my philosophy of life differs from yours. I want to say that I will never forget that you saved my life—twice. Will you drop me at a suitable hotel?"

"No need for that, *mon cher*. I insist on a farewell dinner and a night to ourselves. And I do not want to say *adieu*, only *au revoir*, no? Will you go back to San Francisco after this?"

"No, I'm through with *les Ricains* forever. And they with me, I should think." He held up the passport. "May I keep this?"

Ludivine laughed. "I will have Octave provide you with additional materials to support your new identity, *mon ami*. My parting gift."

Alec settled back in the comfortable leather of the Maybach's rear seat. One last night was more than he'd expected, but it solved another problem for him: how to set the kill switch in Ludivine's 1WeakLink systems. He would have no problem accessing them from her apartment. *His* parting gift, in a way. It would make her work harder, but hard work built character. He'd have to set it up with a scheduler script to kick in after he disappeared. As for *adieu* versus *au revoir*, who knew what the future might hold? But it was *his* future, not anyone else's.

* * *

The painted door in the old building in Kyiv opened, and there was Olyena with a huge smile on her face. Maks stood behind her, noncommittal.

"Alec! We are so glad to see you! Come in, come in! Dinner is on the table, and we have the special *pertsivka* vodka!"

"It's Roland, Olyena. Roland Michaud. 'Alec' is no more."

Alec stepped forward to embrace Olyena and to shake Maks's hand, and the man finally cracked a smile and nodded, but said nothing. He led the way up the stairs to the surprisingly spacious apartment. A small dog greeted them and immediately went for Alec, jumping on his chest with its paws.

Maks said, "This is Daria. She seems to like you, brother."

"The name comes from Daria, a Ukrainian-Canadian model, Alec, er, Roland. That's the affinity," Olyena said, placing plates on a dining table covered with food and bottles. The appearance and smells of the food filled his senses. It would be a fun night. One of many, Alec hoped, as he settled into his chair, petted Daria, and watched Maks pour him some vodka.

Two successful software developers, a country for his home base where they understood software well, and a cute dog. He clinked his glass with the other two and sent the fiery liquid down his throat. Honey and chili pepper, said the label on the bottle. He coughed. To his new life!

What could possibly go wrong?

"Jesus Christ, I thought the boat was bad," moaned Jeff Morrow, sitting across from Elliot Perry in the heaving covered lifeboat.

"Ship. Man up, Jeff. It won't be long now that the typhoon is fading."

"You sure they're getting that distress call?"

"They've replied, Jeff. My rescue team is totally reliable. They needed to travel from Dubai to the Maldives to wait for the storm." The encrypted satellite transmitter for the lifeboats had been Elliot's idea, and having three rescue teams. Big ships had lots of heft and stability, but Elliot preferred to limit risk as much as possible. He'd seen the movie "Titanic" three times. Relying on maritime authorities was not an option.

The free-fall lifeboat was large enough to accommodate twenty people, but claustrophobic. Oscar slept across from him, leaning against one of the coders.

Elliot mentally thanked the ship's designer for the two free-fall lifeboats at the stern of the *Mugwump*. The captain, crew, and a few Seacave inhabitants took the other free-fall, leaving the other 120 crew members to fight it out for the large lifeboats on the upper deck. The rescue team told him they lost communications with all the other boats. He'd have to hire more people when he started up his new operation. And a new captain for his next yacht. Losing the *Mugwump* was a drop in the ocean, as all the software and money lived in the cloud. Huh. Bad metaphor.

"I wish Susie had come on this boat," said Jeff. "She was sweet. Ship?"

"Boat, Jeff, boat. And Susan expressed a definite preference for the other boat. You need to work on your sex appeal, Jeff."

"Fuck you, Elliot." Jeff closed his suffering eyes and leaned back against the bulkhead of the lifeboat.

Elliot smiled.

Acknowledgements

I'd like to thank all the talented software developers I've worked with over the years, who taught me an infinite amount about building software systems. I'd like to thank the Massachusetts Institute of Technology for everything they gave me when I attended during the years 1976-1982 while getting a Master's and PhD in Political Science. It's a different place now, but it will never change its essence. I'd like to thank my fellow founders of Phoenix Bioinformatics Corporation for the opportunity to fill the roles of CTO and CFO for several years, a real education on wheels.

Needless to say, all of the 1WeakLink tools are pure fiction. Blockchains, smart contracts, and dapps are much more secure than the hackers of my fictional world could defeat so easily. The problems with blockchains usually come from transactions taking advantage of bad software or worse security and accounting policies at crypto-related companies that manage to centralize operations on a decentralized blockchain. I hope that skeptics and overzealous regulators don't manage to throw the baby out with the very dirty bathwater.

That said, the hacking activities and the NSA's procurement practices are not that implausible, aside from poor Alec's kidnapping. Those interested should consult Matthew Connelly's great book, *The Declassification Engine,* especially Chapter 5 on Surveillance. For an overwritten but informative look at hacking, consult Nicole Perlroth's *This Is How They Tell Me the World Ends: The Cyberweapons Arms Race.* And for crypto, see Andy Greenberg's terrific tome, *Tracers in the Dark: Global Hunt for the Crime Lords of Cryptocurrency.* Finally, for more on hacking, organized crime, blockchain-related crime, and money laundering, see the excellent book *Rinsed: From Cartels to Crypto: How the Tech Industry Washes Money for the World's Deadliest Crooks,* by Geoff White.

I'd like to thank my writing group at the Mechanics' Institute of San Francisco for their invaluable and unflagging critiques; it's a much better book for their hard work.

Finally, I thank Mary Swanson, my wife, for her patience as I transitioned from software executive to full-time writer.

Thank You!

Thanks for reading *The Blockchain Killing*. If you liked the book, please leave a review on the website through which you bought it.

Sign up to our mailing list for notifications and get a free ebook!

https://www.poesys.com

www.ingramcontent.com/pod-product-compliance
Ingram Content Group UK Ltd.
Pitfield, Milton Keynes, MK11 3LW, UK
UKHW040735200225
455358UK00001B/87

9 781939 386175